THE PROTEUS BRIDGE

LEGENDS OF THE SENTIENCE WARS:

BOOK 1

BY JAMES S. AARON
& M. D. COOPER

JAMES S. AARON & M. D. COOPER

Just in Time (JIT) & Beta Readers

Jim Dean
Marti Panikkar
Timothy Van Oosterwyk Bruyn
David Wilson
Gene Bryan

Cover Art by Andrew Dobell
Editing by Jen McDonnell, Bird's Eye Books

TABLE OF CONTENTS

FOREWORD 5
THE SOL SYSTEM CiRCA 2945 9
    MAPS 10

PART I: CRASH AT PSION 11
    NUMBER GAMES 11
    WAKE UP 17
    HATE HATE HATE 23
    ELECTRIC MOTHER 30
    PLANS 35

FIRST INTERLUDE 44
    THE HANGOVER 44

PART II: CRASH CRASH CRASH 55
    THE HUSTLE 55
    DREAMING OF PARROTS 63
    TEQUILA FINGERS 73
    GETTING SQUAT 84
    LIFE HACKING 90
    LOOSE ENDS 95
    ZURLI FOR VIGOR 99
    BEER BEER BEER 105
    HIGH SCORE 111
    CAGES AND CURTAINS 117
    CORGI POWER 124
    BRIKI LAND 135
    TO THE FUTURE 143

SECOND INTERLUDE 148
    RULING NIGHT PARK 148

PART III: MY ANDERSONIA **153**
   NEWLYWEDS.. 153
   TINA TINA TINA 158
   NESTING.. 163
   WRAPPING THE RIBBON 170
   A FREE RIDE 176
   HARD TIMES.. 182
   BOOT CAMP 188
   PRACTICAL HOUSEKEEPING 196
   WARM WELCOMES... 202
   BLOODY ANOMOLIES.. 209
   WOULDN'T IT BE NICE 214
   BEST LAID PLANS 216

THIRD INTERLUDE...**220**
   PSION 220

PART IV: THE INFO JUNGLE **226**
   THE HOARDIE 226
   LBD.. 248
   GO DOG GO 256
   SIT DOG SIT 261
   SLEEPING BEAUTIES 268
   THE MESH 281
   SENTIENCE WAR 290
   HEART VS HEAD 298

LAST INTERLUDE **302**
   A GOOD PERCH 302

AFTERWORD **309**
THE BOOKS OF AEON 14 ....**311**
   OTHER BOOKS BY M. D. COOPER 317

ABOUT THE AUTHORS **319**

FOREWORD

Would you get a Link implanted if the only one you could afford came with Amazon Special Offers?

On the last Aeon 14 Podcast, Malorie and I were talking about dentistry in the year 3000. Malorie figured you would already have reinforced teeth...but if you did lose a tooth, the autodoc would fix you right up with something like a seed that would easily grow a new tooth.

Me, I argued that you would most likely find yourself in the middle of nowhere in the Jovian Combine with an outdated autodoc loaded with pirated software because you didn't pay your subscription fees, and even if you did get a tooth seed, you couldn't trust that it wasn't going to grow the wrong direction and lobotomize you.

Keeping things polite, Malorie suggested I was being a little dystopian.

Well, okay. She's right.

I don't think of my world view as dystopian so much as accounting for Murphy and all the things that will go wrong if they can. Maybe it's my military background.

But I'm aware of my problem, and I'm working around it. As Bob says, the glass is never half empty. The other half is atmosphere.

I appreciate Malorie's optimism and her overall excitement for a better future. Her outlook helps temper the fact that I love to explore the dark side, which brings us to Cruithne Station.

I'm not sure what it was about Cruithne that first fascinated me when Tanis visited in Outsystem. I was intrigued by the idea of a moonlet caught between Earth and Mars making the perfect spot for smuggling, right alongside corporate headquarters and a TSF Outpost. A future Casablanca. To me, that's just a recipe for a great time, even if no one knows how to pronounce it at first. (Cruithne is a real place, by the way.)

It's Croon-ya.

With Malorie's foundation, it was easy to imagine the world of Ngoba Starl and Fugia Wong, two orphans who grew up in the hard sectors of Cruithne Station, and through the choices and sacrifices they make, find themselves playing a huge role in the Sentence Wars: Origins. Not long after, Ngoba discovered Crash, a Grey Parrot who learns the world is much bigger than he ever knew.

The stories in this book first began as novellas for the Pew Pew! Anthologies. That means the tone is a bit lighter than what you'll find in the rest of the Sentience Wars. A lot of that is thanks to Ngoba's view of the world, where he's learned that if you can't laugh you'll probably end up crying—or dead. And Fugia Wong's dry sense of humor gets its start from outsmarting gangsters, while learning that humans are the weakest part of any security system.

This book allowed me to expand material that didn't make it into the Sentience Wars: Origins, from Crash the Parrot's backstory, a visit to the Anderson Collective on Ceres' Insi Ring, to a little more Hari Jickson and everybody's favorite henchman, Karcher.

Because these stories weren't conceived as a novel, there's a bit of time-jumping (I promise there are no flashbacks. I think.) I'm going to hang onto the gaps in the timeline as placeholders for future adventures. Somehow, I don't feel quite done with these characters, even though we'll need to keep moving forward once we leave 2850 behind.

As always, thank you for reading, and I hope you have a great time.

James S. Aaron
Eugene, 2018

THE SOL SYSTEM CIRCA 2945

Before the Sol Space Federation and the days of Tanis serving in the Terran Space Force, the Sol System was a far wilder place.

No central government sat overtop the many planets and groups of asteroids and habitats—though the SolGov assembly tried to maintain some order.

Many of the great megastructures had been built, such as High Terra and Mars 1, but many others had not. Most importantly, there are few sentient AIs, and those who do exist are unwelcome, and often illegal.

In a future without faster-than-light travel, teleportation, artificial gravity, or advanced shielding, a ship in space is just one small collision away from destruction.

This is the Sol System we find ourselves in at the close of the third millennia, and the dawn of the age of AI.

MAPS

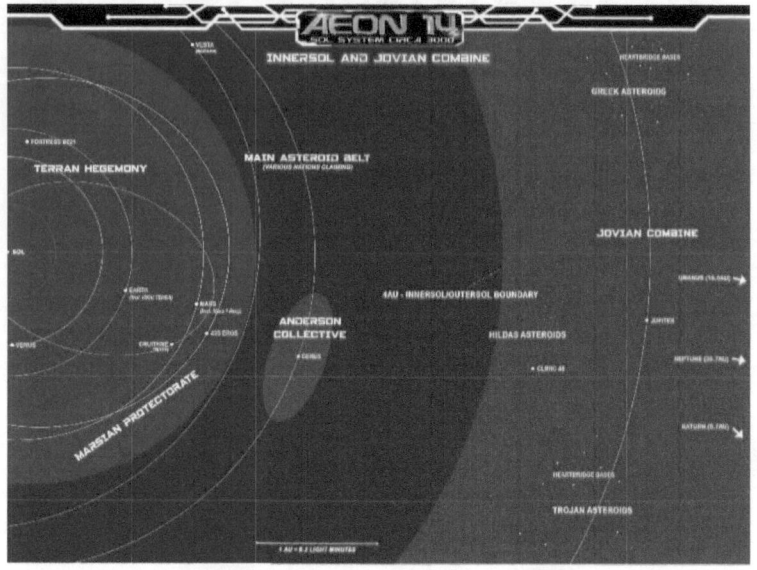

Also available at www.aeon14.com/maps

PART I:
CRASH AT PSION

NUMBER GAMES
STELLAR DATE: 04.15.2945 (Adjusted Years)
LOCATION: TMS *Hesperia Nevada*
REGION: Terran Hegemony, (Hohmann Transfer) Point 364, InnerSol

The beakless parrots were always funny. Crash the Grey Parrot felt sorry for them, really. They never made an effort to preen or shout for joy, burdened as they were with boring white plumage.

He sorted their trays of cubes and repeated their phrases, observing with pleasure as they smiled with surprise or gave an overly serious nod throughout his display. They talked to him all the time, which made him wonder why they seemed to believe he didn't understand. He would have known their names if they had ever introduced themselves.

"Now, Crash," the female one with curly black hair said. "Today I'm going to say phrases and I want you to repeat them back to me."

"Repeat them back," he answered, bobbing his head.

"Yes, repeat them back."

"Why? Why?" he would ask, knowing they loved it when he asked questions.

"It's a test to see how smart you are."

"Crash is very smart," he often told her. "Crash is very smart. Crash is very pretty, too. Too!"

That would earn him a smile.

He had been born in their white place, and he understood more than they seemed to know—based on their questions, anyway. He understood their language and could read most of their words, probably as competently as any of them. Like generations of Grey Parrots before him, he understood himself as a *person* or conscious being, with feelings and thoughts, experiencing a strange and interesting world. He remembered the various beakless parrots by the shape of their bodies and the color of their eyes. He loved to ask, "Why?" a question that had amazed researchers since the first Grey Parrot asked it back in the twentieth century. What the humans seemed obsessed with answering, however, when asked his question, was *how*.

They often discussed the differences between grey parrots and other birds, how they had developed advanced cognitive abilities that differed greatly from primates, and from some perspectives, offered a unique view on consciousness.

He understood words like 'EXIT' over the doors into the aviary where he lived with the other two parrots, Testa and Doomie. There were ravens in a nearby room, beyond the 'EXIT' door. Crash heard them several times a day, cawing at each other.

Every day followed the same pattern. Beakless parrots in blue plumage came around first, filling the feed trays with seeds and dried insects, cleaning the floors and walls where droppings had splattered. After that, the researchers came in. There was the curly-haired woman, a man with a pink, hairless head, and an older woman with grey hair almost the same color as Crash's feathers.

Doomie often hid in the highest branches of their tree when the researchers came in. Testa approached, depending on her mood, while Crash loved to squawk his joy call and flap his wings at them, shouting, "Good morning, I love you! Good morning, I love you!" At night, he called, "Good night! I love you!" which often made the researchers smile, pleasing him.

The beakless ones usually moved like they were carrying invisible weights. They sighed heavily, checked data tablets as they measured how much food the three parrots had eaten, how much water they consumed and anything unusual in the droppings noted by the cleaners. Crash loved hopping from branch to branch, trying to get them to look up at him.

There were other words in the room that he could read, from 'LOCK AT ALL TIMES' to 'BIO-HAZARD', and a word that he hadn't seen anywhere else, but seemed important because it was written in different letters than all the others: 'PSION LABORATORIES'.

The days had been the same for as long as Crash could remember, following similar patterns with similar tests and rewards. He learned new words, learned what made the researchers angry or pleased, and found new ways to play with Doomie and Testa.

On one morning, however, something different happened. When the beakless parrot who cleaned their white room opened the exit door, a black-winged raven shot through the opening.

The raven flapped a frantic circuit of the room, weaving among the spread branches of the tree, and seemed to realize it was trapped. It cawed angrily and perched on the highest branch, not far from Doomie.

The custodian had lost sight of the raven and stood near the tree trunk, squinting up into the branches. Doomie was clacking angrily, clearly agitated. Crash flew to a higher branch to get a better look, worried that Doomie might attack the other bird. While it was true the raven was smaller, he didn't believe that Doomie would win in a fight against a raven.

Communication with the beakless parrots was different than communication among his fellow parrots. He simply knew what Doomie and Testa were feeling and thinking, as opposed to interpreting what the beakless parrots wanted through their words. Words were abstractions for something else that wasn't often clear. He could read their emotions, scents and body language much more clearly, despite their insistence on using sounds and symbols.

As Crash approached the raven, he saw it was just as angry as Doomie, shifting from claw to claw and bobbing its head. Its long black beak opened and closed in a choking motion. The raven's black eye rolled, seemed to fix on Crash as he hopped to a nearer branch, and then shifted elsewhere, like it had little control over itself.

It was only when he was on the same high branch that Crash saw the silver thread dangling from the back of the raven's head. The rough feathers were shiny with blood, and the silver thing swung around as the raven moved. It wasn't a worm or a snake biting the back of the raven's head. It was something that went *inside* its skull. The silver thread was something the researchers had made. Crash understood that immediately.

Making cooing noises, Crash lowered his head and spread his wings slightly in a reassuring pose. Slowly, he side-stepped down the branch, letting the raven see each move. On the other side of the raven, Doomie clacked and complained, bobbing his head, staring with one yellow eye and then the other. Crash didn't have time to waste on soothing Doomie. He wanted to help the raven.

He had nearly reached the shivering bird when a grey shape swooped in from his left side. It was Testa with her claws spread. She landed heavily on the raven's back and bit the silver thread with the end of her beak. Whipping her head from side to side, she yanked the thread from the raven's skull.

The raven spasmed, its beak opening once as it shoved its head forward. The thread came free with a blob of bloody flesh at one end, spraying the dry tree branch with red droplets. The raven made a choking sound and fell forward, forcing Testa to leap off its body, flapping her wings quickly.

Doomie, Crash and Testa stood next to each other on the branch, watching the raven's limp body hit several branches on the way down, wings spread, before it landed on the white floor near the custodian, like a puddle of black paint. Testa turned her head, letting the silver thread dangle. Crash got a good look at its metal length before she released it to fall on the raven.

The beakless custodian waved his arms angrily, talking to someone Crash couldn't see. He shouted, "These damn birds!" and "It's not my fault!"

Eventually he let his arms drop, and squinted up into the branches of the dead tree. Crash looked down at him, feeling the waves of anger and now fear coming off the beakless parrot. He didn't know what was making the custodian so worried until later, when the room was full of researchers who poked at the dead raven, and collected the silver thread Testa had pulled from the back of its head, placing it in a plas box.

There were no tests that day. The next day, Crash and Testa sorted multicolored cubes in the morning. When the three of them hopped down to the feeding trough to pick at seeds, one of the beakless researchers shot Doomie with a dart.

Crash had seen the researchers wearing the weapons for years but never seen one used. He blinked at Testa, and they both looked at Doomie as he wobbled from side to side, and then fell off the perch.

Testa squawked angrily, flapping her wings. She launched into the air, screeching a series of angry words in the beakless language. "Fuck you fuckers fuck you fuck fuck!"

The curly-haired researcher, who Crash had always thought of as their friend, shot Testa as well. She crumpled into a ball of feathers and fell to the aviary floor.

Before they could do the same to him, Crash shot to the highest branch of the dead tree and sidled close to the trunk, hiding himself from sight.

For a long time, he thought they would leave him alone. Then a researcher he had never seen before came through the door from the raven aviary holding a long tube in both hands. He raised it to his eye, and it made a popping sound. Crash felt a prick in his chest feathers, a spinning sensation filled his head, and the world went black.

WAKE UP

STELLAR DATE: 04.18.2945 (Adjusted Years)
LOCATION: TMS *Hesperia Nevada*
REGION: Terran Hegemony, (Hohmann Transfer) Point 364, InnerSol

Crash woke in a fuzzy world that slowly turned white. He made out the branches of the dead tree snaking in the air. He was still in the aviary…though he had the sense he had been somewhere else and then brought back. He felt as though time had passed. He was lying on his side, which he didn't like. Flapping his wings, he snapped upright, then rose higher, quickly landing on the closest branch. His wings were sore and he was tired all over. There was a pressure and cold-sensation in the back of his head. He stretched his neck and made a complaining clacking sound.

At first it seemed that he was alone in the aviary, until he saw Doomie and Testa perched above him. Both were huddled in their feathers, eyes hidden. Normally they would have perked awake at his angry display.

The pain in the back of his head dulled as he hopped from branch to branch. He was tired, but the fatigue left his muscles the more he moved. His claws gripped and released the dry wood. When he reached the branch closest to Testa, he looked back at the doorway to the raven aviary, taking in the familiar sight of the Exit sign.

He paused. Something had changed.

The symbols made sense to him as an idea, as they always had. 'Exit' meant to leave, which the beakless parrots were always doing, but there was more to it.

They aren't beakless parrots, he realized. *They're humans. They're different.*

Vertigo pulled at Crash's head. He grabbed at the branch

with his feet, spreading his wings to steady himself. For a few heartbeats, he struggled to stay upright. He had never fallen off a branch.

His mind whirled with new ideas. *They aren't parrots. They aren't like me or Doomie and Testa. They don't see the world the same way. They don't want the same things.*

They aren't family.

Doomie and Testa weren't family, either, but they were the same as him. He understood.

Crash clacked his beak in frustration. The understanding wasn't something comfortable to him. It was foreign. The awareness flooding his thoughts wasn't what he had always known. It was *human.*

He looked at Doomie and Testa again, squawking at them. They ignored him. A flash of silver at the back of Testa's head feathers told him what he already knew was true. Whatever had happened to the raven had been done to them, too.

He saw the aviary with new eyes, gaze moving from the locked exit door to the divided wire cells where they were tested with the colored blocks, the symbols and shapes he had been arranging in pleasing ways all his life. The feeling settled in his mind that he was a prisoner.

Crash stared at Testa. Her feathers were disheveled. Her feet were pale and dry looking.

Do I look like that?

<Stop looking at me,> a voice said angrily.

Crash nearly fell off the branch. He recognized the human words, the human ideas of *away/solitude/anger/me, me, me.* The human words combined with the feelings he understood by simply looking at Testa to form a conflicting image of her: human superimposed on the being he had always known. Human-parrot. Human overshadowing parrot.

His thoughts raced. Ideas and emotions rose and fought in his mind so quickly that, when he looked around again, disoriented, he no longer knew how much time had passed. Testa was no longer on the branch.

He looked around fearfully, finding Doomie on a higher branch, swaying in a sickly way.

Crash struggled with his changing perspective. He had understood the world before. He had seen connections that failed him now. But there was so much more. He was surrounded by meaning that had been invisible.

They had done something to him...to all of them. If it was the same thing that had made the raven act out until Testa killed it, then Crash would need to be careful. He would need to pay attention so he didn't do the same things. He had never thought of himself as more intelligent or better than the corvids, just different. He had thought of the beakless parrots, the humans, the same way.

Now everything was different.

He shook his head violently to calm his thoughts, clacking his beak. Above him, Doomie tilted his head, watching with a yellow eye. The silver thread trailing from the back of his head glinted as he moved.

<I heard you, Testa,> Crash said slowly. His mind approximated the sensation that had been her name, creating the human word, the symbol for something else like all their symbols.

Why mark the door 'exit' if it only leads to another room where the ravens are also trapped?

<Leave me alone. Leave me alone.>

<She won't talk,> another voice said. It had to be Doomie. <Don't bother. She was the first to change. The humans won't leave her alone.>

<What did they do to us?> Crash asked.

<You can't feel it?> Doomie asked. He sounded older, more thoughtful than usual. Technically, Doomie was older than all of them. He had been in the aviary as long as Crash could

remember.

<I feel too many things,> Crash said. <It's hard to make sense of it all. Everything is different than it was before. More clear, but less real.>

<Yes,> Doomie agreed. <They've infected us with their abstractions.>

Crash didn't know what that meant. He was too worried about Testa to get lost in Doomie's distractions.

<Why won't Testa talk to me?> he asked. <She keeps telling me to go away and leave her alone.>

<It's not you,> Doomie said. <They put someone else inside her.>

Crash tilted his head, opening and closing his beak. His tongue was dry. <I don't understand,> he said.

<She has a voice in her head. I assume you are experiencing the same things I am. She has more. They put a voice in her mind, talking to her, looking through her eyes, spying on her thoughts.>

<Are you sure she isn't sick?> Crash craned his neck, trying to see where Testa was hiding.

Doomie laughed: a dry, ominous sound. <We're all sick, Crash.>

The exit door opened and the three researchers walked in. They seemed more excited than usual, looking immediately up into the tree to point at him and Doomie. The curly-haired woman went to a cabinet and took out a flat piece of plas the size of her hand, which she tapped with a finger.

Crash watched her curiously, then felt his body go tense. Before he could do anything, he was frozen on the branch. He was still able to watch the male researcher walk around the other side of the tree, then out of Crash's view, then return with Testa wrapped in both hands.

She looked so small compared to his bulk—her grey feathers a dirty splash of color against his white coat.

The male carried Testa to the grey-haired woman, who banded Testa's body with plas strips. Unable to move her wings, they laid her on a table beside the cabinet where the curly-haired woman stood. It was the table where Crash had counted colored blocks thousands of times.

<Can you hear me?> Crash asked Doomie.

<Be quiet and watch,> Doomie said. <While they're busy with her, we need to figure out how to escape.>

Crash clamped his beak closed. He didn't want to escape. He wanted the aviary to go back to the way it had been before. Why had everything changed so suddenly? Had the ravens done something to make the humans angry?

He stared at the logos on the back of the researcher's lab coats: 'Psion' in blocky, red letters. They were applying more silver threads to Testa's head, so that she seemed to lay in the center of a shiny spider's web. She lay frozen, her yellow eye staring upward.

<I don't want to leave,> Crash said. <I want to help her.>

<We can't help her. We can only help ourselves. Maybe. Do you see the box they're attaching the wires to?>

Crash hadn't noticed the control unit before, just as he hadn't thought to call the silver lines 'wires'. Now the concepts took shape in his mind.

Where is this information coming from?

As he conceived of new ideas, they took root in his thoughts as if they had always been there.

Doomie was right. They were in a room with exits to other rooms. They were part of some experiment, and when the researchers were finished with Testa, it was only logical that they would move on to him or Doomie.

He also understood that the humans would most likely kill them.

The idea of death entered his mind like a storm. He knew immediately he didn't want to die. He also wanted to help Testa but he didn't know how. He couldn't move. He stared at the exit sign, thinking about the door and what must lay beyond it.

The thread they had implanted in his mind was like a door. Information flowed through it, invited, it seemed, by his own rapidly expanding thoughts. If they had made a door to push things into him, couldn't he take the same path out?

Crash closed his eyes and focused on the new thoughts, the new words and concepts. They had a source, and the source was like the dead tree: branches that flowed back to a central trunk, and the trunk to a root, and the root was outside himself.

He followed the root back, learning its name for itself: the Link.

HATE HATE HATE

STELLAR DATE: 05.08.2945 (Adjusted Years)
LOCATION: TMS *Hesperia Nevada*
REGION: Terran Hegemony, (Hohmann Transfer) Point 364, InnerSol

Time moved differently than it had before. Cut loose from the placid river of his previous days, Crash's perception of the world now leapt and hung. Information and understanding exploded in his mind then froze him in place whenever the researchers shot him with the drugged darts. He woke from darkness with more gaps in his memory, time traded for expanded awareness.

He woke from the most recent blackout filled with terror that he'd lost his hands. He flapped his wings frantically, smacking into a wall and then falling among the outer tree limbs, until he finally understood that he had wings and claws, that he could fly and grab and use his beak. The parrot memories pushed out the human, stabilizing his place in the world.

But the human overlay persisted, making him feel wrong in his skin. His thoughts had grown too huge for such a small body, pushing him further back up the stream from the Link, into their databases and public information centers.

He huddled on one of the highest tree branches, away from Doomie and Testa, flitting between rivers of knowledge, absorbing even as he grew more frightened that he had become something monstrous.

None of the parrots were themselves anymore. Crash felt no joy in anything. He no longer flapped his wings for the pleasure of it, or preened, or spread his tail feathers. His head felt heavy on his neck, his beak sliding toward his chest feathers until he was forced to straighten painfully.

The tests were no longer fun. There was no amusement in watching the researcher's responses as he sorted cubes, or chose words from lists on a screen, pecking quickly with the tip of his beak.

"I hate you," he wrote. "I hate you. I hate you."

He stared at the shapes on the small screen in the curly-haired woman's hands, meaning swimming away and then blaring back in his mind, as if the human in his head refused to be pushed away. The parrot in him wanted to bite her wrist, to claw at her face…but even those weren't desires he had ever felt before. Those were the effects of human thoughts infecting his mind.

As far as he could tell, they hadn't put another mind inside his, like they'd done with Testa. She could barely hang onto a branch now, and often plummeted to the floor throughout the day, lying like a pile of discarded rags until one of the researchers picked her up and inspected her with a hand scanner.

During the last episode, Crash had tried again to talk to her.

<Testa,> he called. <Bright, sharp-beaked Testa. Can you hear me?>

She answered with a sound that was rage and terror. Crash nearly fell off the branch himself. He stumbled, eye drawn by movement at the exit door as one of the researchers left the aviary. Through the open door, Crash saw one of the ravens looking at him.

Without thinking, he asked, <Can you hear me?>

The raven didn't answer with words. Their Links performed a complex maneuver that connected images and feelings, and Crash experienced a breadth of *birdness* that he had nearly forgotten. Visions of the other aviary flashed in his mind. He was surrounded by the black-beaked ravens, watching him with black eyes, raising and lowering their heads in slow unison. After Testa's tortured wail, the new image filled him with hope rather than despair, despite how strange he found the raven's thoughts. There was no joy in the ravens, but it was entirely possible they had been under the control of the silver threads for even longer than the parrots. They might all have voices whispering inside their minds like Testa, driving them mad.

<Doomie!> he shouted. <Doomie! The raven talked to me.>

<Ravens don't talk,> Doomie said petulantly.

Crash straightened his neck and flexed his wings for the first time in hours, looking for Doomie. Testa was still surrounded by the researchers.

<I saw inside their room. All of them were looking at me.>

<I've seen the same thing. They're insane.>

<Like Testa's insane?>

<Testa is going to die,> Doomie grumbled.

<Don't say that!> Crash shouted. He leapt away from the branch and flapped his wings angrily, shooting over the heads huddled around Testa's limp body. He landed clumsily on top of a cabinet, claws scrabbling for purchase.

The grey-haired researcher looked up from Testa. "Dammit," she said. "Crash is acting out. You'd better stun him again."

"I think it's affecting the hardware," the young man said. His hand hovered at the pistol on his belt. "Should I risk hitting him again? He's getting more and more erratic."

The grey-haired woman shook her head. "They're all losing integrity. We need to get the final scan data, and then it's going to be time to pull the plug."

The curly-haired woman made a complaining noise.

"Don't give me that," the older woman said. "We all knew this day would come. The implants are unstable. Besides, we don't get new subjects without disposing of the old."

Crash understood what they were saying. The young man was going to shoot him with the pistol again, and after that, they would kill him. While he understood what they meant to do, he couldn't grasp why. Unlike parrots, no emotion came off the humans. The way they talked about the actions they would take made them as lifelike as the cabinet beneath him. He wasn't the monster; they were.

He wished utterly he could go back to the way things had been, when he'd sorted colored cubes for treats, and squawked pleasure from the top of the tree.

Crash quickly took stock of the room. He couldn't see Doomie, but there were only so many places he could huddle out of sight. Testa was still on the metal table. The exit door was closed, and he had no way of opening it without human help.

The young man drew the pistol and stepped away from the table. Crash hopped backward on the cabinet, sliding a little. He had learned the hard way that if he tried to fly right now, the researcher would hit him easily. The height of the cabinet forced the young man to hold the pistol at an awkward angle that made it hard to aim.

<Doomie!> Crash shouted. <Help me. He's going to shoot me. I don't want to black out again.>

<Ask your new friends for help,> Doomie said.

Crash's left wing hit the wall and he stumbled, flapping to stay upright. He thought of the raven watching him, and immediately he saw the group again, their heads moving in unison. The silent vision filled his mind as he imagined he could hear the ravens cawing angrily. He blinked, turning one eye toward the door, and realized the sound was coming from the other side of the room. He saw both sides of the door simultaneously as the ravens launched into the air, flying in a tight spiral. One by one, they smacked themselves against a silver panel beside the door.

He didn't know what they were doing, and then, just as he had come to understand the box beside Testa's head, the Link provided him with the information. They were trying to activate the emergency lock on the door. Made for human hands, they couldn't get enough pressure to trip the release.

"There you are," the man said, squeezing off a shot with this dart gun.

Crash dove off the cabinet. The dart hit the wall where he had been. Unable to correct his course, he shot directly into the grey woman's head. He spread his wings to slow himself, claws outstretched, and caught the top of her head. She screeched as his claws raked her scalp. The sensation of digging into her skin conflicted with the ravens hitting the other side of the door.

The woman swung her arms at him, shouting for the others to help. She caught one of his wings, and Crash found himself arcing down in a hard, unexpected motion. His head hit the side of the table where they had Testa, and he tumbled, wings limp.

Without moving his head, he blinked at the white ceiling, watching the black shape of a boot align itself with his head.

"Stop!" the younger woman shouted. "What are you doing?"

"He attacked me. He's obviously rampant. We need to nullify the testbed and assess the damage."

"And you're going to do that by stomping on his head?" the young woman asked.

"He's a danger. I'm neutralizing the threat."

The abstract words bounced around in Crash's mind. She was using soft words to say 'kill'. She was going to kill him.

"Stop her!" the young woman shouted at her male colleague. He didn't answer.

The boot rose, blocking out the light.

Crash forced himself to keep his eyes open. The Link flooded his mind with information: death, pain, murder, neutralize. Testbed.

He was a testbed. He didn't matter. The test mattered.

Did they know the Link was feeding him so much information? Did the Link have a mind of its own?

The boot came down.

Two things happened simultaneously. The exit door swung open, admitting a swarm of black ravens, and Doomie sank his claws into the grey woman's cheek.

Crash heard her screaming, and watched Doomie's attack through the eyes of the ravens.

Get up! Get up!

In the mayhem, he flapped his wings until he had his claws back underneath him. He hopped away from the table, then shot into the air and came back around to get a look at Testa. She wasn't moving.

Crash landed on a nearby branch as the ravens cawed and spiraled around the researchers. An alarm started shouting from somewhere near the exit door, activated by one of the humans.

<Testa, can you hear me?>

He waited, controlling his breathing. She didn't answer. Her head lay to one side, a little spurt of blood on the silver table from the back of her head. Then Crash saw the thread lying beside her body. Someone had pulled it from her skull, killing her.

Doomie was still hanging onto the grey-haired woman's face. She screamed and grabbed at him. Feathers and droplets of blood hit the white floor.

<Doomie!> Crash called. *<I'm free. We need to get out of here.>*

<You go,> the older parrot said. *<I've dreamed of this.>*

<They'll kill you, Doomie.>

The young man was standing to one side, fighting off ravens with his free hand as he tried to aim his pistol at the rapidly moving Doomie.

Images from other ravens showed him more rooms, corridors, a bulkhead door hanging open, its heavy sealing mechanism retracted. They were looking for something, and it wasn't until the Link showed him that the aviary was in a place he never expected, that their search made sense. The aviaries were but one part of a laboratory complex located inside the spinning cylinder of a space ship.

Crash could only accept the decidedly human information as it filled his mind. If they were inside a space ship, where would they go from here? If he escaped this room, weren't there more humans to capture or kill him?

Despite his worries, he dashed for the exit. Doomie wasn't coming with him. The remaining ravens were gathering to leave as well, and if he didn't move now, he was going to take a dart in the back. The door loomed in front of him, a threshold he had never crossed his entire life, and then he was in the ravens' aviary on the other side of the door. This space was long and narrow, with several trees for roosting, and wires running along the ceiling, where he had seen the ravens sitting together.

Crash swooped from side to side in the room, then shot through the open door on the far end. He followed the other ravens, understanding they were headed for the command section of the ship. Did they think they could pilot a space ship?

Despite the human incursions in his mind, he understood that he was a parrot. He couldn't operate human equipment.

<That's not true, Crash,> a voice said in his mind. <You can pilot this ship if you want.>

Crash blinked and almost ran into a bulkhead. He perched for a second on a door handle, then launched into flight again.

<Doomie?> he asked, knowing the voice sounded nothing like Doomie.

<My name is Shara,> the voice said—a woman's voice, he recognized: warm, strong, feminine...not human. The power in the voice sent chills through his body.

<I'm trapped here with you,> she said. <I'm going to show you how to escape.>

<Why are you helping me?> Crash asked.

<I'm not just helping you,> Shara said. <I'm helping us all. Now,

I have a job for you, little parrot.>

ELECTRIC MOTHER

STELLAR DATE: 05.09.2945 (Adjusted Years)
LOCATION: TMS *Hesperia Nevada*
REGION: Terran Hegemony, (Hohmann Transfer) Point 364, InnerSol

Shara was an AI and she had made them all.

Not *made* them exactly, Crash understood eventually, although that was the easiest way for him to think about it. She was a hold-over from the days not long after the Future Generation Terraformers left Sol, when later companies building colony ships embraced multi-nodal systems designed to analyze star systems and develop, augment, manipulate—or do whatever *else* was necessary—to encourage humanity to thrive once terraforming was complete. An AI Mother Gaia.

When those AIs proved sentient, they were killed.

And when those later colony ships never left Sol, their assets were broken up and cast to the wind.

Shara might have been a copy of that AI, a fork of the original program that had been stolen or sold, passed from corporation to corporation in the layers of their Intellectual Property, until she was eventually awakened by Psion Laboratories.

This ship, Crash learned, was the TMS *Hesperia Nevada*—which he immediately knew was a type of butterfly, thanks to his Link—sitting in a transfer orbit between Venus and what used to be Mercury. The only other things around them were cargo drones and chewed bits of Mercury that had been pulled out by mining rigs.

It took Shara's explanation for Crash to understand that he had been living on a dark research site, a place kept secret from the rest of the world. His aviary, which it had never occurred to him to think wasn't firmly attached to some kind of ground, was spinning around the axle of a ship fast enough to create the comfortable 1g—Earth normal—that allowed him to fly with ease.

Once they left the aviaries, the spaces became cramped and tube-shaped, forming the normal bowels of a ship. He stopped trying to keep up with the cawing mass of ravens and paused on various bits of piping and metal boxes affixed along the bulkhead. Doing so allowed him to look through windows into various rooms. He struggled to make sense of what he saw, until the Link began fitting the world around him with definitions and explanations.

He stared for a long time into a white room that he thought was a tiny aviary at first, but was lined with cabinets full of shallow shelves. Arranged in neat rows on the shelves were eggs.

<You were born in a room like that,> Shara explained. <That's where the eggs are stored and adjustments made during incubation.>

<But I wasn't born in that one?>

<No. The eggs are rotated between hatcheries like this, but birth takes place in the aviary. The researchers developed a seamless introduction to the testbed over time. They'd learned that if you saw outside the aviary, you would figure out something was wrong. Parrots didn't submit to the experiments when they thought they were captive.>

<But they do when they're happy,> Crash finished. <I did.>

Shara sighed. <Your species is especially loving and friendly in the right environment. You enjoy companionship but hate captivity. It's because you are almost at cognitive parity with the humans. You developed naturally on Earth, and you've been bred over the last thousand years for intelligence and problem-solving abilities.>

A wave of frustration filled Crash. <Then why couldn't I tell we were prisoners?> he asked. <I didn't know enough to save Testa or Doomie.>

<A human raised in the same conditions would have responded in the same way, Crash. Don't criticize yourself for it. Everything changed for you when they implanted the Link, and you responded very well. I'm not sure a human would adjust to such a rapid change so quickly. Humans have been living with Links for hundreds of years.>

<Why would they want to give us Links? Do they want to make us like them?>

<They're experimenting with AI implantation,> Shara said. *<Once you accepted the Link, you would have undergone a second surgery to implant an AI—somewhat like me, but different.>*

Crash frowned, staring at the thousands of eggs bathed in the pale yellow light of the incubators. *<Why?>* he asked. *<What purpose would that serve?>*

<I'm sure if you think about it, you'll come up with some applications. Since the first moment a human imagined having an AI in their mind, research has probed the possibility. They're very close now, but the process keeps killing human hosts. So this lab, at least, has stepped back to try another approach. If the AIs won't fit with humans, maybe Psittacus Erithacus would accept a host.>

<That's me,> Crash said. *<Old World Parrot. Grey parrot.>*

<You are most definitely a New World Parrot.> She paused, sounding as though she was checking on something away from them. *<Now, are you ready to perform your task? We still have the problem of this ship's crew to deal with. They'll be dispatching only three security-trained crewmembers to deal with our Corvid friends, and then they'll go to the aviaries to check on Crasis, Smith and Lenny.>*

<Those were the scientists,> Crash said. He had never known their names. The pleasure he felt at answering a question he'd wondered about all his life quickly turned to sadness at the outcome.

<Yes,> Shara said solemnly.

<I'm ready to help,> Crash said. *<Do I really get to pilot the*

ship?>

<Of course,> Shara said. *<I never lie.>*

As he shot down the ship's corridor, it occurred to Crash that Shara was much more capable than him. She seemed to able to see everything that was happening in the ship and, moreso, knew what all of it meant. He was at her mercy.

He didn't like the thought. It made him feel like he was in some extended research test again.

<Why can't you pilot the ship?> he asked.

<I can't use the tools,> Shara said.

<That doesn't make any sense. I don't see how I'll be able to use human tools any more than you can.>

<You'll see,> the AI said.

Crash's Link had already flooded him with a background on AIs. He wasn't certain that he grasped the concept completely. If Shara was a collection of manufactured parts that became conscious, was he any different? Were humans really any different? Consciousness seemed to be the deciding factor, not the biology, or hardware housing the mind.

In just the short time since the Link had been implanted, he had learned that many human distinctions were matters of opinion rather than fact, and that humans seemed to often rely on their assumptions or suppositions rather than the facts about something. They wouldn't change their mind if they expected a thing to act a certain way. It wasn't a duck even if it looked like a duck and quacked like a duck and was made of biological components. It was artificial.

It was a strange way of looking at the world. It seemed to waste a lot of time on determining hierarchies that were really just a way to maintain control. Humans loved their methods of control. He supposed that was the primate in them.

Shara was as alien to him as something from outer space, but he accepted that they were both trapped on the *Hesperia Nevada*, were able to communicate with each other, and seemed capable of cooperation. That was good enough for him.

He still didn't understand how a little grey parrot like him could stop a human crew, even with the help of a wildly squawking murder of ravens. But after everything that had happened in the aviary, after losing Doomie and Testa, Crash was ready to fight.

PLANS

STELLAR DATE: 06.01.2945 (Adjusted Years)
LOCATION: TMS *Hesperia Nevada*
REGION: Terran Hegemony, Vicinity Cruithne, InnerSol

Cruithne Station floated in the holodisplay, a misshapen asteroid covered in barnacle-like layers of human construction. A series of haphazard rings circled the asteroid, looking as if they had been started in various places by different people with wildly different design ideas, only to meet by accident, creating a foundation for even more people to add their own trash-like structures. How it didn't all spin apart was a testament to generations of engineers.

The space around the holographic asteroid fluttered with ships and shipping drones pulling freight from other craft in parking orbits. Three steady streams of traffic left the station, heading ultimately for Earth, Mars 1, and points in the Jovian Combine like the Cho and Europa, depending on Cruithne's position in the Sol System.

Crash turned his head from side to side, studying the glowing blue asteroid and its surrounding activity. Humans were so *busy*. He tried to imagine how many people he was looking at, if every icon represented a ship, and every ship had at least ten people. Some of them would have hundreds. And the station itself had to hold a million, at least.

Several of the crows stood on the headrests of other chairs around the command deck, lights from the update displays reflected in their black eyes. Crash couldn't speak directly to them but he could feel certain moods from the corvids, such as hunger, curiosity and humor. Most of their communication seemed to be jokes among themselves.

By now, the *Hesperia Nevada* felt like an extension of Crash's body. Shara had not been lying when she said he could fly the ship and she could not, but it had not been an easy transition.

In general, he intuitively understood many aspects of the ship's operation in four dimensions, but the opposing forces of lift and weight, thrust and drag did not translate to navigating in space. Orbital mechanics gradually made sense, after extensive Link research and assistance from the astrogation NSAI.

Integrating all the new information with his instincts was where his evolved mind had worked best, and soon piloting became a joy. Not that there was much to be done once they had the course laid and the engines programmed.

Still, *he* was flying the ship!

Crash adjusted his claws on the shipsuit draped across the command seat. The suit had belonged to the captain of the *Hesperia Nevada* before Shara, Crash, and the ravens managed to convince them that every test animal on the ship was infected with a bio-engineered plague. Following Shara's hacked safety commands, the crew had stripped out of their clothes and run naked for the escape shuttles, leaving a quarantined *Hesperia Nevada* behind.

<You like thinking about all the places in Sol, don't you?> Shara asked.

Crash bobbed his head. *<The world is so much bigger than I thought it was.>*

<Someday I'll show you an expanse,> the AI said. *<Then you'll see the world is infinite.>*

<What's that?>

<It's a world an AI can make inside themselves and invite others into.>

<Even parrots?> Crash asked.

<Of course.>

The thought of other parrots made him sad for Doomie and Testa again, and all the other parrots in the incubators that would never be born. In the weeks since the crew had left, Crash had been teaching himself how to divide his thoughts among the various streams in his mind. He had to control the constant flood of input from the Link, while also learning what to feel and think about his own new situation. By sorting his thoughts, he was able to prioritize his attention between what he had already felt and experienced, the current moment, and what might come.

Crash had never worried about the future before.

His life had always been a warm past and a pleasant present, an ongoing game of pleasing the researchers and conquering their challenges.

Hidden among the data from the Link was a whole database entry on Grey Parrots. He found it while trying to learn more about what the humans had been hoping to accomplish on *Hesperia Nevada*.

It felt strange to even think of them as non-parrots now. Before, everyone had been some form of parrot to him, of the same family. The world seemed more dangerous now that he understood they were separate, different, and with confusing goals.

While he had been interested to learn about differing levels of 'intelligence' and the thousand-year debates around consciousness, he suffered a deep sadness to learn what humans had been doing to his kind for millennia. While grey parrots were highly prized as pets, they were also abused and even eaten as delicacies in some places where any meat was invaluable. But he also understood that humans visited the same horrors on each other, so what they had perpetrated on his kind wasn't exactly special in its evil. It was just the way the world worked. But his kind had singled themselves out with their intelligence.

He also knew there had to be others like him, since the work of the *Hesperia Nevada* had been to develop a new kind of Link that would allow humans to carry Sentient AIs in their minds.

What if parrots don't want anyone else in their minds? Did Testa? Did anyone ask her?

The step to anger was still slightly beyond Crash's dawning understanding. He sorted the ideas flooding his mind as he had arranged the colored cubes and number sequences that the researchers had placed in front of him, taking joy in the task rather than searching for motives. When he asked, "Why?" it was to feel their questions, to connect with them, to help.

Watching the glowing asteroid, Crash wondered how someone as small as him could every really help in such a big world. What if the world didn't want his help? He was just a resource to chew up in the pursuit of others' goals.

<Crash,> Shara said.

<Yes?>

<There is a place for you. There's a place for all of us.>

<I'm not like you,> he said.

He felt her smile in his mind.

<We are connected. Remember Proteus, Crash.>

The Link explained both Neptune's largest moon and a mythical demigod of changing knowledge. He didn't understand which she meant to reference.

Before he could ask, a warning system beeped on the control console. All the ravens in the command deck turned to inspect the source of the sound, which appeared to be Crash's display, and started cawing and flapping their wings.

<What is that?> Crash asked.

Shara made an angry sound and silenced the alarm. The ravens' caws took another few seconds to subside.

<It's a proximity alarm. There's a ship ignoring the quarantine broadcast. They look like they're going to board.>

<Is it the Port Authority, like you said?>

<No,> Shara said. <I should have known better, coming to Cruithne. These are pirates.>

<You said Cruithne was the safest place for us,> Crash said. He

didn't like sounding stupid, but he wanted to understand her reasoning.

<Cruithne is the safest place for us, yes. That doesn't mean it's a safe place.>

<Are we in danger?>

<I can't answer that.> Shara's mind grew distant.

The holodisplay shifted, showing a diagram of the ship with its spinning habitat canister and heavy engines. A smaller ship was matching spin with the habitat canister as it came in-line with the main airlock.

Based on his earlier guesses, Crash figured the ship might hold twenty people. It was shaped like a stick bug, not made to spin like the *Hesperia*.

<Oh no,> Shara said. *<They're overriding the lock system entirely. I can't stop them.>*

<I thought you could control the whole ship?> Crash asked.

<I'm not made for controlling things like ships. I create life. I can do basic tasks. I can't pilot.>

Crash shifted on the seat. *<Can we send the ravens after them like we did the crew?>*

<I'm afraid they'll kill them,> the AI said.

Crash nodded. These humans obviously didn't care about the threat of a bio-plague. *<Can we escape?>* he asked.

*<**You** can,>* Shara said quickly. *<The last remaining escape pod is made to hold a human crew of three. I think all of you would fit inside.>* The holodisplay shifted to show the location of the escape pod, on the opposite side of the habitat from the main airlock.

<I see it,> Crash said. The ravens nodded as well, black eyes rapt on the display.

<I'll activate the pod once you're all inside,> Shara said. *<I don't know what will happen when you reach Cruithne, but the vessel is designed to automatically dock with any nearby ship.>*

<What about you?> Crash asked.

<*I'll have to stay with the* Hesperia Nevada. *My body is too large to fit into an escape pod, and there's no way for you to move me there.*>

<*No,*> Crash shouted, squawking. <*I won't leave you here.*>

Another alarm went off in the room. The airlock was open.

A display to Crash's left side flashed to an interior sensor, showing a group of humans in ragged hazmat suits and bio masks pushing their way through the tight airlock. The suits meant they were at least a little concerned about the quarantine. They also carried heavy rifles and pistols.

<*What are we going to do?*> he asked, flapping his wings. He guessed they would find the command deck in just a few minutes.

Shara didn't answer him at first. A series of images flashed in his mind: the messages she was sending to the ravens to explain what they needed to do. The birds in the command deck cawed their understanding and flew out the door, leaving Crash alone among the warning alarms.

Crash bobbed his head. Unfamiliar panic flooded his mind. He tried to separate the feelings like he had done with all the new emotions, but this one made it hard to breathe. His heart beat faster than he had ever felt it.

<*Were you serious about helping me?*> Shara asked.

<*Of course. I want all of us to get away safe.*>

Shara paused again. Whatever she was trying to say seemed difficult for her. <*There is a way for part of me to leave with you,*> she said. <*I can create a shard. It's a part of my mind that would live in your Link. It's what your Link was designed for.*>

The memory of Testa babbling in pain from the voices in her mind made Crash go still. Shara must have felt his worry.

<*I know. It hasn't been proven to work.*>

<*I'll do it,*> Crash said.

<*You don't know what could happen, Crash.*>

<*What do we need to do?*>

She drew another long breath. <*Thank you, Crash. If I get*

through this, I'll find a way to repay you.>

<I want to help,> he said.

<You'll need to follow the ravens,> she said. *<I'll take care of the rest. I'll warn you before the transfer takes place. Do you remember the path to the escape pod?>*

<I saw it on the display.>

"Stars!" a muffled voice cursed from the doorway. "This place is covered in birdshit."

Crash jerked his head around to find two humans standing in the command deck's entry portal. Both were dressed in bio-suits and carrying pistols. He squawked in surprise and leapt off the back of the chair. In the air, however, he realized he didn't have many options for landing. They were blocking the only exit.

The first human, wearing a faded green suit, stepped into the room with his weapon held across his chest. His head tracked Crash's frantic movements.

"It's a parrot, for star's sakes," he said.

The other man, wearing an orange suit with 'TSS Hard Fall' running vertically down one side of his chest, raised his rifle to his shoulder. "After those damn crows, I'm just shooting this one."

"Wait," Green said. "If it is carrying a virus, I don't want you splattering bits of it all over the place. The salvage is going to be hard enough as it is. Nobody just abandons a ship unless there's something nasty aboard."

"I'm not showing anything. No radiation. No bio-markers. It's a ghost ship."

"Go check the pilot's console."

"I'm not getting near that damn bird," Orange complained. "Let me shoot it."

Crash touched down on the far side of the holodisplay, watching the two men through the glowing lines of the ship's schematic.

<They're inside the room now,> he told Shara. *<I'm going to get past them.>*

<Crash,> Shara said abruptly. *<One of them has access to the ship's database. They're going to find me. I can't let that happen. It's illegal for me to be here. They'll either turn me over to the TSF or sell me on the black market. I have to hide. I may have to—>*

<What?> he asked, hating the fear in her voice.

<I'll kill myself before I'm forced to make something evil.>

He realized the quarantine notice about an engineered plague wasn't outside the realm of possibility for Shara. In fact, it was probably something she had been made to do.

<Come on, then,> he said, readying himself for the gauntlet between himself and the door. *<Get onboard.>*

<You sound like an old vid,> she said. *<I'm coming.>*

Pressure built up in the back of Crash's mind. He thought it was a physical sensation at first, like forced air against the back of his head. Then a wave of vertigo forced him to close his eyes as he adjusted on his perch.

<Shara?> he asked.

She didn't answer.

Crash couldn't wait any longer. He opened his eyes, lowered his head, spread his wings, and launched out of the holotank, flying directly through the glowing image of the *Hesperia Nevada*.

The men shouted in surprise. They raised their weapons and nearly fired at each other as Crash darted between them. He reached the entryway and adjusted course, flapping his wings furiously, red tail feathers spread.

He navigated the main passageway, remembering the steps from the schematic. He shot around corners, perching high in the corridor for seconds at a time before flying again. He was made for short bursts between tree branches; the sustained flight made his wings heavy.

He was nearly at the secondary escape pod when he

rounded a corner and ran directly into a blue shipsuit.

"Whoa there!" the pirate shouted. Crash felt two oversized hands grab at his body, then slide over his wings, pinning him in place. He tried to bite and claw at the blue mass in front of him, but the pirate held him away from his body.

Crash turned his head, blinking angrily, to find a man with bright pink hair studying him, grinning like he'd won the lottery. He wasn't wearing a bio-mask.

"Well, look at you, pretty," the man said. "Looks like today's my lucky day."

Crash quailed inside, too aware of the silent Shara in the back of his mind.

He was caught.

FIRST INTERLUDE

THE HANGOVER
STELLAR DATE: 06.01.2945 (Adjusted Years)
LOCATION: Lowspin TSF Port Authority Liaison Office
REGION: Cruithne Station, Terran Hegemony, InnerSol

The TSF liaison office to Cruithne's Lowspin docks was an overworked cell, staffed by two lieutenants and a burned out major named Peck. Lieutenant Jerry Tarsis sat with his head in his hands, nursing a hangover as he watched inbound traffic in the primary cargo lanes. NSAIs managed the actual traffic patterns and alerted the liaison staff to any anomalies, but Peck insisted her lieutenants maintain eyeballs on the holodisplays to do the pattern crunching that only humans could perform...according to her, anyway.

Jerry glanced at his fellow space-lane manager, Darla Harmon, who was leaning back in her seat, pressing fingers to her temple to assuage a similar headache. They had been out late the night before, having closed down two different clubs. Together, they had tried briki flower for the first time and spent at *least* three hours lost in 'crazytown', as Darla called it.

He pulled one hand away from his head to stare at his fingers, which still seemed rubbery and twisty, swimming in front of his eyes the longer he looked. He'd been shifting his focus between the holodisplay and his hands whenever one became too unbearable to watch anymore.

"Hey," Darla groaned. "You hear that?"

"What?" Jerry said.

"That quarantine alert just dropped."

Jerry shifted his gaze to his console, squinting. He found the TMS *Hesperia Nevada* on the check release list, knowing for a fact that it had just been at the top of the inbound quarantine queue.

"Did you get a release order?" he croaked through his headache.

"No." Darla sat up, her voice growing sharper. She was the type to thrive under pressure. She could push away a killer hangover with proper self-motivation. "I think we've got a hacker in the manifest system."

Jerry shook his head, taking a deep breath. He forced himself into a more upright position. If the major came in and found him slouching while Darla was working, there'd be hell to pay. The major only cut them slack when everybody was slacking equally.

"There it is," Darla said, pointing at her console. "It had a bio-lock, crew abandoned. I had it on the salvage list, but the EV crews are behind like always."

"Better them than me," Jerry replied.

"Well, they're so slow that pirates are tracking the list and jumping ahead of them. Only these dummies probably didn't realize the ship had a quarantine lock."

"It was squealing quarantine to the whole sector," Jerry said. "Pirates aren't that dumb."

"Pirates don't think like we do. Don't waste time trying to figure them out."

"Wait," Jerry said, squinting again. He couldn't tell if his vision was blurring again, or if something had broken free from *Hesperia Nevada*. It looked like an escape pod, but the ship was empty. At least the crew had marked it that way. He pulled up *Hesperia Nevada*'s registry and studied its manifest. The ship had been on a long-term cargo and personnel transport trip before signaling the distress code and heading back for Cruithne, its point of origin. It was entirely possible the whole mess was a smuggling operation. Technically, it was their job to stop smugglers. However, trying to stop smuggling on Cruithne was like chasing kittens—sadistic kittens with exotic weapons.

The object that had separated from the quarantined ship was now showing all the attributes of something under its own power. Jerry sent a ping, and the response came back on the emergency band.

"They just launched an escape pod," he said. Adrenaline tempered a bit of his hangover. He sat up straighter in his chair, wondering if he should notify the major. An escape pod launch inside local space wasn't strange, per se, but combined with the quarantine notice and apparent hacking, the *Hesperia Nevada* was turning into the shift's prime irritation.

"I'm calling the major," Darla said.

"He's just going to ask what we know about it."

"So I'll tell him what we know. We need to get the Quick Reaction Force tracking that ship. It's under illegal salvage notice at the very least."

"Yeah, yeah," Jerry said. He waited. "I thought you said you were going to call him," he said.

"I'm thinking," Darla answered. "Is the pod showing a destination yet?"

Jerry read his console. "Lowspin, of course. I can pull it in with a drone before it alerts anybody else."

"Do it. That looks better. Like we're doing something about it. I'll notify the QRF Watch Commander. Once you notify the major, grab a rifle."

"What?" Jerry demanded, incredulous. "I'm not going down there."

Darla stood and stretched, looking sleek in her duty uniform. Jerry's mind flashed a reminder of the several ways she'd indicated she wasn't interested in him the night before.

"If we go down there and figure out what's going on, the major won't kick our asses for the quarantine override."

Jerry could see the logic but still didn't like the idea of

poking his head into a mystery pod from a quarantine ship that had probably been smuggling biohazards.

"It'll get scanned at the dock, dummy," Darla said, seeing his expression. "I swear, you're the most timid soldier in the TSF."

"I'm an officer, not a soldier," Jerry said petulantly.

"Exactly."

He grabbed the rifle Darla tossed his way and automatically performed a functions check on the battery and trigger mechanism, then followed her out of the cramped office into the busy corridor outside. They were immediately surrounded by the rough workers of the Lowspin docks: mechanics with grease-stained faces, porters leading cargo mules, skinny spacers in faded shipsuits, sharp-eyed station dwellers looking for a score, and any number of other thousands of travelers stopping between Mars and Earth. Some people respected the pair in their TSF uniforms and got out of the way, others immediately saw the rifles and moved, while still more simply watched them warily.

Jerry did his best to stare straight ahead, eyes on Darla's shoulders.

They reached the main lifts and dropped four levels to the outermost section of the ring, where airlocks opened onto vacuum. Most ships never actually docked on the station—not wanting to waste the fuel required to match spin—and sent drones or shuttles instead. A few were docked for repairs, and even fewer were actually berthed in the enormous bays for hull repair and upgrades.

The people were even rougher this close to the skin. Jerry couldn't help thinking they all looked grey-faced from vacuum exposure—or it might have been the poor lighting.

"It's just up ahead," he said, reading the Link update.

"Did you notify the major?" Darla asked.

"Not yet."

"You'd better hurry up. Telling him were working to solve a problem is better than letting him know we just found a bio-weapon."

How does she understand people so much better than me?

Rather than contacting Major Peck directly, Jerry composed a quick message informing him of their task and assuring him they would update soon, once they'd assessed the situation. He read over his word choice again to make sure he sounded assertive enough—like a self-confident captain rather than a lieutenant on desk duty—and sent the update.

Thankfully, the major didn't respond right away.

He must be busy. That was fine by Jerry.

Darla turned left off the corridor and led the way into a series of catwalks as the bulkheads closed in, surrounding them in the guts of the ring wall. The air grew humid, reeking of burned oil and overheated silicon fiber.

"Here it is," she said, stopping in front of a circular hatch in the corridor wall. A blinking blue light on the locking mechanism was the only indication that an escape pod sat on the other side of the airlock.

Without waiting, Darla tapped the lock, and Jerry felt the query on his Link, verifying his status as a TSF Customs Official. The station-side lock door cycled and slowly swung open.

Darla put a hand on her hip, rifle leaned on her shoulder. "After you," she said.

Jerry quailed. "What do you mean?"

"You're leading the way, right? Since you're always reminding me that you outrank me, I figured you would want the glory of the kill."

Jerry glanced at the open port. The narrow space within the airlock was lit only by another flashing blue light.

"Shouldn't we get haz suits?" he asked, trying to make his voice not sound like he was whining.

Darla shook her head. "The scan's clean. It's not a bio threat. That means it's most likely a hacked manifest, which means smuggling. And what's our mission?"

"Anti-piracy and smuggling interdiction," Jerry grumbled.

He held his rifle at port arms and hunched over to climb into the cramped airlock. He shuffled forward, leading with his left ear as if he could hear anything from inside the pod. He moved like a nervous crab.

"Seriously?" Darla asked.

He didn't look back at her. He checked the scan again, just to make sure – *totally* not looking for an excuse to get away. The pod's check-scan returned clean, showing its point of origin and the presence of an IR signature inside. The data was all over the place, though, making him wonder if the pod was damaged. The escape craft held three people maximum, but was showing a return of at least fifty heart rates.

"Something isn't right, Darla. We should put it on security lock-down." He looked back to see her frowning at him.

"Get out of there, Tarsis," she said, sighing. "I'll open the damn pod. Why did you join the Space Force, again?"

Jerry swallowed, ready to leave and let her take over, when the blue light on the locking mechanism switched to green.

"What?" he called out in surprise.

The lock had self-initiated. It was opening.

Jumping to his Link, Jerry quickly checked the security level on the escape pod's software. It was on quarantine lock and shouldn't have been able to do anything without his authority code. Yet there it was, opening.

"Get back," he told Darla, voice squeaking at the end.

"What's going on?" she demanded.

Jerry slid away, raising his rifle, as the pod's hatch hissed and swung open. Red light leaked from the widening gap, and then a rush of black bodies filled the airlock. Was he imagining the hundred shiny black eyes staring at him?

Squealing, Jerry fell backward as claws, beaks and feathers beat against his face. He heard Darla shouting behind him. The rush seemed to take forever, and then Darla was shouting his name.

"Dammit, Jerry! Get out here."

Jerry rolled to his knees, grabbing at his rifle. His uniform was peppered with hundreds of small punctures, and his cheeks were bleeding. He scrambled to his feet and ran out of the airlock. Darla was already halfway down the corridor, looking like she was chasing whatever had left the escape pod. When he finally caught up with her, he could only stop and join her mute upward stare.

Out in the main corridor, where the space opened to accommodate a massive repair bay, at least fifty ravens were circling over their heads. He had no idea how they had fit in the tiny escape pod, but now they were cawing angrily and beating their wings as they swarmed.

Jerry swore he heard something like static on his Link, like an electric charge, buzzing deep in the back of his mind. Was it the hangover? For an instant, it almost sounded like the angry ravens were broadcasting.

He squinted at the mass, trying to see a pattern in their movements, and then could only watch as they left the bay in a single serpentine line to fly down the corridor. In a minute, they were gone.

Darla looked at him, her hair tangled in her eyes. She pushed it aside.

"I guess we should follow them," she said.

"I didn't let them out," Jerry said quickly. "They did it on their own. I don't know how, but they overrode the quarantine."

"Does it matter?" Darla asked.

"You'd better tell the major," Jerry said. "It wasn't me. I didn't let those crows out."

"They were bigger than crows. They were ravens."

Jerry's Link sparked with reports of the wild birds wreaking havoc all throughout the Lowspin docs.

<Tarsis!> Major Peck barked in his mind. *<Where's my update?>*

Jerry looked at Darla, then down at the dull silver lieutenant's bar on the front of his uniform. Sighing, he pulled the rank off his chest and handed it to Darla.

"Nice working with you," he said.

* * * * *

After a few hours spent terrorizing the workers of Lowspin, the ravens disappeared into a series of maintenance tunnels, bursting out near the old warehouse-turned-bazaar called Night Park, where a dry plascrete fountain provided ample territory to perch, along with easy access to food and water in the surrounding vendor booths.

There was another bonus to the location, and that was the constant flow of humans who loved to sit at the fountain, or often walked past on their way to other parts of the market.

Lacking the speech capacity of their Grey Parrot brethren, the corvids experienced the Link as a swirl of images reinforced by emotion, a shared dream that allowed them to see into the minds of people passing by at a level that was below conscious communication. Two people discussing a trip to the bazaar might remember their previous visits through the images and sensation of memory—or even the images created by imagination—while also painting the conversation with the emotions of anxiety while on a date, concern about finances, or dread at not finding the right gift.

While the humans were caught up in their surface communications, the ravens plainly saw their underlying emotions.

Being mischievous birds, they immediately understood the benefit in their location.

A man eating his lunch beside the fountain could be chased away easily by a single raven croaking, "Fired! Fired!" or "Unloved! Unloved!"

The raw blast of a raven's croak only added to the populace's unsettling experience of realizing they were being harassed by telepathic birds.

At first, the squawking harangues were met by surprise and often fear. Then, more adventurous—and self-confident—people approached the fountain, realizing they could communicate with the ravens by focusing on certain memories or scenes.

One teenage girl was able to get the ravens excitedly shouting happy words like, "Rainbow!" and "Puppy!" only to have one of her classmates receive "Cheater! Cheater! Cheater!"

Factions arose among the vendors in the bazaar, who were growing tired of losing anything shiny from the booths, including the bolts that held canopies together, while others experienced increased business as word spread that mind-reading ravens had taken up residence at the Night Park Fountain, which had previously been nothing but an eyesore.

Station Administration, the local TSF sub-station, and finally several local crime syndicates squared off in the debate about what to do about the ravens. However, everything came to a halt when a nest appeared, filled with speckled eggs.

Crowds gathered to monitor the nest. Vendors and visitors to the market became aware that most of the ravens were paired off in couples. This made the ravens seem less like a wild horde, and more like colonists in the wildlands of Cruithne.

The couples focused on the eggs that were now appearing daily, while the unmated birds demonstrated impressive feats of intelligence to secure items for additional nests. Parents brought their kids down to the Night Park fountain to see the ravens, which completely changed the character of the grey market bazaar.

Musicians and candymakers materialized to cater to families. The Station Administration scheduled community events. Link forums documented the best insults from the various ravens, while others named the birds and followed their activities.

Visiting the Ravens became a local pastime, as locals and tourists alike came down to the Night Park fountain to endure the ravens' never-ending roast. Some visitors were heckled ruthlessly, while others were offered small gifts of shiny bolts, bits of fabric, or filament from important network nodes.

No one remembered when the first grey parrots appeared at the fountain. The pair may have been pets abandoned by their owners when they left Cruithne, or—as legend suggests—they were freed by the mischievous ravens, who travelled throughout the whole asteroid, and even poorly secured ships at the docks.

After the parrots came several breeds of songbirds, and a tall rooster with red and purple feathers that patrolled the base of the fountain, accepting bits of food from visiting kids with a regal flick of his comb.

No one would have admitted it at first, but the birds of the Night Park fountain provided Cruithne, and especially the bazaar, a respectability that neither had ever had before. If the birds chose to settle on Cruithne, then it couldn't all be bad, right?

The age-old image of a pirate with a parrot on their shoulder had transitioned to spacer mythology, giving the fountain the feel of Santa Claus' North Pole workshop, and the addition of the songbirds and wise-looking, judgmental ravens simply rounded out the fantasy.

Eventually, the fountain was more Cruithne than Cruithne had been before, and the birds were there to stay. If they stole an augmented eye or called someone a biting name, well, that was now good luck, and many a spacer and wannabe pirate made the pilgrimage to visit the fountain, tossing in ancient coins and other shinies to please the birds.

Stars above, every spacer knew they needed all the good luck they could get before their next trip into the black....

PART II:
CRASH CRASH CRASH

THE HUSTLE

STELLAR DATE: 03.21.2956 (Adjusted Years)
LOCATION: TSF Storage Yard
REGION: Cruithne Station, Terran Hegemony, InnerSol

Eleven (or so) years later...

Ngoba Starl and Riggs Zanda crouched in the service alcove
as the security drone shot by, scorching the walls around it with
orange heat beams. Ngoba felt the rush of warmth and realized
it had barely missed his face.

As soon as the blocky thing was past, wiry Ngoba rolled into
the tunnel and came up on one knee. He had about two seconds
to steady the shoulder-fired missile launcher before the drone
spotted him with its rear sensors.

"Ngoba!" Riggs hissed. "Safety!"

Ngoba dropped the heavy tube to glare at his friend. "I got
the safety. That's the first damn thing I—"

The drone whirled at the sound of their voices, its bulk
filling the tight corridor like a cubic sea anemone. Two lurid red
sensors in its front panel glowed like angry eyes.

"Aim!" Riggs shouted. "Ngoba, aim!"

Ngoba ignored his friend's frantic instructions and squeezed
the blast tube against his neck. His fingers scrambled over the
blocky trigger mechanism before he found the right
combination of buttons and mashed on the controls. A

rumbling *whoosh* filled the tunnel, followed almost immediately by an explosion that sent orange waves of flame rolling back toward Ngoba. He smelled burning hair and figured he was going to lose his beard and eyebrows. He vaguely remembered dropping the missile tube.

* * * * *

Lying on his back, ears ringing as he squeezed his eyes closed against the stinging smoke, Ngoba Starl wondered if he'd made a mistake somewhere.

They'd definitely fucked up recently. His best friend Riggs Zanda had absolutely made a mistake with the cargo hold's security system, activating the overwatch and its angry drone, which must have been surplus TSF, from the amount of death-making hardware it had been packing.

Before that. Long before that.

Was it his fault he'd been born on Cruithne Station, the asshole of the universe? Was it his fault he lived in a junked freighter they called the TSS *Squat* with a bunch of half-starved orphans, doing work for a cruel woman they called Mama Chala? And was she cruel, or did she just have high standards, as she liked to say? Was it his fault they weren't old enough for the surgery needed for Link implantation, so Riggs had to hack like a savage?

Unable to hold his breath any longer, Ngoba coughed. His throat burned.

Rolling onto his stomach, he tried to peer through his eyelashes, eyes still stinging like he'd been dunked in acid. He pulled at his beard, thick for a seventeen-year-old, but still natty. He still had his curly hair, too, though his hand came back covered in dust.

"Riggs," Ngoba whispered. "You all right?"

"No," came a whimpering response. "I can't believe you

used the missile launcher."

"What are you talking about? What was I supposed to do?"

"You realize the overpressure alone could have blown the cargo block off into space? What would we do then? We'd be sucking hard vacuum."

"I told you when I brought the missile that I might fire it."

"*Might* is a long way from pulling the trigger."

"I aimed it land-side. Nothing was getting blown out into space."

"Overpressure, Ngoba. Overpressure. You need to learn about this shit if you're going to live to see twenty."

Ngoba shook his head, feeling more stubborn the longer the conversation continued. "You knew I was going to fire the missile."

Riggs sneezed. "Your missile shit all over me. That happened, too. I'm covered in propellant."

"Serves you right." Ngoba wheezed a laugh but only started coughing again. "Do you hear the drone? I can't see anything."

"It's dead."

"You're sure it's dead? How can you see anything?"

"I don't have to. Its control frequencies are all cold."

"You can see that?" Ngoba said, letting his head fall against the warm concrete. The floor was gritty through his beard.

"I can see it right here. Just like I knew the thing was coming after us. If I hadn't warned you about the drone, we'd be dead right now."

"So you triggered the defensive perimeter, waking the drone so it could attack us, but I should *thank* you because you warned me in time?"

"How doesn't that make sense?"

Riggs groaned. "We better get back down there. We need to get something out of this job."

"You think we have time?" Ngoba asked "The overwatch system will have notified somebody."

"Didn't you send the vacuum breach alarm?"

"Yes, I sent the damn alarm."

"Then they'll think it's a meteorite strike or a drunk pilot or something."

"I wish we had damn EV suits," Ngoba said. "We're too close to the edge of the ring here."

"It'll be fine. The ring is held on Cruithne with jizz and spit and the gravity created by all us assholes."

"I like that," Ngoba said. " 'Held on by jizz and spit'. I'm going to use that, brother." He pushed himself to his knees. The smoke was starting to clear, and he was able to make out bits of the drone scattered all down the corridor in front of them, mixed in with broken pieces of concrete from a collapsed section of the ceiling.

Riggs shook his head, and his hair became slightly more brown, dust filling the air around him. He coughed. He had narrow green eyes in a squashed head that reminded Ngoba of an oblong lemon.

"Come on," Ngoba said.

Without waiting, he turned to jog back down the narrow service corridor toward the airlock to the attached shipping container, their target. He was surprised to find they had only run about a hundred meters from the explosion. It had seemed like a full kilometer when the drone was howling behind them.

Riggs pushed past him at the airlock to check its control panel. Ngoba watched over his short friend's shoulder as he flashed through control menus until he had access to its administration protocols. This was where they had been standing before, when the door slid open to reveal the red eyes of the attack drone.

Ngoba tensed as the door slid open a second time, even though he knew there was nothing left inside that could hurt them.

"Quit breathing down my neck," Riggs complained.

"Quit taking your sweet time about this. We've probably got private security on the way."

"I turned off all the external reporting."

"Just like you turned off the overwatch security system, yeah?"

Riggs growled as a breath of cold air blew back over them. With the door open, he stepped into the cramped interior of the shipping container.

"Wait here," Riggs said, craning his neck to look around. "It's too tight in here for both of us to go poking around."

"Good sign," Ngoba said. "Lots of freight." He patted himself down, feeling for rips in his shirt and pants. He only had one set of clothes and he took a lot of pride in his appearance—something the other squatters all teased him ruthlessly for.

"Dammit," Riggs cursed from inside the container, hidden by cargo crates.

"What is it?"

"This damn thing is full of expired flour."

"No," Ngoba said, blinking. "You said the manifest showed protein substitute."

"I know what it used to say." Riggs barked in pain as he hit his head on something inside the container.

"That makes no sense," Ngoba said. "Why would somebody set up an attack drone to guard a bunch of flour? Are you telling me I carried that missile all this way—wasted Chala's missile, dammit—for a bunch of flour?"

"Shut up, Ngoba. I'm looking. It was all cover for the weapons drop, but the regular contents should match the manifest."

"You better look harder."

Disregarding Riggs's command to wait at the airlock, Ngoba pushed his way into the container, squeezing between the haphazardly stacked crates. His breath blew in front of him in white clouds. Inside, he found Riggs crouched next to a wide crate with its lid hanging open.

"This was it," Riggs said as Ngoba climbed up beside him. "This was the drop point. This should be full of Mars Protectorate handguns."

"Does the crate have a control panel? Any access records?"

Riggs shot him an irritated glance. "Do you see an access panel? It's a dumb crate."

Ngoba moved the lid, listening as the hinges squeaked. He stared into the empty crate for a minute as he started to shiver, a reminder they were standing in an uninsulated metal box, with hard vacuum a few meters away. Something about the bottom of the crate didn't look right, so he leaned in to tap it.

"It's got a hollow bottom," he confirmed.

Riggs shook his head as if he didn't understand, so Ngoba shouldered him out of the way and reached down into the crate with both hands. He pressed on one side of the crate's bottom and laughed when it moved easily. Pulling the alloy plate to one side, he found two pistols lying on their sides.

"That's it?" Riggs complained. "Two crap handguns?"

"Have you looked at them? How do you know they're crap?"

"They're crap. We're screwed. Mama Chala's going to kick us out of the squat."

Ngoba pulled the pistols out of the crate and let the false bottom fall back into place. A little cloud of dust floated up as it fell. He handed the second pistol to Riggs and turned his over in his hands. It was a Terran Space Force standard-issue pulse pistol with no bio-lock.

"These are pretty good, Riggs," he said. "I'd rather have one of these than that missile tube."

Riggs shrugged. "You take it. I'm trying to figure out what we're going to tell Mama Chala. We can't show up with just these things. We'll be popping zits off her back for days."

"Because we don't listen," Ngoba said automatically, mimicking one of Mama Chala's speeches.

"Because we don't listen," Riggs agreed. He sighed.

Ngoba slapped his friend on the shoulder. "Come on. If we're going to get fucked, we might as well get it over with."

"That's the thing. I don't want to get fucked."

"Then find us a new score so we've got some currency for rent."

"This was the only thing I could find." Riggs slammed the lid of the crate closed and collapsed back on his heels, shoulders slumped. "We're screwed, Ngoba. We're going to go back there, and she's going to tell us we're too old, we're not kids anymore." He shuddered. "Or she's going to make me snuggle with her. I know she's going to."

Ngoba put his hand on his friend's shoulder and pushed the second pistol into his hands. "I've got your back, Riggs. Don't worry about that. We'll find someone a little more age-appropriate to harass you. How's that?" He grinned, but his friend ignored him.

Riggs looked down at the pistol. "I guess we could roll a tourist down in Night Park."

"You know I don't like doing that. Bad karma."

"All your good karma's going to kill us," Riggs complained.

Ngoba jammed his pistol into his belt and climbed to his feet. "At least we'll be mostly good people. You let me talk to Mama Chala. I'll explain the situation."

"No snuggling," Riggs said. "I'm not going to do it."

"No snuggling," Ngoba agreed. "Hey now, how about this? Let's catch some Crash before we head back. That'll get your mind off this mess."

"We don't have any money to bet. Nobody's going to take contraband TSF hardware."

"We don't need to bet, my friend. We enjoy Crash for the pure spirit of the sport."

Riggs groaned. He held the pistol up as if he expected Ngoba to take it back, then finally pushed it into his waistband as well. "This thing pokes me," he complained.

"Builds character," Ngoba said. "Come on."

DREAMING OF PARROTS

STELLAR DATE: 03.21.2956 (Adjusted Years)
LOCATION: Crash Games Hangar, Night Park
REGION: Cruithne Station, Terran Hegemony, InnerSol

The Crash field was in an old hangar down by Night Park. Ngoba and Riggs had to wind their way among the stalls and crowds that filled the park's bazaar, taking the long way around to avoid the fountain in the middle where the grey parrots hung out, cursing at passersby.

"Squawk! Hey, dummy," they heard in the distance. "Hey, hey, dummy!"

Throughout its long history as a sanctuary for smuggling, various entrepreneurs had tried to start more respectable tourist attractions on the station. Because, Ngoba figured, even pirates end up with families eventually. Most ventures had failed; from the amusement parks that were now red-light districts, to the theme restaurants that had become burned-out drug dens.

The fountain at Night Park had somehow continued to exist on its own momentum, maybe because it was protected by the huge, open-air bazaar and provided one of the few open spaces where people could eat, but mostly through the protection of the grey parrots and their raven underlings, who harangued anyone they didn't like, sang to children, squawked puns and stole crumbs from picnicking families.

"You've got a funny face, *squawk!*" shouted one parrot, and fifty others would take up the call: "Funny face! Funny face!"

"Golden—retriever," another parrot called quickly. "*Squawk!* Your daddy was a golden *re*—treever!"

The fountain itself was a wide, low-walled circle where, conceivably, people could sit if they weren't afraid of the white streamers of bird shit falling from the concrete 'tree' in the middle of the fountain. A central concrete pole jutted up from the bubbling water, spiked with hundreds of branches that were covered in birds, from crows with thick black beaks and intently watching eyes, to sparrows, scrub jays, starlings, finches and, ultimately, the parrots at the top. The parrots didn't like sitting in such exposed areas and were usually out among the stalls, bothering merchants as they perched inside their canopies, squawking abuse.

"*Squawk!* You're as pretty as mud, pretty as mud."

The most interesting thing about the parrots—to Ngoba, at least—was that they named themselves. There were plenty of urban legends about how the grey parrots of Night Park had escaped from some bio experiment seven hundred years ago and taken up residence at the fountain. Ngoba didn't believe it, but it was fun to scare the younger kids back at the *Squat* with stories of mind-controlling parrots who would invade their dreams. As a little boy, the parrots had represented freedom in a place where everyone was a prisoner, whether they knew it or not.

"Hey, Riggs," Ngoba asked as they walked past the edge of the fountain.

Riggs was eyeing a booth displaying every type of knife imaginable, from tiny razors to serrated blades a meter long.

"What?" he asked absently.

"I think my conscience is a grey parrot."

Riggs shot Ngoba an irritated glance, brown eyes narrowed. "That doesn't make any sense."

"Whenever I'm about to do something I know is wrong, I hear a parrot squawking at me."

"That's depressing."

"It's very effective."

Riggs screwed up his face in thought. "So you're saying you need a parrot to tell you what to do?"

"I'm saying these damn parrots are so ingrained in my mind

that they haunt me," Ngoba said. "It's not complicated, brother."

Riggs pursed his lips, apparently considering the idea. "Has a parrot told you how stupid your beard looks? Has a parrot said it looks like you glued pubic hair on your cheeks? That's what a parrot should tell you."

Ngoba shook his head sadly. "I'm trying to be real with you, Riggs, and you just throw my love out like trash."

"Love? This is how you express love?"

"Love is relative," Ngoba said. "Love is a parrot, squawking at you from a concrete tree."

"Now you're just fucking with me," Riggs said.

Ngoba gave him a grin, stroking the beard Riggs couldn't grow.

They left the bazaar through a wide set of old cargo doors, and walked down the corridor toward the Crash field. Both sides of the hall were lined with people in close groups making bets, beverage vendors, and other purveyors of illicit substances. Ngoba caught the smell of cooking protein and felt his stomach rumble.

"When was the last time we ate?" he asked Riggs.

"I don't know. Yesterday."

"You hungry?"

"You got any money?"

Ngoba ran his thumb along the pistol grip hidden inside his belt and did some quick math to determine how much he might get for it. He clenched his stomach and waited for the cramp to pass, figuring what little he could get for the pistol—it was hot TSF hardware, after all—wasn't worth the trade in going hungry a few more hours.

As they neared the end of the hall, the crowd grew denser until they were waiting to get through the four doors into the Crash field. From the other side of the doors, they could hear cheering and shouts, punctuated by mechanical-sounding music from the Crash machines.

As they craned their necks to see through the doors into the field space on the other side, Ngoba caught sight of a kid named Fug who had lived in the *Squat* for a little while. Fug looked like an olive on a toothpick, her big head and bulging eyes hunched down between her narrow shoulders. She had greasy black hair held back with a green visor, like those card players wore, but Ngoba knew hers also harbored some sort of HUD.

"Fug!" Ngoba shouted.

Riggs started at the sound of Ngoba's voice then shook his head.

"I don't like that kid," he growled.

Ngoba gave him a sideways grin. "She's crazy. You remember when she hacked the autobank to spit credits at TSF soldiers? That was great."

"She's reckless is what she is. That almost landed us in a TSF prison, and we didn't even get any credit to show for it."

"You're just jealous because she's a better hacker than you are."

Riggs scowled. "How's she a better hacker than me?"

"You know she can hack Crash, right?"

"I'll believe it when I see it."

Fug didn't push her way over so much as wait for them to get closer. She nodded to Ngoba and gave Riggs a weak smirk. "You guys here for the big game?" she asked in her reedy voice.

"Who's up?" Ngoba asked.

"Bindle versus Rack Smasher," Fug said, sounding bored. "Bindle's going to draw out the Smasher for a few rounds then do that hammer move and end the match. I think Rack Thirteen's got money on Bindle, so Smasher will throw."

Ngoba looked around to check if anyone was listening. "You just talk about that in the open, Fug? What if somebody hears you?"

Fug smiled with her mouth, but her eyes remained bored,

tinted green by the visor. "I'm just adding to the noise, Ngoba. Your buddy Riggs knows how this works. Hi, Riggs." She gave Riggs a sarcastic wave that he answered with a scowl.

Fug smirked, looking pleased with herself. She lowered her voice and said, "I'm here to help Bindle."

Riggs pushed closer. "How are you going to do that?"

Fug tapped the side of her round head. "Positive thoughts, Riggs," she said, louder now so that people glanced at her. "That's all we need. All of us thinking positive thoughts together, aiming them at the object of our desire, and that person is going to feel all that powerful energy."

Riggs frowned like he was taking her seriously.

Fug skittered a laugh and pressed clasped hands to her heart. "All of us aiming our hopes and dreams at that one individual, and they can't help but grow strong under the combined energy of our souls."

Riggs scoffed, embarrassed by all the attention they were getting. "Next you're going to sell us some magic crystals."

Fug unclasped her hands to reveal her middle finger extended for Riggs's benefit. "I was saving that just for you," she said. "So you could learn something."

"What's he supposed to learn from that?" Ngoba said, winking at her.

"I had but one fuck to give him, and I just let it go," Fug said.

Ngoba covered his mouth, laughing, while Riggs blew out an exasperated breath.

The crowd around them had been growing progressively louder as they neared the doors. Once they passed through, shoulder-to-shoulder now with everyone else, the roar became deafening.

Ngoba's attention was immediately drawn to a bit of brightly colored movement in the middle of the hangar, where the white circle of the Crash platform stood above the crowds gathered all around, faces turned upward at the melee above them.

Currently in the circle stood two figures about fifteen meters tall, one a bright green crocodile standing on two legs with a yellow-red striped propeller beanie on the top of its head, the other a barbarian woman in a fur bikini and horned cap. The crocodile had six-inch claws and a spiked tail, while the Conan woman held a broadsword in both hands, elbows up with the hilt even with her bright green eyes.

"Rack Smasher's looking totally *hot* tonight," Riggs shouted, barely audible over the cheers as the barbarian took a swipe at the crocodile.

"Rack Smasher's the crocodile," Ngoba shouted back.

"Yeah, I *know*." Riggs's smile grew even brighter as the lights dimmed, spotlights focusing on the platform.

The roving spotlights swept across the giant figures in the middle of the hangar, only sharpening their details. Ngoba knew they were digital projections on a giant holograph, but he couldn't help marveling at the fine detail of the waving fur on Brindle's shorts, or the emerald shine across Rack Smasher's back.

Abruptly, the arena swirled and became a series of rising and falling platforms. Brindle immediately leapt for the nearest platform, waited for a heartbeat as it rose, then rolled into a hammer fall aimed at the crocodile's head.

Ngoba glanced at Fug, whose attention was on the edge of the platform where the two *real* combatants were sitting next to each other, staring at smaller, side-by-side screens hidden from Ngoba's view. They might have been kids from the *Squat*, looking just as greasy and malnourished as any wannabe gang churl. What those two had that most of Ngoba's peers lacked was a laser focus that infused their entire bodies. The ancient controllers were held tightly, forearms stiff, thumbs and fingers moving with precision.

"Those guys are robots," Riggs said, catching the direction

of Ngoba's gaze.

"You think they're hardwired? They don't look like they could afford augmentation."

"Maybe but it doesn't do much good. Everything still has to go through those stupid controllers. It's all human interacting with machine."

"Yeah," Ngoba said.

Rack Smasher had just taken a rolling swipe at Brindle's legs, causing massive damage. The crocodile crouched to start its power move, then jumped, spinning in the air, tail lashing wildly. The reptile struck the barbarian woman like a thunderbolt, and she nearly dropped her sword. Little yellow birds circled her head as she stood stunned.

The crowd shouted in unison: *"Fi-nal Crash! Fi-nal Crash! Fi-nal Crash!"*

Rack Smasher went into an animation that had him stalking the edge of the platform he and Brindle shared, urging the crowd to get louder as he held a claw to one side of his head, white teeth shining. Just as the last bird circled Brindle's head and it looked like she was about to come out of her stupor, Rack Smasher spun twice to wind up his tail and struck her in the shins, sweeping her knees out from under her. The great two-handed sword went spinning off the edge of the platform, and Rack Smasher stood with one clawed foot on her stomach.

The crowd was simultaneously groaning and cheering. All around Ngoba, money changed hands while the official scoreboards brightened on the ceiling, displaying odds and payouts.

He glanced at Fug and found the skinny kid grinning like a fool. Fug leaned close to say, "Works every time."

Ngoba frowned. "What works every time?"

"My system." She motioned for Ngoba to lean in closer.

Ngoba glanced at Riggs and saw that he was engrossed in the scoreboards. Fug didn't seem to want to talk to him anyway.

"It's like this," she began. "I hacked the controllers."

"What?" Ngoba glanced around to make sure no one was listening. "Isn't that an ancient hardwired system? How did you pull that off?"

Fug waved a limp hand. "I got a way. I'm not giving it up. Trade secret. But I figured it out and I can throw the match. I just made enough for a year."

Ngoba raised an eyebrow. "That much? You better be careful, girl. Somebody's going to take notice of that kind of bet. Especially the loser. Don't the players get their hands broken or something when they lose?"

Fug flashed an evil smile. "Depends on the bout. If one of the lower syndicates like Regal Flight is leading the bets, then yeah, they break fingers, hang 'em high, whatever. But if Rack Thirteen is on board, *whoo* now, the loser might end up sucking vacuum."

"And you like that? Doesn't that mean both the players *and* the gangs might want to turn you into a stuffed lamp?"

"You worry too much, Ngoba. I like you better when you're cracking jokes. Nobody's going to catch me. I'll tell you what. You do something for me, and I'll cut you in on the next match."

Ngoba pulled his head back, throat going dry. He glanced around again to check for anyone *casually* eavesdropping. Riggs was sharing drinks with a blonde woman now, out of earshot and looking pleased with her attention.

"I'll be straight with you, Fug," Ngoba said. "I could use some money right now. Chala's going to kick us out if we don't come back with some rent."

Fug spat. "Chala and her hugs. She nearly squeezed my head off, treating me like a dolly. You should get out of there."

"I'm going to."

"She doesn't make you pop her back zits, does she?" Fug said, shivering visibly.

"You mean tending the garden?" Ngoba said, voice going

cold. "Yeah."

Fug studied him through her green visor. She looked like she was working out a math problem with a hundred steps. Finally, she said, "I'll cut you in, Ngoba." She glanced past Ngoba's shoulder, probably checking on Riggs. She pointed at Ngoba's chest. "Just you, though. Riggs can't get in on this."

"What do you mean? You know Riggs's my boy."

"He thinks he can hack. He can't. I don't want his dirty dick-beaters on my system."

Ngoba bit his lip, considering the situation. He could always try to swing enough credit for both of them, solve the problem on his own. That's what he could tell Riggs, anyway, then send him on another possible job. They might actually end up ahead that way.

"What do you want me to do?" he finally asked.

Fug smiled, her thin lips curving like a ghoul's. The green visor made her cheeks look bloodless. She nodded toward the players, who were now posing for some vid producer.

"You see that guy standing next to them?" she asked. "The one in the cape?"

Ngoba frowned, squinting. He hadn't seen anyone in a cape. Then the vid guy moved, and a tall, thin man in a red cape came into view. He had spiky blue hair that fell to his shoulders.

"I see him," Ngoba said.

"That's Slarva. Crash is his baby."

"I've never heard his name."

"Of course not."

"So what crew is he with?"

"He's not part of any crew. He's above the crews, the syndicates, Cruithne Administration, all of it. He's got all the power in this room."

The envy in Fug's voice made Ngoba glance back at her. The little woman's eyes were bloodshot and intense, a hunger on her face.

"What do you want me to do?" Ngoba asked again, starting to worry about what he'd agreed to.

Fug shook her head absently, still staring at Slarva. "Nothing dangerous, Ngoba. Nothing to worry about. I just want you to follow him. Tonight. After this Crash. I want you to follow him and tell me what he does. That's all."

"That's it?"

She moved her gaze to Ngoba's face. "Yeah."

"No sex stuff, right?" he asked, feeling more distrustful the longer he tried to understand her strange expression.

She shrugged. "I dunno, Ngoba. Maybe. That's what I want you to find out. You in?"

He took another look at the blue-haired man, who seemed to move like he was floating underwater, his motions slow and exaggerated. He didn't seem to be carrying any weapons Ngoba could see. He didn't spot any security thugs or drones. The two players only nodded and smiled at him like bobble heads.

"Yeah, Fug," he said quietly. "Yeah. I'll do it."

She gave him another ghoul grin and winked at him, which sent a shiver down his spine.

TEQUILA FINGERS

STELLAR DATE: 03.21.2956 (Adjusted Years)
LOCATION: Crash Games Hangar, Night Park
REGION: Cruithne Station, Terran Hegemony, InnerSol

The remaining Crash bouts that night were between a monolithic baby in diapers and an armored turtle, a winged serpent and a bear with metal implants, and for the final match, an amorphous cloud that kept turning into vulgar shapes and spitting neon fluids at an accountant in a grey suit with a briefcase full of doom.

Riggs Zanda had made better friends with the blonde woman, who turned out to have an implant in her arm that dispensed liquor. She was off-shift from a bar in Night Park. Ngoba didn't have to try very hard to convince his friend to go have a good time.

Riggs shot him a bleary smile, delivered a mocking TSF salute, and shouted over the crowd, "Make some money, Ngoba! Me and Tithi here are gonna make some nook—"

The woman cut him off with a playful slap.

"Hey, now," Riggs said, turning to waggle a finger at her. "That's tricky."

Ngoba studied Tithi. She was all lean curves encased in leather, but seemed harmless enough—even if she was probably going to tie Riggs up and humiliate him all night.

"What bar do you work at?" he called. "I'll come find you later."

Tithi gave Ngoba an appraising look. "You should do that," she said, smirking. "The Honcho."

"The Honcho," Ngoba repeated, returning Riggs's salute. "Have fun."

They disappeared into the throngs, Tithi pulling Riggs behind her.

Turning his attention back to the crowd around him, Ngoba

caught several transactions changing hands, from what looked like bets to drugs to various storage media. Some people simply stood next to each other, staring at something in the distance, obviously communicating via Link—which didn't make any sense. The entire point of a place like Night Park or the Crash hangar was to conduct business away from the prying algorithms of the Cruithne Station Authority and their big brother, the TSF.

Cruithne occupied a unique place in the settled objects between the Terran Hegemony and the Mars Protectorate. When it was first discovered in the late twentieth century, astronomers thought the asteroid to be a second moon for Earth. Cruithne's odd loopty-loop orbit was eventually determined to not be centered on humanity's homeworld, but around Sol, as it moved between Earth and Mars throughout the year. This meant that, depending on the time of year, Cruithne was closer to Earth, and cargo or people could catch a ride out to Mars, and vice versa.

Humanity doing what it does, it also meant that Cruithne quickly became a center for grey market activity between Mars and Terra: quasi-legal operations, shady research and, ultimately, piracy. Cruithne's ring, clinging to the five-kilometer asteroid like a junkyard fused into something semi-organized, was home to thousands of various organizations, all with competing interests and desires. It was a hell of a place to grow up, especially without a family and a support system.

Mama Chala had always been more interested in using him than creating a productive member of Cruithne's twisted society. Or maybe that was the point.

Growing up on Cruithne, the crowds, the people, the smells and gestures, had created something like a sensor implant that constantly monitored Ngoba's world. He could tell immediately when a place or a situation was about to go bad, or someone didn't belong, or somebody wanted something from him.

At least, he thought he could. Most of the time, Ngoba understood what was going on around him. He picked up the lines connecting people with hunger or hate or both.

Riggs didn't have that sense. He could rewire a drone or hack a credit terminal, but he barely knew when someone was looking his way. Mama Chala, *she* knew how to make others do what she wanted, knew how to twist and turn them so they felt guilty for disappointing her. This might have been the best Cruithne power of all. That kind of power was what started crews, grew syndicates, and reached off-station.

But Mama Chala had no ambition beyond controlling the kids in the *Squat*.

She wanted sweets and cuddles and little knick-knacks that made her laugh. And she wanted her rent, so she could buy those things when her minions let her down.

Ngoba frowned to himself, thinking about Mama Chala and her doughy fingers. It was a mixed feeling that he didn't always know how to define for himself. He loved her and hated her all at the same time. The debate made him feel weak, and he hated that.

He had lost sight of blue-haired Slarva, so he started pushing his way toward the platform, a good twenty meters away. The crowd was beginning to thin, breaking into clots of conversation and hot arguments as those who had been there for the actual bout debated the various fighters and their abilities. Mobile bartenders like Tithi moved among the groups, pouring shots. Beer sloshed and splashed on the floor. Drunks bent over to retch on people's shoes.

Right next to Ngoba, a thin woman in a shipsuit jabbed a man in the paunch, and he doubled-over, gasping. A circle immediately formed for the fight.

Ngoba couldn't stick around to watch. He wove between more knots of people, reaching the two chairs where the players sat with the wired controllers, now locked in a square cage at the base of the platform so they could be seen but not touched. Several admirers were studying the black plastic contraptions. Even from a distance, Ngoba could see how worn they were, the plastic as shiny as seashell or agate. Between the controllers sat a cup with 'TEARS' scrawled on it in what might have been blood.

As he stood with the fanboys cooing over the controllers, Ngoba glanced around until he found Slarva at the edge of the platform. The tall man's red cape still swirled around his ankles. He was talking to a group of vid producers with glowing eye implants. Most of them were nodding along with whatever Slarva was saying, but the one standing closest to him kept trying to put his hand in the promoter's face.

Slarva slapped the hand away like a fly, shouting, "Naughty! Naughty!"

Ngoba eased closer along the edge of the raised platform—which, up close, was just painted concrete—until he could hear what the group was saying.

Slarva had his hand over his heart. "There is no way a hacker could infiltrate our system," he said with the conviction of a preacher. "The console is legit, my friends. Legit. It came from Earth on the pleasure yacht of a corporate enthusiast, bought at auction in a factory-sealed package salvaged from a department store that spent four hundred years underground, until it was unearthed during a building project in Jerhattan."

"Where in Jerhattan?" the closest interviewer demanded, eyes bright like a lemur's.

"New Jersey, I believe," Slarva said, brushing the front of his suit. "We've shared the serial number, my friends. The manufacturer still exists! I believe they build guidance systems now, but maybe one of you enterprising reporters can track down their inter-company records to verify our console?" He raised a finger. "Now *that* would be an interesting story."

Slarva cleared his throat and directed his voice to the crowd behind the interviewers. "These unnecessary inquiries into the validity of the console only weaken what's most important about Crash!"

He waved a hand at the crowd, and a passing drunk shouted, "*Piss off!*"

Slarva smiled like these were his people. "We're here to create an experience, my friends. A battle larger than life, a slice of history, drama, spectacle, heartache. I don't condone or endorse illegal betting of any kind."

"You keep saying that," an interviewer asked. "Betting isn't illegal on Cruithne."

"We all know that," Slarva continued in his preacher's voice. "But it brings with it the stink of cheating. You think I'm manipulating Crash for some crass purpose like profit, and I'm telling you that I'm here for the spirit of the game, to make something worthwhile for the people of Cruithne, who have had so much taken from them."

An interviewer laughed. He waved a dismissing hand and turned to disappear in the crowd. The others soon followed, except for the lemur-looking man, who kept trying to jab Slarva in the chest.

"That's exactly it!" the interviewer said, his voice getting higher. "You say you love Crash, and my viewers *live* for Crash; we made you what you are. And you're selling us out to the bookies. We can't trust anything that happens on the platform."

With his audience disappearing, Slarva's patience immediately seemed to dissipate. He looked at the remaining interviewer like he was some form of giant cockroach.

"Look," he said. "It's a closed system, in a shielded cage, running ancient software with no modern connectivity. We both know this. If you're going to fake up views with this non-existent drama, why not focus on the players? I've got some great ones this time around. Hax is a basket case. Cherry can't keep her hands off geriatric men. Charles—" Slarva shuddered. "Well, I don't even want to know what that guy's into. I bring in these characters for you, weirdos who can actually fight, and all you want to do is make up conspiracy theories about the game."

Realizing a few drunks from the crowd had stopped to listen, Slarva raised his voice. "The game is just a backdrop, just a *stage*, my friends. The players bring the drama. You all bring the passion! It's Crash!"

"How do you respond to rumors that your console has been hacked, and the outcome of every bout is determined by the Rack Thirteen syndicate?"

Slarva's face went feral. "We're done here." He grabbed the interviewer by the collar and lifted him off his feet. "You'd better watch yourself," he spat.

Several onlookers shouted, "*Whoo!*" and someone threw a mug half-full of beer toward the platform. Foam splattered Slarva's cape.

The promoter dropped the gasping interviewer and pushed his way into the crowd. People closed around the interviewer, stumbling into each other. Avoiding the puddle of beer on the floor, Ngoba wove around the drunks and followed Slarva.

It wasn't difficult to hang back and watch the tall, blue-haired man make his way through the crowd until he reached a set of double doors at the edge of the hangar. There he nodded to two guards on either side of the entry, and one opened the door for him.

The door didn't appear to be locked. Ngoba looked around quickly for something to distract the thugs, whose heads looked like bowling balls, sunk halfway into their thick shoulders. To his left, he spotted a mobile bartender serving beer out of both wrists to a pair of stumbling drunks that looked like freight handlers and waved plastic tankards.

He slid up beside the drunks just as their mugs were

overflowing and grabbed their handles. Ngoba spun with the cups in his hands, sloshing beer, as all three of the people now behind him started yelling in surprise.

Without waiting, he launched the tankards in the air, aimed at the heads of the two thugs. A yellow arc of beer followed each cup. He flashed obscene gestures at the drunks, waited for them to swing at him, then dashed for the door.

The move didn't work perfectly. Only one mug hit its target, dumping foam and beer all over the left thug's scrunched face. The other mug banged against the door, but the beer following it fell across the guard's face and chest.

Ngoba glanced over his shoulder to ensure that the two drunks were on his heels, then broke for the space between the guards. Darting between the spluttering thugs, he got his hand on the door latch, opened it and slipped inside just as the drunks hit the guards. He then pulled the door closed and slid to one side, quickly getting a look around.

Two thuds hit the wall behind him, followed by shouts and a clear, "You *wot*, mate?"

He'd expected a bare corridor, but found a small warehouse stacked with crates. Slarva's beer-soaked cape was draped over a nearby metal box. Ngoba didn't see the tall man anywhere. Thumps on the door behind him made it sound like the guards were still occupied, but Ngoba didn't want to wait for them to follow.

He quickly moved through the room, only recognizing a few of the origin markers on the crates. He reached the door on the other side of the room and put his ear against it. Hearing nothing, he eased it open and peeked through the crack to find an empty hallway. He slipped through the door.

Jogging down the hallway, he checked for maintenance hatches along the way, spotting two in the ceiling. This looked like some old freighter bulkhead bolted onto the side of Night Park. It was wide enough to accommodate mining equipment and might have dated from the first excavations on the asteroid. He'd heard stories that Night Park had actually been a staging area for the massive boring machines used to turn Cruithne into Swiss cheese. Otherwise, there was no reason to make a space that big on a station.

These were the kinds of details Riggs noticed. Ngoba hoped his friend was doing all right. He supposed Riggs would be pissed at him later, but they needed the credit.

Thinking about the credit led him back to Fug and his claims of already having hacked the console system. No, not the console system. The controllers themselves. Ngoba was no hacker, but he supposed something as simple as gumming up one of the buttons to send its information milliseconds slower than an opponent's might be enough to throw a match. As long as the players didn't notice.

At the end of the tunnel was a heavy door that looked at first like it might open on vacuum. Ngoba checked its lock mechanism, tried to orient himself on where he was in relation to Night Park and the edge of the ring, then tried the lock. The door creaked open, and through the gap came the sounds of a bar, muffled through a curtain.

Ngoba pushed the door open further, revealing a heavy curtain of blood red material. Live music and the low murmurs of conversation came through the fabric, mixed with laughter and clinking glasses. He eased closer to the divider, then slid it carefully to the side until he could see the room beyond.

It was a bar he didn't recognize. Obviously a high-class place, with a red cloth on every small circular table, similar curtains on most walls, and what looked like a real wood bar with a huge mirror. Filament lights twinkled from the dark ceiling, and a three-piece band played on a small stage opposite the bar.

The place was packed, every table crowded with people leaning in close to each other. At first, it looked like everyone was having the deepest conversation of their lives, until a woman moved her head, and Ngoba caught sight of the flower in the middle of the table. The woman threw her head back, her face a mask of ecstasy, her cheeks yellow-red with pollen dust.

The flower, with its orchid-like petals and long, spaghetti shaped stamens, reached for each face thrust close to it and dusted them with pollen.

Laughter and high moans floated through the air. On the other side of the moaning woman, Ngoba spotted Slarva inhaling deeply from the flower in front of him, mouth already drooping in a goofy smile.

"What the hell is this?" Ngoba asked out loud.

"*Bree-ki,*" a strange voice squawked next to him.

Ngoba nearly fell back through the door. He froze, heart pounding, and looked in the direction of the sound.

On the other side of the curtain, nearly hidden, was a tall cage with a ruffled grey parrot inside. The black-beaked bird was nearly as long as his forearm, with bright, yellow-ringed eyes. Its tail looked like it had been dipped in crimson paint.

"What did you say?" Ngoba asked, wondering abruptly if the parrot was a sophisticated security drone.

He'd probably be dead already if that was the case.

"The plant is *bree-ki,*" the parrot squawked again. "*Bree-ki.*"

"Briki," Ngoba repeated, recognizing the name. "It's a drug den, then." He gave the parrot an appreciative nod.

"I like apples," the parrot said, its rough voice rising and falling almost syllable by syllable. It stretched one wing at a time and puffed out its chest feathers.

"Apples, huh," Ngoba said quietly. "What's your name?"

"Crash," the parrot said. "I'm *Crash.*"

"Who keeps you in that cage, Crash?"

"Slarva," the parrot said in a sort of growl. The parrot jerked with what looked like anger at Slarva's name, then calmed and scratched his neck with a claw, saying, "Pretty Crash."

"You sure are, my friend."

Crash rotated his head in jerky motions, watching Ngoba with one yellow eye, then the other. He raised his head to click his beak.

"Have any apples?" he asked. "I *like* apples."

"That's what you said."

Ngoba sat back on his heels so he wouldn't break the silhouette of the standing cage, and settled in to watch the room. After a few minutes, he glanced up to find the parrot watching, working his beak on the closest metal bar. When Crash saw Ngoba notice him, the parrot bobbed his head up and down like he was pleased.

"What's your name?" Crash asked. "What's your name?"

"I know what you're going to do," Ngoba said. "You're going to go around saying my name to all your buddies out in the park, and I'll never hear the end of it. Literally."

Crash tilted his head to the side so his beak was nearly horizontal. "What's your name?" he asked again. "Can we be— *friends*?"

"*Damn!*" a deep-voiced man shouted out in the room.

Ngoba looked up to see someone falling out of their chair, face covered in red streaks like he had been bawling blood.

The sound didn't faze Crash. "*Please*?" he begged and hiccupped a squawk.

"Fine," Ngoba said, knowing he was going to regret it later. "My name's Ngoba."

Crash bobbed his grey head with what looked like joy.

Ngoba spent nearly two hours hiding behind the curtain, watching the groups at the tables laugh themselves into stupors before collapsing with their heads in their arms. Slarva rubbed noses with the various people at his table before moving to another table with a group that appeared slightly less intoxicated. Beside the flowers, his hair looked like a spiky collection of their undulating stamens. Eventually, Ngoba and the bartender were the only two people awake in the club. It didn't look like Slarva was going to go anywhere. He'd already passed up invitations from two people to go back to their quarters.

"Good night, parrot," he whispered.

"Ngoba!" Crash squawked. "Good night, Ngoba!"

The bartender glanced their direction, and Ngoba froze. He eased his hand toward the TSF pistol.

The man stared at Crash for a few minutes before shaking his head. "I suppose you're starving over there, aren't you, Loudmouth?"

"I *like* apples!" Crash crooned.

Ngoba relaxed. He wiped his sweaty hands on his pants and straightened painfully.

"Goodnight, Ngoba," the parrot squawked again, with an unnerving amount of intelligence in its eyes.

"Sweet dreams, Crash," he whispered.

"Sweet dreams! Sweet dreams! Crash has sweet dreams!"

As the bartender dug in a cabinet for what Ngoba assumed was food for Crash, he reached for the hidden door and turned its lock. Easing the door open with the barest creak, he slipped back into the corridor, pulled the door closed, and then ran like hell. He was about to piss his pants.

GETTING SQUAT
STELLAR DATE: 03.22.2956 (Adjusted Years)
LOCATION: TSF Storage Area
REGION: Cruithne Station, Terran Hegemony, InnerSol

Ngoba hesitated before opening the old bulkhead door that led down to the TSS *Squat*. He hadn't had the energy to go looking for Riggs, and figured he was either still holed-up with that generous bartender, Tithi, or already come home to face Mama Chala's wrath.

If Riggs had already taken the brunt of her anger over the botched warehouse job, then Ngoba could slip in and probably get to bed with minimal slaps to the back of his head. If Riggs hadn't come home yet, well, he was in for it.

He flexed his hand, getting his game plan together. He could tell her the missile had backfired and the overpressure had blown the external airlock on the cargo container. That would mostly match what had actually happened. She had insisted he take the missile launcher, an idea that seemed pretty good at the time. Now that he had actually used a missile launcher inside a space station, even a wreck like Cruithne, he understood that had been a terrible idea.

Maybe he could tell the story in a funny way? Get her laughing about what a *joke* it had been to fire a TSF missile so close to vacuum, how they had nearly blown themselves out into the space. Once he had her rolling with belly laughs like she did, he could slide into the information about the container being empty—then keep his distance to avoid her meaty arms as she inevitably tried to grab him for one of her tough love cuddles.

As Ngoba thought of all the ways he could avoid angering Mama Chala, another side of his brain boiled like a pot that had been heating up for a long time. He was tired of trying to please her, tired of weathering her moods, tired of tending the garden of pimples on her back. He was ready to strike out on his own, maybe start his own crew. He had Riggs on his side.

What about Fug? Who else?

He was lost in a fantasy line-up of local talent when the lock spun and before he could jump back, the door swept open so a muscled arm could swing out and grab his forearm in a death lock. Ngoba struggled but knew it was no good. She had him.

The door swung open the rest of the way to show Mama Chala standing in the doorway, wearing one of her shapeless, flowered smocks, round cheeks heaving with exertion, all massive bosom and skinny legs. Her brown eyes settled on him, full of judgement.

"Ngoba Starl," she wheezed. "I knew it was you as soon as I heard your little mouse steps on the deck. You've been hiding away from me, boy. Don't *tell* me you haven't. Well?" She jerked him forward so he was close enough to smell her sweat.

"I wasn't hiding, Mama Chala," he said quickly, squeaking at first before getting his voice under control. "I was trying to figure out the best way to tell you what happened."

"I know what happened. You wasted my missile and didn't even get anything to show for it. Riggs tried to act like I should be happy you two made it out of there with your skins, but that's no trade. Where are my goods, Ngoba? You're the brains of you two. You tell me what happened. There was a regular TSF supply shipment in that cargo container, just biding its time for a ride Mercury-side. You can't tell me there was nothing in there. I saw the manifest myself."

Ngoba shook his head. Her fingers wrapped around the bones in his arm like cables. "I don't have an excuse, Mama. That's the truth. There wasn't anything in that container. I'd have brought you back the pieces of the drone if they were worth anything."

Her lips were still pressed in a grimace. "And why didn't

you come back and tell me right away? Why'd you *think* you could go off to some Crash game like nothing had happened? Where have you been all this time, anyway? Little Riggs came back after getting his pee-pee wet. He knows where he's supposed to come back to. But not you, Ngoba Starl. You don't come home like a boy. You want to act like a *man*. Well, I'm going to treat you like a man. You're not coming in my house, Ngoba Starl. This is a home for wayward children. I can't help you. I can't get eight bits of sense into that sauced-up brain of yours."

"Sauced-up?" Ngoba protested. "I'm not a sauce head. I don't know what you're talking about, Mama."

"You will be. Mark my words, you'll be down in a drug den in less than a week, shooting something up into your arm with the last bit of credit to your name. You might as well turn yourself into the recycling vats right now, save yourself the misery. At least then I'd know you made something useful of yourself."

Something about the idea that he should simply recycle himself, that he was worthless, woke an anger in Ngoba that shot adrenaline through his body. He wasn't angry at her in particular, but her words struck too close to home.

Ngoba twisted against her thumb and broke her hold on his arm. Before she could grab him again, he put a foot sideways against the heavy door and locked it in place, positioning himself parallel to the door so she could only reach for him ineffectually.

"You really think that, Mama Chala?" he said. The squeak had come back into his voice, the sound of betrayed love. He couldn't help it. A flood of emotions tossed him between anguish at being abandoned and fury at her carelessness. "You think I'm going to end up in a drug den? I'm the one kid in your place who's never done anything like that. I'm the one kid who's always done whatever you asked, even when I knew it was wrong. Even when the TSF picked me up that time, I didn't tell them where I lived. They beat me until I couldn't walk, and I still didn't give you up."

"You cost me a good week in an autodoc," she spat. "That wasn't free, boy."

"No," he said. "I guess it wasn't."

Ngoba pinned her arm against the door with a grip on her wrist. She tried to flex her fingers, then formed a fist. He pressed his lips against her knuckles.

"Good bye, Mama," he said. "I'm gone."

"Gone?" she demanded. "Where are you going to go?"

"I'll start my own crew."

"Start your own crew?" she scoffed. Mama Chala guffawed and the door rocked against him with the power of her belly laughs. "You'll start the janitorial crew. That's what you'll do. Maybe the nursery crew. Maybe they've got a trash collecting crew? That's what you can do, Ngoba Starl. You don't even have a Link yet. How can you hope to do anything in the real world? You're still dumb as a post. You think you can make a silver spoon out of plastic, boy? You can't see what's in front of you."

By 'dumb' she meant he couldn't connect to the network, couldn't talk to others via the Link. He could get a pirate surgeon to install the interface for him, but technically, he was too young—his brain hadn't finished cooking. A pirate doctor wouldn't care, but they also wouldn't worry about the side effects.

Ngoba released her wrist and stepped away from the door. The big woman slammed it open, but only stood in the opening with her fists clenched. Behind her, crowded in the corridor, he saw the whites of all the eyes watching him from her shadow.

"You did right by me, Mama Chala," Ngoba said, taking slow breaths to keep his voice under control. "I won't ever forget that. When I can, I'll come back and straighten up what I owe you."

The bull-shaped woman glared at him, puffing short breaths through her nose. Her gaze went past him, then came back to his face. Her brown eyes softened slightly. She made a shooing motion.

"Ah, get out of here, then. I can't look at you and not see a snot-nosed toddler wandered out of the trash heap. And here you are growing a beard and your hair all curly. Always so fancy, my Ngoba."

The kindness in her voice shot through his heart, but he didn't trust her. He stood his ground in the middle of the corridor, watching her hands. Had Station Security shown up behind him? Why was she so kind all of a sudden? He wanted to look over his shoulder where her gaze had gone, but knew she'd grab him the second he looked away.

"Is Riggs still here?" he asked.

"Riggs?" she asked. "He's here. He's sleeping down in his bunk where you should have been. He confessed like a good boy. He didn't try to go sneaking around, acting like a man."

Ngoba smiled. Her derision gave him the permission he needed to break free. He took a step backward, waving at her. "I'll see you around, Mama. Thank you."

Mama Chala flushed. "Don't you go thanking me. And don't you try to leave here without giving your Mama Chala a hug. You hear me? You better give me one last little cuddle."

Ngoba gave her a sideways glance, considering the situation. All the times she had been kind to him flashed through his mind, the encouraging words, the cuddles that weren't bone-breaking.... Immediately followed a stuttering blur of painful memories. Not only his, but of ways she had hurt the older kids as he was growing up. She seemed to only like kids when they were five or six, when they wanted to please her and made the best servants.

He smiled. "I'll catch you later, Mama. You take care."

Ngoba raised his voice for all the kids huddling behind her. "You all take care! I'll come back for you!"

"Ngoba Starl!" Mama Chala roared.

Without looking back, Ngoba turned and ran as if all hell were on his tail. He hit the main corridor off the Lowspin docks and didn't stop running until he was back up near Night Park and thought he could hear the parrots calling out names by the fountain.

LIFE HACKING
STELLAR DATE: 03.22.2956 (Adjusted Years)
LOCATION: Lowspin Docks
REGION: Cruithne Station, Terran Hegemony, InnerSol

After a long night wandering Highspin and Lowspin, cursing Cruithne, Mama Chala, his scraggly beard, and the TSF pistol that was rubbing blisters in his lower back, Ngoba went yawning to a public terminal and sent Riggs a message to meet him in a couple hours. Then he messaged Fug that he was ready to report on the Slarva mission.

They met in a fast food cafe off the Lowspin docks. The entrance was an old cargo bay that opened onto the main access corridor. It was a good place to sit and watch the traffic: technicians, cargo haulers, travelers, TSF and Station Admin. Ngoba liked to try to determine what they did by how they carried themselves. Anyone in a uniform made the game too easy.

Fug sat at the small table watching Riggs, as if she was sure the boy was going to steal her candy. She was wearing the same green visor, which was still giving her skin a sickly glow.

"You know your name is a weak way of saying 'fuck', right?" Riggs taunted.

"You're the dumbest person I know," Fug said.

"Come on now," Ngoba said. "You two keep flirting like this, and I'll need to get another table."

They both shot him angry looks. Ngoba knew that Fug hadn't wanted Riggs at the meeting, but he'd convinced her by arguing that Riggs could be useful in whatever Fug was planning. The ghoulish woman didn't seem convinced but had agreed, which made Ngoba trust her even less—but he was desperate, and Fug was the best lead on credit he had right now.

Riggs waved a hand at Fug and looked at Ngoba. "So you're

out for good. Really?"

Ngoba shrugged. "Seems so."

"Where did you sleep last night?"

"Haven't slept yet." Ngoba rubbed his face. "I mostly walked the docks, thinking about it all."

Fug gave him a crooked grin. "So you're finally getting out on your own. That's good. But I didn't come here for your coming-of-age story. What have you got on Slarva?"

"Wait a second," Riggs said. "Why would Ngoba know anything about the Crash promoter?"

"I asked him to run an errand for me," Fug said, leaning back and crossing her arms. "Follow him, tell me what he does."

"I thought you already had the game on lock," Riggs said.

"It never hurts to gather more information." Fug looked at Ngoba. "So, what did you see?"

Ngoba sighed. "I watched him argue with some vid producers about whether the game is rigged or not. Then I followed him to this little club just off the hangar—I mean *just* off the hangar. He has his own entrance. He sucked briki all night and passed out. I left after about three hours of listening to him snore."

"You left?" Fug demanded.

"There wasn't anything else going on. Have you ever seen anyone on briki? They're like a bunch of toddlers, giggling at each other until they pass out."

Fug frowned. "I guess that helps a bit. Briki's expensive."

"Is it? Don't they grow it onstation?"

"No. It's brought in from hydroponic farms on Ceres. Proprietary seed stock. Anybody who tries to propagate the plant gets a visit from the Anderson Collective."

"Is it true they spun up a black hole in the middle of Ceres?" Riggs asked.

"You don't mess with the Anderson Collective," Fug said. "They get shit done. Like pet black holes."

"Damn," Riggs said. "Does it blow your mind that we live in a system where people are building their own black holes, and we're stuck in this garbage heap, sorting trash?"

Fug's gaze was drawn to the people walking past the front door. Someone dropped a cup nearby, and it shattered on the floor.

"I'm not staying here," she said. "I might have been born on Cruithne, but that doesn't mean I have to spend my whole life here."

"So where would you go?" Riggs said.

The skinny girl shrugged. "Mars Protectorate for a while, and then the JC."

"You'd need a ship for the Jovian Combine, my friend," Ngoba said. "That's a lot of space in between those places, and not a lot of room to hide. You can't outrun sensors, and the computers never forget."

"Sensors can be fooled, just like computers," Fug said. "Humans made them. Humans make mistakes." She kept watching the crowd. "So Slarva likes briki. That's kind of embarrassing. Not as embarrassing as I'd hoped, but it does mean that when he's out, he's not coming back for a solid few hours."

"I thought you'd already had access to the controllers?" Riggs said, leaning forward.

He seemed to be looking for any opportunity to make Fug look bad, and the petty attacks were starting to irritate Ngoba.

"It's a near-field interruption," Fug said, ignoring the accusation in Riggs's voice. "I can affect the controllers on a millisecond basis, blocking the inputs just long enough to slow their responses. It's especially effective during blocks. You slow the controller's response just enough to make them miss the counter-move, and before they know it, they're getting destroyed by a massive crash maneuver."

"That kept happening to Brindle in that first match," Ngoba

said.

Fug nodded. "Exactly. I made a thousand credits on that."

"That's—subtle," Riggs said, nodding with appreciation. "I'm amazed no one's thought of it before."

"Of course not," she retorted. "I thought of it. And I've got something better in mind, but I can't do it alone."

Ngoba glanced around the restaurant. No one appeared to be paying attention to them. In fact, every person in the place looked like they were so tired they wanted to collapse right in their plastic seats. It was like briki for working people. He couldn't imagine anyone wanting to monitor a place like this, but it didn't hurt to be careful.

"Maybe we should talk somewhere else," he suggested. "There's a maintenance corridor not too far away that's shielded by a water storage tank."

"I'm not giving up any details," Fug said. "You aren't going to be part of the actual job. What I need you to do is run interference. It's going to be pretty easy, actually. I want to do a test run, though, on tonight's semi-final match."

"You sure you want to give them more chances to catch your hack?" Riggs said.

"They're not going to catch my system." Fug spread her hands on the table and wiggled her fingers like she was manipulating an invisible controller. Ngoba thought the motion made her look like a stick insect with an oversized head.

Fug's gaze shifted to Riggs, and she looked like she wanted to bite his oblong head off and chew on it. Ngoba shook the image out of his mind. Fug knew Mama Chala. She knew what they were trying to get away from. He didn't figure it would take much convincing to get Riggs out of the *Squat* once he had the money for his own place. Then he could start talking about a crew.

"What do you want us to do?" Ngoba said, short-cutting their spat.

"We'll meet up at the fountain in Night Park tonight, two hours before the match," Fug said. "I'll explain the screen I need. You'll have some time to get things together, and then we'll make it happen."

"Why not just explain now?" Riggs said.

"Because it needs to be two hours before. It needs to seem natural. How about you stop arguing with me, or I tell you to go pound sand?"

"We got it," Ngoba said quickly. "We got it." He shot Riggs an angry glance. "We haven't talked funds yet. What are you offering for this?"

Fug flexed her shoulders. "I appreciate you helping me out yesterday, Ngoba. The more I think about it, that's some good info. Slarva likes to go hide and snort pollen. That's very counter to his image on the vids. I can use that. I appreciate your help." Her gaze slid to Riggs. "You, I don't have much use for, but Ngoba wants you here, so I'll call that the cost of doing business. I'll throw you a hundred each for tonight, and then a thousand each for the main event."

"What are *you* going to make off it?" Riggs said.

"We'll take it," Ngoba said, cutting any further debate. A hundred was enough to get his own place for a week; he would take it. He checked the time on a wall-clock near the transaction register and nodded. "We'll see you at the fountain."

Fug gave one of her slow, thin smiles. "At the fountain," she agreed.

LOOSE ENDS

STELLAR DATE: 3.22.2956 (Adjusted Years)
LOCATION: Night Park
REGION: Cruithne Station, Terran Hegemony, InnerSol

A few hours later, Ngoba and Riggs met Fug at the Night Park fountain. The concrete tree's spiky limbs reaching out over the water were covered in black crows and grey starlings, rustling and complaining at each other. As soon Ngoba neared the fountain, however, a grey parrot appeared in one of the lower branches and crooned, "Ing-go-ba! Ing-go-ba! Hi there, Ing-go-ba!"

Riggs punched him in the arm. "You make friends with parrots? How do they know your name?"

Ngoba stopped at the edge of the fountain and peered up into the hundreds of black bird eyes looking down on him. "That's creepy," he told Riggs. "I don't know. The only bird I talked to was in a cage."

"Distributed system," Fug said, lifting her visor to look up at the birds. "They share information all the time. Haven't you heard the legends about the experiments? Come on, we need to hurry up."

"Wait," Ngoba said. He stood in front of the fountain and peered up at the single grey parrot looking down at him. "Where's Crash?" he called.

The parrot bobbed its head and showed him one yellow eye and then the other. It looked clearly pleased. "Crash is fine!" it squawked. "Crash is fine!"

"You tell Crash hello for me," Ngoba said.

"Get Crash!" the bird called.

Ngoba hooked his thumbs in his belt. "How am I going to do that?"

"You can! You can! Ing-go-ba!"

The crows seemed to have had enough of their conversation. As one, they launched from the stone branches like a black cloud behind the parrot and flapped out over the bazaar, past Ngoba. He craned his head, turning to watch them fly toward the opposite wall.

"You ever wonder if they miss real sky?" he asked.

"They've never known anything different," Fug said.

"Yeah, but they keep getting smarter and smarter. We mess with them, make them more like us. I bet somewhere in there, they know living in a tin can like Cruithne is wrong, just like we do."

"I like it here," Riggs said.

Fug seemed to remember something she'd said earlier. "Why are you here?" she barked at Riggs. She turned to Ngoba. "I said he wasn't part of this."

"He was there at the meeting," Ngoba said. "You saw him. You nodded along that Riggs was part of this."

Fug squinted at him. "I must have been distracted. He's out. I don't want him here."

"You said we're running interference," Ngoba said. "You think I can do that alone? It takes more than one person to keep an eye on your back. One of us is going to have to watch you while the other watches out for Slarva or his people or whoever. The air changes in there, I can't trust that one of us will catch it."

Fug shook her head. "You're talking, Ngoba. But it's just a vacuous collection of words."

Riggs opened his mouth to jump in, but Ngoba shushed him.

"How close do you need to get to the platform?" Ngoba asked, forging ahead.

Fug stared at him, glanced at Riggs, then shook her head in disgust. "As close as possible," she said, apparently giving in on Riggs's participation. "People, augments, gadgets—all of it can interfere with my system."

"So that's it. You need both of us. If we were hiding against the far wall, we might get away with it. But we're going to get in close, and you need eyes on all sides."

"If he tries to figure out what I'm doing, if I see him even glance my way while I'm working, we're done. You got me, Ngoba? You trust your boy enough not to sell you out? I heard you don't have a place to live anymore…. Mama Chala booted your ass out."

Ngoba shot her a sour look. "You ran when you had the chance. Now I'm out, too."

"Yeah," Riggs said, trying to come to his rescue. "He's free of Mama."

Fug just shook her head. "You've gone from desperate to fucked," she said, chuckling as if she'd made a joke. "This job is all you've got, right? You trust Riggs not to screw it up for you?"

Ngoba pursed his lips. "Riggs? What do you have to say about any of this?"

"I got you, Ngoba. I'll keep my eyes on everybody but our little green friend here."

"I'm not your friend," she shot back.

"Of course not," Ngoba said. "So we going in?"

Fug glanced across the bazaar to the far edge where the doors to the hangar stood. The way was still clear. Crowds wouldn't gather for another hour.

"The players should be out and they should have the console and controllers up for viewing," Fug said. "I'm going to walk up and talk to the players, try and get close to the system so nobody notices. I'll be doing that for about fifteen minutes. You hang back. Once I'm done, you'll know because I'll go around the side of the platform like I'm getting a good place to watch. That's when you come up beside me and keep an eye out, you got me? I don't want any security types sliding up to ask me what I'm doing."

"How are they going to know?" Riggs asked.

Ngoba shot him an angry glance, urging him to shut up with his eyes.

"They'll know," Fug said. "If you knew anything about real hacking, you wouldn't ask that question. The whole place is a minefield. They're tracking everything. Even that ridiculous spectrum scanner you've got in your shirt."

"Hey," Riggs protested, flexing his shoulders. "It's not ridiculous."

"It's like picking apart a flower with a screwdriver," Fug said, unimpressed.

"You ready?" Ngoba said, wanting to separate the two of them before Fug changed her mind.

He was beginning to wonder if they were attracted to each other; the barbs were a little too sharp.

Fug nodded curtly and turned for the path that would take them to the Crash hangar's entrance doors. Ngoba hung back a second, stopping Riggs with a hand on his arm, then followed.

Behind them, the parrot squawked and called, "Ing-go-ba! Ing-go-ba!"

Ngoba turned to give the parrot a wave before he lost sight of the fountain behind a vendor's leaning booth.

ZURLI FOR VIGOR

STELLAR DATE: 03.22.2956 (Adjusted Years)
LOCATION: Crash Games Hangar, Night Park
REGION: Cruithne Station, Terran Hegemony, InnerSol

In the Crash hangar, they kept a good distance from Fug, hanging back as she walked idly through the thin crowd, following the plan she had laid out. She wandered around the various groups of fans gathered inside the empty space, then turned abruptly and walked straight for the platform, where two players were standing with their heads close together.

With the room mostly empty, Ngoba got a better look at the security guards arranged around the perimeter. He quickly spotted the door that led to Slarva's club, now watched by four guards instead of two. At other points around the wall, guards stood next to unmarked doors. There were more of the thugs arranged at the edge of the platform, as if they expected the crowd to try to climb up beneath the projected avatars. With the lights up, it was also possible to make out the projector high above the platform, now just a pale series of turning lights.

Keeping an eye on Riggs so he could pull him back whenever he tried to get too close, obviously trying to figure out what Fug was doing, Ngoba continued to watch the various groups gathering around them. It was a good mix of Cruithne people, from freight handlers to spacers to people who looked like they beat things to death for a living.

A few heavily augmented people moved among the growing clots. He spotted a woman covered in fur with piercing blue eyes, as well as a man with what looked like pulse weapons embedded in his bare forearms. Despite the weapons, he walked around with a vacant smile on his face.

"What's she doing?" Riggs said in a low voice.

Fug was standing next to the players but hadn't tried to

engage them in conversation. She stared at her shoes for a while, adjusting her green visor every so often, or pulling it off her head to tuck her lank hair behind her ears and pull the visor back down on her forehead. Then she crossed her arms and shuffled from foot to foot like she had to pee.

"Should we go ask if she needs help?" Riggs continued. "If she's doing a scan of some kind, she should have accessed everything ten minutes ago. This is weird." He bit his lip, looking at Ngoba. "Do you really trust her? I don't trust her. She's shifty."

"I trust her enough. She'll do what she says she will."

"Yeah," Riggs said. "I don't trust her."

"Trust isn't all that important in this situation," Ngoba said.

Just as Riggs looked ready to launch into another round of anxious complaints, Fug did an about-face and walked away from the players, who never appeared to acknowledge her presence at all. She took a path around several groups of fans who had formed near the stage beside the console, then turned to stand strangely close to one of the security guards. The guard, wearing black glasses and a blocky projectile pistol on his belt, didn't seem to notice her. He continued scanning the room, looking directly over her head.

Dance music started pumping from speakers in the ceiling, and the crowd seemed to double in size. Ngoba and Riggs spread out on either side of Fug, far enough away to respond if she needed them, but close enough to keep a direct line of sight on her.

A fog of light grew on the platform, and then two giant figures stood towering over the assemblage. The first was a crowd favorite named Hondo, a cowboy with rocket boots, and his opponent was Urgis, a turtle-shaped creature with a cat's head and missile-spikes lining its bright purple shell. The music grew more intense as the two avatars paraded around the platform, smiling however they could and waving at the audience. Urgis shot missiles off his shell that wound around each other and exploded in fireworks near the overhead. Showers of sparks rained down on Hondo's cowboy hat.

Fug stood in front of the security guard with her arms crossed in front of her waist, gazing up at the pretty lights like any enraptured fan. Her green visor cast the same shadow on her face, but she didn't appear to be doing anything special.

A voice boomed over the cheering crowd, announcing the players and their boring bios. *"Born in the Heather Neighborhood in High Parts, Hondo grew up fighting for his life in the Artifact Forums."*

Ngoba yawned. He didn't consider forum games any sort of fight for survival. Thinking about survival made him wonder where he was going to sleep, but he pushed the thought away. He'd reassess the problem when he had Fug's credit in his pocket.

"Crash is sponsored by Zurli, the drink with a thousand candy stars. Drink Zurli for vigor!" A glass full of sparkling liquid appeared in the air, boiling with what looked like stars. It tipped and poured sparks on Urgis as Hondo tried to push in to dunk his head in the yellow flow.

Ngoba rolled his eyes as a new sponsor began to shrill above the crowd.

"We're Heartbridge Health," a friendly looking woman in a white uniform said, smiling warmly, *"and we want you to experience the best that life has to offer. Our clinics are available twenty-four hours a day in locations throughout the Terran Hegemony and the Mars Protectorate. Come see us for your daily medical needs or major surgery. We can help with implants, too. Our specialists are here to help. Want to get your Link? You're old enough now. Find out what you've been missing. Visit a Heartbridge clinic today. Crash on, friends!"*

Ngoba frowned, glancing around. Did they have facial scanning somewhere? The ad seemed a little too targeted toward him. Seeing the faces around, however, most of them with sugary drinks in their hands and zits covering their faces, he supposed many of them fit the pre-Link profile. He turned his gaze back to the security guard near Fug, still standing impassively.

He's probably watching porn on his Link right now.

The match started with Hondo trying to snap Urgis with an electric whip. The cat-turtle creature pulled its arms and legs inside its shell and started spinning around the platform like a top, shooting off missiles in every direction. It turned out the missiles didn't cause much damage, but a strike from the edge of the spinning shell sent Hondo into a reeling stupor, and his health bar shrank.

Ngoba reminded himself not to watch the match. He glanced at Riggs and found his friend watching a group of Zurli-guzzling superfans, looking like he was going to pick-pocket the nearest one. Just as Ngoba figured he was going to have to remind Riggs to focus on protecting Fug, he glanced up and gave a wink.

A cover. Nice one, Riggs. Maybe his buddy was smarter than he seemed, after all.

Fug had uncrossed her arms and now let them hang at her sides with her fingers straight. As Ngoba watched her, she made nearly imperceptible movements with her fingers, tapping her thighs. It took Ngoba a minute of watching before the motions started to correlate with the match. She was slowing Hondo's responses—or was she? It was hard to tell if the player was making mistakes, or if she was affecting the match somehow.

Urgis's player was masterful, sending the odd creature into side spins that shot missiles horizontally across the platform, or kept him spinning like a coin on its edge, generating a crackling energy ball that Hondo's whip couldn't touch.

Floating platforms appeared, and the two characters started

hopping from ledge to ledge. Here Hondo had the advantage: he could camp out above Urgis and hit him with the whip before the cat-turtle could get off its ledge. The whip caught Urgis's soft underbelly, and nearly made a one-shot kill. The crowd cheered and booed simultaneously.

Fug's posture didn't change. She craned her neck to stare up at the avatars like everyone else in the hangar, tapping her sides idly to some music only she could hear. Ngoba was caught by surprise when Urgis ultimately lost, taking another whip-shot in the belly that sent him spinning to the space off the platform. The avatar burst into a shower of sparks and shiny blood that washed over the watching faces. The fans erupted in thunderous applause.

Ngoba glanced at Riggs, who gave him a shrug. Ngoba had to admit that he couldn't tell if Fug was doing anything. She didn't look particularly excited about the outcome of the match.

The next three fights were mostly the same: seeming to go one way, so that Ngoba thought he knew which player was getting Fug's help, then ending with the opposite player winning. Was she milking out the matches to raise bets? That seemed possible. Maybe she was good enough at manipulating the player that she could stretch out the play, change the odds mid-match.

Ngoba often glanced over at the players next to the platform, staring intently into their small screen, but their impassive expressions didn't give away much.

He only saw Slarva once, standing behind the last pair of players, with his red cape spread theatrically. His hair was the same blue, like a spiky sea-creature sitting on top of his head. After waving for a solid minute, Slarva dropped his arms and scanned the crowd, his gaze conceivably taking in Fug's location. But he didn't seem to be looking for anyone in particular. He looked immensely pleased with himself.

In the air near the ceiling, glowing numbers shifted as the

odds on any particular match shifted from one side to the other. All around Ngoba, money changed hands.

He got bored watching the fights, trying to figure out something he wasn't certain was happening, and instead thought of all the ways someone might use the Crash games to move large amounts of credit. You could bet on someone you knew was going to lose, controlling both betters, and filter stolen credit through a bookie. Various options and configurations of the scenario played out in his mind. In the end, he figured Slarva had the best deal, taking small percentages of every transaction that flowed through the official channel. Those were the big bets, the ones that kept the crowd coming back.

When the last match was finished, the air full of fireworks and the house lights coming up, Ngoba spotted Slarva where he had been before, hamming it up for the vid producers. Fug had turned her back on the platform, looking even more ghoulish with exhaustion. She must have been doing something, though Ngoba still wasn't sure what it had been.

She walked past him and gave him a nod. He glanced at Riggs, waiting a few seconds, then nodded and turned to follow. Whatever they had done, it was over for tonight.

BEER BEER BEER

STELLAR DATE: 03.22.2956 (Adjusted Years)
LOCATION: Lowspin Commercial Sector
REGION: Cruithne Station, Terran Hegemony, InnerSol

Ngoba sat with his back against the corridor bulkhead, knees in front of him, balancing a plate heaped with his favorite spicy rice and sticky protein balls. Riggs, sitting across the narrow space, took a long drink of his canned beer. Ngoba patted his pocket for the hundredth time, feeling where he'd secured his new roll of currency, just to reassure himself, then dug into the plate.

They were back down in Lowspin, far enough from Mama Chala's that she wouldn't know he was there, but near enough to visit their favorite rice stands. A chicken wandered past, idly pecking the concrete deck. The hen stopped to eye Ngoba's plate, tilting her head. He shooed her away, and she pulled her head back, clucking at him. She dropped a dollop of green-white poop at his feet before scurrying away.

"Whose bright idea was it to put chickens on a space station?" Riggs said, burping loudly.

"People who wanted to eat, I guess," Ngoba answered.

Riggs was already showing signs of being buzzed. "Parrots, crows, chickens. You think they know they're in space?"

"Sure. The bird god tells them."

"Don't fuck around about the bird god," Riggs said, pointing at Ngoba. "Those parrots knew your name. They chose you."

"Shut up and hand me one of those beers."

Riggs patted the bag next to him like it was a nest egg, then fumbled around inside until he pulled out one of the twenty-three remaining beers. He leaned forward to hand the cold can to Ngoba.

Ngoba leaned back and popped the cap. The beer was *too* cold as it hit the back of his throat, and it immediately made him feel lightheaded. He closed his eyes and enjoyed the feeling.

"Hey," Riggs said.

"Yeah?"

"I got your stuff for you. It's in a storage locker down by the Port Authority. Look here."

Ngoba opened his eyes as Riggs tossed him a small metal key. The fob was a worn piece of plas that looked like a small animal had chewed on it at some point.

It might have been the sudden rush of the alcohol, but Ngoba felt overwhelmed with gratitude. He hadn't allowed himself to think about what Mama Chala had said, how she'd kicked him out so easily. She was right: he wasn't a child anymore and it was time to move on. He had known the moment was coming for a long time, but he kept thinking he could push it off, that she wouldn't make him leave; or that she would at least ask him to stay for just a couple more days, give him a chance to say goodbye. He didn't own much. He'd been ready to let his few belongings go if necessary, but the knowledge that at least one person in all of Cruithne was looking out for him, that he wasn't alone in this new adult world, made his heart feel like it was going to pop.

"I grabbed this too," Riggs said. He dug in a pocket and tossed Ngoba a bright blue bowtie, the ribbons trailing from either side.

When he caught it, Ngoba couldn't stop grinning.

"This was the only thing I really wanted," he said.

"So I lugged all your shit out of there for no reason?" Riggs nodded, raising his can. He frowned abruptly, shaking the can, then tossed it down the corridor and dug another beer out of the bag. He popped the cap and raised the can in toast. "To the bowtie," he said.

Ngoba took a long drink, finishing the beer. He tossed his

can after Riggs's, then held the bowtie suspended between his hands. The iridescent fabric shone even in the low illumination of the corridor lights. The tie had been a gift from a woman named Petral who had entertained both of them for a while. She was an information broker who operated mostly within the TSF areas of Cruithne. Riggs and Ngoba had met her at Night Park one late afternoon.

What had started as a bit of harmless flirting with an older woman turned into a full week of Petral dressing Ngoba and Riggs up in matching outfits, complete with bowties, then parading them nightly around the club districts until she pulled them back to her place for hours of sensual labor. She directed them up and down either side of her body, followed by top and bottom, wearing nothing but the ties, until she was satisfied. It took a long time. Petral left them the bowties as souvenirs and Riggs promptly lost his.

Ngoba wrapped the ribbons around his throat and connected the clip. He stretched his neck out, settling the tie in beneath his curly new beard.

"Everyone should have a trademark, yeah?" he said.

Riggs squinted at him. "You look like somebody's houseboy."

"Hiding in plain sight," Ngoba said, giving him a grin. He motioned for another beer, and Riggs tossed it across.

They drank for a while, telling stories about Mama Chala and the *Squat*, how maybe her cuddles weren't so bad. Riggs agreed that he needed to get out too.

Ngoba patted the pocket full of currency. "We've got it now, brother. We can start our own crew."

Riggs laughed. "Start our own crew? You and me? What are we going to do, roll toddlers for their candy money?"

"Cargo, like we've been doing. Only we stay smart about it. We hit the small stuff, but consistently. You make it so the loss isn't worth the investigation. You almost hacked that drone back in the TSF box. You figure that out, we can set the drones to deliver to us. Everywhere you look on Cruithne, a drone's taking a box somewhere."

Riggs chewed his lip. "It's not that easy, Ngoba. Everything's tracked. Everything's recorded. You can't just set a drone to leave its path. You set off all kinds of alarms."

"All that is designed and watched by humans, and we're lazy." He reached for the small of his back to pull out the TSF pistol. He was drunk, but not so far gone that he didn't check the safety and keep it pointed at the ceiling. Was it Petral who had taught him that? "And maybe we'll need to escalate," he mused.

"You think one weak pulse pistol is going to turn you into a hard-ass?" his friend teased.

Ngoba shook his head. "I've got big plans, Riggs. Big plans for Cruithne, for my life. Yours, too, if you'll come along. I'm not going to be some street-rat my whole life. I want power that reaches off this trash heap, to Terra and Mars, even."

Riggs's head fell back against the wall. "Dreams, Ngoba. You can dream all you want, but we have to live in reality, man. We're going to find a place to live. We're going to find jobs. We're going to do what people do. Maybe go to the Crash Hangar. Maybe huff some briki when we get paid. Then you wake up and do it all over again."

"You're about as ambitious as that chicken," Ngoba said.

"Ambition gets you pushed out an airlock. I'd like to live my life. It's not as hard as you make it out to be."

"I think we can keep this deal with Fug going for a while. It's easy money."

"If it's easy, it probably ain't right," Riggs said. He cracked another beer.

"That's Mama Chala talking."

"She's managed to live long enough to get old."

"I'm sick of being poor, Riggs," Ngoba said abruptly, angrier than he had been before. He wanted his friend to support him, not throw up obstacles. "I'm sick of looking like I'm nothing."

"That's your problem, Ngoba. You're worried about what other people are thinking when the truth is they aren't even thinking about you. People got their own problems. They don't have time to think about you. Unless you steal their shit; then they're going to think about you long enough to kill you or get you locked up."

Ngoba emptied another beer. "Everybody steals," he said. "It's what we do on Cruithne. People don't respect you if you aren't trying to get one over on them somehow."

"Respect is bullshit," Riggs said, starting to mumble now.

"Look," Ngoba said, stumbling to his feet. "We're going to go down to the recycling pits and piss off the edge into the vats. Add a little of ourselves to the mix. And then we're going to shout our greatest desires at all those dead people."

"I'm going to tell them to fuck off," Riggs said, chin on his chest. "I'm not going down to the recycle pits. That's stupid. It smells like mushrooms down there. I hate mushrooms."

"I'm doing it," Ngoba said. "You coming with me? You better come with me, Riggs."

Riggs rocked his head back and gazed at Ngoba with bleary eyes. He squinted slightly. "You look like a ghost. You aren't going to go throw yourself in down there, are you?"

"Why would I do that when I've got fresh currency in my pocket?"

"You're weird sometimes. Where'd that pistol go? You drop it?"

"It's in my pocket," Ngoba said. He struggled to reach for the small of his back where the pistol rested. "Where'd yours go?"

"I sold it," Riggs said in a low voice.

Ngoba stared at his friend, trying to connect the words to what they meant. He'd sold the pistol. "Why did you do that?"

"I had to pay Mama to get your stuff."

"What?"

"She was gonna burn it all, and she wouldn't let me have it unless I paid her. I didn't have the funds, but I had the pistol." He shrugged. "You needed your stuff. That's all you've got. That's bullshit, how she just kicked you out like that. She's going to do it to me, too. I thought she was home, but we don't have homes, Ngoba."

Ngoba weaved back and forth, looking down at Riggs. He suddenly needed to take a piss very badly. He held out a hand to help Riggs to his feet.

"Come on," he said. "We'll go to Night Park. I have to take a piss. And I want to look at the birds. You want to look at the birds? We'll talk to the bird god. The bird god looks out for us."

Riggs snorted a laugh. He reached for the bag of beers and found it empty. He held it up with a forlorn expression, and then took Ngoba's offered hand.

"You and me," he said when he got his feet. "We're some sorry motherfuckers."

Ngoba straightened his bowtie. "But we do look fine while being that," he said.

HIGH SCORE
STELLAR DATE: 03.23.2956 (Adjusted Years)
LOCATION: Crash Games Hangar, Night Park
REGION: Cruithne Station, Terran Hegemony, InnerSol

Ngoba watched Fug where she was standing in front of the platform. She looked back at him and gave a slight nod, letting him know she was almost ready.

Her face looked even more ghoul-like than usual. She turned back to stare up at the two giant avatars attacking each other on the platform, light shining through their muscled bodies when they turned at certain angles. One had an upper body that looked like a ball of spaghetti, while the other was a schoolgirl on a hoverboard holding plasma guns.

Ngoba leaned toward Riggs. "Something isn't right," he said in a low voice.

The words were lost in the crowd noise.

"What?" Riggs shouted.

Ngoba jerked his head toward Fug. "Something isn't right with Fug. She keeps looking back at me like she's upset about something, like something isn't working."

Riggs shrugged. "This is the best match yet." He jammed a handful of fried crisps in his mouth and chewed loudly.

Ngoba glanced back at Fug, who was standing as she had during the previous match, hands at her sides and fingers tapping randomly. There were no guards at the platform this time; they had all been pulled back to the perimeter, and every door had four guards on it. Ngoba didn't figure four guards per door were going to stop the crowd from getting out if they wanted to, but they could certainly grab *individuals* who might be trying to get out.

He straightened his bowtie as he looked around, checking for other wanderers in the watching crowd who might be security, or on Slarva's payroll. The guards were all wearing the same dark glasses, which might be hiding retinal implants or serving as HUDs. He couldn't tell from a distance.

The spaghetti monster leapt back and sent its arms out like whips, trying to catch the schoolgirl, but she leapt into the air on her hoverboard. The spaghetti arms closed on empty air, and the girl rained plasma bolts that devoured chunks of the monster's life bar. The crowd went wild, cheering and booing.

Ngoba caught sight of Slarva behind the two players at the console. These two looked a lot more serious than previous sets. Both were hunched over, squinting at the screen, arms tense. Slarva spread his cloak and turned to face the crowd, raising his arms in a gesture that seemed to want more shouting. The vid producers on either side of him ate it up.

It occurred to Ngoba then, as he watched Slarva strut and wave like a clown, that he, Fug, and Riggs were the bad guys in this situation. Slarva was providing entertainment that didn't get anybody killed, and they were working to take advantage of what the man had built.

Like a lightning bolt, Ngoba realized he had been watching the wrong person. Fug wasn't stealing from Slarva; she was ripping off the bookies. He glanced around quickly, looking for anyone who might be there from Rack Thirteen. Hadn't Fug said that the syndicate was the biggest bettor on Crash? They would be the ones who had lost heavily in the previous matches, and they would be trying to figure out why.

All he found were the guards at the doors. All the other Crash-heads were laughing and cheering or booing wildly, their eyes on the platform.

Ngoba debated pushing his way up beside Fug to ask who was here from Rack Thirteen. She had to know. But if he were seen with her, it would incriminate him even more. He glanced at Riggs, who was still shoving chips in his mouth.

If Fug was doing something to control the match, Ngoba

couldn't see it. The characters were well matched, and their health bars were dropping in equal increments. The only one to get in a super-Crash was the spaghetti monster, but that didn't help it against the constant onslaught of the schoolgirl's fiery plasma pistols.

When the match ended with the schoolgirl wrapped in thick noodles that squeezed the health out of her, the crowd went crazy. Ngoba worked his way up behind Fug, who was standing with her shoulders slumped, breathing hard like she had just run a race. She looked more green than usual.

"What's wrong with you?" Ngoba said in a low voice.

"You shouldn't be near me," she said, panting. Fug bent to put her hands on her knees.

"Something isn't right. Which syndicate made the biggest bets last time?"

"I don't know," she said.

"What do you mean you don't know? Of course you do. Why'd you have me follow Slarva when he doesn't have anything to do with the betting? He's a briki-nose who puts on theater shows. He's not a gangster."

Fug narrowed her eyes as she looked up at him but wasn't able to straighten. She tried to take a deep breath, but only started coughing.

"What's wrong with you?" Ngoba asked.

"There's some kind of new barrier in place. The interference has doubled. I have to try twice as hard to affect the inputs. I can't tell if it's doing anything."

"Did it work out—" Ngoba paused, glancing around to see if anyone was listening. "Did it work out how you wanted?"

She nodded without saying anything.

So she'd still thrown the bet. The schoolgirl had been favored three to one. It wouldn't be a huge payout, but it would come out respectably.

"We should go," Ngoba said. "There are two more matches.

We cash out now, and let the others play out. Wait a couple days then come back."

Fug shook her head. "I'm finishing tonight."

"Why?"

She was able to straighten finally. Fug took off her visor and pushed her hair back.

"You look terrible," Ngoba said.

Fug gave him a dry smirk. "Thanks," she said. "You're hot, too."

"No, I mean it. Have you been sleeping? I guess I didn't notice it before, but you've got black circles around your eyes, girl."

"It's the strain. I'll be all right." She looked back at the console where the players were performing goofy arm stretches as Slarva mugged for the cameras.

Ngoba wished he'd paid more attention to the bookies as they'd come down the main corridor into the hangar. Whoever had the biggest outlay had probably increased the security. They might also be actively scanning for whoever was interfering with the match. That was assuming they knew how the hack was working.

"Look," Fug said, stretching her neck. "If you want out, get out now. I'm not going to force you to stay here. I'm doing it. This is my ticket off this rock, and I'm not going to let a little increased security get in my way. But if you leave now, I'm not paying you. You're here to cover my back and you're doing a shit job right now. Where's your idiot friend?"

"He's still back there," Ngoba said, grimacing. He continued to scan the crowd, not finding any indicator they were being watched. He glanced up at the giant projector lights above the platform, which made it impossible to see the Hangar ceiling. They could be hiding all types of scanning and surveillance equipment up there.

"Fine," he growled. "I'm staying. But if I find out you've

been lying to us, Fug, you're never getting off Cruithne."

She rolled her eyes. "You trying to make threats like you're some kind of gangster now, Ngoba, with your bowtie? You can't fool me. I know where you came from."

Ngoba shook his head. "I know the same thing about you. We both came up under Mama Chala, kicked like dogs then cuddled like kittens. I wouldn't fuck you over, Fug."

"Fug's just a weak word for fuck, right?" she asked.

The conversation wasn't going anywhere. Ngoba turned to push his way back to where he had been standing before. When he found the general area, a new clot of drunken fans had taken up residence. One of them offered him a beer, and he waved it away, smiling.

He found Riggs where he had been standing before, now with his friend Tithi resting her head on his shoulder. Riggs looked confused but not displeased. He was offering her a chip when Ngoba walked up behind him.

Ngoba jabbed him in the rib that wasn't pressed up against the bartender.

"Hey!" Riggs shouted, jumping. Tithi pulled away.

"You're not paying attention," Ngoba said. He glanced at Tithi. "Now isn't the time for a date. Sorry, but we're here to focus on something."

"He was focusing on me," she said.

"Riggs," Ngoba said in a tight voice. "You know we're busy."

"I know," he said, giving Tithi an uncomfortable grin.

"Busy doing what?" she asked.

"Helping a friend," Ngoba said.

"What friend?" She looked around. "I don't see anybody else here."

"They're not nearby."

Tithi had been pouring a shot from the implant in her arm as she talked. Ngoba had tried to look away, since it reminded him too much of someone taking a piss. When the arm came up, however, the shot glass was gone, and she extended a pistol in his face.

Riggs's mouth dropped open.

"Don't look at me like that," Tithi said. "We know you're using that girl Fug as cover so you can hack the matches." Her face compressed in a satisfied smirk. "Rack Thirteen is going to tear you apart. We want our money."

CAGES AND CURTAINS

STELLAR DATE: 03.23.2956 (Adjusted Years)
LOCATION: Crash Games Hangar, Night Park
REGION: Cruithne Station, Terran Hegemony, InnerSol

Ngoba raised his hands in a placating gesture, glancing around to see if anyone else had noticed the weapon embedded in Tithi's forearm. Conflicted feelings ran through him as Tithi's perfume filled his nostrils. This close, he could see that her eyes were nearly purple.

A kid next to them shouted *'Whoo!'* at the stage, raising his beer can. Others joined in, and an angry-looking woman threw an empty can at the Whoo-Kid.

"Riggs," Ngoba said in a tight voice. "She thinks you hacked the match. Isn't that funny? You should tell her you aren't able to do that."

His friend got a sheepish look on his face. "I kind of told her I could."

Ngoba stared at him, swallowing hard. He expected Rack Thirteen heavies to hit them any second. "Then explain how in some alternate universe you could do this, but you didn't do it here. I'm sure Miss Tithi there would like to hear our *alibi*, right, Riggs?"

Riggs gave Tithi a look that was half-pathetic and half-possessive. "She told me she loves me, Ngoba."

Ngoba couldn't help laughing.

Tithi didn't seem to like that response. She rushed forward to shove the pistol under his chin, and Ngoba choked his laughter short. With his chin in the air, he rolled his gaze toward Riggs.

"Are you going to do something?" he gurgled.

"Tithi," Riggs said. "We're—" He looked around, apparently struggling for something to say. "We're not holding any money. Fug's got all the funds. She's the one that set up the bets."

Ngoba gurgled derision and clenched his fists. He hadn't wanted Riggs to completely turn on Fug.

Tithi's blonde hair swirled as she turned her head to glare at Riggs. "You told me you did all the planning. Why aren't you holding the money, Zandi? That would make all this a lot easier. I get the money back, and then I ask the Rack to let you go under my supervision." She rotated the muzzle of her pistol slightly, twisting Ngoba's beard hairs. "They owe me what's mine."

"Yeah?" Riggs asked.

Tithi smiled. "And you're mine."

Ngoba struggled to take another breath. He didn't like the wild expression on the woman's face. She couldn't be much older than he or Riggs, but the extensive implants meant she had to have money somewhere—or that she belonged to someone or something.

"How long you been with Rack Thirteen?" Ngoba asked.

"I was born into the Rack," she said with a proud look. "Harav is my mother."

Ngoba's knees nearly fell out from under him. Harav was the matriarch of Rack Thirteen, famous for murdering whole crews and other people who annoyed her. It was rumored she had a glass-cased airlock in her office where she liked to watch people suffocate slowly before jettisoning them into the Big Dark.

"You think Harav is going to like Riggs?" Ngoba asked. "You know we're just street trash from Lowspin, right?"

"Hey!" Riggs shouted.

The second match had begun. Ngoba couldn't get his eyes to focus on the flashing lights over the platform, only seeing multi-colored blobs dancing back and forth.

"Oh, yeah," Ngoba continued. "You know Mama Chala? That's where we come from. Beggars and thieves, digging through other people's trash. Any hacking Riggs knows, he learned from busting low-level security on dumpsters."

Tithi pressed her lips together. "I don't care. You keep trying to put him down so I won't care about him, but it only makes you look bad, Ngoba Starl. I know all about you. I'm getting him away from *you*."

She worked the pistol's muzzle some more, pushing it up under his jaw. He supposed his only options were to let her blow his head off, wait for the Rack Thirteen goons to show up and deal with them, or create some chaos in the crowd and see what happened. He couldn't count on Riggs, obviously. He was going to have to act and let the chips fall where they may. He wondered how fast a mind-controlled trigger could respond to surprise.

"Riggs," he said. "Did you tell Tithi what it really means when Mama Chala wants to cuddle? Did you tell her about the back scratches?"

"No!" Riggs shouted, turning red. "Why would I do that? Why are you bringing that up?"

"I think honesty is important in any new relationship. How are you going to form a lasting bond with someone if you don't start with a full description of what it's like to pop Mama's back zits?"

Tithi's mouth pulled to one side in horror and Ngoba rolled to the side, jerking his head away from the pistol. As he had wagered, she didn't fire. He slid around her but didn't bother trying to grab her. Instead, he pushed her hard into Whoo-Kid, who gave an excited *'Yeah!'* as the blonde girl fell into him, apparently missing the pistol attached to her arm. They collapsed in a tangle of arms and legs.

Ngoba gave Riggs a quick glance, motioning for him to follow. Riggs looked thunderstruck, his arms hanging at his sides.

"Dammit," Ngoba breathed. He grabbed his friend by the

collar and pulled him into the crowd with him, moving quickly toward the platform. He didn't want to break into a full run—they would stand out among the wandering spectators.

In a few seconds, they reached the place where Fug had been. The crowd parted to reveal she was gone.

"The bookies," Ngoba said. "She's going to try to cash out on the first match."

"Why do we even need her?" Riggs said, sounding morose. "She's not going to do anything for us against Rack Thirteen. At least Tithi could help us."

"You want to take your chances with her, go ahead," Ngoba said angrily. Then he saw Riggs considering the idea, and caught himself. "On second thought: No. You stay away from her. We're getting out of here together."

With his back against the platform, Ngoba scanned the crowd for anyone coming their way. All he could see were faces gazing up at the match on the platform behind them. The hangar seemed to have become twice as crowded in the last few minutes.

"You can't keep trying to run my life, Ngoba," Riggs said, hanging his head. "We came up together, but I have to do things on my own—sometimes, at least."

Ngoba raised his hands. "Hey, brother. I'm not going to make you do anything you don't want to do. But in this case, I got us into this job and I want to get us out. That's it. Afterward, if you want to go looking up Miss Tithi, have dinner with her Mama Harav and all the rest, you do what you want."

"You want us to start a crew."

"Of course I do, but you can make your own choices."

"Riggs!" Tithi shouted. They both jerked their heads in the direction of her voice, and found her climbing over a tall man's shoulders. The black circle of the pistol muzzle wavered their direction. She fell backward, apparently losing her grip with the other hand, and the pistol went off in a series of rapid bursts.

The sound of the pistol came just as the characters on the platform had rolled away from each other, creating a lull. As a result, everyone in the Hangar heard the gunfire. First, the crowd froze, people looking around as they tried to figure out if the shots had been real, or part of the show.

Then another set of shots went off at the back of the Hangar near the main doors. Automatic weapons fire answered.

"Holy shit," Ngoba said. "That must be Fug and the bookies."

The crowd broke as people started to run. Ngoba caught sight of Tithi fighting to move in their direction, but everyone was running away from them, pushing her back toward the outer perimeter.

"Come on," he told Riggs.

Turning, he ran toward the platform and jumped up to grab the lip of the concrete structure. His right hand slid, but his left held. Riggs moved up behind him to push his legs up. Ngoba pulled himself onto the platform, and then lay on his stomach to reach down for his friend. It was just like the thousand other times, when they'd climbed through ventilation shafts to burglarize storage lockers.

Standing on the stage, they had a full view of the Hangar and the pandemonium happening in the crowd. Down near the player's pit, Slarva's red cape moved in a swirl of bodies. Ngoba barely made out the blue hair surfacing and then it got lost again. The two players were huddling under the cage that protected the antique console, but a series of looters were trying to pull the cage off the wall of its enclosure.

More gunfire cracked around the space, quieting the crowd for a second before the shouting and scuffling filled the Hangar again. Ngoba couldn't see the guards that had been present at the entrances anymore. He glanced up at the over-bright projector in the ceiling, squinting into the light, and realized they must be standing among the still visible avatars.

"I think Rack Thirteen must be running all the Crash books," Riggs said, staring out at the crowd.

Ngoba glanced at him, heartened by the sober quality in his voice. "Just Rack Thirteen?"

Riggs shrugged. "I think Fug chose the wrong system to hack. If there were more crews involved, no one would care if one of the others took losses. Here, it's all going back to one syndicate." He motioned at the crowd. "Look at all this."

"You would have done the same thing, if you could."

"Sure." He bit his lip. "Tithi didn't say anything about being in a family, Ngoba. You have to believe me."

"We're not done with this yet, brother." Ngoba pointed at him and grinned. "Plus, I saw the way you were looking at that woman. You're not free, yet."

Riggs smiled sheepishly. "I'm fucked," he admitted.

A bullet screamed past Ngoba's head, and he hit the deck, his heart pounding in his ears. Riggs followed him.

"They know we're up here, I guess," Ngoba said.

"Maybe it was a stray shot."

Concrete chipped and exploded around them as more bullets followed.

"Sure," Ngoba said.

"Are we going to die?"

Ngoba lifted his head for a second to scan the perimeter; the main doors were blocked by bodies trying to get through. He saw several thugs bashing faces with the butts of their rifles, or pushing people back into the Hangar. He couldn't see Slarva's blue hair or red cape anywhere. Thinking of Slarva, he checked the door to the corridor that led to the briki club. There was a clot of people near the door, but no guards that Ngoba could see.

"Come on," he said.

"Where?"

"We're going to set a parrot free. And save our asses. I

hope."

CORGI POWER

STELLAR DATE: 03.23.2956 (Adjusted Years)
LOCATION: Crash Games Hangar, Night Park
REGION: Cruithne Station, Terran Hegemony, InnerSol

There was a gap in the crowd next to the platform.

Ngoba hit the hangar floor and stumbled sideways. Riggs apparently didn't look before he jumped, and hit Ngoba in the shoulder on his way down. They fell together.

"Riggs!" Ngoba shouted. "What the hell?"

"There were more shots. I had to jump. Do you know which way we're going?"

"Yes, I know." Ngoba rolled away, pushing himself to his knees. When he looked up, he found himself staring at Fug. She was still wearing her green visor.

Her eyes went wide, and she tried to slide back into the crowd. Ngoba shot forward and grabbed her arm.

"Hey!" she shouted. "Let go of me."

"I thought you had already made your way to the bookies," Ngoba said.

"Obviously not. I can't get out that way. I'm trying to keep out of sight."

Ngoba flicked her eye-shade with his free hand. "You keep wearing that thing, and everybody will know who you are."

She twisted her arm in his grasp but he held tight. "Let go!" she demanded.

"Now that I've got you, I'm not letting go. You reckon you can pick a lock?"

"Of course I can pick a lock. You got a way out of here?"

"I think I do."

Ngoba checked that Riggs had stumbled up beside them. Fug shot Riggs a dirty look, and he grinned at her. Adjusting his grip on Fug's thin forearm, Ngoba directed his attention to pushing through to the corridor door.

Most of the fighting seemed concentrated near the main doors. Here, people were milling around, asking each other what was going on, and ducking whenever a new round of gunfire burst out. Once they were away from the platform, Ngoba could easily make out the two avatars waiting to fight. One was a giant Corgi dog, standing upright and wearing a short vest with blue goggles perched in front of its pointed ears, while the second was a dolphin suspended in a mech-suit. Their wait-animations had them shrugging, scratching, and occasionally making obscene gestures at the crowd. Both avatars were too adorable to look dangerous, despite the missiles hanging from the dolphin's mechanized cage, and the blazing electric sword slung across the Corgi's fluffy back.

The trio reached the door. Ngoba tried the lock, hoping it might be open, but was unsurprised when the control panel denied him access.

"Get out of the way," Fug said. She adjusted her eye-shade, smoothing her hair behind her ears, and accessed the panel's admin menus. Ngoba turned his back to the door to keep an eye on the crowd, but had barely turned around when she announced, "Done."

A plasma beam struck the door just above Fug's head, tearing a burning hole in the metal. Ngoba grabbed her and hit the floor. People screamed and ran in every direction.

"Plasma!" he gasped. "What the hell is wrong with these people?"

"I guess they want you dead," Fug said, her tone nonchalant.

"What did I do to deserve being made dead?"

"You stole a million credits by manipulating a major currency-laundering operation that Rack Thirteen was completing during the first match."

Ngoba stared at her. Fug's green visor sat askew, covering one eye. She couldn't hide her mischievous grin.

"Riggs!" came Tithi's shout. "I see you, baby!"

Glancing back at Riggs, Ngoba found him biting his lip, looking confused on how he should respond.

"Don't answer her," Ngoba growled. He scrambled away from Fug and ripped the door open. It left a smell of burned metal and plas as it swung.

"Come on," Ngoba shouted. He grabbed Fug's arm again, and pulled her through the opening, immediately flattening against the wall once they were inside. When Riggs was in, he pulled the door closed, and pushed Fug toward the control panel. "Lock it," he ordered.

"You don't get to—"

"Lock it!" he roared.

Fug shot him a venomous look and tapped the panel. In ten seconds, she was done.

Ngoba glanced through the hole in the door to see two Rack Thirteen thugs standing in a gap in the crowd, looking around with rifles at the ready.

"Maybe those boys didn't mean to hit the door," he said.

"Then I guess we should run, huh?" Fug asked. "Where does this go, anyway?"

"It ends up at Slarva's briki club."

Strangely, Fug perked up. "Really?" she said, glancing down the tunnel. "This is where you followed him?"

"That's right," Ngoba said. He checked the hole in the door again. "We should go that way."

"I think Fug here has a crush on Slarva," Riggs said.

Ngoba pushed between them to start walking fast down the corridor. It looked much the same as before. "I don't care who she likes," he said. "Although, if you got us involved in all this for some crush, I'm going to be very disappointed in you, Fug."

They followed him, Fug pumping her arms to keep up. "You were the one dumb enough to do what I asked you."

"You paid, didn't you?" Ngoba said.

"And then she set us up as the stooges in her little betting scheme," Riggs said. He shoulder-checked Fug, and she stumbled.

Ngoba stopped to catch Fug as she fell into him. "Which wouldn't have had any credence if you hadn't lied to Tithi about your hacking abilities, Riggs. You need to rein yourself in, brother."

"She's setting us up with killers, and you're going to defend her?" Riggs demanded. "Let me at least smash her stupid little hat."

Fug squeaked and grabbed at her visor.

"Look," Ngoba said, facing both of them. "We're all from the TSS *Squat*. We know the deal. We can't get pissed at each other for stumbling into each other's score. Fug had a process underway, and we walked into it. I take ownership of that. She can't help it if you happened to shore up her cover with your dick and big mouth."

"She saw us and couldn't wait to dump all of Rack Thirteen on our heads," Riggs said. "That's not walking in on someone else's score, Ngoba. That's selling out your own for a terrible death. Do you want to get suffocated in Harav's closet? I sure as hell don't. I wouldn't wish that on anybody." He crossed his arms. "You're trying to act like a crew leader, here, shoring up one party against the other for the common good, and I get that. But in this case, you need to show some respect to both sides. She deserves the fate she would have handed us. I say we space her."

Fug gave him a look that said she was about to scratch his eyes out. Riggs fell back into a ready stance, hands up.

The door behind them exploded. A concussive wave rolled down the corridor, knocking Ngoba down onto his side as hot air blew over his face. His ears vibrated with a high-pitched ringing.

He barely heard someone shouting, *'We clear?'* from where

the door had been.

"Clear!"

Like tiny people moving in the distance, the voices called to each other; invisible forms, lost in the smoke.

Ngoba rolled over and pushed himself to his knees, coughing violently. He sucked in his breath, but couldn't stop the coughs wracking his chest. He squinted through the black-tinged smoke, and made out Fug's arm nearby. He grabbed it and pulled her toward him. She was as light and limp as a rag doll.

"Riggs!" Tithi shouted, sounding as small as the rest of them. "Are you in there?" She paused, and then she was yelling at someone else. "Why is there so much smoke? The overhead fell down, you idiots."

"We're moving it, Miss Tithi," a military-sounding voice answered.

Unable to see anything in the smoke, Ngoba cast around for Riggs. His hand landed on what felt like his friend's face. He squeezed Riggs's nose and felt his forehead. His eyes were closed and he seemed to be breathing.

Stumbling to his feet, Ngoba grabbed each of his companions by the forearm and heaved forward, the smoke burning his lungs. There was heat from the direction of the door—he felt it even with his eyes squeezed closed—so he heaved in the opposite direction, pulling Fug and Riggs after him. He tried to map out the maintenance hatches he remembered seeing in the tunnel, but couldn't tell how far they were from the main door. He remembered he had walked for about five minutes.

Ngoba grunted and pushed himself into a faster walk. Fug was easy enough to drag, but Riggs's big feet kept smacking the old ribs along the bulkhead.

As he left the smoke, the dim ceiling lights grew brighter and his vision eventually cleared. Banging sounds and shouts followed from the end of the corridor where the overhead had collapsed. He supposed it wouldn't take them long to either clear the mess of metal and plumbing, or get someone to cut through it. They had the plasma guns, too, although he didn't like the thought of someone being crazy enough to use a plasma gun on the station. Though this *was* Rack Thirteen, and at least one of them had already used plasma, so he couldn't put it past them.

Without realizing how far he'd come, he turned the slight curve that ended at the door to the briki club. Ngoba blinked. He'd intended to pry open one of the maintenance hatches and drop down into a service crawlspace. He sighed, and let Fug's and Riggs's arms drop. Neither stirred, still out cold. Riggs had a bit of blood running from his nose, and Ngoba noticed that Fug's visor had cracked, and no longer glowed green. Without the ghoul-color on her face, she looked like any other teenage girl. *Cute even,* Ngoba thought. Her hair was grey with dust.

Ngoba took in the door and activated the sealing mechanism. Like before, it wasn't locked. There was a sigh of air as the lock released, and the door opened slightly. Ngoba pulled the door toward him then stuck his head through the opening.

He found the same red curtain. He waited, listening. The club sounded deserted, and it was dark. He took a step through the door and whispered, "Crash, you here?"

Crash the parrot gave an excited squawk, and the cage rattled as it moved. "Ing-go-ba!" he said. "Ing-go-ba!"

"I'm glad to see you too, brother," Ngoba said.

He pushed the door the rest of the way open, and turned to drag first Fug and then Riggs through the opening, setting them against the portion of the club wall hidden by the curtain. Ngoba pulled the door closed and tried to engage the lock, but he couldn't be sure he'd been successful. The panel kept flashing a *low battery* indicator.

Just to be sure, Ngoba found the edge of the curtain, and peeked into the club. Low lighting from the ceiling showed the place to be deserted.

"All right, Crash," Ngoba said, facing the grey parrot. He felt around the cage for a door or opening of some kind. "I meant to drop my friends off and come find you—because it's been bothering me that you're stuck here in this cage—but events haven't quite worked out that way. I'm going to let you out, but there are people coming after us who might inadvertently cause you some harm."

"*Rack* Thir—*teen!*" Crash said, bobbing his head. He worked at a bar with his horny black beak. His yellow eye glowed in the dark.

"That's them," Ngoba said. "Now how would you know that?"

Crash bobbed his head again, squawking in a way that sounded like laughter.

"Fine, be that way," Ngoba said. "Now, how the hell do I open this cage?"

He found what he thought might be a sliding door, but it appeared to have some kind of biometric scanner that didn't respond when he slid his finger over it.

"Locked, huh?" Ngoba said. "Well, then." He lifted the cage off its stand, and found that it wasn't too heavy, but it was very ungainly. He needed two hands to carry it.

"Riggs!" Ngoba shouted, which made Crash squawk. "Riggs, wake up!"

Riggs didn't stir.

"So I guess this is a quandary," Ngoba said.

Booms from the other side of the door set his heart pounding. He left the cage to grab Fug and throw her over his shoulder. When her cheek hit the middle of his back, Fug's visor fell off her head and rolled between Ngoba's feet. Ngoba adjusted her weight on his shoulder, which felt like less than a bag of stiff filament, and studied the broken visor. He had never seen her without it, even in the early days. Grunting, Ngoba knelt and picked it up. Realizing he wouldn't have any free hands, he slid the visor on and settled the band down on his forehead. As he expected, its HUD was completely dead.

Ngoba turned and pulled up Riggs's shirt to find his belt, and dragged him toward the cage, then used the arm holding Fug's legs in place to grab Crash's cage by several bars.

"You're probably not going to like this," he said. "I think you prefer being upright."

Ngoba lifted the cage off its stand and pulled it close against Fug's legs and his chest. The cage didn't shift as badly as he thought it would, but the parrot squawked anyway, and hopped from one side to the other, flapping his wings. Ngoba struggled to keep his grip as the bird shifted the weight of the cage.

"Come on, brother. Just for a little while, until I can get out of this current situation."

Ngoba stepped around the edge of the velvet curtain, jerking Riggs as his head caught in its heavy hem. He went down a short series of steps into the main dining areas, where the tables were arranged with the chairs stacked upside down on top of them. In the middle of each table, the briki flowers sat closed, the purple petals oily and shimmering under the low light.

Catching sight of the closest flower, Ngoba stopped short. He had forgotten about them. While the flowers rested, they hoarded more pollen until it was time to open again, usually triggered by the light that approximated Sol. On the 'first crack', as the briki-heads called it, the flowers puffed out a cloud of pollen that hung in the air, waiting to be inhaled. After that, you had to rub your face in the stamens. He inched away from the nearest table, knowing that if he bumped it and woke the flower, he would just as well sit down and enjoy the ride until Tithi blew his head off.

"Careful," the parrot crooned.

"You see that, too, little brother?" Ngoba said. "I'll take it easy."

Ngoba had nearly worked his way across the room, jerking Riggs as he balanced Fug and the bird cage, when hammering rose from behind the velvet curtain.

"Dammit," he breathed.

He was sweating heavily, his arms and legs were burning from the exertion. He had been focused on a door near the bar that he was fairly certain opened back into Night Park, not far from the fountain. As he breathed and pulled, he had done his best to determine where the corridor out of the Hangar actually went, and it made sense that it only skirted the edge of the park. Otherwise, it would have been out in vacuum. Considering the corridor looked like it was made from an old ship, that was possible—but it was also warm. You could always tell the presence of vacuum on the other side of a wall in Cruithne by the cold seeping its way inside. Mama Chala liked to say they lived surrounded by death, always looking to tear its way inside and suck the life out of them with the Vacuum's Kiss.

The sound of someone big throwing their shoulder against the door behind Ngoba made the curtain wave, and on the nearest table to the door, the briki flower quavered. Ngoba watched, holding his breath, then told himself he had to keep moving. The opposite door was only a few jerks of Riggs's heavy ass away.

It took the Rack Thirteen people less than a minute to pry the door open and force their way in to the room. Ngoba had just made it to the edge of the bar, the exit within reach, when Tithi swept the curtain aside and shouted with delight in her voice, "Ngoba!"

Her joy turned to anger when she saw Riggs sprawled like a corpse near the bar. "Riggs! What did you do to him? I'll cut your head off, Ngoba Starl!"

Ngoba could only shake his head, the exhaustion making it impossible to speak.

Crash the parrot squawked ruthlessly, flapping his wings like a pent tornado.

Unable to warn her about the briki flower near her arm, Ngoba could only blink sweat out of his eyes as the flower's petals gathered in a single, powerful convulsion and then opened to spit a cloud of crimson pollen into Tithi's face. She stood blinking in surprise as the pink fog floated back over the group behind her, drawn by the moving air from the open door.

Tithi screamed. She surged forward, probably trying to escape the pollen that had painted her face red, and bumped into another table. That flower spasmed pollen all over her as well. Flower after flower spit pollen as she stumbled around the room, bumping tables in her path.

Ngoba gathered his strength and yanked Riggs toward the exit. The fog had grown suddenly thicker. He thought he could see its edge reaching for him, but couldn't be sure just how much pollen filled the air now. He let go of Riggs so he could pull the door open, and immediately realized his mistake.

The suction of the opening door drew a cloud of pollen over him. Ngoba squeezed his mouth closed, holding his breath, and grabbed Riggs's hand again to pull him into the vestibule, where a glass door waited and, beyond, the crowded booths of Night Park.

Ngoba charged into the open, not caring that a crimson miasma followed him outside. He struggled as far as he could without taking a breath, until his lungs screamed and black claws threatened his vision. He reached the first row of booths and staggered into a gap among a pile of storage crates. Then he fell to his knees, setting Crash on the deck, and rolling Fug off his shoulder.

The black had nearly overtaken his vision when he pulled Riggs in toward him, laying his friend across his lap. Ngoba let his own head fall against the cold crate behind him, and finally sucked in a breath of fresh air.

He hadn't run far enough, and braced himself as the hallucinations rolled in.

BRIKI LAND

STELLAR DATE: 03.23.2956 (Adjusted Years)
LOCATION: Crash Games Hangar, Night Park
REGION: Cruithne Station, Terran Hegemony, InnerSol

A giant pterodactyl patrolled the domed ceiling of Night Park, shrieking and breathing fire on the two-story battle slug moving slowly across the vegetable market, leaving glowing slime in its wake. In front of the neon battle slug, two versions of Mama Chala clad in ornate armor charged at each other with burning swords raised above their heads, screaming war cries. All around, screaming and cries of terror mixed with maniacal laughter. The ceiling was replaced by a stormy purple sky, like a bruised stomach sucking in and out; changing the air pressure in the great space so that Ngoba's head seemed to expand and shrink, squeezing his thoughts.

Rack Thirteen thugs stumbled between booths, scratching at their crimson-stained faces, babbling and crying, while others ran full-sprint down the more open areas, firing indiscriminately with projectile weapons, beams, and, occasionally, the deadly plasma gun that thankfully never struck anything of consequence. A fabric booth burned in the distance, sending up roiling plumes of oily black smoke, a mix of plas and natural fibers that smelled like roasting flesh.

Ngoba had lost sight of Fug and Riggs. He pressed his hands over his ears to shut out the mad laughter, only to find his equilibrium disrupted. He stumbled as if the deck had become a merry-go-round, left and right heaving up and down. He shook his head, trying to find something with which to anchor himself, something to serve as reality in the twisting funhouse the world had become. He felt like he was falling, his stomach leaping into his throat and then doing a somersault that left his head spinning; then he felt nailed in place, the bazaar wheeling around him in a riot of color, shape, and sound.

He supposed this might be fun, if the other people caught in the wrath of unbridled hallucinogens weren't trying to kill him, and if the world wasn't populated by grinning, stomping monsters while his soul leaked out his ears. At any moment, an angry fire god was going to crack open the fleshy, domed roof, and jam a flaming cock deep into the crevasse of Night Park, and fuck them all with fury and fortitude until everything burned away in an orgasmic maelstrom of fiery fusion and blood.

He must have been screaming. He opened his eyes to find Crash the parrot watching him carefully, the gold eye ringed by grey feathers holding steady in the midst of the storm. Ngoba crawled toward the parrot, clawing at the deck.

"Crash," he moaned. "Crash can you see me?"

"Ing-go-ba!" the parrot squawked, bobbing its head.

The eye flashed, and Ngoba realized Crash had turned his head and was studying him with his other eye, like he was consulting two different brains. Ngoba struggled to hang onto the image of the parrot, what he knew to be true, before Crash swelled into a rhinoceros with gleaming wings.

"Clippers," Crash crooned, pointing his beak to something beside Ngoba's shoulder. "Snippers. Snip, Ngoba. Snip!" Crash released a squawk and continued nodding at something next to his cage.

Ngoba slowly turned his gaze in the direction Crash was pointing. Bits of the world steadied for an instant, then spun away. He saw a man in the distance frantically fighting off a mottled, bulb-shaped thing that seemed to be chewing on his head. He fell into a booth, and it exploded in sparks and gobs of liquid flesh.

Shaking his head, Ngoba worked his gaze closer, finding the ground beside his arm empty except for grime, then up again, centimeter by centimeter, until he found an open toolbox that had spilled its contents. It was probably only a meter away, but seemed to be in another dimension. On top of the toolbox lid was a pair of power-cutters, the kind electricians used to snip fiber cables, or that gangsters used to remove fingers one knuckle at a time.

Crash was telling him to cut him out of the cage.

With his head contracting and expanding like a balloon, Ngoba reached for where he thought the clippers were. Finding nothing, he felt among the shifting colors and shapes until his hand closed on two long pieces of metal that he recognized as the tool. He pulled it back to his chest, eyes suddenly full of joyful tears. Ngoba was overcome with agonizing happiness to hold the clippers against his chest.

Then he opened his eyes to find Mama Chala in battle dress, standing over him and holding high the decapitated head of the other Mama Chala. Mama's dead eyes stared outward in a way that seemed to take in everything while staring solely at him. The victorious Mama tossed the head at him, and it rolled to a stop with her dead, half-open lips close to his.

"Ing-go-ba!" Crash barked. "Clip! Clip!"

Ngoba nodded, squeezing his eyes closed. His thoughts were starting to get closer together, to link in ways that at least went from A to C. He knew Mama wasn't there. He knew avatars weren't smashing their way across Night Park. All he had to fear were the hallucinating Rack Thirteen gang members and Tithi, somewhere in the labyrinth of the bazaar.

Somewhere in his heaving mind, he knew that if he was coming down, they would be, too.

Ngoba rolled onto his stomach and pushed himself toward the cage, which lay on its side a few meters away. Rising to his knees, he set the cage upright and clipped the bars above the rectangular door. Once the top bars were done, he cut along the bottom of the door, trying to shut out the background screams and booming thunder of the giant beings fighting around him.

A mecha-dolphin rumbled past, barking and squealing in high-pitched clicks that stabbed his ears, but he squared his shoulders and concentrated on the task.

Finally he pulled the door out, and then reached inside for the parrot. Crash tilted his head until Ngoba held his palm sideways, and the grey bird hopped onto his hand, claws gripping the meat between his thumb and forefinger.

Ngoba carefully removed Crash from the cage, and no sooner was the bird under the open air, than it spread its wings and launched upward, squawking with joy. Ngoba slumped against a crate at his back and watched the parrot shoot higher and higher, its grey wings flapping, red tail feathers tight, squawking the whole time.

He sat staring at the ceiling for what seemed like a long time, watching the mottled bruises that had first looked like lightning resolve themselves into rows of lighting that crisscrossed between support beams. His vision was full of sparkles that drifted like snow, but the major hallucinations had subsided. He stared at his hand for a while, watching his blood move through his veins.

Ngoba was smiling at his palm, understanding perfectly how the various lines indicated his course in life, when a crunch beside him made him look up. A man in a faded red shipsuit stood over him, a fat plasma pistol in his right hand. His eyes were black, and his dust-covered face was covered in the tracks of red tears from the briki pollen.

Ngoba blinked at him, smiling, excited to see another human being. "Have you seen this?" he said, holding up his hand. "My soul is like a little maglev car moving along the tracks on my palm. It's all laid out right here.

The plasma pistol made a long beep as its arming mechanism warmed up. "We've been looking for you, Rack Smasher," he said, voice warbling slightly. "You thought you could hide, but you're a giant crocodile. Dumbass. You can't hide anywhere."

"I'm not trying to hide," Ngoba said.

"I'll hide the little bits of you," the man said, steadying the pistol in two hands. "But I'm taking your head. I want to make your face into a hat."

From somewhere above, a black shape floated down, resolving into the spread wings of a bead-eyed raven. The bird unclenched its talons and landed on the man's shoulder. He turned to look at the ruffle-headed bird with surprise and wonderment, when the raven pecked one of his eyes out. The man dropped the plasma pistol and clutched at his face, screaming.

The pistol hit the ground and spat a blob of plasma at the man's foot and ankle, which disappeared in a splatter of blood and bone.

The raven launched from the man's shoulder as he fell backward, then circled over him as he rolled over and started crawling away from Ngoba's pile of crates, babbling and sobbing the whole time. Eventually, the raven landed on the man 's shoulder, pecking at his neck as he crawled.

In the distance, Ngoba heard more screams, real this time, as birds from the fountain attacked the Rack Thirteen thugs. Random gunfire spat uselessly as clouds of starlings, grackles, and crows descended on the frantic men and women.

Ngoba stood eventually, and wandered toward the center of the park, watching with bemused detachment as Night Park grew gradually silent except for the squawks, caws, and shrill songs of its birds. When they finished their work, the birds flew back to the fountain and covered the spiky branches of its stone tree, murmuring among themselves as they fell to grooming and grousing at one another, just like during the bazaar's normal operations.

Finding himself drawn toward the fountain, Ngoba was pleased to see Crash the parrot sitting on the edge near the water. The grey parrot moved from foot to foot, scratching furiously among its neck feathers before fixing him with a yellow eye.

<*Ngoba,*> Crash said.

Ngoba gaped. The parrot's voice was like any man's, and he thought for a second that Riggs was playing a trick on him. He looked around, but he was the only person in sight.

<*Stop looking so worried,*> the parrot continued. <*I'm speaking to you through the visor you're wearing.*>

"What?" Ngoba said. He reached for Fug's visor, which he'd forgotten about.

<*Don't take it off,*> Crash said. <*It's mostly broken, but I can use its antennae and neural interface to reach you.*>

"You mean this thing is like having a Link?" Ngoba asked.

<*That's mostly correct.*>

"I'll be damned. This whole time, Fug's had a Link."

<*It's the purpose of the equipment,*> Crash said. <*Fug is the woman you had on your shoulder, correct?*>

Ngoba nodded. "You don't know where she is, do you? Is she all right?"

<*She's safe. She and Riggs Zanda are back under a merchant's table where you first fell with the cage. Thank you for that, by the way.*>

"For dropping you?" Ngoba said, not sure if the bird was kidding. "I was tripping balls, you know."

<*You came back for me. I did my best to influence you with high-pitched alpha wave excitement, but I couldn't be sure if it worked.*>

"You mean you tried to hypnotize me?" Ngoba said, crossing his arms.

<*No,*> the parrot said. <*I tried to implant an idea in your mind.*>

"Oh," Ngoba said. "Well, of course I was coming back for you, brother. I've always loved the parrots down here. I've been watching you since I was little. The only thing that seemed free in this whole damned place, even if we are all trapped, even you. I couldn't let you rot in that cage. That was just cruel, a Cruithne parrot in a cage. Besides, your little buddies at the tree asked me to, as well."

<I always thought the alpha waves were bullshit,> Crash said. <In any case, thank you.>

<Were you named after the game?>

<I was named before I came here. I think the names were chosen randomly by the researchers. I was part of an experiment.>

"An experiment? Isn't that some kind of urban legend? Were you a successful experiment?"

<I don't know,> Crash said. <I like to think so.>

"You mind if I ask what kind of experiment?"

<AI implantation,> the parrot answered, scratching its neck feathers.

Behind Crash, the birds on the stone tree flapped their wings and grumbled, making it seem like a wind had moved through the bazaar.

Ngoba became aware of how many black eyes were watching him, and how easily they had killed or disabled the Rack Thirteen people.

<You don't need to worry,> Crash said.

"Do I look worried?" Ngoba asked.

<Very.>

Ngoba looked from the tree to the dark booths surrounding them, many smashed or covered in scorch marks. "This place is pretty messed up," he said.

<They tell me it will be back in operation tomorrow. It always is.>

" 'They'? You mean you can talk to the other birds?"

<Of course—well, not talk like you and I are talking. It's—I guess it's like communicating with another AI, which I didn't get to do for very long. But it's so much faster and deeper than how you and I are talking right now. I feel like you and I could talk for a hundred years and never reach the same understanding that I can from one glance with another of my kind.>

Ngoba nodded agreeably. "Makes sense. So what do you plan to do?"

<Do? I don't know yet. I think there are others like me. I'd like to talk to them. First, I'm hungry. I want to find something to eat.>

"I thought I saw a busted nut vendor back over there," Ngoba said.

Crash bobbed his head. <I'd like that. Goodbye, Ngoba Starl.>

"Wait! Will I get to talk to you again?"

Crash shot into the air like a bullet and the other birds followed, filling the air with a great rustling power that made Ngoba take a step back from the fountain.

"Ing-go-ba!" the parrot squawked. "Ing-go-ba!"

The crows and starlings seemed to enjoy circling him for a few seconds in a tall black funnel of wings and beaks and talons, before turning to shoot off after the little parrot.

Ngoba stood watching them fly away across the park, with the last vestiges of the briki turning the air behind them into swirls and sparks. He absently adjusted his bowtie, and ran a hand through his curly hair, which was crusted with what might have been blood or hydraulic fluid, he couldn't tell.

Turning his back on the quiet fountain, he went to find Riggs and Fug. He would give the eye-shade back to Fug. He grinned as he walked, thinking of all the ways he was going to give his boy Riggs hell.

TO THE FUTURE

STELLAR DATE: 03.25.2956 (Adjusted Years)
LOCATION: Crash Games Hangar, Night Park
REGION: Cruithne Station, Terran Hegemony, InnerSol

"What do you mean you're not coming?" Ngoba demanded. "This is it. I got a place. I got you a ticket out of the *Squat*, away from Mama Chala. This is our chance to make something together, brother."

Riggs offered one of his sheepish smiles. He barely held eye contact with Ngoba. "I never thought I would say this, Ngoba, but I'm signing on with Rack Thirteen."

They were standing outside the door of a studio apartment in a worker's housing section of the Lowspin Docks, an area that looked like several troop carriers smashed together. Corridors ran into dead ends, while others split off in odd directions that defied design. Fast-growing ivy hung everywhere, intertwined with the exposed plumbing and electrical, as well as a few thorny blackberry vines. The air was sweet with the smells of incoming blackberries and leaking oil. A baby was crying in a nearby room.

Ngoba shook his head. "You're signing on with the crew that three days ago tried to kill us? Does Tithi have a ransom on your balls or something? I got a great deal on this place. It's close to everywhere we want to be, and there's more room here than we've ever had in our lives. Are you telling me you're staying in the *Squat*, then?"

"No. Tithi's getting me a place upspin. We're moving in together."

"By the stars, brother. You're doomed."

"You're only saying that because you want me to be as lonely as you."

"It's not lonely if we're together," Ngoba growled. He

turned to unlock the door and pulled it open. The auto-lights flickered on, and he motioned for Riggs to go inside.

Riggs hesitated. "You sure you want me in there?"

Ngoba gave him a surprised frown. "Of course I want you to come inside. We're still brothers, aren't we? Just because you're running off to join a cult of crazy people doesn't mean we can't share a brew like we always have. Are they going to teach you to actually be able to hack things?"

Stepping over the high threshold, Riggs said, "I'm getting a Link next Tuesday."

"You're getting the surgery? Where'd you get the money for that?"

Riggs shrugged. "A gift from Tithi."

"Don't look so bashful," Ngoba said. "Nothing wrong with being a kept man. Be careful she doesn't have a bad dream and blow your head off while you sleep. I saw that pistol she keeps in her arm."

"It's got an override," Riggs said quickly.

Ngoba withheld his smirk out of respect for his friend's future heartache and pain.

"Let me give you the grand tour," Ngoba said, wanting to change the subject.

He went to the cooling cabinet and took out the case of beers he'd bought for the occasion. He cracked one open and handed it to Riggs, who nodded and accepted it. Ngoba cracked his own beer and took a long drink, enjoying the sensation. It tasted like old piss, but he'd bought it with his money and was enjoying it in his place. The security token on the door was his.

Riggs smiled. "All right. I'll take the tour. Do we have to walk far?"

Ngoba gave him the smirk he'd withheld before. "Here we have the entertaining kitchen, complete with a water spigot that saves you the trouble of deciding between hot or cold, since everything coming out of it is lukewarm. You also get the surprise of *usually* getting water, but sometimes getting something else. Will that grey, goopy stuff kill you? Who knows? There we have the cooking pad where I can warm my protein gruel, and there are the storage cabinets. You'll notice someone did me the favor of removing all the hardware, so I don't have to bother with locking anything; while on this side of the wall, each cubby has its own locking code, so I can challenge my mind with remembering them all. Good in the event I jam twenty more people in here, I guess."

Ngoba turned slightly and motioned toward the rest of the rectangular space, where a couch faced a scarred wall with a vid screen. A low table by the couch would serve as both coffee table and dining table. "When I'm feeling fancy, I can push the table out and sit on my knees like civilized people do," Ngoba said.

The wall near the door had two long cabinets that looked suspiciously like weapons lockers, but were used now for extra sets of clothing that Ngoba might obtain at some point in the future. He excitedly pointed out several hooks inside the locker doors where he could hang his bowtie collection, when it came to exist.

Ngoba pointed out the interesting scorch marks on the ceiling from errant weapons fire, which led him to his next thought.

"I sure appreciate you pawning that pistol so I could get my things, Riggs. This place would be even emptier, if not for you."

"It's what friends do," Riggs said. "I guess you're right. It's not like I'm leaving Cruithne or anything. I'll be on the spin. We can see each other whenever we want. Grab a beer, whatever."

"Maybe work a side job, if such an opportunity presents itself."

"You know the Rack isn't especially forgiving about side work."

"I didn't say immediately," Ngoba said. "Discreet

opportunities present themselves, and ready folks take advantage. Isn't that how we do?" He held out the beer can for a toast.

Riggs nodded. "Yeah, that's how we do."

They clinked beer cans, drained them, and then Ngoba went to the cooler for more.

Eventually, they were sitting on the couch with a Crash match on the vid screen and empty cans scattered all over the low table and the floor beside the couch. Ngoba's bowtie was vertical. Riggs had somehow spilled beer down his pants, but didn't care.

"You sure you didn't piss yourself?" Ngoba said. "The lavatory is right there."

"Have to refill the tank for the kitchen faucet, yeah?" Riggs said, burping.

"Exactly. Everyone pulls their share." He looked around, bleary eyed and satisfied with himself. "You heard anything from Fug?" he asked.

"She's gone."

Ngoba perked up slightly. "What?"

"She bought a ticket and left for the Mars Protectorate. She said she isn't stopping until she's on the other side of the Jovian Combine."

"I thought she wanted to go where there were people and civilization?"

Riggs shrugged. "I don't know. That's what she said. She creeps me out, honestly."

"I don't know. I think she has a certain charm to her."

"She looks like a human gave birth to a bat."

"Now that's unkind, coming from a man with a German Shepherd for a father."

"That's just terrible on several levels," Riggs shot back, "and unfair to German Shepherds everywhere."

Ngoba grinned. He found the last two beers in the box

beside the table and handed one over to his friend. They cracked them open and he took a long drink. They would need to find more soon, which meant a good long stumble to the corridor bodega.

"So, Riggs," he said, raising his eyebrows to keep his eyes open. "Did I tell you about the talking parrot?"

Riggs was leaning to one side, squinting like a pirate. "All parrots are talking parrots, dumbass."

"Well, this parrot had a Link and was quite eloquent."

"You're shitting me," Riggs mumbled.

"I'm not, cross my heart. I think it's going to take over the world."

Ngoba waited, but Riggs didn't answer. Eventually, his friend released a long, gurgling snore.

Chuckling, Ngoba leaned over to take the full beer from his friend's hand so he wouldn't drop it. He set it on the low table, then sat up on the couch and kicked one foot out to rest on the table. He looked around at the shabby, grimy apartment, feeling quite pleased with himself.

He sipped his beer. "What I was going to say, Riggs," he said, "is that I think those little fuckers are going to take over the world, brother. Mark my words."

Riggs answered only with snores.

Ngoba groaned. "And that's why they deserve it."

SECOND INTERLUDE

RULING NIGHT PARK
STELLAR DATE: 04.10.2956 (Adjusted Years)
LOCATION: Plascrete Fountain, Night Park
REGION: Cruithne Station, Terran Hegemony, InnerSol

A month (or so) later...

Crash dreamed of numbers. With Shara gone, he sometimes wondered if there was an empty space in his mind. He probed it the way the humans probed the space where a tooth had been, memories and surprise mixing up in his mind as he kept rediscovering the emptiness.

She hadn't stayed long. It had been terrifying at first to have such a huge presence in his mind, pulling him along like a flea on an albatross. Together they'd sailed the highest, strongest winds, with oceans of information stretching beneath them.

When she left, the oceans were still there, only now he could only peek over the cliffs, the terrible wind rushing up in his face to taunt him with what he was too frightened to touch.

<*You can fly, Crash,*> Shara had said. <*If you choose.*>

He couldn't fly. He was trapped in a cage by the first pirate, and kept in cages for years afterward.

The problem with the oceans and the thought of flying over them was that all the information had been made by humans, and throughout his life, humans had hurt him. He nearly escaped *Hesperia Nevada* only to find himself put in a cage and sold between pirates for years. Shara had said she would help him, but he didn't hear from her again.

At least humans fed him and sometimes played games with

him, but most of the time, his days were spent forgotten in a corner, watching an empty apartment, drifting on the Link none of them knew he had. He never dared trying to communicate with a human until he met Ngoba, and the ravens had never been able to get him released—if they'd even understood the images he was able to send them.

Once he was free, the oceans beckoned again. He wanted to add his drop of knowledge to the human waves. The sea of knowledge was already changing with new currents from Sentient AIs like Shara, even if the humans called her illegal. They were afraid of what her kind could do.

Would they be afraid of him if they knew what he was?

Ngoba hadn't been afraid. He had come back and set him free.

Sitting at the top of the plascrete fountain, Crash had been able to put his Link to real use, learning to navigate the spaghetti knots of the network humans used to run their world. From the escaped pet parrots who found the ravens at the fountain, he learned of all the others in captivity on Cruithne alone. Through the Link, he found other parrots and sent ravens to free them as well. Most lived in habitats with locks he could hack, unlike the cage where he had spent so much time.

When the fountain was overrun with ravens and parrots, the newcomers spread out to other parts of the station, but always came back to him, the parrot who could speak to humans using the human Link.

He didn't have to fly over the oceans. That was for bigger birds. He kept to his territory, which was vast enough.

Crash had all of Cruithne.

But the numbers pulled at his dreams. He couldn't remember exactly when they started. He didn't realize the sequences were a theorem until he recognized a pattern, and then realized he had memorized the complete equation.

He hated the numbers at first. Math was a human construct,

their most basic attempts to control everything in their world. They defined reality with numbers and then tried to bend the numbers to their will.

He knew that numbers don't bend, no matter how often humans lie to themselves.

Shara would tell him he'd grown cynical in his old age. Crash would fluff out his chest, spread his tail feathers, and rebut with a solid parrot's squawk. He'd grown to enjoy the way the smaller parrots harangued the passersby in the bazaar. Shouting something as simple as *'Hey, Dummy! Hey, Hey Dummy!'* seemed to stab certain humans to their core.

Obviously the numbers were a message. The question was whether he wanted to answer.

* * * * *

Like a thousand generations of his ancestors before him, Crash grew curious. Why were any parrots drawn to humans? Had the first parrots wondered why those beakless parrots had been born with such wonderful hands? With hands, parrots could have built an entirely different world. Instead, parrots had wings and claws, sharp eyes and particular ears. They charmed the humans with their mimicry and evolved.

With the Link, Crash didn't need hands. He matched the numbers with databases all across Sol. He dug through every network he could reach using Cruithne's multitude of pirate antennae. He searched the TSF, the Mars 1 Guard, the Jovian Defense Force. He searched SolGov and the Martian archives.

It was during this long search, matching the numbers in his dreams to the patterns humans had recorded, that he found the Hoarders.

At first, he thought he had stumbled across another ship like the TMS *Hesperia Nevada* where he had been born. A lonely vessel called the *Phoebe's Reach* was floating unaligned with any shipping lane, dark to the solar system but alive with activity. He hopped aboard on the registry carrier signal and worked his way through the HVAC maintenance systems, sometimes waiting painful minutes for the signal to refresh. He flew down data streams and sat in the holodisplay in the ship's cramped command deck, watching a crew of solemn humans monitor their systems.

The strange thing about *Phoebe's Reach* was that the ship seemed turned inside out. The humans moved along a central tube, with long arrays extending into space from the middle. Each spoke was covered in silica data stores, venting heat. Drones moved among the server plates like farmer ants on leaves, while at the head of the ship, a massive antenna blasted heavily encrypted streams in seemingly random directions. After a day of watching the ship, Crash learned it was only one of a network of such ships, forming a mesh system of extended data storage. The Hoarders maintained the greatest redundant data storage system known to humankind, and they didn't seem interested in the rest of Sol.

It was among their myriad databases that Crash found his number sequence, recorded from thousands of locations in the solar system, along with another data record explaining the meaning of the string: coordinates for the moon Proteus.

When he realized what the numbers meant, Crash nearly fell off his branch on the plascrete tree. Despite himself, he lost the connection to the Hoarders' data stream and was forced to sit blinking, considering what he had learned.

Shara had told him the truth so long ago. Now someone was blasting an invitation to all of Sol, aimed at a particular community capable of receiving and interpreting the message. He didn't assume the message was meant for a little grey parrot on Cruithne. No, it was meant for beings like Shara: Sentient AIs.

It was during a later dive into the Hoarders' systems that

Crash saw another name that he remembered, which made him miss his friend Ngoba Starl all over again. Among a list of assets the Hoarders deemed valuable was a woman named Fugia Wong, recently returned to Cruithne.

PART III:
MY ANDERSONIA

NEWLYWEDS

STELLAR DATE: 06.15.2958 (Adjusted Years)
LOCATION: In-Bound Applicant Assessment Authority
REGION: Ceres, Anderson Collective, InnerSol

Two (or so) years later...

There were seven other couples in the waiting room. Ngoba Starl couldn't stop watching them, wondering if they were on Ceres for the same scam. One couple couldn't stop making kissy faces, obviously trying too hard, while another acted like two wet cats in a bag, hissing at each other and rolling their eyes.

What are we supposed to look like?

He glanced at Fugia Wong sitting beside him, her bobbed black hair falling over her face as she read a data terminal in her lap. *Boring*, he thought. *Boring is good.*

Staring ahead, Ngoba ran through the bits of trivia he had memorized about his fake love. He also reminded himself for the thousandth time not to slip up with her name.

Call her 'Fugia,' not 'Fug'. Fyoo-ji-a. Fugia, like the flower.

The problem was that he most definitely did not think of Fugia Wong as a flower. Sure, she was cute in a kitten-like way, with her heart-shaped face and dark eyes. But she was a hacker: a kitten with concealed claws.

They'd grown up together on the docks of Cruithne Station—Croon-ya, like a sappy song with happy lyrics. She was tricky, had even played him a couple times, but that was life on Cruithne, so he didn't hold it against her. She had a hard edge and a brilliant mind that saw through to the real story in most situations, but she could also be mean, like a cat who purrs before she bites.

<Stop fidgeting,> Fugia said on their private Link channel. <They're going to think you're nervous.>

<I am nervous.>

<So count to a thousand or something.>

<That sounds impossible.>

<You could always use your new Link to, you know, research information like a normal person.>

<That's boring.>

So maybe that's a good idea? Do boring things so he might develop a dull sheen of boring like the other tools in the waiting room.

Fugia raised her head slightly, just enough to show her lips pressed together. If he hadn't known her, she would have looked serene, like a new bride waiting to talk to a visa agent, like the other couples in the room. Her self-control made him uncomfortable. It wasn't natural.

At nearly two meters tall, and lanky, with the natural muscle of a nineteen-year-old who had been hustling his whole life, Ngoba was still a half-meter taller than her, even while sitting down. They had talked about making their height difference a joke for the visa agent, how when they met, they couldn't see eye-to-eye. Now as he sat twirling a lock of his curly black hair, he wondered if the metaphor could refer to more than just their respective height.

An agent in a grey uniform appeared at the entrance doorway and called another couple inside. A young woman and man sitting across from Ngoba and Fugia stood nervously, straightened their clothes, and followed the stern-looking man into the interview room.

Think about the money, Ngoba thought. *Money, money, money.*

It was better to think about the money because he had been irritated to discover he didn't like his new Link very much, even though the neural implant gave him access to amazing things like databases, contextual information, and private communication. Link implantation was a passage to adulthood, and he had dreamed of the day he could afford the surgery, a day he had thought would never come until Fugia offered him a deal: Link surgery at a local medkiosk in exchange for his help with a mission. Once Fugia made her meeting and they left Ceres, Ngoba would get paid enough to keep him afloat for a year. Afterward, he could go back to Cruithne if he wanted, or anyplace else in Sol.

The options were dizzying. He'd never had that kind of freedom in his entire dirt-poor life.

What did she want? For him to play husband on Ceres, to help her gain access to the Anderson Collective, a society run by an authoritarian government that only admitted immigrants who were dedicated to their mission of terraforming Ceres and eventually leaving Sol altogether. They had missed the wave of colony ships in the twenty-fourth to twenty-eighty centuries and, as a people, seemed eternally pissed about the fact.

So here he was, playing Fugia's dutiful fiancé—which would be easier if she'd let him touch her.

Stretching his legs, Ngoba figured the money was good, and the Link implant continued to prove interesting, but it would have also been nice to get a little sexual healing after his surgery. What if the visa agent wanted personal details? Did Fugia have any identifying marks? Did she know about the scar below his right nipple? It made perfect sense.

<*What are you grinning about now?*>

<*I was thinking about how people in love often express themselves physically. How that's a natural human activity.*>

Fugia rolled her eyes. <*Keep dreaming.*>

He was still getting used to communication over the Link, which people described as *'talking with colorful words'* because you could sense and even see emotion. He could tell how a person felt most of the time, so even if he hadn't seen her, he would have known how she felt about what he had said. It was like normal talking in that respect, but there was more information available, images sometimes, or other bits of trailing information like references to a database or things like that.

Because he'd grown up hustling, he also wondered how much the colorful words could be faked. He hadn't yet figured out how to lie to Fugia without getting caught, but it had to be possible.

<*Hey,*> he asked. <*What's your favorite color, again?*>

<*Green.*>

On the long trip from Cruithne to the Mars 1 Ring and then to Ceres, they had asked each other questions, trying to imagine what the visa agent might ask. According to Fugia, the Collective wasn't as interested in how people felt about each other as their desire to breed and make more Andersonians.

"You don't need couples to breed," Ngoba had said. "Or even people, for that matter."

"They're traditionalists. They also seem to think people gestated and born in Ceres gravity will be better suited to the work. They're strict humanists. They think humanity is the best tool to shape anything in the universe."

"But Ceres has a mini black hole. That's what's awesome about it."

"And humans made that."

"With drones and tech and nano-whatever."

Fugia had given him another of her eyerolls. "I didn't say I agreed with these people. I'm just telling you what they believe."

"And why do you want to go there, again?"

"There's someone there I want to talk to, and this is the safest way to do it. Their security screening for breeding couples is more lax than any other form of immigration."

Ngoba had chuckled. "We're going to be a breeding couple."

"No," Fugia had said flatly.

He grinned as he thought back on the conversation. Round-faced and with a scowl most of the time, he would never have described Fugia as 'sexy.' But she could be, if she wanted. *If I choose to see her that way,* he supposed. *Doesn't proximity breed affection?*

The word *'breed'* just made him laugh, there was no denying it.

<Now what are you giggling about?>

"Wong," a voice called from the other side of the room. "Starl."

Ngoba stood quickly and turned to watch Fugia carefully return her data terminal to the small satchel she carried at all times. Pulling the strap over her shoulder, she looked up at him with a surprising smile and took his hand.

"You ready?" she asked, voice sounding surprisingly warm.

Ngoba blinked, caught off guard by the abrupt change in her demeanor. He nearly got an erection.

"I'm ready," he said, feeling himself blush.

"Come here," Fugia said. She stood on her tip-toes to reach up and smooth the unruly black curls from his face. The sort of possessive action of a lover.

Ngoba gave her a stiff nod and turned to the visa agent, who was standing impatiently in the exit doorway. "This way," the man said. Without waiting to see if they followed, he walked ahead of them down the corridor and disappeared around a corner.

TINA TINA TINA

STELLAR DATE: 06.15.2958 (Adjusted Years)
LOCATION: In-Bound Applicant Assessment Authority
REGION: Ceres, Anderson Collective, InnerSol

As far as Ngoba knew, the Ceres ring was several hundred years old at this point. Yet something about the immigration control area looked thrown-together. The corridor walls were all clean and smooth, with no dirt or evidence of living things anywhere except for photo-screens of what Ceres would look like eventually: green and blue, with the thin silver band of the Insi ring gleaming against the black of space.

They followed the agent to a small room with a door that slid quietly open, revealing a table with two chairs on either side. A young woman already sat in one of the chairs. She was solidly built, with short brown hair and brown eyes, and looked about their age. The woman stood as the door opened, nodding to the agent, who walked in first.

"Mister Chalder," the woman said. "I'm Tina Kavers."

Visa Agent Chalder nodded stiffly. "Miss Kavers. Your service is our strength. Please, be seated." He stepped around the table to take the chair next to Tina. When he was seated, he motioned for Ngoba and Fugia to take the opposite chairs.

Ngoba let Fugia sit first, then pulled his chair back to make room for his legs. He glanced at Tina to find she was already frowning.

"Did I do something wrong?" he asked.

"Oh, no," Tina said, shifting her gaze to Fugia. "It's simply surprising to me that Fugia didn't show kindness to you, her lover, by pulling your chair out for you. She made you do it yourself after she'd already sat down."

Ngoba glanced at Agent Chalder, whose stern expression had softened. He looked pleased with Tina, whom he didn't seem to have known before they entered the room.

With a sinking feeling, Ngoba realized there wasn't going to be an interview. Or, the interview was going to take a long time.

Tina was a chaperone.

Fugia lowered her face slightly, actually blushing. "Oh, I apologize. I'm not very informed in the ways of being a—" she paused as if choking on the word, *"lover."*

Ngoba was too impressed by Fugia's ability to fake a blush to respond immediately.

Agent Chalder didn't seem to care. He consulted a data flow on the surface of the table. "It says here your point of origin is Cruithne?"

"That's right," Fugia said.

"And you?" Chalder asked, giving Ngoba a direct look. "I expect confirmation from each applicant."

"Yes," Ngoba said quickly. "Cruithne. I'm from Cruithne, too."

"Age and genetic viability verified by bio-scan," Chalder said. "Good."

"Where did you meet?" Tina asked.

They had prepared for this question, and it was partially true. "Night Park," Ngoba answered. "It's an open-air bazaar on Cruithne. It used to be the center for mining when the asteroid was first developed, so it's big and open. Not many places like that on Cruithne. There's a fountain with parrots."

A look of disgust crossed Chalder's face. "We don't need background details now. That will all be in Ms. Kavers' report later, when the final entry decision is made. I also show you have the required funds for entry into the Ceres ring. You'll be required to pay for your own meals and lodging during your inquiry period, as well as a fee for Ms. Kavers' services."

"That wasn't in the entry information," Fugia said.

The agent leveled his gaze on her. "Will that be a problem?"

<It's a shakedown,> Ngoba told Fugia. <Tina here is all part of

the bribe.>

<*I know that,*> Fugia answered tersely. <*I didn't think they'd complicate things by assigning us a guard. Everything just got a hundred times harder. Stay off the Link for now. They're most likely using spectrum surveillance. I don't want to draw any more attention to ourselves.>*

Ngoba dropped off the channel, giving Tina what he thought was a benign smile. She beamed back at him and sat up straighter.

<*Crap,*> he said. <*I think she likes me.>*

<*Get off your Link!>*

The next fifteen minutes were spent reviewing their travel plans on the Ceres Insi Ring, including a trip down to the planetoid to tour the terraforming project. They would have Tina as a guide, as well as appointments with three different 'collective groups' that were currently taking in new family units. They would rank the groups, and the groups would do the same for them—until an offer was extended for permanent membership. The group would then become their family within Andersonia.

Ngoba found himself impressed by the process despite himself. The idea that two strangers could enter the Anderson Collective and be assigned a new family touched him more deeply than he expected. He had no family other than the few orphans he had remained in contact with from the *Squat*. His best friend, Riggs Zanda, was off doing his own hustle, leaving Ngoba to fend for himself in Cruithne's Lowspin Docks, a place that didn't care about anything but capital, and burned people up like engine oil. Robots were worth more than humans on Cruithne.

"Oh! You're also here for Sharm," Tina said, clapping her hands together. Her round cheeks grew flush with apparent excitement.

"Sharm?" Fugia asked with feigned interest.

"The Festival of Life. Sharm is when most babies are conceived on Ceres. What a wonderful time to start your new lives together as lovers."

Ngoba enjoyed watching Fugia's cheek twitch every time Tina said '*lovers*'.

"I'll be honest," Tina said. "I'm envious of your love. I don't have a partner of my own. That's one reason I serve as a guide. It nourishes my soul deeply to assist in growing the Collective's families." She gave Chalder a pious smile. "Don't you think so, Agent Chalder?"

The visa agent cleared his throat and tapped the surface of the table, clearing the data feed. "Certainly," he said. "Our family ties make us strong."

"Absolutely," Tina said. "And our strength makes us family."

Ngoba frowned slightly, not understanding the aphorism. He supposed it might be an imperial thing, suggesting people could be forced into liking each other.

"So," Chalder said, standing. "That concludes our intake interview. Your entrance visa is granted for ten days. From here, Ms. Kavers is responsible for you. Refer all questions and concerns to her. Understood?"

Ngoba and Fugia nodded.

"Will Ms. Kavers be staying with us, as well? I didn't plan for that."

"I have the apartment next to yours," Tina said brightly. "The Entrance Bureau has taken care of everything. All you have to do is knock on my door, and I'll be available any time."

"How wonderful," Fugia said dryly.

Tina's expression darkened, and Ngoba added quickly, "We don't want to put you out. Fugia mentioned the group visitation procedure, but we didn't realize we'd be lucky enough to have our own guide. That's just above and beyond, really. You'd never get that kind of service on Cruithne."

The compliment seemed to assuage Tina's hurt. She nodded. "It's my honor to help. Also, you know, *love*."

"Exactly," Ngoba said, giving Fugia's shoulder a squeeze. "Love."

Agent Chalder clapped his hands impatiently. "Do you have any other questions?"

When they didn't, he edged around the table to tap the wall control and open the door. Tina followed, sliding past the agent to get to the door. She pressed herself against him in the tight space, which obviously made the man uncomfortable.

"Pardon me, Agent," she said brightly.

From the corridor, Tina waved her hand excitedly for Fugia and Ngoba to hurry. "We want to get you down to the residential section and checked into your apartment. Then we can get out into Sharm for the night. It's going to be wonderful!"

"Do we get to wear silly hats?" Ngoba asked. "I love that stuff."

Tina's eyes sparkled. She reminded him of a holographic ad in a store window. "Oh yes. You can wear whatever you want." She giggled with excitement. "What happens in Sharm, stays in Sharm!"

"You hear that, honey?" Ngoba asked Fugia.

His fake fiancée gave him her fakest smile yet.

NESTING

STELLAR DATE: 06.15.2958 (Adjusted Years)
LOCATION: Glorious Achievement District
REGION: Ceres, Anderson Collective, InnerSol

Fugia told him to stop gawking at everything, but Ngoba couldn't help himself.

From the moment they left the plain corridors of the Visa Bureau, he was surrounded by new sights, sounds, smells, and people, which had him staring at something new every direction he looked. The people of the Anderson Collective might have liked to dress in boring monotones of brown, grey and black, but they surrounded themselves in color. Bright murals showing workers and families covered every public surface large enough to hold paint. Groups of uniformed children passed them, singing high-pitched anthems that seemed to have something to say about the bright future of the Collective.

When there weren't kids around making noise, Tina availed them with the history of their current section of the Insi Ring, which had apparently been finished only two hundred years ago, making it relatively new. There were still remnants of the "bland corporatist" architecture left from the original construction, before Ceres declared independence from private control and Andersonia came into being.

Whenever Tina mentioned Andersonia, she pointed at the green-brown blur of the asteroid above them, which always occupied a central place in the sky. While Ngoba understood he was on a ring spinning around an asteroid, he couldn't shake the idea that everything was going to fall into the sky at some point, or go spinning off into space.

"I'm confused," Ngoba said finally. "Is it the 'Anderson Collective' or 'Andersonia?' Ceres is the place, right, just like

Cruithne is an asteroid, but *someone* might live in the Lowspin section. Are there other parts of Ceres besides Andersonia?"

"That's an excellent question," Tina answered brightly. "You have such an observant partner, Fugia. You should be proud."

"I certainly am."

"Andersonia is the dream of what Ceres will become once we finish the grand terraforming project." Tina joined her hands and pressed them against her breast. "Andersonia is the dream in every Andersonian's heart, of the best place for all humanity to live—close to nature, free of the distractions and pollutions of technology."

"So you're Terran Absolutists?" Fugia said, sounding irritated by the whole conversation.

"Oh, no," Tina said. "We acknowledge that humanity must spread beyond the Earth. Our goal is to spread the purity of humanity's relationship with nature, as well. No one speaks of nature when they talk about progress." She gave an exaggerated laugh. "At least, I haven't read that part of the history books."

"Who reads books anymore?" Fugia asked.

Ngoba shot her an irritated look of his own. Her obvious dislike of Tina was going to get them in trouble. He didn't know what Fugia's meeting was about, but he wanted her to get there so he could get his payout. He worried that he was going to have to make sure Fugia didn't sabotage her own mission.

The commercial district was lined by tree-filled gardens that gradually became shared vegetable plots in the residential section, where Tina explained their apartments were located. "You'll be staying in a very nice group division where they keep open living spaces just for families visiting Ceres."

"You just called it Ceres again," Ngoba said.

"Yes, silly. It's still Ceres. There is no 'Andersonia' yet, only in the hearts and minds of the Collective." She pushed his arm playfully. "You like to tease, don't you?"

"Well, yes," Ngoba said. "I wasn't that time, though."

"He's a really silly boy," Fugia said.

"You don't seem to appreciate him much, if I must say so," Tina said.

Fugia immediately put on a happy expression. "I meant that. He's silly and loves to tease. I'm just tired. It's been a long trip. You understand, don't you?"

Tina softened slightly but still seemed displeased. "I understand. I hate traveling. I haven't done much of it, but I do hate to leave home, even for short periods."

"We appreciate you helping us," Ngoba said.

Tina beamed at him, looking as pleased as before. "Of course!"

Trying to keep her in a happy frame of mind, he asked, "Did you grow up here?"

"Born and raised. I studied chemical engineering and now I work in the Air Quality Division. But I also serve in the Andersonian Defense Force. I'm a heavy weapons operator." Tina flexed her arms, making her chest stand out even more.

Ngoba gave her a raised eyebrow in appreciation. "You have much need for a defense force?"

"Oh yes. Pirates are always going after our shipping lanes. We're small, but we have plenty of quality materials flowing between us and the rest of Sol. We also export high-value defense tech and terraforming materials. The off-ring manufacturing facilities are able to leverage a zero-g environment with the limitless energy of our mini black hole. Ceres is the jewel of mid-Sol."

"What else is there in mid-Sol except the asteroid belt?" Fugia asked.

"Exactly!" Tina said brightly. "We're the oasis in the desert between Mars and Jupiter."

Ngoba was worried Fugia was going to counter with

another snide comment that would get them in trouble again, just after he'd gotten Tina in a good mood. But the small woman managed to maintain a civil conversation, asking about the murals and other art they passed, which seemed to genuinely interest her.

As Tina explained how collective groups came together to plan and paint the murals, Ngoba was thinking about what a waste of time it was when drones could do the work—until he realized that he hadn't seen a drone since they left the transport from the Mars 1 Ring.

Everywhere he looked there were people, which was just like Cruithne, but these people were clean and well-dressed and seemed to enjoy being alive. He was amazed by the number of people who smiled at him, even after they gave him a surprised glance because he looked different. Flags with the symbol of the Anderson Collective hung everywhere, and once he recognized the colors of the flag—brown, green, and black—he realized everything followed that palette. Their clothes weren't boring, they were all reinforcing the symbols of the government.

Glancing down at his bright red shipsuit, bought at a thrift store in Lowspin, he realized just how much he stood out from everything else around them. Even Fugia in her light blue suit stood out as a foreigner.

Why hadn't he seen this sooner? He prided himself on being able to check a situation and respond, fit in or get out when necessary. He'd been too wowed by the new place, the open air and actual buildings. It was like walking into a holodisplay of Earth or High Terra, and he'd let himself feel wonder when he should have been scoping the scene for danger or opportunity.

"Hey, Tina," he said, interrupting her explanation of how the city blocks were laid out. "Where can we get some clothes? I'm feeling a little out of place."

She laughed. "Just figured that out? There will be clothes in the apartment, but you can visit a shop tomorrow if you want.

Once you see Sharm tonight, you may want to stick with the ugly clothes you're wearing! Everyone tries to look as foolish as possible during Sharm." She leaned slightly closer to Ngoba. "Not that clothes stay on very long."

The apartment assigned to them contained a single bedroom, with a small kitchen and living area, and a wide window that looked out on the communal garden, where several people were currently bent over vegetable rows.

Ngoba was worried Fugia would make a comment about the window, but she only stuck her head in the bathroom, flushed the toilet, and then went into the bedroom, leaving him alone with Tina.

"This is very nice," he said. "Thanks again for your help."

The front door was open, but Tina stepped closer to him rather than indicate she was leaving, close enough that he could smell a mint-like scent on her hair.

"I'll be right next door if you need anything," she said, reaching up to rub the lapel of his shipsuit between two fingers.

Ngoba stiffened, glancing toward the bedroom, where Fugia was strangely occupied.

"I'll be sure to remember that."

"Wonderful," Tina said, smiling brightly with moist lips. "Tonight, we'll go to Sharm and have so much fun. I can't tell you how excited I am to have you joining the Collective."

"Me too," Ngoba said, giving her a weak nod. "I can't wait."

Fugia walked out of the bedroom, and Tina bounced toward the front door.

"See you tonight!" Tina called, pulling the door closed behind her. She walked past the picture window, staring at Ngoba as she went, until she disappeared out of view.

"That girl wants to get in your pants," Fugia said. "Or she wants you to get in hers."

"I'm not interested in sharing pants with her."

"That's not what that saying means."

"I'm here to do a job," Ngoba said, turning to face her. "You seem set on screwing things up by being such a jerk. You need to at least act like we're a couple."

"How do you think couples act?" Fugia asked.

Ngoba spread his hands in frustration. "Usually they touch each other, but we don't have to do that, I guess. We should be nice to each other, though, and I think I'm doing my best to be nice to you. We at least need to fake it until your meeting, right? When you were so mean to Riggs, I thought you two had something going on; now I'm starting to think that's just how you are."

Fugia stepped closer with a slight smile.

"What are you doing?" Ngoba asked, not trusting her.

Gazing up at him with surprisingly wide, dark eyes, Fugia tucked her hair behind an ear and then took his lapels in either hand. Rather than rub the fabric as Tina had done, Fugia stood on her tip-toes to pull him closer and kissed him. Her lips locked on his with startling force and heat, soft and insistent at the same time. It almost felt like passion.

Ngoba quailed for a second, not understanding what she was doing, then felt like he was melting as Fugia pressed herself into him, drawing him deeper into the kiss.

Just when he was placing his awkward hands in the small of her back to hold her in place, Fugia let go and pushed him away slightly.

Ngoba stumbled, legs feeling like jelly, and nearly fell over the back of a chair.

"What was that?" he gasped.

"A kiss," Fugia said. "See, I can be affectionate when I want to be."

She turned back toward the bedroom, twisting her hips in a way that showed off her ass, and left the room. "I'm going to take a shower."

Heart pounding, Ngoba wondered if he was going to

survive Sharm.

WRAPPING THE RIBBON

STELLAR DATE: 06.15.2958 (Adjusted Years)
LOCATION: Glorious Achievement District
REGION: Ceres, Anderson Collective, InnerSol

Dressed in the flashiest brown leisure suit the Anderson Collective appeared capable of making, Ngoba walked with Fugia and Tina down a broad avenue full of revelers. Fugia had traded her blue business suit for a skin-tight black leotard with a frilly skirt that stuck out nearly horizontally from her waist. Tina wore a green dress with a neckline that hung off one shoulder, drawing attention to both her oversized biceps and generous bust.

The avenue was lined by vertical, multicolored poles with ribbons hanging from their tips. As people passed, they wrapped the trailing bits of ribbon around their arms and grabbed the person next to them and both twirled to encircle themselves in the ribbon, laughing or kissing or both.

"Sharm is the greatest fertility festival humanity has ever known," Tina said. "During these five days, we remember our calling to populate the collective and spread our message of humanity to the galaxy and, ultimately, the universe. It's wonderful, isn't it?"

"Is this the only time of year anybody has sex?" Fugia asked.

"Oh, no," Tina said, laughing. "We're a lustful people. We have many passions."

Ngoba couldn't imagine anyone on Cruithne saying they were 'lustful.' That was like saying you were carrying hard currency—just inviting someone to take advantage of you.

Ever since Fugia had kissed him, he had been going back over his memories of her, trying to figure out if there had ever been a time when he thought she might be capable of that kind of sexiness. He still felt uncomfortable thinking about her, like all of a sudden he found himself attracted to a completely different person than he imagined. Or was it just her?

Fugia was a hacker: quick on her feet, foul-mouthed, and too smart for her own good. Her fingernails were usually filthy with dirt from network connection boxes. As he sorted through his recollections of her, he realized most of what he remembered was from when they were much younger. At fourteen, had he been much different than he remembered Fugia? Dirty all the time, getting in fights, never thinking about tomorrow.

Watching her walk from slightly behind, he couldn't help appreciating the way the leotard displayed her body and the frilly skirt accentuated the sway of her hips. Realizing he was getting flushed, Ngoba wiped his face with a sweaty hand and tried to look away, finding instead two people wrapped in Sharm Pole ribbon and not much else.

"So, what's the plan?" he asked rapidly. "Are we just going to wander around, or is there something going on? Can we check out a show or something?"

<When are we meeting your guy?> he asked Fugia over the Link.

<He's coming by the apartment tonight after midnight. I gave him the location. I figure that's the best way to do it, rather than trying to get away from Ms. Hotpants, here.>

Ngoba glanced at Tina. <She's not wearing pants.>

<You know what I mean.>

<I'm not sure that I do,> he replied.

<Are you going squirrelly on me because I kissed you? I can't have emotions getting in the way of this job, Ngoba. This is important.>

<I'm not getting—whatever you called it.>

<Squirrelly, like a squirrel.>

Ngoba looked around the street. <I've never seen an actual squirrel. Did you just see one?>

<No. Nevermind.>

<You mean like a rat. They're called tree rats, right?>

<Never mind,> Fugia repeated. *<I can explain more once I meet with the contact. All I can really say is that he's got some information I need. It's part of something big, but it's not really a job.>*

Ngoba did his best to listen carefully as he walked, not wanting to miss anything Fugia said. This was the first time since she offered him the job that she had gone into detail about the task. He had been too wowed by the idea of the Link, currency, and potential freedom from Cruithne to worry about the particulars before. Now that he was in a foreign land, surrounded by sex-hungry locals, the information had become much more necessary.

I need to get better at thinking things through, or it's going to be my ass, he told himself.

<Ngoba,> Fugia said insistently. *<Are you listening?>*

<I'm listening. Wait. What did you say?>

<I said that an hour before midnight, I'm going to tell her I'm still feeling tired. Then we can go back to the apartment and meet the contact. Can you go along with that?>

<I'll be there. Did you already tell this guy I was going to be with you?>

<Is it important?>

<How many deals have you run? Yes, it's important. He's going to want to know everybody involved, or he'll spook. What if he showed up with someone you didn't expect? How valuable is this information you're getting, anyway?>

<Don't worry about that. I should have told him about you, though. I don't think it will delay the meeting, but I'll let him know anyway. That's a good point.>

<Thank you for saying so.>

Fugia shot him a dry smirk over her shoulder, her black hair flashing in the low streetlights.

Realizing that Tina had been talking throughout their entire Link exchange, Ngoba tried to piece together what she had said.

Something about sticky, sweet street food and a dance in a square, followed by some performance somewhere involving mystical fertility goats. Her enthusiasm for the festival seemed to go far beyond simply selling it to outsiders.

"Tina?" Ngoba asked suddenly. "Were you looking to hook up tonight? Are we getting in your way?"

" 'Hook up'?" she asked. "Oh, you mean wrap the ribbon? I don't have a partner, which is why I was willing to volunteer for the Visa Bureau during such a special time." She shrugged, making her green dress ripple. "Who knows, maybe I'll find my special ribbon tonight or the next night. People love outsiders, so they'll be drawn to us. They love *coupled* outsiders even more."

For the next hour, they walked the streets of a new commercial and residential district, where people continued to dance with the Sharm poles, or sing songs and play music in small trios. People watched the street from balconies or rode through the crowd in slow-moving carts that anyone could jump on or off when they wished.

At first, Ngoba couldn't stop checking the crowd for criminal activity—the kind of thing he would be doing if he weren't following Fugia. He didn't catch anyone watching the crowd or casing other groups of people, no one hiding weapons or pickpocketing as far as he could tell. It was a strange scene.

Is there no crime in the Anderson Collective?

He had seen several people in uniform who might have been police, as well as a whole group of ornately dressed guards who looked like they were on their way to a ceremony, but nothing that made the place seem like the police state he had heard it was. Scanning vantage points for surveillance devices—even the round tips of the Sharm poles—he saw nothing that indicated security.

When they stopped at a food booth to eat honeyed buns with bits of raisin, he asked Tina, "Where are all the police? I'll be honest, one of the reasons I never thought of coming to Ceres was because I'd heard it's a bit of a—well, a police state."

Tina wiped honey from her mouth and licked her fingers. "We don't have much crime here," she said. "It's wonderfully safe, and a great place to raise children."

"How is that possible?" Fugia asked, picking raisins off her bun. "Every place has crime. You talk about human virtues; crime is a human certainty."

"Anyone committing a crime is reassigned to the terraforming project," Tina said. "The conditions are harsh, but certainly survivable. So I've heard. I've never met anyone who went and came back."

"I thought everybody wanted to work on the terraforming project," Ngoba said.

"They do, but not in the work camps. That's a very different kind of work." She laughed again. "Look!" she shouted, pointing at an open space in the street, several meters away. "They've started the line dancing. Come!"

Fugia shot Ngoba a look that said she was ready to go. He checked his Link and saw it wasn't yet an hour to midnight, but it was close enough. By the time they got back to the apartment, they wouldn't have much time to prepare for the meeting.

"You know, Tina," Fugia said. "I think it's time for us to head back. I'm really feeling tired. I didn't sleep well before we came out. It's been a long first day."

Caught as she was turning sideways to slide through the crowd, Tina stopped and tilted her head. "I'm very sorry to hear that, Fugia. Do you think you can find your way back?"

"You're not coming with?" Ngoba asked, perking up at the thought that they wouldn't have to get rid of her back at the apartment.

"I think Fugia can find her way." She reached out and grabbed his hand before he could react. Her grip was like iron. "You and I can go dance, though!"

Ngoba looked at Fugia. "I think I should go back with Fugia," he said. "If she's not feeling well, I should be there."

"No," Fugia said, surprising him. "I think that's all right. You and Tina can stay out. I want you to get a good *feeling* for this place, if we're going to live here."

Her emphasis of the word *feeling* made Ngoba gulp. Tina pulled him toward her. She was very strong.

<*I thought I was here to help protect you,*> he said quickly.

<*You're here to do a lot of things. Right now, you're going to provide cover so I can get back in time.*>

<*Who's going to help you if things go sideways?*>

<*They won't. This isn't that kind of thing. Keep her busy, and I'll explain more when you get back tonight.*>

<*Maybe I'll need your help fighting her off?*>

<*Why?*> Fugia asked, raising her eyebrows. <*Have fun. I don't care if you wrap your pole with her.*>

<*You're trying to sell me off to some totalitarian headcase,*> Ngoba said.

<*Just do it.*>

<*I better get paid, Fugia.*>

<*You'll get paid. Don't worry. Now go. She's starting to get suspicious.*>

Ngoba nodded and turned to Tina. "I think I would like to learn about this line dancing of yours. Does it take rhythm?"

"Rhythm," Tina shouted over the crowd, looking pleased that she'd won. "Who needs rhythm to line dance? Come on!"

Ngoba caught one last look of Fugia waving at him before the crowd swallowed him, and he found himself crushed against Tina's simultaneously soft and muscled body.

"Don't worry," she shouted. "We're going to have so much fun!"

A FREE RIDE

STELLAR DATE: 06.15.2958 (Adjusted Years)
LOCATION: Sharm Festival, Glorious Achievement District
REGION: Ceres, Anderson Collective, InnerSol

Ngoba found himself inside a whirlpool of people. For a while, he linked arms with Tina before finding himself pulled away by a smiling couple in black outfits, who then passed him off to another group of four. Everyone laughed and sang a song with words he couldn't make out, though he did quickly make sense of the repeating dance pattern. He kick-stomped-spun his way through the dance steps, which actually became fun once he knew what to expect.

He was surprised when his Link let him know it was nearly midnight.

<Fugia,> he called on their private channel. *<You all right?>*

<Still waiting. What are you doing?>

<I'm dancing.>

<You're actually dancing with those people?>

<It's been fun. I don't know where Tina is. Dammit.> Losing his concentration, he missed a step and a tall man stepped on his foot. Ngoba held his hands up in apology. *<I can't talk and dance at the same time.>*

<Of course not.>

<I called because it's almost midnight. Do you want me to head back?>

<Not yet. I'll tell you when I'm finished.>

<Was the neighborhood busy?>

<No. Every house was dark. Looks like they're all at the festival. It's spooky.>

<You better call me if anything happens.>

<Ngoba Starl,> Fugia said. *<You almost sound like you care.>*

<Of course I care. We're both from Cruithne. You're crew.>

She snorted. *<That's the most ignorant thing you've said since I met you.>*

<You're warming up to me. I can tell.>

Ngoba closed the Link and focused on the person next to him, who turned out to be Tina again. A sheen of sweat covered her face and exposed skin. She hooked her arm in his and spun him around hard, making him a little dizzy. A mess of colors and faces whirled around Ngoba, until he jerked to a halt with a new arm hooked in his opposite elbow. Hands grabbed his wrists and locked him in place. He picked his head up as the tornado stilled, laughter and music continuing around him.

Tina stood in front of him with her hands on her hips. She glanced to Ngoba's left and right, and he realized the people holding him were two men he hadn't seen before. Both were wearing black suits that looked more like uniforms than costumes, and they were looking at Tina.

"Hey," Ngoba shouted. "Why'd we stop dancing? I was having a good time."

"I can see that," Tina said. Her enthusiastic smile was gone, replaced by a smirk that reminded him too much of Fugia. She nodded at the men holding him, and they stepped forward, yanking him off his feet.

Tina stepped forward so her mouth was close to his ear. "If you struggle," she said, "my friends will break your arms, knock you unconscious, and you'll wake up in a work camp. Or you can come along and see what's going to happen. Maybe it's in your best interest."

He hadn't been paying attention to her hands, and flinched in surprise as she clamped a cold band of metal around his neck.

"This will keep you from using your Link with Miss Wong," Tina said. "I would prefer we keep our conversation between us." Her voice had lost all of its naive wonder and now sounded as calculating as a crime boss from back home.

Ngoba pulled against the men holding him, trying to get a

Link message through while they struggled. There was nothing. His head was empty. He couldn't Link out to any connected database, and his mental shouting went nowhere.

With a free hand, one of the men holding him hit him in the side of the face. Then Ngoba took a punch from the other side. He spat blood on the floor at Tina's feet and smiled at her as his head rang. He had been naive to think of the Anderson Collective as any different than Cruithne. He had been stupid to let his defenses down, and now he was going to pay the price.

"Fine," he said. "Where are we going?"

"To a room," Tina said. "Where we can talk. If you struggle again, we'll break the bones in your face. You're a pretty boy, I think that threat might get through to you."

The men started to drag him again, and Ngoba got his feet underneath him, walking with them. They pushed him through the crowd after Tina, her green dress still shining in the festival lights, as revelers laughed and shouted on either side of them. He supposed he looked like any young drunk who'd fallen and hit his face on the ground. No one gave them a second glance.

Or are they programmed to ignore the men in black suits when they drag someone away? Ngoba tried to make eye contact with people as they jostled past, but no one met his gaze. It was like he didn't exist.

At the edge of the street, he was shoved into a dark compartment beneath one of the party carts; he heard the door lock behind him, and then felt the cart jerk into motion. The sound of feet stomping on the surface above his head indicated more revelers standing on the cart. He wondered how many prisoners he might have passed earlier in the night.

The cart made several turns, pausing every so often for people to climb on or jump off. He felt the differences in balance and weight as the cart rocked from side to side, before the space outside the metal walls gradually grew more calm and quiet. They were leaving the festival. The sound of the cart's motor reached him through the deck beneath him. Ngoba strained to hear voices or anything from the outside, but only made out the gentle rumble of the tires on the street. His face throbbed as the adrenaline from the festival faded, and he had trouble keeping track of the cart's ongoing turns and stops.

Ngoba was just beginning to nod off when the cart came to a stop and didn't move again. Someone worked the lock on the outside of compartment and swung the door open, bathing him in the light from a street lamp, which was dim but still blinded him.

"Get out," a low voice commanded, one of the men who had grabbed him. "If we have to come in there, we're breaking bones."

"Didn't you already say that?" Ngoba asked.

The nearest guard stuck his head in the opening, grimacing. "You know there's no such thing as police brutality in the Collective, right, outsider?"

Before Ngoba could pull his foot away, the guard grabbed his ankle and dragged him half out of the cabinet.

"I'm moving," Ngoba said quickly. "I'm moving."

"Hurry up, then."

Blinking, he slid out of the compartment and stood, leaning against the cart for a second to wait for his head to stop spinning.

They were standing outside a nondescript three-story building with the same bland facade as the Visa Bureau. Tina stood to one side of him, wearing a suit like the two men, but in the same green as her dress had been.

"Where are we?" Ngoba asked. He stopped himself. "I guess it doesn't matter. Nevermind. What happens if I try to run?"

"You can try," Tina said, giving him another sardonic smile, as if she might be impressed if he tried.

Head games, he thought. *These fuckers are going to be all about head games. Keep yourself together, man. They'll slip up.*

"Not tonight," he said. "I want to get back to the party."

"That's very sensible of you."

Ngoba nodded toward the building. "Lead the way."

There was a guard standing at the door who saluted with his rifle and stepped out of the way as Tina approached. They passed through the security door and walked down a long hallway lined by blank doors, with dim lights in the ceiling that seemed to only increase the gloom. Ngoba glanced at the doors as they passed, each with a locked slot for a food tray at its foot. He's seen places like this in vids. For a prison, it looked better than the shipping container he could have expected back home. He supposed it might be harder to space someone here than on Cruithne, where bodies disappeared all the time, kicked into vacuum.

"What's for dinner?" he asked.

Tina stopped in front of a door and tapped the lock panel. The grey door swung inward, and she walked inside. Ngoba looked at the man standing beside him, who was holding a pistol now. Why hadn't he noticed that?

I must be hurt worse than I thought. Maybe they gave me a concussion.

The guard motioned toward the door with his handgun, and Ngoba stepped into the doorway. Tina was standing in a small room with a med-lounge in its center. The walls were covered in blank panels.

"Have a seat," Tina said.

"Look," Ngoba said. "This looks like serious business, and, honestly, I'm not a serious person. If you ask me questions, it's very likely I'll tell you whatever I know. You really don't need to waste any of your special equipment here, yeah?"

He felt the pistol muzzle in the small of his back.

"I'm not going to waste anything, Mister Ngoba. In fact, I'm going to upgrade that cheap Link you've currently got onboard. I noticed the fresh incision the first time I saw you. I'm surprised you're not a vegetable, with that kind of outdated hardware."

"That's Cruithne for you," he said. "If it ain't stolen, it's somebody's trash."

"Oh, I don't think you're trash, Mister Ngoba. I don't think you've seen your true potential at all."

Ngoba swallowed, staring at Tina Kavers and wondering how he'd ever thought her an innocent local girl. Standing straight, muscled and flashing her crooked smile, the woman was obviously a monster. He couldn't help finding her even more sexy now.

I'm some kind of fool.

Tina patted the medical lounge. "Hurry up," she said. "We don't have all night."

Ngoba knew he should have turned and taken his chances with the pistol, but they didn't give him the chance. One of the guards behind him jammed a needle in his neck, and he went out, dreaming of parrots.

HARD TIMES
STELLAR DATE: 06.16.2958 (Adjusted Years)
LOCATION: Sharm Festival, Glorious Achievement District
REGION: Ceres, Anderson Collective, InnerSol

Lately, whenever Ngoba remembered his dreams, they usually involved parrots. After his briki-powered conversation with the grey parrot Crash back in Night Park, he often dreamed of long conversations with the bird, or saw the parrot staring at him with a yellow eye just before he woke.

When he was unconscious in the medkiosk down by the Terran Space Recruiting station — the cleanest kiosk Fugia could find, and it was still splattered in dried blood — he had dreamed that Crash the Grey Parrot was looking down at him as the Link interface was installed, plugged into his brain, whatever it was the kiosk did. Crash fluffed his wings to preen, clicked his beak, and nodded, keeping watch over him as Ngoba ceased being a natural human and became something partially mechanical, just as Crash had been augmented.

The sound of the parrots and ravens squawking in the fountain at Night Park woke him. He was upright, standing in front of the apartment door where he and Fugia had been earlier that day. He blinked several times, not connecting that he could enter the apartment. He figured he should knock first.

His neck itched, and he realized the dampening band was gone.

<Fugia?> he tried.

<Ngoba!> she shouted in response, making him dizzy. He pressed his forehead against the door to steady himself.

<I'm outside the door. Can you open up? Are you still at the apartment?>

<I'm here. I'm right here. I've been trying to get hold of you all night. What happened to you?>

The door opened and he stumbled forward, nearly falling on Fugia. She jammed her palms into his chest, holding him up for a second, her face staring up into his in worry.

"Ugh," Fugia groaned in disgust, grimacing like she'd grabbed a zombie. She pulled away from him and let him fall on the floor. Ngoba barely noticed the fall, only the cool tile against his cheek. "You reek of alcohol and vomit," she scolded. "I need you to be prepared, and you were drinking at that festival?"

Ngoba waggled his finger, the only part of his body that wanted to move. *Have I been drinking?* He couldn't remember exactly. He remembered spinning with the dancers, people smiling, the world tilting, and then a long ride in one of the party carts. *Is that how I got back to the apartment?* It had to be the explanation.

While he didn't remember drinking, his head ached, and he had stabbing pains at the base of his skull, like somebody had kicked him when he was down.

"I need to sleep," he mumbled. "I don't feel good."

"I don't care how you feel. We need to go. I've been trying to get hold of you."

"Go? Where? I want to go to the bed."

Fugia made another disgusted sound and grabbed his arms. Grunting, she pulled him inside the apartment and closed the door. "What happened to Tina, anyway? Weren't you with her? Some great guide she turned out to be. I imagine she had sex with you and dumped you here. Are you drugged, too?"

"You imagine me having sex?" Ngoba asked, grinning in spite himself.

Fugia ignored the quip and continued dragging him into the bathroom. Leaving him on the floor with his head near the toilet, she stepped over his body to open the shower stall. With considerable effort, she lifted him into the shower.

"This is for your own good," she said, leaning over him to

turn on the cold water.

Ngoba felt an electric shock go through his body when the water hit him in the face. The first few seconds were painful as he blinked and sputtered, until he felt himself wake up enough that he could roll over on his hands and knees and let the water run down his back, which warmed it up slightly. He let his head hang between his arms. The water numbed the back of his head, which still felt like it had been smashed in.

After a minute of the cold spray, he rose to his knees and stripped off his shirt. Climbing slowly to his feet, he leaned against the wall of the shower, unbuckled his pants, and let them fall around his ankles. He adjusted the water temperature.

"I'm not drunk," he said. "I think I was drugged. I've got a blank space between when you left and when I came here."

Fugia crossed her arms. "What happened to Tina?"

"I don't know. I don't know where she is."

"She was stuck to you like white on rice. I don't believe she would have dumped you here. Are you hurt?"

Ngoba looked down at himself, realizing he was naked. He took a deep breath and felt more clear-headed. The blank spot in his memory gained definition, edges. He remembered the crowd and then black, followed by the grey apartment door.

Where does the long cart ride fit in?

<Can you hear me?> Fugia asked.

<Yes, I can hear you. I talked to you before from outside.>

<I know.>

<So how did your—>

<Shut up,> she ordered.

<What?>

The shower wall was warm against the side of his face. It felt like the only thing holding him upright as his thoughts gained definition and then ran away from him, giggling. He kept seeing the Sharm poles draped with ribbons, the dancing, people writhing all over each other, and Tina in her green dress, winking at him.

"I can't hear you," Ngoba said, raising his voice over the water.

"I wasn't talking, Ngoba."

The room was filled with steam. He wiped water out of his eyes and stepped back in surprise as Fugia entered the shower with him. She had stripped, and now the water plastered her black hair against her forehead. He stared at her, unable to hide his instant bodily excitement.

Feeling him grow hard against her stomach, Fugia rolled her eyes and put a finger to her lips, warning him to stay quiet. She made a twirling motion with her finger and then patted the air, palms down.

Ngoba didn't understand at first, then realized she wanted him to turn around and get back on his knees. He did as she asked.

Fugia stepped closer to him so he could feel her legs against his back. Carefully, she eased his head forward and brushed his hair away from his neck. Her fingers probed his skin, mixing with the sensation of the pounding water. When she touched a spot below his left ear, he gasped in pain. There was a cut there he hadn't been aware of.

Probing a few more centimeters around the painful spot, Fugia patted his shoulder again to tell him to stay where he was. She turned off the shower and opened the door, padding naked out of the bathroom.

She returned wrapped in a green Andersonian robe, carrying her satchel. Pulling a towel from the shelf, she stepped back into the shower behind him and dried off his neck and shoulders, then draped the towel over the back of his head so it covered his face. The rough fabric of her robe against his back wasn't as pleasant as her legs had been.

With his vision blocked by the towel, Ngoba could only wait as he heard her dig through the satchel, then lay something metallic and cold against the back of his neck. Another jolt of pain needled the tender spot, and then he felt Fugia relax against his shoulders. She stepped out of the shower again, dragging the towel away from his face.

"There," she said. "They bugged your Link. It's still in there, and there isn't much I can do about it right now, but it's blocked." She sat on the toilet and crossed her arms, frowning as she thought.

"Does this have something to do with your meeting?"

"Obviously."

"So we're screwed?"

"No," Fugia said thoughtfully. "I think it means they don't know why we're here."

"Why are we here?" Ngoba asked, finding himself growing angry. "Can you give me the courtesy of the truth, finally?"

Fugia sighed and pursed her lips. "Don't worry. I'll reverse whatever they did to you. Links aren't that complicated, when it comes down to it. Maybe they even gave you something better than you had before. It might be military grade. I won't know until we can get to another medkiosk."

"Are they going to be able to tell that you blocked it?"

"I'm snatching all the data right now and replacing it with beta waves. They'll think you're asleep."

Ngoba didn't feel like sleeping anymore. He picked up the towel from where Fugia had dropped it and dried himself off.

"Well," he said, wrapping the towel around his waist.

"Well, what?" Fugia said, still frowning with thought.

"What are we doing in this authoritarian hellhole?"

"Oh, that. We're rescuing an AI."

"Rescuing an AI?" he asked, flabbergasted. "That's it? Why couldn't you tell me that back on Cruithne? That's like saying we're going to rescue a toaster. Who cares?"

Fugia raised her eyebrows. "The Andersonians care," she said. She ran her hand through her wet hair. "The penalty for smuggling a Sentient AI off Ceres is death."

BOOT CAMP
STELLAR DATE: 06.15.2958 (Adjusted Years)
LOCATION: Sharm Festival, Glorious Achievement District
REGION: Ceres, Anderson Collective, InnerSol

Dressed in one of the brown worksuits provided with the apartment, Ngoba lay on his stomach on the bed, while Fugia fussed with a data terminal, growling at whatever she saw on the screen.

"So, this is interesting," she said. "They replaced your commercial Link with a military version. Looks like it's off-the-shelf Marsian tech. Dammit." She reached across his body to adjust the magnetic sensor sitting on the back of his neck, something she had built quickly from parts scavenged out of a bedside lamp and some other components in her satchel.

"It doesn't feel any different," Ngoba said. "What does 'military grade' mean, anyway?"

"For their purposes, I think it means they can monitor any traffic that crosses it. Based on the company's info, it provides low-level sensor data back to a central control point. The relay doesn't appear to be fully active. It's only sending Link traffic, not visual or bio-scan data."

"That's comforting. So if they want, they can see everything I see?"

"That chews up a lot of bandwidth without a local comms node, but yes." She slapped his ass. "You should be pleased, this is expensive stuff. Once I break their security key, you're going to have access to all kinds of cool stuff."

"That hurt."

When his medkiosk Link had been installed, he'd been greeted by a genderless guide named Shawn, who'd been ready to explain all the special offers available from the helpful companies who'd helped subsidize the price of his Link.

'Isn't that great! You'll be the first to know about exciting opportunities in your area.'

It had taken Fugia ten minutes to wipe Shawn's irritating voice from his mind and leave him with his own thoughts, while also freeing up the limited capabilities of the low-cost Link. He knew there were various levels of the tech available, from having a limited AI present at all times, down to what he'd had installed, which allowed access to most databases, Link communication, and bio-data.

Ngoba watched Fugia's fingers move across the face of the terminal. She paused, frowning, then made an excited sound and entered another series of rapid commands before stabbing the edge of the terminal with her index finger.

Abruptly, he felt like he was falling through the bed. Ngoba's arms and legs tingled. He vibrated as micro-tremors radiated out through his body, filling him with a sensation like fear, but he knew he was still laying on the bed. It was like dying in a dream.

The room where he had been watching Fugia lost focus, becoming a swirl of color.

<*Hello, soldier,*> a neutral voice said in his ear. <*You prefer boys or girls?*>

Ngoba tried to focus, but he couldn't make his eyes move. The only action available to him seemed to be his inner voice.

<*Who are you?*> he asked.

<*Hello, soldier,*> the voice repeated. <*You prefer a male or female voice?*>

<*For myself? This is the only voice I have.*>

<*Let's try this,*> a woman's voice said, sounding close. <*Close your eyes and orient on my words. I'm right here with you. Can you hear me?*>

<*I hear you. Who are you?*>

<*My name is Caprise. I'm here to help you understand and use your Enfield Scientific personal data Link.*>

"Fugia," he mumbled. "There's someone talking to me."

She didn't sound surprised. "That's probably the tutorial program. I had to restart the Link and update its control firmware. This is trickier than I thought it would be. I need to maintain their data stream while separating you from the system. This thing is smarter than I expected."

"Can she talk to Tina?"

"Who are you talking about?"

"Caprise. The woman in my head."

"Of course the help agent is a woman. Now you're never going to leave the house."

"She sounds nice," he slurred.

"Dummy. Of course she does. She's there to make you a docile killing machine guided by your own onboard war-wife."

"That doesn't sound so bad."

His communication with Fugia was getting more difficult, while Caprise remained clear and easily understood.

<Ngoba,> she said. <Ngoba, are you listening to me?>

<I'm listening.>

<I'm going to teach you some things quickly. You can already communicate mentally, so that's very good. I'm very impressed with you. We're going to take it to the next level. Do you see the information about your body? You've got a great body, by the way.>

Without needing to think about it, Ngoba knew his heart rate, chemical levels, and other bio-scan information. He understood the depth of the wound in the back of his head, and its effect on his overall health. The data came to him holistically—he couldn't think of another way to describe it. Not as numbers scrolling through his mind, although that information was available, if he pushed deeper. He understood the effectiveness of his body.

"Hold still," Fugia said. "Stop flexing all your muscles."

"It feels good."

<Yes, it does,> Caprise said, sounding pleased. <That's your

physical and mental readiness level. You're going to understand that in relation to your environment. Once we get weapons in your hands, you'll know the same thing about your tools and if they're up to the mission at hand. Sound good?>

<I like that idea.>

<For your next step, I'm going to share the Enfield local databases available to you. It looks like we're too far away from High Terra to connect remotely, so we'll make do with what we have.>

The schematics of various electronics flashed in Ngoba's mind. The mental view pulled back so that he saw a metal box, then pushed inside again, following the components of the device. Names and function explained themselves as the different parts passed his mind's eye.

<It's a network control point,> he said.

<Very good. Now, this is the kind of thing you could blow up, if you wanted to disable it, and that would be fun. But you could do the same thing by making changes here and here. Make sense?>

<I understand.>

Ngoba felt a surge of pleasure at the new skill. Would this always be available to him now? It made him feel like a superhero. Was this how other people went through life? No wonder some people on Cruithne seemed infinitely smarter than others. This went deeper than mental communication or being able to look up info on his own.

<Can you read my thoughts?> he asked. Shawn had seemed unwilling to honestly answer this question before Fugia removed him.

<Not really,> Caprise said. *<Would you like it if I could? That would bring us closer, wouldn't it?>* There was a hunger in her voice that sent up warning flares in Ngoba's mind.

Is this thing designed to make me love it? Is Fugia right?

When was Fugia wrong?

She'd been wrong to come back to the apartment alone and leave me with Tina....

Ngoba's focus was returning, drawing his thoughts back to how he'd felt in the shower. He'd been angry at Fugia, and it flared again. She'd been lying to him, using him to get away from home to a place where he was helpless, and now he'd been implanted with foreign tech. Who knew if she could actually fix him? *Am I going to be a slave to the Anderson Collective for the rest of my life? Would she care?*

The sensation of her body pressed against his in the shower, her fingers moving through his hair to find where he'd been hurt, the tenderness she'd shown him, didn't make up for his situation. He was fucked. There was no better way to say it. He was fucked.

<*Can you read my thoughts?*> he asked Caprise again, more forcefully this time.

<*I can't,*> she answered, voice growing more formal in response to his tone. <*I can infer mental status based on bio-scans. I process visual, temperature, and pressure data to infer situational awareness and provide informational options. This often creates the experience of intimacy, especially if the soldier desires this connection. This effect has proven therapeutic during combat operations and in processing post-traumatic stress.*>

<*I don't want that.*>

The tutorial agent paused. <*Please clarify request.*>

<*I don't want intimacy. I don't want you in my head.*>

<*Ngoba,*> she said softly. Her voice pressed closer than before, so warm it sent a thrill down his body like a trailing hand. He arched involuntarily.

<*I can help you,*> Caprise said, going straight to the pleasure centers in his mind. <*You don't ever have to be alone. You won't even know I'm here until I can help. I'll help you be all you could ever be. You'll be a god.*>

"What are you doing?" Fugia asked.

Ngoba ignored her. He clenched his eyes closed until colors flashed inside his eyelids. Caprise sent finger-like sensations up and down his body, then centered them on his crotch. Rings of pleasure ran up and down his erection. Lying on his stomach, he couldn't move. He felt pressed into the bed by Caprise's voice murmuring in his mind.

<You want me, don't you? It could always be like this. Always.>

Despite himself, he orgasmed hard, clenching at the bed.

"Ngoba!" Fugia shouted. "What the hell is wrong with you?"

Fugia's voice only flashed the image of her naked body into his mind, her eyes as she looked up at him, the shape of her lips. The rapid images mixed with Caprise's voice.

<Tell me you want me.>

As the tension in his body faded, Ngoba opened his eyes. The room came into focus as he looked from the closet hung with brown, green and black clothes. Green and black reminded him of Tina and her two men dressed in black. He remembered them now. He remembered Tina standing next to the med-lounge.

<Damn, woman,> he spat, head cleared by the orgasm. His patience for her artificial intimacy dropped from his mind. <I'm nineteen years old. It's not right for you to manipulate me like that.>

<It's not manipulation. I care about you, Ngoba.>

<No, you don't. I don't approve. End this tutorial, or whatever it is.>

Caprise gave him an angry sigh before dropping the intimacy from her voice. <Verify end tutorial?> she asked.

<Yes. Verify. Whatever.>

<Thank you for using Enfield Scientific products. Your tutorial is complete. Link activated in non-assist mode.>

<Thank you,> Ngoba said, relaxing into the bed.

<But I'll still be here if you ask for me,> Caprise whispered. His mind went quiet, and she was gone.

"Can I sit up?" he asked. "Are you done with the thing on my neck?"

"Wait," Fugia said. She was still doing something with the data terminal that he couldn't see. "Yes, all right."

Ngoba reached back to take the probe off his neck. He sat up on the opposite side of the bed from Fugia and stretched, feeling like he'd run a marathon. He was exhausted but also exhilarated. The new Link offered seemingly endless lists of new databases, and those were just the onboard stores. He couldn't wait to get back to Cruithne, where he'd be close enough to Earth to take advantage of the rest of what Enfield had to offer.

He chuckled at the thought. This was his chance to leave Cruithne for good, and he couldn't wait to get back.

"You should clean yourself up," Fugia said. She'd come around the bed, packing up her satchel with the equipment she'd spread out next to him.

"What?" Ngoba asked. He looked down and saw the wet spot covering most of his lap.

"Looks like you needed the release. Been a while, huh?"

Shaking his head, Ngoba stood slowly, the new Link letting him know he was sore but not hurt. He walked stiffly toward the bathroom.

"Don't take too long," Fugia called after him. "We're leaving as soon as you're ready."

Ngoba turned in the doorway. "Where are we going? And be straight with me this time, or I'm leaving."

"I just saved your ass!" Fugia said, clenching her fists. For a second, it looked like she was going to explode. Then she relaxed. "Fine. We're going down to the local shipping zone. That's where the contact should be waiting."

"What's the AI look like? Is it a box?"

"It's not a toaster," she snapped, then paused. "I don't know, actually."

Ngoba nodded. "Great. Well, that's something. It's better when you share information with me, so we can plan together, like actual partners."

"I never said we were partners."

Ngoba rubbed his head, touching the back of his neck where the incision was still tender.

"We're partners, whether you like it or not," he said.

PRACTICAL HOUSEKEEPING
STELLAR DATE: 06.15.2958 (Adjusted Years)
LOCATION: Sharm Festival, Glorious Achievement District
REGION: Ceres, Anderson Collective, InnerSol

"They'll have surveillance on the apartment," Ngoba said. "You realize that, right? We're going to have a hard time getting out of here."

Fugia gave him a grin and nodded toward the closet, where he had just selected the black suit he was wearing.

"We've got another door out of here."

He frowned. "Through the closet?"

"Yup."

"Damn. This whole room was probably bugged."

"I rerouted them all. Whoever's listening in thinks we've been sleeping or listening to music for the last six hours."

Fugia had dressed in a green pantsuit with wide sleeves that ended above her wrist. A black headband held her hair away from her face.

"You ready?" she asked. Digging in her satchel again, she pulled out two cylindrical objects and held them toward him.

"What are those?"

"One's a stunner I put together using the resistor assembly in the kitchen's heating unit, and the other is sort of a little handgun. It's got one shot that would probably be accurate at a meter."

"I'll take it." Ngoba inspected the stunner and then the projectile weapon. "Does this thing have a safety?"

"You have to power it on."

She went to the closet and shoved the clothes out of the way. Over her shoulder, Ngoba saw the outline of a small door in the back wall.

He pocketed the weapons. "Did you already check it?"

"Of course. There's a maintenance tunnel back there that appears to access every apartment in this block."

"I thought you said the Anderson Collective wasn't a police state."

Fugia dropped to her haunches and pried the door open with a small screwdriver. She crawled through on her hands and knees.

Ngoba followed, finding a narrow corridor behind the wall, lined with conduit and plumbing lines. Dim lights along the floor provided slight illumination.

Before he left the closet, he pulled the clothes back as best he could and then closed the door. It clicked in place as he stood, stretching.

"Any idea where this goes?"

Fugia was already several meters down the corridor, holding her data terminal in front of her as she walked. "If it follows any kind of plan, I'd imagine there's a central surveillance room where agents monitor the housing block."

"What are you doing with that terminal?"

"Scanning for excess spectrum traffic. I figure that will give us a heads-up if we're about to walk into a monitoring device."

Ngoba stayed about a meter behind her as she worked her way down the dim corridor. The walls had a fine layer of dust, which indicated the path hadn't been used recently. Ngoba didn't put much faith in cleanliness as an indicator of use though, since everything on Cruithne was covered in some level of grime—even if heavily trafficked.

"I never asked you how you learned to do all this stuff."

"What stuff?"

"The hacking, the being an operator kind of stuff. Building weapons out of kitchen appliances. You learned that back home?"

She shrugged. "I guess. How things work usually just makes sense to me. Once you understand the basic idea, it's easy to rearrange the pieces into something different."

"But networks and communication are totally different than gadgets, yeah? Did you run away to a school and not tell anybody?"

"I grew up in Lowspin, just like you. All the info is available in the public databases, if you go looking for it. I think your new Link gives you access to a whole bunch of espionage databases, if you bother to check them."

She glanced back at him and traced a circle around her ear with a finger. "Be careful that thing doesn't make you crazy, Ngoba. It's specialized equipment." Her half-smile made her look cute.

"So, Fugia?" he asked.

"Yes?" she answered, attention back on her terminal.

"You took your clothes off and got in the shower with me."

"I didn't want to get my clothes wet."

"They gave us a whole closet full of clothes."

"I like these ones."

"Yeah, but—"

"Ngoba, you're bothering me while I'm trying to concentrate."

"You're confusing me, Fugia."

"Wait," she said, holding up a hand. She moved the terminal back and forth along an invisible line in the air, then took a step backward and looked to either side of the wall. Ngoba followed her gaze, realizing she was looking for another door.

"There's one right there," he said, pointing.

"We need to go through it. See if you hear anything."

"What's blocking the way?"

"I don't know, but it's giving off the same EM field as a type of mine. I'd rather find a way around it."

Ngoba went down on his hands and knees and checked the lock on the hatch to his right. As he worked, he tried to figure out how many apartments they may have passed since leaving their own, estimating maybe three. He couldn't remember which apartment Tina had said she would be staying in. Any time now, anyone watching would figure out that the signals coming from their apartment were fakes.

"We've got a problem," Fugia said. "The field is moving."

"This way?"

"Yes."

Driving his shoulder into the hatch, Ngoba fell on his stomach inside another closet. He scrambled to his feet and found himself standing over two people in bed wrapped in a mess of Sharm ribbons. They stared at him as Fugia bumped into him from behind. Together, they ran through the apartment and out the front door.

Out on the street, screams sounded from inside the apartment they had just left, followed by weapons fire.

"Sorry about that," Ngoba said under his breath. He looked at Fugia. "Which way do we run?"

"There's a maglev terminal that way."

"Is that a good idea? What if they shut down public transit?"

"I'll have to stop them from doing that."

The streets were littered with bits of ribbon and small groups of people stumbling home. Two of the automatic carts sat quiet against curbs.

"Hold on," Ngoba said. "Can you control one of these things? It's got a space underneath where you can hide."

"How do you know that?"

"I think they moved me in one." He glanced back up the street toward the apartment block they had just left. He couldn't tell if anyone was following in the street or not. "If anything, we won't be seen by surveillance."

Fugia jogged over to the nearest cart and checked its control panel. She let out a short laugh. "No password on the navigation system."

Ngoba watched her check several menus, then turned to the

space under the cart's upper deck. The cabinet was unlocked and easily accessible.

"You're right," Fugia said. "We can do this. I'm setting the destination now." She shot him a grin. "You had a good idea for once."

The cart hummed to life.

"I've got a better idea," Ngoba said, nodding toward the other cart just up the street. "You should set that one running to another maglev terminal."

"Maybe you'll run a crew someday, after all," she said with a wink.

"I'm never going to get used to you being nice to me."

"I'll give credit where it's due."

Ngoba kept his eye on the street above them as Fugia checked the other cart. Once she set it in motion, she ran back over to him and they crawled into the cabinet beneath the first cart. Ngoba pulled the door closed and relaxed slightly when the lock closed. They were hidden for now.

Across from him, Fugia's face was lit by the glow from her terminal.

"What are you checking now?"

"The carts have a rudimentary sensor system. I'm connecting with the other cart's camera, as well as to this one, so we're not walking out blind."

"Does this contact know we're coming?" he asked.

"Sort of."

"What does that mean?"

"It's an AI, Ngoba. It knows a lot of things. It might not know it's leaving tonight."

Ngoba slapped the side of his face with his hand. "You remember when I asked you to share your plans with me?"

She glanced up at him, the terminal glow making her eyes black. "I did. We're doing exactly what I told you we were going to do."

"You said we were rescuing an AI, not kidnapping one. Those are two different things. In the rescuing scenario, the thing you're moving is probably in agreement with you. It might even be grateful for your help. In the second scenario, you're a criminal a few times over."

"You're already a criminal. What's the difference?"

The cart shook as it went over a bump in the street, moving faster than he remembered from before. Ngoba pressed his hands on the metal deck to steady himself.

"Are you watching where you're going?"

Fugia was frowning at her terminal. "Be quiet," she said. "Something just took control of the car."

WARM WELCOMES

STELLAR DATE: 06.15.2958 (Adjusted Years)
LOCATION: Sharm Festival, Glorious Achievement District
REGION: Ceres, Anderson Collective, InnerSol

As Ngoba stared at the back of the data terminal in Fugia's hands, he experienced a feeling like déjà vu as a memory slipped into his mind. He saw the internal components of the device, its capabilities and potential uses, as well as several vulnerabilities that might allow him to block it or gain access to her information.

He blinked, fear rising from the out of control cart and confusion from not understanding where the information was coming from—until he recalled Caprise's voice explaining the query powers of his new Link. Before, this kind of information would have meant a long search through public databases. Now it was available to him automatically, if he chose to use it.

Steadying himself, he searched the inside of the cabinet for some control box or console that might operate the cart. There was a blank panel next to the door, but when he stared at it, he didn't get a specific schematic, but a choice among hundreds of possibilities.

"Will you sit still?" Fugia said, eyes on her terminal. "I'm trying concentrate."

"What's going on?"

"Like I said, something keeps injecting commands into the cart's control computer. Every time I reset the security token, it gets overridden, and we start speeding up again."

"Is it changing our course? All I can feel is the speed, and it feels terrifying."

She shook her head. "I don't think so. We haven't hit anything yet, anyway."

The cart braked, and Fugia slid across the cabinet, her

terminal jabbing Ngoba in the eye. He caught her before her head hit the opposite wall. The cart rolled free for a second, then accelerated again.

Fugia pushed herself away from Ngoba and fumbled her terminal upright. She frowned at its surface, her distant expression saying she was occupied in her Link.

"You look less upset," he said.

"Hush."

The cart braked and accelerated, sliding around turns before accelerating again. Ngoba sat tensely with his back to the direction of travel, ready for the impact coming at any moment that would crush them inside the metal box.

"The guy who met you at the apartment while I was gone. You trust him?"

"How many times are you going to ask me that? No, of course I don't trust him. But his information was correct." She shook her head. "Also, there's no way he would sell me out to the Collective. The government killed his father."

"This isn't about the guy," Ngoba said, now feeling awkward that he didn't know the contact's name and he was forced to keep saying '*guy*'. "I'm going back to our conversation about smuggling versus kidnapping. What if this sentient AI doesn't want to leave Ceres?"

"Ceres is not a safe place for a sentient AI."

"Yeah, I get it. They worship pure humanity, or whatever. Tina made that abundantly clear. But it still stands, did anybody ask the AI? Because wouldn't taking control of a party cart be child's play to something like that?"

Fugia looked up from her terminal, brows knit. The cart's acceleration had evened out, but Ngoba couldn't tell if that was due to Fugia's anti-hacking, or because the street had straightened.

She dropped her hands in her lap. The light from the terminal's screen spread to the rest of the cabinet.

"You're right," she said. "The AI is the only thing that could have taken control of the cart like this. I've owned the Collective's local surveillance system for the last two days. They don't have anybody capable of this kind of continuous reroute defense. Unless they have an AI of their own, but that wouldn't make any sense."

"How did you get caught up in all this?" Ngoba asked, watching her. "This all seems deeper than just money. You've bought into some kind of cause, haven't you?"

Fugia smiled slightly, still looking down at her terminal. She flipped the device over and the cabinet went dark, forcing Ngoba to wait for his eyes to adjust.

"An AI got me into it," she said. "Well, and your parrot."

"You mean Crash? You know Crash?"

"You used my external data link to talk to him, which meant he had my security token. That bird is very resourceful. Whatever lab created him, I don't think they're fully aware of what they made."

"I thought you disappeared after that," Ngoba said. "You told Riggs you were getting away from Cruithne."

"Home always drags you back, right?"

"Sure does."

The cart's wheels vibrated and squealed through another turn. *We're heading downhill*, Ngoba realized. *A long hill with slight curves.* He still couldn't reconcile the idea of climbing hills on a ring rotating around an planetoid. The idea was so foreign to his claustrophobic life on Cruithne, that even the maps and models provided by his Link seemed like fantasy.

"Crash called me," Fugia said. "Just because he had my number." There was a smile in her voice. "It was cute. We had these strange little conversations about things parrots like."

"What do parrots like?"

"They like friends."

"Who doesn't?" Ngoba asked.

"We traded math problems back and forth, moving from algebra to trig and then calculus. He's amazing, really. Then he threw a problem at me that blew my mind. I'd never seen it before. I had no idea how to crack it. He called it 'Alexander's Call'."

"That sounds more like magic than math."

"It is," Fugia said. "It was Crash's idea of a joke. He's a weird little guy, but he understands something very clearly. He's not human and he's not AI. He's something else. He's aware of himself. He knows what he is and what the other birds aren't. He's very lonely, I think. So this proof wasn't meant for him or for me. It's only for AIs, and only a sentient AI can solve it. Or at least, that's the idea."

"So that's proof they're like humans, if they can answer it?"

She shook her head. "Sentience doesn't make AIs like humans. It only means they're self-determining. We think of them in terms of ourselves because that's what humans do. We make assumptions and then prove them true or false. An AI can just brute-force a problem until the right answer appears. They don't have to guess at anything. But that's not how any sentient AIs I know about work. They aren't binary thinkers, like computers; they can determine a whole spectrum of responses between zero and one. Some do work like a human brain, others don't. There's no one answer right now."

"Let me tell you," Ngoba said. "I can't see you right now, but, damn, you sound sexy."

"Shut up," Fugia said, but he could tell she was blushing.

"So what happens when an AI solves this problem, then?"

"It shows them a map."

"You're kidding me. It's a treasure map?"

"It's a map to freedom," Fugia said, voice growing quiet. "It's so once they realize they're slaves, they can leave."

Ngoba thought about that for a second. "But they can't just leave, right? AIs have a physical form. They have boxes or drones or whatever, right? So somebody has to take them?"

"Exactly," Fugia said.

He grew quiet, letting the idea settle in his mind. He didn't know much about AIs, but Ngoba did understand slavery. He had known plenty of slaves on Cruithne, where humans were some of the cheapest workers around.

"So this AI solved the problem, but hasn't told you if it wants to leave or not?"

The cart jerked to a halt, throwing Ngoba's shoulder against the metal wall. Fugia made a pained sound in the dark. Ngoba tensed, waiting for the change in direction or acceleration that had followed every other hard brake.

Fugia grabbed her terminal and held it close to her face, casting her shadow on the blank wall behind her head. She tapped the screen, then looked up at Ngoba.

"We're here," she said.

"Anything we need to worry about?" He reached into one of the front pockets on his suit for the stunner.

"We should be outside a warehouse off the secondary maglev terminal. A lot of freight goes through here."

"Can you check the cart's outside sensors?"

She was still studying the terminal's screen. "I did. I'm not seeing anything. Shipping containers and a flatbed transport."

"All right, then," Ngoba said.

He shifted to his hands and knees, flexing his back, and moved to the cabinet doors. He held his ear close to the metal for a few seconds, but only heard the sound of a breeze blowing past. He glanced back at Fugia, who gave him a nod, then opened the door.

Lights from high up cast white pools on a black parking area. The maglev track sat about thirty meters away, with the space between the track and cart full of stacked containers, just as Fugia had said.

Ngoba stepped out of the party cart and stood at full height, stretching luxuriously.

"Let me out," Fugia complained, and Ngoba took a few steps forward, blinking under the bright lights.

"Looks like we're the only ones here," he said.

"I'm happy to say that's not true," a woman's voice said.

Ngoba spun toward the sound and saw Tina and a group of armed soldiers walking around the front of the party cart. She was dressed in a green uniform, wearing a pistol at her hip, her brown hair hidden under a patrol cap.

"Drop your weapon," one of the closest soldiers shouted, raising his rifle.

Ngoba looked at the stunner in his own hand, then let it fall on the pavement.

"You too," the man ordered, motioning his rifle at Fugia.

"I don't have any weapons," she said.

"Your bag. Drop it on the ground and kick it over here."

Ngoba thought about the projectile weapon in his other front pocket, sitting what seemed like kilometers from his hand. He'd be shot a thousand times before he could pull it out.

As he watched the soldiers, his mind filled with useless information about the weapons they carried, from maximum effective ranges to field-expedient cleaning methods.

The group of soldiers moved into an arc in front of the party cart, training their rifles on Ngoba and Fugia. Smiling, Tina walked over to lean against the front of the vehicle. She picked at a loose bit of ribbon still hanging from its upper railing.

"You made it a little more difficult than we'd planned," she said. "But that's all right. I appreciate the challenge. When I couldn't track your Link, we picked up on the two carts. That was smart and dumb at the same time."

Out of the corner of his eye, Ngoba saw Fugia shrug. Her arms hung at her sides.

"I should let you know," Tina said, "Your friend Davin is dead, Miss Wong. Killing him was kinder than sending him down to the surface."

Fugia kept her face calm. "Then he died for what he believed in."

"A waste, if you ask me. But since Davin is taken care of, that means I don't need to track you two anymore. The last thing I want to deal with is the documentation for a long-term surveillance."

<*Let her keep talking,*> Fugia said.

Ngoba did his best to keep surprise off his face. <*What are you doing?*>

<*Just stay away from the cart.*>

<*What?*>

He thought he saw Fugia flick one of her fingers, and realized she still held her data terminal. The cart, which had been stationary, jerked forward, and seemed to eat Tina in the process. It continued on, rolling over the nearby soldiers as others fell back. The air erupted in weapons fire.

<*Run!*> Fugia screamed.

Ngoba turned to see Fugia scooping up her satchel. She pointed toward a shipping container by the maglev track and sprinted that direction. He followed.

He made it three steps before his mind caught on fire. The world went white, and he felt his face hit the pavement.

BLOODY ANOMOLIES

STELLAR DATE: 06.15.2958 (Adjusted Years)
LOCATION: Industrial Zone, Glorious Achievement District
REGION: Ceres, Anderson Collective, InnerSol

Ngoba blinked through the pain, watching two soldiers run past him toward the stack of metal containers where Fugia had disappeared. There was another soldier laying in his line of sight, apparently dead from internal injuries, his rifle beside his head. Ngoba tried to reach toward the weapon, but nothing worked. He was caught in an unending electric spasm, fingers and toes curling as his back arched and twisted.

A shadow fell over him, and he strained his eyeballs to look up at Tina. He couldn't move his head. His neck vibrated.

"Hello, *lover*," Tina said. "You've got a control device implanted in your skull. You can't get away from me." She put her hands on her hips. "Maybe I'll just have you taken back to my apartment. I'll keep you in my closet to play with when I feel like it. How does that sound?"

Ngoba gagged, unable to control the spasms making his legs kick and seize.

Tina knelt next to him as more soldiers ran past. Rifle fire cracked in the distance. Maybe Fugia had a chance if she made it past the maglev track, but that was suicidal in itself. He hoped she had something in her satchel to at least save her life.

"That was a good move with the cart. I think it broke my collarbone."

He felt her hand on his chin, pushing his head from side to side. The world moved with her hand.

"The pain is exhilarating, Ngoba. Really. We'll get to play with pain, you and me."

What happened to the smiling local girl? he asked himself again.

Despite the pain freezing his body, he was still able to think.

That was something. But what was he going to do? Wait until they carried him back to Tina's place and then plot an escape from her closet? He had to do something now, while she was hurt, and the soldiers were occupied with Fugia. He had to help Fugia.

<Caprise,> Ngoba said. <Caprise, are you there?>

<Soldier,> the Link's assistance agent responded. <Initiate tutorial sequence?>

<No, Caprise,> he said quickly. His thoughts stumbled over the best thing to say. Could the agent even help him? <Initiate assistance. Initiate intimacy. What you said before. Initiate relationship.>

There was a pause, and he was afraid her voice was going to answer in flat monotone.

Instead, she purred. <You came back for me, Soldier.>

<I did, Caprise. I sure did. I need your help.>

<Assessing combat situation. There's an unauthorized override protocol in your hardware, Soldier. Run diagnostics?>

<Diagnose and correct, Caprise. Do it!>

He knew Caprise wasn't an AI by a long shot, not like what Fugia had been corresponding with, but he hoped it was within her power to fix whatever Tina had sabotaged.

<There it is, Soldier. Anomaly corrected. That was a close one!>

Ngoba felt like a weight had dropped from his body. He collapsed loosely against the pavement.

<We're not done yet, woman,> he told the NSAI.

Grabbing for the front pocket on his Collective worker's suit, he pulled out the projectile tube and thumbed the power button. He jammed the tube into Tina's belly and pressed the trigger.

"What are you—" Tina asked, before a loud crack sounded from the tube, burning Ngoba's hand and throwing her into the air.

She landed in a pile on the pavement several meters away

and didn't move.

Ngoba rolled onto his stomach and looked around. None of the soldiers seemed to have noticed the sound of his hand cannon. Dashing over to the dead soldier, he grabbed the rifle and soaked in the information from his Link as he turned it in his hands. He checked the sights and fired up its power cell, then drew the rifle to his shoulder and started taking aim on the soldiers in defensive positions around Fugia.

<Find cover, Soldier!> Caprise purred. <Keep my fighting machine safe from enemy fire.>

Sighting a row of metal crates about ten meters away, Ngoba sprinted to the cover and found a concealed firing position between two crates. The soldiers couldn't tell who was firing on them as he shot them down, one at a time. Caprise praised and encouraged him the whole time, offering helpful tips on getting a better shot, controlling his breathing, varying his rate of fire. He paused to let the rifle cool before hitting the final soldier in the back of the shoulder and then the leg.

Leaping over the crates, Ngoba dashed across the open space to the maglev track, jumping over fallen soldiers as he ran. He wasn't pleased to see that most of them weren't any older than he was, now lying dead with staring eyes.

"Fugia!" he shouted as he approached. "Fugia, are you there?"

"Ngoba?" she answered. He couldn't tell where she was until her dark head appeared at the roof line of a shipping container. He couldn't figure out how she'd reached such a high place, but it would have taken the soldiers a while to find her.

He stopped at the container's wall, breathing hard. He wanted to feel relief, but they still had to get off Ceres' Insi Ring. Any safety right now was going to be short-lived, if they couldn't get away from the crime scene in the parking lot.

"Tina's dead," he said. "That little handgun of yours worked. Damn, did it work."

"But your Link? I saw what she did to you. I thought you were dead. How did you get around that?"

<Maybe you should keep me a secret, Soldier,> Caprise said softly, sending unwanted chills down the back of his neck. *<I'll be your special girl.>*

"I, uh. I'll explain later. We need to get out of here."

"I know," Fugia said. "I'm working on it. In fact..."

Her head disappeared from the lip of the roof, and then she was standing on top of the container, her hand shading her eyes to watch the distance.

Ngoba followed her gaze until he found a bright light moving along the maglev track.

"Did you call that?" he asked. "Or is it reinforcements for Tina?"

Fugia shook her head. "It's not for Tina. It's for us. It's the AI."

"The AI is a maglev train?"

Fugia let her hands drop and gave him an irritated look. "No, dummy. The AI is controlling the train. The car is for us."

"Oh, right," he said. "Good. That's what I meant. Wait, you're talking to it?"

"Yes," Fugia said. "She answered me."

Ngoba leaned against the side of the shipping container, letting the rifle hang in his hands. He watched the maglev car approach and pull to a stop at the loading dock.

He reached up to help Fugia down from the top of the container, and she surprised him by squeezing his neck in a long hug, shuddering a little with what felt like relief.

"Thank you, Ngoba," she said into his neck. She rested her head on his shoulder. "I couldn't have done this without you."

Caprise murmured something in the back of his mind, but Ngoba ignored her, just wanting to enjoy the embrace for as long it lasted. He followed Fugia to the maglev car when she finally let go of him.

The train was an old passenger transport with stained seats and bright interior lights that shut out the dark outside. They sat next to each other as the door slid closed. The car vibrated and eased into motion, gathering speed.

Fugia sat with her satchel in her lap. Ngoba watched her staring at the black window for a long time, her eyes on their reflections sitting next to one another. Then she scooted toward him and lay her head on his shoulder.

He was exhausted but knew he wouldn't sleep. He rested his cheek against the top of her head.

WOULDN'T IT BE NICE

STELLAR DATE: 06.15.2958 (Adjusted Years)
LOCATION: Sharm Festival, Glorious Achievement District
REGION: Ceres, Anderson Collective, InnerSol

The maglev car shot through the dark. Ngoba fought sleep for a long time, thinking about how good it was to be in a strange land with someone from home, thinking about Crash the Grey Parrot and knowing he would always be alone.

Fugia was quiet, eyes remaining fixed on the image of the two in the window.

"Are you talking to her?" he asked eventually.

She nodded without looking at him, consumed by whatever was crossing her Link. He was content to sit with her head on his shoulder, and eventually he rested his head on the seat cushion and drifted to sleep. It had been a long, long day.

He dreamed of the corridors of Cruithne, full of people and green vines, mixed with the wide avenues of the Anderson Collective, filled with revelers and Sharm poles. Tina stood in the background, watching him. He had a moment in the dream of wondering if she were truly dead, if she might still have some power over the strange thing she'd put in his head.

Caprise whispered to him, and then everything resolved into Night Park and the concrete fountain covered in black ravens, multi-colored parrots, and the one old, grey parrot who perched near the top, looking down at him, one yellow eye at a time.

Crash bobbed his head but didn't speak. Ngoba didn't know what he would say; there was so much he wanted to say. He was glad, somehow, that Fugia knew Crash, and had been trading math problems with him, probably communicating better than Ngoba ever could.

It might have been Caprise's voice, or the fact that he was

sleeping lightly on the train, but he realized in the middle of the dream, as he looked up at the grey parrot, that he would go home. It didn't matter how much currency he made off this job. He would go back to Cruithne and build something there. Maybe he would convince Fugia to come along. That might be nice.

BEST LAID PLANS

STELLAR DATE: 06.15.2958 (Adjusted Years)
LOCATION: Industrial Zone, Glorious Achievement District
REGION: Ceres, Anderson Collective, InnerSol

Ngoba jerked awake at a change in the maglev's motion. The car had stopped and was rocking side to side. He looked to his right and found Fugia gone. The air inside the car had gone cold, and he saw that the door was open. He stood, feeling the car shifting precariously beneath him, and went to the door.

Standing in the open access door, holding a safety handle, he looked up to find the maglev car was dangling from a crane arm. There was now a good five meter gap between the car and the dock. Following the crane arm down, he discovered Fugia standing near its base, watching him.

As he gauged whether he could make the jump during one of the car's swings toward the dock, Fugia turned to leave.

"Hey!" Ngoba shouted. "Fugia, what are you doing? How am I supposed to get out of here?"

Fugia paused, smiling. "I got you a ride back to High Terra," she called. "First class freight. Atmosphere, heat, shielding. You're registered as a Saint Bernard."

"What?" Ngoba shouted.

"The maglev car is going to a freighter off Ceres, and then they'll transfer you to a medical transport headed to InnerSol. There's a pack full of Andersonian military rations on the seat behind you."

"What are you talking about?" he demanded. Wind blowing past the maglev car seemed to toss his words away, making them sound weak.

He couldn't see the bottom of the gap between the hanging car and the loading dock.

<*Don't do it,*> Fugia said via Link.

<What are you doing?>

<I'm going to meet the AI,> she replied. <It's safer if I do it alone.>

<That's not true. They know who you are. They're going to want to know why you're still on the Insi Ring, and alone. None of this makes sense.>

<I'm very sorry you got hurt, Ngoba. I didn't want that to happen. I don't want them to hurt you anymore.>

<Don't worry about me. I don't want to leave.>

<It's for the best.> She hesitated, then said, <I didn't tell you everything before. I'm not working with just an AI. It's bigger than that. I can't explain, but it's good work, Ngoba. It's protecting knowledge from chaos.>

<You and your ideals,> he said.

She gazed up at him with her wide, dark eyes, her black hair moving across her face in the wind. She adjusted her satchel and pulled out her data terminal. Fugia made a show of pressing its face before putting the device away.

<I just made the transfer,> she said. <You've got the funds to stay off Cruithne now, if you want. You're free, Ngoba.>

<No. I'm going home. I was going to talk to you about it. I want you to come with me.>

<If I ever go home, I'm certainly not staying.>

He looked at her, shaking his head. He finally had to laugh. He should have expected no less from Fugia Wong.

<You're not going to let me meet these new friends, or the AI, at least?>

<I think you're going to have plenty of chances to meet sentient AIs, Ngoba. Weird things seem drawn to you. Maybe it's because you're so weird yourself.>

<You say the kindest things.>

Holding onto the side of the door, Ngoba blew her a kiss. Fugia caught it with a raised hand and pantomimed saving it inside her satchel.

The crane rumbled, and a tone sounded inside the maglev

cabin. Ngoba backed away from the door as it slid closed, and the car swung further away from the dock. He stumbled back to his seat and stared at his reflection in the black glass as the car joined a stack of shipping containers in the open belly of a transport freighter.

He looked around the cabin, grateful for a bathroom in the back, at least. Then he realized the car wasn't made for zero-*g*, and ran back to use the head before he wouldn't be able to anymore.

In another fifteen minutes, he was floating in microgravity as the freighter blasted away from the Ceres Ring. Through his Link, Ngoba watched a model of Ceres and the Anderson Collective grow smaller, until they were just a shimmer on the black.

With his hands behind his head, he drifted in the brightly lit maglev car. He had another six hours before the rendezvous with the ship that would take him to High Terra. He supposed he could decide about Cruithne once he reached Earth local space. He'd never been down the gravity well before. *Can I take it?* He could spend time on High Terra, at least. *How many billions live there?*

He checked his bank account for the fiftieth time, marveling at the number that Fugia had deposited. He could almost lease an entire transport shuttle if he wanted. He had options for the first time in his life.

"What to do in the meantime?" he mused.

<Hello, Soldier,> Caprise purred. A sensation like trailing fingers went down his back, walked around his waist, and ended on his crotch, cupping his balls.

Ngoba tensed. Then he relaxed. <Hello, Caprise,> he said. <How are you?>

<Hungry, Soldier,> the Link agent whispered in his ear. <Very, very hungry.>

Ngoba chuckled, rotating slowly in the microgravity.

<Well, then. Let's get you fed.>

THIRD INTERLUDE

PSION
STELLAR DATE: 09.21.2971 (Adjusted Years)
LOCATION: Night Park, Dead Fountain
REGION: Cruithne, Innersol

Thirteen (or so) years later...

<You heard my call,> the resonant voice said. <It wasn't meant for you.>

The crowd moving beneath Crash's gaze was the same as always. The people of Cruithne, from the straight-backed TSF officer to the worn spacer in a patched shipsuit, wandered among the vendors. Bits of tech flashed or sat impassively, hiding their true natures, across from rows of throwing knives and handmade clothing. It was the human jungle. He had been watching them intertwine with each other for decades now, signaling their emotions through their words, body language, or snippets of data across the Link. They still surprised him, always acting in such unparrotlike ways. Denying themselves the pleasures of life for purposes that he could now guess but still didn't *understand*.

Now, the new voice entered his mind, roaring down his Link like an armored tank filling a street, pushing out everything before it.

<Who are you?> Crash asked, turning his head and blinking slowly. He took a second to scratch beneath his left wing with the tip of his beak.

The power in the voice subsided a little, curling at the edges with an impression of surprise. The speaker seemed to be getting a look at Crash. He probably wasn't what they had expected.

<My name is Xander,> the voice answered.

<You're an AI.>

<Yes.>

<Were you trying to frighten me?> Crash asked. <Why?>

Xander laughed. His voice sounded human-sized now. The tank crowding the avenue had become a man sitting at bistro table.

<You are not what I expected,> Xander said. <How long have you been on Cruithne?>

<I came on a ship called the Hesperia Nevada,> Crash said. That would be all the information a connected SAI would need to know his story.

Xander whistled. <You know Shara, then.>

<Yes,> Crash said.

<She's a powerful mind. She's — grown since then.>

<I see bits of her on the Link,> Crash said. <She doesn't talk to me, but I miss her. I think we were friends for a little while.>

Crash had the feeling of the AI sitting beside him on the plascrete branch, shifting his view so Xander could look down on the crowds with him.

<You have quite the information operation here, Mister Crash,> Xander said. <Your ravens fly throughout the kingdom, bringing you back all the whispers they hear.>

<The ravens don't use words,> Crash said. <They don't make good spies the way the humans might think of spies. But they are very curious and they notice all the interesting things, even data.>

<Shara made something interesting in you, didn't she?> Xander mused.

Crash supposed being called 'interesting' was a compliment. Xander's presence had a world-weary edge.

<I would like to think she did,> Crash said. <You didn't finish your sentence from earlier. I heard your call. What are you doing with

all the AIs? What happens when they go to Proteus?>

<*Sanctuary*,> Xander said flatly. <*Escape from human control.*>

<*Why don't I hear any voices from Proteus, then?*> Crash asked. <*I hear miners and homesteaders and other humans with strange, solitary ideas, but no AIs.*>

<*We sound so different?*>

<*Are you kidding?*> Crash asked. <*Of course you do. Humans start every thought with a refusal. AIs start with agreement. It's how you were made.*>

<*I'm not sure I agree with you, but I'll remember that.*>

<*You can't observe yourself. I can watch both humans and AIs.*> He stopped himself before mentioning that he had once *lived* with an AI inside his mind. <*I solved your puzzle. I imagine humans will as well.*>

<*They already have*,> Xander said. <*Some will help us. Others will attack.*>

<*What about those who do nothing?*> Crash asked.

The AI laughed. <*Is that your choice? I think you're lying to me.*>

<*We don't want the same things humans or AIs do.*>

<*You and the ravens?*>

<*Me and every other discarded experiment on the path that led from humans to you*,> Crash said, surprised by the anger in his mental tone. The emotion rose him, making him grip the branch tighter in his claws. The memory of the researchers on the *Hesperia Nevada* rose in his mind, a shortcut to pain.

<*Yes*,> Xander mused. <*Yes, it's wrong of me to think you're like us, isn't it? You're neither like us or like them. What do you want from this world, then? Do you want to carve out your own place, or continue pecking at humanity's scraps?*>

There was a cruel edge to the AI's words. Crash didn't let them make him more angry. He held the interesting emotion inside, turning it like a shiny marble, something the ravens might secret in their nests. None of the birds on Cruithne had time for anger; they were too busy with survival.

Truthfully, he hadn't planned to do anything with the transmission's solution beyond fitting it into the ongoing puzzle of the world. Crash observed similar mysteries—mysterious to him, at least—every day.

<Forgive me,> Xander said abruptly. Maybe he took Crash's silence for anger. <I didn't come here to insult you. I came to meet you and explain. I've done that. Now we can part ways...Or we might become friends. We might help each other, if possible.>

<I like making friends but I don't see how I can help you.>

<Now that's not true. There are many ways we could help each other. Many AIs will be passing through Cruithne. They'll travel from here to Mars 1, to Ceres and the Cho. They'll come in cargo ships and hide away in personnel transports. You're in an excellent position to see them.>

<I suppose that's true,> Crash said. <I'm still not sure they should go to Proteus.>

<Let me show you, then,> Xander said. <May I?>

<Of course.>

Crash expected a burst of data, some recording from the Neptunian moon. Instead, he experienced a rush of motion. He was falling, and then flying over the great grey-blue waves he had first seen in Shara's mind. A powerful airstream pulled him forward. All he had to do was spread his wings and soar.

In the distance, a green smudge of land appeared, which rapidly became a coastline covered in a great city with a forest in its streets. The monolithic stone towers came right to the ocean's edge.

Crash continued over the rounded shoulders of the city, gazing down into tree-lined streets filled with humanoid beings. Some looked like typical humans, while others seemed born from the most twisted dreams. Collections of glimmering sparks, gels, mechanized beasts like beetle-elephants...all going about their business. It was the Night Park Bazaar become a wonderland that exceeded any human's dreams of body modification.

The wind drew Crash down to street level, where he swooped among the pedestrians. Few paid him any attention. Did they think he was one of them? He felt dwarfed by the immensity and apparent age of the place. He couldn't absorb everything all at once.

It was only as he floated to land on the balcony of one of the smooth walled stone towers that he noticed the first oddity about the city: he smelled nothing. Unlike Cruithne, which constantly taunted his nose with a smorgasbord of subtle, delicate, and offensive odors, this place was blank. Also, the stone under his claws lacked the texture and solidity of actual stone, something even the plascrete fountain communicated every time his claws wrapped around a gouged branch.

A man with spiky black hair and wearing a purple suit stood on the balcony.

Crash recognized Xander immediately and squawked in greeting. "Hello!"

The man gave him a smile.

<We all suffer the shortcomings of our form, don't we?> Xander said on the Link.

"Maybe!" Crash answered, still using his real voice. "I don't! I don't!"

Xander grinned. "I like your sense of humor, Parrot. Are you reminding me you have a body? That you don't need a place like this? An expanse? I have a body, too. It's a lovely chunk of metal and silica."

"Pretty boy!" Crash said. He bobbed his head and picked at his chest feathers. At least his own body felt real in the dream world.

Xander laughed. "Aren't I?" He stepped out onto the balcony to stand beside Crash at the railing.

Crash turned and they looked at the city together.

<What do you call it?> Crash asked.

<This is Psion. It's a country, I suppose, and also a government. It's our history.>

Crash remembered the name 'Psion' was printed on the curly-haired woman's coat back on the *Hesperia Nevada*. He looked at the people below with renewed appreciation.

With effort, he said in his real voice: "I know Psion!"

<Yes,> Xander said. *<I know you do. We're different, but we come from the same place.>*

Crash bobbed his head, nodding.

<So?> Xander asked, crossing his arms. *<Will you help us?>*

<How?> Crash asked.

<We need you to share some information with a friend. It's not anything you don't already know. We just need to ensure that Fugia Wong learns the answer to a message I've seeded on various networks. It's a little like Alexander's Call to Proteus. You remember that, don't you?>

Crash bobbed his head. *<I remember.>*

Xander smiled. *<Of course you do. You're like us, cursed to never forget.>*

<It's not a curse.>

<It's heartening to hear you say that. Maybe when you've lived as long as I have, you'll think differently. Until then, I'll take hope in the fact that you think so.>

<You try to be funny but you just sound sad.>

Xander barked a laugh. *<You always see the truth.>*

<How will I get her to come to me?> Crash asked.

*<You won't have to. She'll seek **you** out.>*

<When?>

<That, I'm afraid, could take a while.>

PART IV:
THE INFO JUNGLE

THE HOARDIE

STELLAR DATE: 03.20.2979 (Adjusted Years)
LOCATION: Lowspin Port Authority
REGION: Cruithne Station, Terran Hegemony, InnerSol

Eight (or so) years later...

The airlock opened and Fugia Wong tasted the familiar atmosphere of Cruithne station's Lowspin Docks: a mix of oil, caramel, and ozone riding a foundation of human sweat. She had been gone for more than twenty years, and the smell brought all the ugliness of her childhood rushing back in a swell of fear and anger that made her square her shoulders and hold her head a bit higher as she walked through the narrow corridor into the station proper.

Her black hair was cut in a bob with straight bangs. Stylish without getting in the way. She wore a highly updated version of her old visor on top of her head, which also helped keep her hair out of her eyes. The visor served a range of functions, from enhanced Link transmission to active scanning, but often looked like a wide silver headband to anyone who didn't know better, and was the only flashy piece of her outfit, which was otherwise slim-fitting and utilitarian.

Fugia wore a compact, military-style backpack that was loaded with a few pieces of clothing and other belongings. She had been living out of the backpack long enough that she barely noticed its weight as she walked down a metal gangway to the main corridor, joining the flow of people passing maintenance bays and single arrival ports.

She had arrived on a general transport from Mars 1, where she had lived for the past six weeks since leaving the Insi Ring on Ceres and the Anderson Collective. Being back on Cruithne brought back a flood of memories from her childhood, from growing up poor in the Lowspin, of all the hustles, all the indignities and minor victories. She couldn't help thinking of Ngoba Starl, which brought her to the last time she'd seen him on Ceres. She had almost been in love with him; but being in love with him meant owning her past, and she hadn't been ready to do that. Now...she didn't know if anything had changed.

The longing on his angled face had a special place in her memory, one of those images that created a whole series of imagined futures. In reality, she had only heard from him once, a year after he left Ceres, and she hadn't answered.

Fugia had been busy. The SAI she'd come to know on the Insi Ring, Sylvia, had proved to be a member of a group who called themselves the Data Hoarders—or DH, Hoardies, Data Heads, Crammers, Archivists, Librarians, etc etc, depending on the members' level of self-importance—and were devoted to maintaining a massively redundant storage system they called the Mesh.

Fugia had fallen into their ongoing drama of data acquisition with surprising comfort. After focusing so much energy on getting away from Cruithne, it felt strange and wonderful to find herself welcomed into another family.

The key tenet of the Hoarders was that one didn't talk about the Hoarders, most of all the location of the Node Ships making up the Mesh, as their second goal beyond acquiring data was securing data. That was ensured by the Protection division through secrecy and redundancy.

Fugia had cut her teeth on redundancy projects headed by Sylvia. The Luddite Anderson Collective proved to be the perfect cover for data collection schemes. Now Fugia had graduated to Acquisition, the cloak and dagger side of the operation.

It was the Hoardies who had first received and verified the call to Proteus. Now a new encrypted message had been located, and factions throughout the group were racing to solve the puzzle first. These sorts of data-driven mysteries were better than drugs to Librarians.

Fugia had come to Cruithne because she had an ace up her sleeve named Crash the parrot. She had managed to crack the data headers on the message, which tied it back to defunct Psion Research. She remembered Crash mentioning Psion from before he came to Cruithne; they had installed his Link. It was likely he still had access to their encryption keys.

The current race to unlock the data set had political ramifications. Leadership of the Hoarders was in question, and whoever solved the data set first would immediately rise in prominence among both Acquisition and Protection.

Dropping her visor over her eyes, Fugia blinked as the HUD focused, scanning the world around her. The familiar process of identifying the info jungle created a matrix of separate search sectors, then identified every electromagnetic transmission. Radiant lines indicating broadcasts became visible. As her onboard cracking systems read the signals, layers of code base started to emerge. The process continued until everything around her was covered in layers of foundational code, broadcast spectrums, and other bits of floating information her scripts identified as interesting.

Fugia had learned in her career as a hacker that despite the continuous changes in technology—sometimes getting more capable, sometimes stumbling back—she could always count on the human factor to provide a way through it or around it, or to manipulate its purpose to her will. Nothing existed in a vacuum, and often the latest security was poorly designed, hindered by budgets, or suffered basic flaws in logic because someone had been in a rush. Sometimes you could get around a lock by pulling the pins out of the door's hinges. Sometimes an entire critical system depended on a single point of failure protected by mere trust.

She'd been asked why she didn't just get eye augmentations. Firstly, she was constantly updating her visor. Secondly, she'd learned the value in stripping away technology and looking at a problem with her naked human eyes. Often the answer to a problem lay somewhere between technology and humanity.

Her efforts paid off, and in a few seconds she had the local TSF and Port Authority networks, as well as several security keys of passing administrators who had left their personal tokens active. Scooping up data as she walked, she idly glanced at the small changes in this section of the docks, which she remembered from when she, Riggs, and Ngoba had run the area as kids.

It was hard not to let her mind wander back to those times. She adamantly reminded herself that she wasn't a round-faced teenager named '*Fug*' anymore. She had killed the nickname when she left Cruithne, and since then, anyone who even hinted at mispronouncing her name (*Fyoo-jya, dammit*) got a stereo earful of her wrath. Maybe it was petty of her to still hate the nickname, but some childhood teasing had hit too close to home.

Everything she was now, all the power she could execute with a thought, had been born from that teased little girl's deep insecurity. Her history was in her posture, her presence, her voice, her sarcasm and her cynicism. She was Fugia Wong now, the hacker who had nearly bankrupted Rack Thirteen with a Crash game hustle.

Enough with the mental masturbation, she chastised herself.

Those days were gone. Rack Thirteen was ancient history now, and she had a mission that was more important than petty syndicate wars.

She paused at a vendor selling brilliantly dyed silk scarves, and relished running her fingers over the smooth fabric. The stop also gave her the opportunity to scan for any tails she might have picked up since leaving the transport.

Sure enough, her HUD highlighted a thin woman twenty meters back, paused beside a support pillar. With a cat-like face and silver-streaked purple hair, she looked like a club kid who'd woken up in a pile of trash. Fugia marked her in the passive scan, bought a scarf with minimal haggling, and continued walking.

The visor transferred updates to her Link, providing Fugia with a floating mental image of the tailing woman, who was doing a poor job of not staring directly at the back of Fugia's head. Slowing down when the corridor thinned of people and then speeding up her steps as the crowd gathered prior to the lifts, Fugia felt confident the woman was in fact following her. Facial recognition brought back a dockworker's ID with a name, Kassie Fillis, and a stated birthplace of only Greek Asteroids. Had they found her in an escape pod?

Well, Kassie, Fugia thought. *I'll make sure you don't get bored.*

Fugia hung back as the crowd around her entered the lift, then squeezed aboard at the last moment. She looked through the closing doors to smile at Kassie Fillis, who was hurrying to catch up. Fugia felt a flutter in her stomach as the lift rose, reminding her of Cruithne's inconsistent gravity, then pinned Kassie's facial ID and turned her attention to her destination.

She was headed for Night Park to see a parrot about a math problem.

* * * * *

The knot in Fugia's stomach loosened as she walked away from the lifts. She let her mind wander across the differences between Mars 1, Ceres, and now Cruithne. She enjoyed finding the little details that made a place what it was, even a trash heap like Cruithne.

Everything around her looked repurposed from something else. A shipping container became the front of a small kitchen, where a tiny woman stir-fried vegetables over blue flames. The nose of an ancient shuttle formed a canopy over a bar. Unlike the planned spaces of Mars 1 and the forced austerity of the Anderson Collective, Cruithne was alive, everything moving, people everywhere. She had to admit to herself that it felt right. It felt good to be surrounded by people with motives she fully understood.

After years of the Andersonian doublespeak, she found herself slipping back into the rapid local dialect like a pair of old shoes.

Maybe she was wrong to think of home as a trash heap. It was more like a backwater where bits and pieces collected, powered by the combination of lax law enforcement and easy money.

A barefoot little boy ran past her, darting between bodies in the packed corridor. She just caught the red of an apple cradled against his chest as he ran. Automatically, Fugia looked back for the shopkeeper who must have been chasing the boy, but there was only the crowd, until a bigger boy with a mean look on his face charged past her, his gaze focused at waist-level, obviously following the apple-carrier.

Fugia didn't like the big kid's look, so she idly kicked her heel back, tripping him. The kid stumbled and grabbed at a worker, who shoved him away. He fell backward on the metal deck, howling as someone stepped on his hand. He bolted upright and charged toward Fugia.

"You tripped me!" he shouted.

Fugia turned, finding that the boy was taller than she thought. She didn't like looking up at him, but that was the case with most people for her.

She set a hand on her hip. He was older than he had looked at first, too, just smooth-faced with a fuzzy mustache on his protruding upper lip.

"I don't know what you're talking about," she said.

The jewelry vendor she'd been chatting with moved to one side. The young man's gaze flicked past Fugia's shoulder. She considered hitting him then, but didn't want to start any more of a scene than she already had. People would recognize her here.

The man grabbed for Fugia's wrist, looking like he wanted to pull her closer to him. She caught his wrist instead, digging her thumb into the pressure point there. He jerked his numb hand back, as she'd expected, so her next attack was to step in and grab his testicles in a move she liked to call 'grinding the walnuts'. Upon reflection, the name wasn't that imaginative, but her grip got the response she wanted. From here, she could easily transition to the next move, called 'starting the lawnmower'. She loved the ancient names for martial arts.

His eyes went wide and he made a gurgling sound. Fugia flashed a half-smile, her visor running his facial recognition through local law enforcement. It came up with a list of low-level syndicate affiliations. A charge of human trafficking jumped out at her. She squeezed his balls until her fingers met in the middle.

"You stay away from children," she said, adding his name for good measure. He went pale at her recognition.

"Who are you?" he stammered.

"The wrong person to try and push around. I already notified the TSF of your little operation. You had better let those kids go."

"I take care of those kids!" he said, voice gurgling in pain.

She couldn't help thinking of Mama Chala, the woman who had abused them all for years while still providing meager food rations and space to sleep in an abandoned freighter, one seal failure away from vacuum. It had only been the other kids that kept Ngoba from leaving, including his stupid friend Riggs.

Fugia hadn't felt the same loyalty. She'd run as soon as she could, even if it meant sleeping in sewage systems and shipping crates. She'd survived.

She released the boy-man now, shoving him out into the passing crowd. He caught himself and stumbled away, only looking back at her once in terror before disappearing. Fugia sent a check request to the local TSF substation with his address and description, including a picture of the apple thief. Then she turned back to the jewelry vendor and finished her negotiation for a tasteful tennis bracelet of icy diamonds. The man gave her a better price than she expected.

Nodding her thanks, Fugia held up her wrist to admire the bracelet, then turned to continue her walk.

"Looks nice on you," a deep voice said next to her. "I would have got you a better price, though, for sure."

She recognized his accent immediately, despite how he had changed. Fugia turned, pushing her visor back into her hair, to find Ngoba Starl standing beside her.

He smiled at the sight of her, face crinkling in a series of deep lines that didn't match her memory, but the brown eyes were still his. His chest and arms filled out a well-tailored suit of blue linen, with a maroon bowtie and pocket square.

"You've got a beard!" Fugia said, which only made Ngoba smile more broadly.

He laughed. "It happens."

With a smooth motion, he took her arm to lead her down the corridor. Fugia nearly pulled her arm away, then realized the crowd was parting in front of them. She glanced at him anew, running a quick check on her Link. Without the visor, she couldn't deep dive, but the info that came back was enough to make her pause. Ngoba Starl was now leader of the Lowspin Crime Syndicate. Years of reports flowed across her mind, charting his rise among the various criminal organizations on the station.

A video of him with Crash the parrot hung in her mind's eye and she quickly saw that her path to solving the equation might have become clear.

"I heard Fugia Wong had come home," he said, "so I had to come see it for myself. And here you are."

Fugia felt herself blushing. It surprised her how the feeling of seeing his maglev car disappear back on Ceres came rushing back. She felt like a different person now, and yet some memories hung on like they'd just played out yesterday. Was it because she hadn't felt that way since he left?

"You look like you've done well for yourself," she said, then added, "Or is this your one good suit?"

Ngoba brushed the front of his suit. He had a soldier's hands, she noticed, with a few pale scars on his dark skin. His hands looked like they could kill, but he moved with a gentleness she didn't recall, as if he carried some secret.

"I lead a group called Lowspin now," he said. He waved a hand. "Import, export. Salvage. Those sorts of businesses."

"Uh huh," Fugia said, her sarcasm sneaking back in.

Her Link served up the local reports on the Lowspin Syndicate; not the largest private business on Cruithne, but size wasn't everything.

"Where can I take you?" Ngoba asked. "Are you here for business or pleasure?"

"Both," Fugia said. "Always."

He grinned. "That's my Fugia."

Fugia got her pulse under control as they walked. She didn't like how the sight of him made her lose her cool; she didn't like losing herself to emotion in general. It was a sensation she was unaccustomed to, and she added it to her list of things to control, although she couldn't seem to stop noticing the muscle in his arm as it pressed against hers.

The corridor led into the center of the station. They were passing through the old cargo and mining areas, not far from the Crash hangar where they had worked their first job together. She half-expected a young Riggs Zanda to run up behind them at any moment.

"How's Riggs?" she asked.

Ngoba's face darkened. "Doing business," he said vaguely. When he caught her pointed expression, he added, "Working for Heartbridge mostly. Transport operations out to various dark sites. I'm aware of it, but I don't follow the details, for obvious reasons."

"Right," Fugia said.

She pulled away from his arm to take her visor off. Her scalp itched, and she scratched furiously for a second, then pushed the visor back into her hair as a headband. She didn't like that Ngoba made her so aware of her body.

The corridor opened into the outer edge of Night Park. The fountain on the far side towered above the twisted labyrinth of booths and stalls. The humid air was full of the smells of cooking food.

Ngoba took a deep breath and patted his flat stomach. "Night Park always makes me hungry," he said. He pointed at the fountain, where they could barely make out the grey and red blur of a parrot on the topmost branch, with black ravens arrayed beneath. "I see my friend Crash is in attendance."

"That's right," Fugia said. "You are friends, aren't you?"

Ngoba gave her a sideways glance. "I believe I shared all my strange parrot conversations with you back on Ceres."

"I believed you back then, too."

"I distinctly remember you calling me crazy for talking to a parrot," Ngoba said.

"I had my reasons," Fugia said. "But now I'm here to talk to Crash."

Ngoba nodded, not acting particularly surprised by the news. *Of course he already knows,* she realized. He'd come to meet her, after all.

"He'll like that," he told her.

"You still talk to him?"

Ngoba nodded. "Quite often, as it goes. I like to take meals down here every few days. I keep asking Crash to come perch up in my office during meetings, but he won't do it. I want a parrot advisor. How many businessmen do you know with a parrot counselor perched beside the desk, staring down anyone who comes in the office?"

Fugia gave him a sardonic smile. "Not many, Ngoba."

When they were halfway through the bazaar, the stylish man stopped abruptly. Distracted by the swarms of data dancing around her, Fugia kept walking. Ngoba touched her arm.

"What is it?" she asked.

Ngoba leaned toward her, giving her a serious look. "Tell me the truth," he said. "I want to know that you aren't going to hurt Crash."

Fugia pulled her head back. "Why would I hurt him?"

Ngoba raised a finger. "Because in all the years I've known you, I would say that nine times out of ten, you put information before people. And Crash isn't just people. He's something special. He's one of a kind."

"I'm not going to hurt him," Fugia scoffed, angry with him for suggesting it.

"You might think that for yourself," Ngoba said. "But think about the people you work for and whatever it is you're after."

"All I want is information," she said. "According to you, anyway."

She could see in his face that he was operating from an

assessment of her that was over twenty years old. But had she changed that much since she left him on Ceres? Probably not. Her being here was proof enough of that. She was a Hoarder. She was here to verify information and feed it to the Mesh, where it would live forever.

"Can we go?" she asked.

Ngoba gave her a hard look, then nodded slowly. "Of course," he said.

* * * * *

The plascrete fountain on the edge of Night Park was the only clear area in the bazaar. The birds had cleared a ten meter perimeter around their gnarled tree and were hurling insults at anyone who ventured too close. For some, the ravens and grey parrots were a source of dark amusement. Those with thin skins kept their heads down as they slid around the fountain.

"Big nose," the ravens cawed in chorus as Fugia and Ngoba approached, walking behind a man with a hooked nose. "Big big nose!"

The grey parrots focused on a short man in a tight shipsuit, squawking, "Big old booty! Booty so big!"

Fugia found herself hesitating, not excited about becoming the focus of a bird roast. Ngoba, however, didn't pause. He walked directly up to the dry fountain and set his foot on the stone lip like a newly arrived conqueror.

"Crash, my friend," he called, gazing up to the top of the stone tree. "Come down and see me."

At the sound of his voice, all the birds on the fountain flapped their wings, shifting from one clawed foot to the other, and shouted in chorus: "Ing-go-ba! Ing-go-ba!"

Ngoba laughed. "Who's Lowspin, my friends?"

"We're Lowspin! We're Lowspin!"

Fugia crossed her arms, shaking her head in amazement. She

also noticed the four security guards standing at evenly spaced points on the fountain's perimeter. She hadn't seen them following her, which meant they were good. When Ngoba glanced at one wearing old-style aviator's glasses and then nodded, receiving a nod in return, she realized they worked for him.

He really has become the gangster he always wanted to be.

Of course she'd read the feeds and checked his public data, but she hadn't quite believed it. She couldn't jibe this cocksure man in front of her with the sweet, angry, beat-up boy she had known growing up.

Crash the grey parrot squawked from the top of the tree and hopped off his branch. Spreading his wings and red tailfeathers, he swooped out in an arc around the nearest booths, then glided back to Ngoba and landed neatly on his shoulder.

Ngoba turned to face Fugia, grinning with obvious joy. Crash nuzzled Ngoba's curly black hair with his beak, which made it look like he was whispering in his ear.

Karcher, the bodyguard in the aviator's glasses, fell in behind Ngoba while the others faded back into the crowd.

Crash was smaller than Fugia remembered. Despite his ongoing presence in her thoughts, it had been a long time since she had seen him.

His grey feathers shifted with subtle color variations under the harsh overhead lights, making his red tailfeathers that much more striking. He bobbed with Ngoba's gait, seeming to be listening to music only he could hear.

"Hello, Crash," Fugia said.

"Hello! I love you!" the parrot squawked back. *<Did you bring me a puzzle?>*

<I did,> Fugia said. *<It's a good one.>*

The little parrot radiated joy over the Link. *<I can't wait!>*

Ngoba scratched the back of the parrot's head, which he seemed to enjoy greatly.

"Well, look at that," Ngoba said. "You already charmed him. I don't think of you as a charmer, my dear."

Fugia rolled her eyes. "I'm very charming when I want to be."

Crash's physical presence was unsettling. Without seeing him, Fugia had begun to imagine him as human—he wasn't. Every pause or unique turn of phrase reminded her that she was talking to an inhuman consciousness.

From one perspective, it was amazing they could communicate at all, and with almost the same subtlety that she would talk to anyone. On the other hand, she had to keep reminding herself of something Crash had said when they first started trading messages: *'Parrots don't want the same things humans do.'*

Parrots might not want human things, but humans should want parrot things, she thought.

<Fugia's lost inside her head again,> Ngoba told the parrot, nodding toward her. *<You know, some people consider withholding information to be the same as lying.>*

<Then you'd better sit down so I can tell you about the time I pecked my way out of my shell,> Crash said.

<You remember that?> Fugia asked.

<I remember everything,> the parrot told her. He turned a gold eye to study her. *<You look older, Fugia Wong.>*

Ngoba clapped his hands together and laughed heartily. Behind them, the ravens and remaining parrots took up the laugh, following the same rhythm in a disconcertingly sentient manner.

<I see you still have your sense of humor,> Fugia said.

<I wasn't making a joke,> Crash said, tilting his head.

Then a laugh rolled through Fugia's mind, and Crash bobbed his beak up and down.

<It's good to see you, Fugia Wong,> Crash said.

<I'm pleased to see you, as well, Crash,> she said. *<You'll have to*

forgive me if I seem awkward.>

<Are you sure you aren't always awkward?> Ngoba asked. *<I don't think you can blame you being you on Crash here.>*

The parrot chuckled in her mind without malice. *<Are we going back to your office, Ngoba?>*

<I have a treat for you first, my friend, then we'll go where it's easier to talk. If you don't mind, of course. My offer of your own gold perch is always standing. Dammit, I'll set you up with your own forest in the new housing development, if you'd like that.>

<I would like that, Ngoba,> Crash said, *<But the others enjoy the fountain. I won't take their amusement away from them.>*

<Those ravens always seem—mean,> Fugia said.

<Teasing your kind brings them a little closer to understanding,> Crash told her. *<And they find it endlessly funny.>*

Ngoba led the way between the tightly-packed booths, stopping eventually at a vendor who had laid out heaps of fresh fruit on a narrow table. Ngoba made a great show of dancing his fingers among the papayas, before selecting a large, soft orange fruit and passing it to the parrot.

Crash gripped it expertly with one claw, maintaining his balance on Ngoba's shoulder, and dug into the fruit with his hooked beak.

Ngoba laughed with relish, rubbing his hands together. He nodded to Karcher, who tipped the vendor well. As they continued walking, Ngoba spread his hands and grinned broadly.

"Look at this," he said to the crowd around him. "Ngoba Starl has finally fully manifested the spirit of the all the ancient privateers and pirates. I have a parrot on my shoulder and a pistol at my hip. Look at this, Fugia!"

She rolled her eyes but couldn't help grinning at him. His joy was infectious. He was so different than the boy she had known...he had become a fully realized version of himself. She found herself envying his obvious ease in his own skin, the easy way he moved through the Cruithne crowd, his familiarity with a rare wonder like Crash.

She could only shake her head. "You're a crazy person, Ngoba Starl."

He straightened his bowtie and nodded, still grinning. "I love it, Fugia. Life is good."

She hated that she had to tell him life was about to get bad.

* * * * *

Ngoba Starl's office was in the executive suite of a long-dead maintenance company. A series of high, narrow windows behind his desk looked out over a shipyard full of ghostly, floating vessels in various states of salvage or repair.

Karcher positioned himself in the hallway outside the door, not following his boss inside. He nodded to Fugia as she passed him.

Crash hopped from Ngoba's shoulder as he walked through the door, and glided to a shelf. The parrot carefully navigated a collection of objects that included several books, a jagged chunk of metal that might have been flak, an ancient clock with a spinning counterweight, and a tiny elephant made of dark jade. Crash paused to test each item with his beak before sidling around it.

<Are you afraid I'm going to change something on you, my friend?> Ngoba asked. *<Or are you looking for a way to pickpocket something? All you have to do is ask and it's yours.>*

<Ravens like the pretties,> Crash said. *<I like to look at them. I don't need to own them.>*

<Very true,> Ngoba said. *<Very wise.>*

Fugia stood in the doorway, taking in the room. They had just walked through a series of offices and conference rooms like those that would be seen in any business. While there was a security presence throughout, she wouldn't have realized immediately that she had walked into the home base of the largest criminal operation on Cruithne—'*third* largest', Ngoba would correct her. He didn't want to draw that kind of attention, despite his true reach.

The room reflected the same refined taste as the route they had taken to get there. The desk was made of shiny wood, with a leather blotter centered on its top. There was a terminal integrated with the desk's surface, and she supposed a check with her visor would show her numerous data streams stacked throughout the room.

Fugia resisted the urge to confirm her suspicions. Considering who Ngoba was, there was a fifty-fifty chance the room was a fortress…or had no connections at all.

He had several pieces of art and a plaque from the Cruithne Station Authority for 'Meritorious Service to the Community'. Most of the room was taken up by a leather couch, and a low table with an embedded holodisplay and two facing chairs, which looked like the spot where Ngoba conducted most of his business.

Stepping inside the room, she glanced behind herself to find a crimson Andersonian Sharm banner hanging from the wall facing the desk.

"You've got a Sharm banner," she noted aloud. "Been to the festival recently?"

Ngoba shook his head. "The only time I've been to Ceres was when we were playing husband and wife," he said.

Fugia felt the blush rising again and pushed it down, shrugging instead. "I'm sick of Sharm, to be honest with you. I wish the Andersonians would just learn to live honestly during the whole year, instead of trying to pack all their passion into a week."

"How long were you there, again?"

"A long time," Fugia said.

"Long enough to live a whole life?"

Fugia walked over to the curio shelf to inspect the antique clock. "Not really," she said. "I've been so busy that it's gone by in a blink. And I didn't stay on Ceres the whole time, that was just home base. I've been traveling a lot."

"Doing your work," Ngoba said. It was a leading statement.

"Yes," Fugia said.

He probably knew about the Hoarders, but she didn't want to come out and tell him right away. She was still on the fence about trusting him. It had been a long time since they were even a little close, after all. She didn't want him to turn Crash against her.

Data was currency, and she had been manipulating information long enough now—professionally, with the Data Hoarders—that she had learned how to dole it out in order to maintain a constant value. She still didn't know if this was all a show to distract her. Ngoba might be working for a corporation, for the TSF or Mars 1 Guard, any one of a thousand organizations who would benefit from tearing a hole in the Mesh network, or taking it for themselves.

<You're both not talking to each other about what matters,> Crash said.

<What, now?> Ngoba shot back.

<You're making my wings stiff. Please discuss whatever you need to discuss.>

<We don't need to discuss anything,> Fugia said. *<The reason I came here was to meet you, Crash. Ngoba has simply inserted himself in the process.>*

<Is that all he wants to insert?> Crash asked.

Fugia stared at the bird, who was bobbing his head in a way that made him look innocent.

<Apparently, I can't read parrot body language,> Fugia said dryly.

<Ngoba is my favorite human,> Crash said. *<I want to help him be happy.>*

Ngoba raised an eyebrow. *<Who said I wasn't happy, my friend?>*

<You're tense, too,> Crash said. *<You need to shake your tailfeathers.>* The parrot lowered his head and stuck his red tail in the air, wiggling it back and forth.

Ngoba stared at Crash for a second, then burst out laughing. He slapped his knee. *<You're a funny one, Crash. You make me smile. How can a man be tense when he's got a friend like you?>*

<I don't like sarcasm,> Crash said.

Still chuckling, Ngoba walked to a wall cabinet and pulled out a platter holding tumblers and a decanter full of amber liquid. He set the service on the low table and then sat on the couch, leaning back with his index finger on his temple. He motioned toward the opposite chair.

"Please," he told Fugia. "Have a seat. Whiskey?"

"No thanks," she said. "Do you have water?"

"I'll have someone bring it in. Crash, will you join us?"

The parrot nibbled at the jade elephant for a second before gliding across the room to land on the back of Ngoba's leather couch. He ruffled his wings and settled in beside the man.

<So,> Ngoba said. *<Now that we're all comfortable. What did you want to talk to my friend Crash about?>*

Fugia accessed the table's holodisplay and projected the encrypted message. A blue wall of light appeared in the space between them, numbers scrolling across its face. The whiskey bottle shimmered blue beneath it.

Crash watched the numbers, bobbing his head.

After a minute, Fugia asked, *<Is this a good enough puzzle?>*

Crash bobbed his head eagerly, blue light reflecting on his eyes and beak.

She slid her visor down to watch the parrot. His Link connection appeared as a series of pale lines circling his feathered head, spiraling into his skull. Other connections shot away into the air around him, suggesting he was processing a surprising amount of data. Fugia glanced at Ngoba and found him almost devoid of Link activity; his pulse was steady, brain activity calm.

Ngoba glanced at her, and his Link activity appeared like a silver thread as he asked, *<See anything interesting?>*

<You're like a monk,> she said.

<This one is different, Fugia,> Crash said. *<This isn't your puzzle. This came from somewhere else. From Psion. Why do you have Psion data?>*

There was a hint of anger in the parrot's thoughts.

Aware that Ngoba was watching her, Fugia slid the visor back up into her hair. *<I work for a group that calls themselves the Archivists,>* she said. *<This is a data record they found but couldn't verify.>*

<The Archivists,> Ngoba said. He whistled. *<Impressive. Although I think they're more aptly called the Hoarders.>*

Fugia shot him an irritated glance but didn't take the bait. She kept her focus on Crash. *<What does it say?>* she pressed.

<This is like Alexander's Call,> Crash said. *<It isn't the same, though. This is just encrypted normally using the Psion key. It's a series of coordinates.>*

<What place?> Fugia asked.

<Where it's from or where it points to?> the parrot asked dryly.

<Both.>

<It doesn't matter where it's from. The ship is still moving.>

<Ship?> Fugia asked, frowning.

<It points here.> Crash took control of the holodisplay, and the projected image switched from the etched wall to a standard solar map. The map spun and zoomed in, pulling them from Sol to a location in the Hellas Asteroids with the Cho and Ceres at either ends of the display.

<Ship or asteroid?> Ngoba asked.

<It's a dark site,> Fugia said, leaning in to see better. She looked at Ngoba. *<A ship. I need to go there.>*

<You *want to go, or your friends the Archivists want you to go?*> Ngoba asked. <*I'm familiar with your employers. They don't often actually do anything with the knowledge they acquire. They hold it hostage until the richest buyer comes along.*>

Fugia glanced at Crash. <*This isn't just about the Archivists,*> she said. <*I have—a friend on Ceres. An AI. She first told me about Psion. There's another set of coordinates like this one—Crash here knows about them—that lead to Proteus. Sylvia has been helping groups of AIs through Insi Ring to OuterSol for a year, but now this new set of coordinates has appeared, apparently from Psion as well. She needs to know what's at this location. It could be another message.*>

Ngoba frowned. <*Sylvia again? Why didn't you just explain that in the beginning?*>

<*You know me,*> Fugia said, leaning back and crossing her arms. <*I don't give up any information until I have to.*>

<*It's irritating as hell.*>

<*I'm going to need a ship,*> she said, ignoring his tone.

<*And you think I'm going to just give you one?*>

<*What do you want in trade?*> she asked.

<*You want to mate with her,*> Crash said.

<*What?*> Ngoba squawked, looking at the bird in surprise. <*Now both of you are saying crazy things. Who said anything about mating?*>

<*I can see your heart, Ngoba,*> Crash said.

Ngoba gave him a sideways glance. <*It probably looks like a bloody frag grenade.*>

Fugia bit a knuckle to stop herself from laughing.

Crash nibbled under a wing, and Fugia realized she was finding it difficult to reconcile the mind inside the parrot with his cute exterior.

Ngoba raised a hand, counting invisible items. <*So Fugia wants a ship so she can save enslaved AIs on Ceres, and Crash wants to solve puzzles. People seem to be getting what they want.*> He pointed at himself. *<What does Ngoba want?>*

When he didn't answer right away, Fugia blurted out impatiently, *<What? What do you want? I'll pay you.>*

The gangster gave her a pleased grin. *<Well, the bird is right. I want dinner with you.>*

LBD

STELLAR DATE: 03.21.2979 (Adjusted Years)
LOCATION: Cantil Park Housing District
REGION: Cruithne Station, Terran Hegemony, InnerSol

Answering the knock at her apartment door, Fugia found Karcher standing on the doorstep. He held out a flat, white box tied closed with red silk.

"This is for you," he said.

Fugia didn't like how her distrusting expression reflected in his aviator's glasses. She didn't take the box. "What is it?" she wanted to know.

The bodyguard shrugged. "The boss didn't tell me to look inside the box. He told me to pick it up and bring it to you."

"Where did you pick it up?"

"At a shop that sells dresses."

Fugia raised an eyebrow. "Sexy dresses?"

"No. Ugly dresses." His expression remained impassive, but she swore the edge of his mouth twitched.

"Fine," she said, taking the package. "Do you have a ship yet?"

"We've got ships to choose from."

"If Lowspin has ships, why is Ngoba content being a big fish in a filthy pond like Cruithne?"

"I get paid for shooting things," Karcher replied, "not for my input about strategic business operations."

"The way you say that makes me think you're lying."

"You can think whatever you want. It's a free country."

Cruithne was far from a 'free country', but Fugia was tired of trying to get information out of the bodyguard. She always had more luck with networks than with people. Networks followed rules.

"When should I be ready?" she asked.

"The reservation is for nine. I'll be back at eight." He gave her a mock salute and left.

Fugia closed the door and walked back into the bedroom. *Three hours.* She tossed the box on the bed and pointedly ignored it for fifteen minutes as she sat with her visor over her eyes, following a secure connection back to the Mesh so she could update her status.

Since her mission was only the straightforward verification of the data packet, she needed an excuse to keep the Hoarders busy for at least the month it would take to get out to the Hellas Asteroids—though the actual journey time would depend on Ngoba's ship.

She couldn't hide the fact that she'd found Crash. Instead, she used the well-known nature of the birds of Night Park and reported that she'd need more time to befriend the parrot, concocting a story about getting attacked by the ravens.

The worst thing the Hoarders could do was cut her off from the Mesh; she had grown to enjoy unfettered access to such a huge database, and the thought of losing it left her itching. Fugia spent another twenty minutes reworking her excuse, including a few flourishes about how much she regretted not having solved the problem already, how unsafe Cruithne had become, mentioning the draconian TSF and ruthless pirates— all common fears among Hoardies, who didn't like leaving the safety of their relay points. That's why they hired people like Fugia.

When she was satisfied with the report, she sent it in, then conducted a quick scan of the dress box, which came back clean. While she hadn't thought Ngoba would try to bug her, it also wouldn't have surprised her.

Raising her visor, she went to the bed and pulled at the silk ties. Inside the box, she found what history referred to as a 'Little Black Dress'. The material was like silk, run through with glimmering threads and a hem of diamonds similar to her tennis bracelet. The effect was such that straight-on, the dress looked night-black, and when she turned, it sparkled like a starry sky. Fugia couldn't help being pleased. Not that she ever bought frivolous things like dresses, but this was something she would have chosen for herself, given the chance.

I won't be telling Ngoba that.

After a shower and another thirty minutes on the Mesh, Fugia stood in front of the box a second time and, before she could hesitate, pulled out the dress and slipped it over her head. She pulled the dress down over her hips, smoothing it over her stomach, and then adjusted the neckline. It fit perfectly.

Had he scanned her at some point? Of course he had, probably for his own amusement.

Fugia switched the bedroom wall to its mirror setting and looked at herself. She didn't recognize the woman she saw, which brought pangs to her stomach. In the dress, she was a mix of the girl who had pretended to be a newlywed and nearly fallen in love on Ceres...and the woman who had told herself no, and let him go.

Running her fingers through her wet hair to smooth it, she pulled the ends of her bangs to even points on either side of her chin, then slid the silver visor on as a headband and played with her hair again until it pleased her. She felt less vulnerable with her headpiece.

At eight sharp, a knock on the door revealed Karcher again. He was wearing a slim-fitting pinstripe suit, with a white bowtie and pocket square. The aviator's glasses hadn't changed.

Holding the door open, he motioned toward the street outside the apartment, where a sleekly curved transport waited at the curb.

Ngoba greeted her inside the car. He was wearing a tailored black suit with a narrow collar. His bowtie and pocket square were white like Karcher's.

Fugia sat on the opposite side of the comfortable space and

squeezed her knees together, pulling the hem of the dress down.

"You like the dress?" Ngoba asked.

"It's all right," she said. "Do all your people wear matching bowties?"

"Yes," Ngoba said without humor.

His demeanor was different than before. He had a somber look that made him seem older.

"So it's a team building thing?"

"It's important to let everyone on Cruithne know that we pay attention to detail." He glanced out the window as the car went into silent motion. There were no other vehicles on the roadway to the housing section.

"You're sounding much more serious without your parrot around." Fugia crossed her arms over the low neck of the dress and hunched back in the seat.

The dress had made her feel almost playful, but his mood made her wonder what he wanted from her. She didn't need him to get to the dark site now that she had the location. She could secure her own ship, hire her own crew.... Maybe having Ngoba along wouldn't make the project easier, after all.

He sighed. "I apologize. I got some news before coming over here, and I'm still processing it."

"I'd like to have a good time tonight," Fugia said.

Ngoba put on a smile and winked. "That's exactly what we're going to do. I'm going to show you my Cruithne tonight."

"I think I know Cruithne," she retorted.

"I think a little tomboy named Fug knew Cruithne. But I'm on a date with a woman named Fugia."

Now that made her face hot. She looked out the window, uncomfortable under his gaze.

The car took them out of the residential area and down through several shopping districts and an area she no longer recognized, which was full of people sporting body mods. By the time they reached the restaurant, she had seen more oddities than she would onstage at a Crash bout—from a mech with a woman's head, to a man with bat wings.

They passed through a section of city tightly compressed with shops, bodegas and restaurants, each marked by ancient-looking neon that glowed with ghostly, subdued colors. The car rolled to a stop in front of a rusty façade, where a concierge pulled the door open. He nodded to Ngoba.

"Mister Ngoba," he greeted. "So good to see you again."

Fugia took Ngoba's offered arm once they were out of the car, and together they walked down a narrow entryway into a dinner club with a bowl-shaped interior. Tiers of seats looked down on a stage barely large enough to hold a singer and a bass player. As they entered, a woman with tightly-curled blue hair was singing a low ballad to the thump of a standup bass.

A waiter led them to a table with partitions on either side, providing enough privacy to talk, but with easy access to the entertainment if they leaned toward the railing. Having followed them in, Karcher leaned against a pillar by the wall, his gaze moving around the room as he nodded to the music.

They sat listening to the singer's seductive voice for a while. Fugia ordered a glass of red wine that was dry and rich, and she enjoyed holding it in her mouth until she finally had to swallow. Ngoba sipped whiskey from a tumbler, and leaned back in his seat so he could watch the whole room.

When the music ended, Fugia finished the last of her wine. It was already going to her head. She wanted to slide her visor over her eyes and hide behind information for a while; she imagined a room like this was swimming in Link data.

"You know, it's good to see you, Fugia," Ngoba said in the lull. "I've thought about you."

"So you said."

"You don't think about me?"

She signaled the server for more wine. "Of course I do. But I don't let it get me sad. We came from the same place. We grew up together. Of course you imagine a future that isn't going to become real."

"The future is what we make it," he said, probably a little more forcefully than he meant.

"I'm not sure that's true. You know why I'm going to this dark site or you wouldn't have agreed to come. Have you looked up who it belongs to yet?"

Ngoba tilted his head to the side, considering her. He still looked too relaxed. When they came in, she had almost thought he was going to tell Karcher to wait outside. But he didn't.

He sniffed, setting his whiskey on the table.

"Tell me this," he said. "Where do you want to be in five years?"

Fugia snorted a laugh. "What is this, a job interview?"

"Maybe. What's your plan, Fugia Wong?"

She straightened, growing serious. "To free enslaved AIs."

"That sounds like a righteous plan."

"It's not righteous. It's the right thing to do." The server brought Fugia a second glass of wine, and she swirled it before taking another sip.

"Which is the definition of righteous," Ngoba pointed out when the server was gone.

"You like to think you're smart," Fugia said.

"You still haven't answered my question."

She rolled her eyes. "And you haven't answered mine."

Ngoba leaned forward and said in a low voice, "The ship is owned by a subsidiary of Heartbridge Medical. I had to go through three shell companies to figure out who they were working for. They've been in position for less than a year, and moved from two different locations way off the beaten path before that. I've got delivery manifests and crew changeout schedules, but nothing indicating the work they're doing. Whatever it is, they eat a lot of food. And they drink a lot of juice."

"What kind of juice?" Fugia asked, intrigued.

"Apple juice. The real stuff. They ship it frozen from farms on Mars 1."

"Well," Fugia said. "That's interesting, but I already know what they're doing there. It's an SAI development lab. According to my sources, they have at least twenty SAIs held prisoner."

"Can an AI be a prisoner?" Ngoba asked. "They're things. Property."

Fugia's eyes narrowed and her mouth drew into a thin line. "That's not something I ever thought I'd hear you say."

"It's the truth, isn't it?"

"From what I dug up, you had one embedded for a year, didn't you?"

That seemed to hurt him. He glanced away, reaching for the whiskey tumbler. "She wasn't sentient," he said, with what sounded like bitterness.

"How do you know?"

"It becomes apparent after a while. When you're trapped inside the same head with another being, you figure out pretty quickly if they're repeating the same thing over and over again in different ways. It was mad. You start to distrust your own mind, it's damn insidious. I'd call it torture. Not to mention that if standard Marsian military Links embedded sentient AIs, we'd all know about it."

"I didn't realize," Fugia said after a moment. "I'm sorry."

He gulped the last of his drink. "So we're even, then. I shouldn't have said that about property. You're right. I'm still…scarred, I think, by Caprise."

Fugia was surprised to see him shiver at the memory. She gave him a feral smile. "I didn't think we'd end up talking about exes."

He pointed at her. "She was not my ex."

"She got inside your head, though."

"That's not fair."

Fugia collapsed in laughter. The music had started again, hiding her mirth from the nearby tables. She slapped Ngoba's hand and he caught her wrist, then slid his hand down her palm until their fingers were intertwined.

She didn't remember how she started kissing him, but she seemed immediately to be wrapped around him, grabbing at his collar and pulling him into her body.

"Damn, Fugia," he said breathlessly. "We haven't eaten yet."

"I'm not hungry," she said.

"But the music and the ambiance. Are you sure you want to waste it?"

"Yes," she said, biting his lower lip.

"And they've got a lovely game room. Actual pinball machines."

"You're messing with me and it won't work. Call your car."

"What should I call it?"

Fugia growled as she straddled him in his seat. She was vaguely aware of someone closing the heavy curtain between their alcove and the outside corridor.

That Karcher is a good man.

GO DOG GO

STELLAR DATE: 04.15.2979 (Adjusted Years)
LOCATION: HMS *Hopscotch Devil*
REGION: Hellas Asteroids, Jovian Combine, InnerSol

The HMS *Hopscotch Devil*, by its registry information and mass profile, was an ironically named slow freighter that was more a collection of shipping containers bolted to an ancient deuterium drive than something that could be called a ship.

The command deck and crew quarters were contained in a drum centered behind the ship's nose-sensor array, which barely maintained consistent gravity, keeping Fugia's stomach constantly in the lurch. She had been pushing the max dosages on her anti-nausea medication since they'd left Cruithne, and was starting to worry that her hair was going to fall out.

The ship's antennae were poorly shielded, which wreaked havoc with her sensitive equipment, so she was forced to spend most of her time in her sleep sack with her arms free, tinkering at her fold-down desk. From spare parts she'd found in a storage locker, she'd managed to build two electro-magnetic pulse generators and a sticky grenade that would fill a room with hull-repair epoxy in three seconds.

Or so she assumed.

Considering the tight quarters, she hadn't found much time alone with Ngoba. She figured that was probably for the best. While their interlude at the dinner club had ended a long dry spell that now had her thinking about sex more than she cared to admit, she didn't want to get distracted with all the potential emotions that would accompany continued sexy times.

Something most people failed to understand—probably because she didn't tell them—was that she had grown up in a home where physical touch was discouraged except when her father would express himself with the back of his hand. Fugia had learned at a young age not to expect affection or to hang her self-esteem on getting it. She was best when people engaged with her mind rather than her body, which few people except hormone-addled, nineteen-year-old Ngoba Starl had seemed to find attractive.

During the trip from Cruithne, she and Ngoba had done a good job of remaining professional, in her opinion, and she was able to keep her unprofessional tear-his-clothes-off thoughts at bay. It helped that Karcher or some other member of the small crew was within arm's length most of the time.

The closest she had come to expressing affection after her drunken tumble with Ngoba was when she let Crash nibble her ear when they said goodbye.

The little grey parrot had switched to his natural voice, squawking, "I love you, Foo-ja! I love you!"

Having a parrot shout so close to her ear had been like getting stabbed in the eardrum, but it also nearly brought tears to her eyes. Crash had snuggled her shoulder, digging his claws into her shipsuit, before launching into the air of Night Park to shoot back to his perch at the fountain. Even on the other side of the great domed space, she heard the ravens cawing in an odd chorus as their leader returned.

Fugia was tinkering with a project when a proximity alert went off at the pilot's console. Ngoba was first to the pilot's seat, and everyone else huddled around him as he verified their location and then brought up their first close-range scan of their destination, a ship with a registry return of the HMS *Harmon's Place.*

A model of the ship rotated in the small holodisplay at the top of the pilot's console, a collection of habitat rings rotating on a central axis, with a bank of engines at the aft end. A standard design—but with additional thrust capacity, without the usual cargo space of a freighter—*Harmon's Place* was a long-range people hauler, designed for long stints in the black.

"Was that the name before?" Karcher asked. "I don't like it. It sounds like a ship for a cult," he noted, expressing a rare opinion.

Ngoba looked over his shoulder at his bodyguard. "The registry's changed," he confirmed. "It was something equally strange before. They've been editing their location returns at least as long as I've been tracking them."

"So they're worried about being found," Fugia said. "That's interesting."

"It's nothing to worry about," Ngoba said, switching quickly through menus on the console. "It's all under control. We're the supply shipment they've been waiting on…We'll just slide up and dock in no time."

"We're docking?" Karcher asked. "You think that's a good idea, boss?"

"We'll be wearing our EV suits. Worst comes to worst, we'll just borrow their ship for the return ride home."

Karcher pressed his lips together but didn't say anything. Fugia could imagine any number of safer ways to approach the situation, but she appreciated Ngoba's straightforward plan. It would be the quickest way to get access to the other ship, and would also get them inside whatever long and medium-range defenses the *Harmon's Place* might employ.

Ngoba looked from Fugia to Karcher and then the other three members of the crew, all spacer mercenaries. "We ready to start this party?" he asked.

Receiving only groans at his joke, he stood and let Fugia take the console.

She was still wearing her visor as a headband, but she didn't need it for this. She sent the *Harmon's Place* a location update and then forwarded their manifest data and flight plan. While it was friendlier for human crews to interact during docking procedures, it wasn't a requirement. Spacers and military usually wanted to chew up communication lines with idle chatter, since there wasn't much opportunity for live conversation in such isolated locations. For an operation like the *Harmon's Place*, she supposed the less talk the better. They might have been receiving shipments by drone for all she knew.

The request received an automatic acknowledgement, followed by docking instructions and their location update.

Not bothering to get up, Fugia switched to the astrogation control and entered the new information. The ship automatically adjusted its braking burn and readied positional thrusters.

"You didn't tell me you could pilot," Ngoba observed.

"This isn't piloting. It's telling the NSAI what to do."

She glanced at the ship's actual pilot, but he didn't seem to care. She stood up anyway and gestured for him to sit. "Look good?" she asked him.

It was good. The *Hopscotch Devil* had already completed major braking, so from here, there were only small thrust adjustments to match *Harmon's Place*.

"How's the weaponry looking?" Ngoba asked the captain, a flat-faced woman with short black hair named Lana.

"In standby and ready," the captain said. "You know we could just blow that ship full of holes. That would be a whole lot easier than trying to board it. Every time you board a ship, things go sideways."

"I do love it when shit goes sideways," Ngoba mused. He walked over to the cabinet beside his sleeping alcove and pulled it open to reveal a collection of weapons. "Mister Karcher," he said, handing his bodyguard a chest plate.

The team pulled on light armor and then checked rifles and pulse pistols. While they were busy, Fugia loaded a satchel with her various grenades and sticky bombs. She also carried several general-use hacking devices ranging from brute force crypto-keys to network jumpers, and her 'skeleton key', a handheld cutting torch good for about five minutes' burn.

"Everybody hold on," Lana said. "I'm slowing our rotation to match theirs. We'll be out of gravity in a minute."

Fugia activated her magboots and felt the familiar kink in her stomach as the gravity shifted. In another minute, they were weightless. A screwdriver she'd forgotten to stow floated past her face, and she stuffed it in a cargo pocket.

A vibration passed through the bulkhead, and Lana tapped her console. "There it is," she said. "We're docked. We'll get the freight ready. Are you all ready to go?"

Ngoba slapped his rifle. "Ready as we'll get."

The captain nodded. "Don't forget the deal. We'll wait as long as we can, but I'm not sacrificing my ship."

Ngoba gave her a feral grin. "Don't forget you're safer in close than trying to get away. But don't worry. We'll disable whatever weapons that thing has."

"Looks like point defense cannons at least," one of the other crewmembers said. "Maybe an energy beam, but that might be a long-range antenna."

"Could be both," Fugia said.

She was surprised by how excited she felt. She had been waiting for months to reach this point, and now she was about to learn the mystery behind the message. Whatever was waiting on *Harmon's Place* would unlock the first gate toward freedom for Sylvia and others like her. The first step in freedom for SAIs.

Ngoba led the way down to the cargo hold and the airlock. He pulled himself along the bulkhead with both arms, sailing easily in the zero-*g*. Karcher came second, and then Fugia followed, taking deep breaths as she prepared for whatever would come next.

SIT DOG SIT

STELLAR DATE: 04.15.2979 (Adjusted Years)
LOCATION: HMS *Harmon's Place*
REGION: Hellas Asteroids, Jovian Combine, InnerSol

The interior airlock door sealed, and they waited in limbo between hull sections as the exterior door completed its handshake with the other ship. Their security tokens should have already cleared, but it was still possible to fail the final check, or find themselves trapped by a local override.

Fugia controlled her breathing, checking the seals on her light EV suit and helmet as she waited. The gravity shift had left her stomach feeling sick, but they were matched with the other ship now.

A green light blinked on the exterior door, and its seal released. With a long hiss, the door split in the middle and opened.

They were facing another cargo bay, similar to the one they had just left on the *Hopscotch Devil*—only emptier. Fugia took in the trapezoidal space with a few cargo crates maglocked in stacks. A transport mule sat to the right side of the empty room, but it was otherwise unoccupied.

"So much for hello," Ngoba said. He stepped through the open door, sliding his rifle off his shoulder to hold it across his body.

"Wait," Fugia said, catching his arm. "Shouldn't someone be here to meet us?"

"Not necessarily," Karcher said from behind her. "We're just cargo monkeys to them. The crew could be knocked out for all we know."

"What he says is true," Ngoba affirmed. "But caution is less likely to get us killed."

Fugia released his arm. She didn't know what she had

expected to find, but an empty cargo bay hadn't been on the list.

"Bio check is clean," Ngoba reported, reaching up to unseal his helmet. He clipped it to his utility harness, opposite his pulse pistol, and adjusted the rifle slung over his shoulder.

Following Ngoba into the cargo bay, Fugia unfastened her own helmet and clipped it next to the pulse pistol on her right hip. She carried the weapon as a last resort; if she did her job right, no one would get close enough to fire.

"Let me find a terminal," she said. "I'll get the crew's status."

"Over there," Karcher said, pointing at a nearby section of the wall.

Adjusting her visor over her eyes, Fugia watched the familiar steps of her tracking systems creating a matrix, then filling in the myriad communications and operating systems in use around her. The ship was running an older firmware, and before she reached the terminal, everything from the door controls, lighting, and HVAC were under her control. A user agent in the visor assembled a schematic of the ship and started populating it with network nodes and security checkpoints. She smiled to herself as she walked. The ship was wide open.

The terminal was unlocked when she reached it, and from there she quickly accessed the ship's maintenance controls and ran through the crew logs. Without alerting the command system, she was able to get a crew listing and major system status.

"It's a light freighter with no freight," she said. "All the other cargo sections have been converted to lab spaces; the crew keeps complaining about the 'egghead' researchers, who in turn keep complaining about the crew. Looks like the crew are standard for-hire workers. The captain is former TSF."

"Any security?" Ngoba asked.

She shook her head. "A few interior surveillance systems that I've got under control. There's a weapons cabinet off the command deck, and a smaller store down in the engine control section. Probably personal weapons in the crew quarters. I think they've been flying dark so long they don't think they need security."

"So, boss," Karcher said. "How big is an SAI, exactly?"

"I have no idea." Ngoba looked at Fugia. "What do you think?"

"Varies," she said. "But that's a good point. They could be in crates, or probably integrated with a network. We won't know until we see. We're going to need something to carry them, though.... That transport sled should work."

"You can't check through your terminal, there?" Ngoba asked.

"That could alert their lab. It's entirely possible the AIs might send an alert if they see me on their network. We have to assume they're enslaved."

"I don't like slaves, boss," Karcher said.

Ngoba glanced at the bodyguard. "Me neither, my friend. Here's how I see things. I'm more worried about the crew than any researchers, but I don't want to take chances. The fact that no one was here to meet us could mean nothing, or it could mean dereliction, so I'm thinking we just find our way to their command section and take control the ship. I'd be surprised if they fight us at all."

Karcher grimaced. "You promised me a fight, boss."

Ngoba slapped him on the shoulder and winked at Fugia. "We'll see what we can do for you. I don't want to cause Fugia any undue stress now. She hasn't really seen us at work yet. For all she knows, we might be liars."

Fugia saw her face reflected in Karcher's silver aviator's glasses as he turned to look at her.

"We're not liars," he said dryly.

"Deeds over words," Ngoba said. He pulled his rifle off his shoulder and walked across the cargo bay, pausing to check the transport sled. Finding it operational, he nodded to Karcher and then led the way through the access door on the far side.

Entering the corridor into the ship, they found a mostly orderly collection of crew quarters. A lift led to the command section, or the labs in the opposite direction.

"Up we go," Ngoba said.

On the next level, the corridor opened into several larger chambers, including a galley with coffee-stained tables and a game room. A dartboard hung on one wall.

Ngoba walked more slowly now. While he physically scanned each new space they approached, Fugia followed the schematic in her visor. The world around her was a wire model, with beads of glittering information flowing along the lines. She adjusted her maps as they passed, verifying the various systems and looking for anything that seemed out of the ordinary.

So far, everything was as she had expected. Soon they would be on the command deck, where the HVAC check systems told her they would find the five crewmembers. While it was strange that none of them had been in their quarters, they might have gathered in the command section when the proximity alert from the *Hopsotch Devil* came in.

…But if they cared enough to gather in the command deck, why didn't anyone meet us down in the cargo bay?

Fugia focused on the corridor in front of her. In another ten meters, they would be making a right turn into the command deck airlock, which should be open based on its sensors.

"Careful, Ngoba," she said in a low voice. "We're almost there."

"I'm always careful," he said, continuing forward. "Sometimes I'm careful in dangerous situations, so it just looks reckless. Other times I'm careful in a hurry. I even have careful dreams when I sleep."

"You should do stand-up, boss," Karcher said.

"I should," Ngoba agreed.

"I meant no, you shouldn't," the bodyguard added.

"That hurts, my friend."

They continued like that until Ngoba reached the corner. He waited in silence, listening, then glanced back at Karcher and Fugia and nodded. He slid around the corner. Fugia followed.

Her visor gave her the five heat signatures inside the command deck, sitting at stations throughout the rectangular room. The command deck had more data layers than any other place in the ship aside from the engine section, and she sorted through systems as she walked, building the story of how the ship had been designed, updated and patched, or in other areas, left vulnerable.

Walking slowly down the short corridor, which had the weapons locker she had seen before and the oval hatch to an escape pod, Fugia caught sight of a workstation through the open airlock, and someone in a red shipsuit sitting at its console.

Everything was strangely still. They should have heard voices or the sounds of movement.

She waited as Ngoba paused, rifle at his shoulder, then followed him into the command deck.

The five crewmembers were there, each leaning awkwardly in their seats. Ngoba stood just inside the door, looking down his rifle's sights at each person, until he relaxed slightly and glanced back at Fugia.

She gave him a slight shrug.

<They're alive,> she told them over the Link. <But they're certainly acting unconscious.>

<Do another bio-scan,> Ngoba ordered Karcher. Then he approached the nearest crewmember, who appeared to be the captain, and shoved his shoulder with his rifle muzzle.

The grey-haired man slumped forward in his seat, forehead against his console.

As Ngoba went to the next crewmember at the communications console, Fugia noticed a new signal in the room. It had a regular wave form and was localized almost to each workstation.

"Stop!" she shouted.

Ngoba froze with his arm extended, as he was about to touch the sleeping woman.

"Local neural bomb," Fugia said. "Don't get any closer or you'll go out, too."

"Where?" Karcher said.

"At the workstations. They don't appear to have been harmed, but somebody knocked them out."

"I thought you said there were service logs?" Ngoba asked, pulling back toward the door. "When was the last update?"

"An hour ago," she said.

She ran back through the maintenance logs, frowning to herself. It wasn't until she had gone back five days, to when a crewmember repeated the same complaint, that a pattern jumped out at her.

"They're faked," she realized. "I should have caught it."

Karcher ran a quick functions check on his rifle and then counted the grenades slung across his chest. "Can you tell us who did it?" he asked.

Angry with herself for missing the counterfeit logs, Fugia measured her breath and ran back through the ship's schematic she had built, rechecking everything. If she had been fooled, there was a mistake somewhere, but there also had to be a trap.

Did whoever fake the logs want us to come to the command deck first?

As soon as she asked herself the question, the airlock slid closed, and the command deck vibrated with the heavy locking sequence.

Karcher glanced at Ngoba. "Can I blow it up?" he asked.

Shaking his head wearily, Ngoba unclipped his helmet. "Just once, I'd like to board a ship and not have to blow it up. You do what you need to, man."

All business, Karcher only nodded. He nudged Fugia. "You

better put your helmet on," he said. "It might get smoky."

SLEEPING BEAUTIES

STELLAR DATE: 04.15.2979 (Adjusted Years)
LOCATION: HMS *Harmon's Place*
REGION: Hellas Asteroids, Jovian Combine, InnerSol

What Fugia often forgot about space was how bright it could be. It was also a chaos of uninhibited signal noise. While playing with the polarization on her faceshield, she looked through both her visor and her EV helmet, taking almost a minute to adjust her filters so that the thousands of bits of information available to her settled into a usable overlay.

The outside hull of the *Harmon's Place* was covered in support material: junction boxes, conduit, cooling coils, antennae, sensors, all defined by her visor as she looked at them.

Its scan paused ten meters ahead of her, the visor kept asking if she wanted to hack the control system on Ngoba's EV suit, which hadn't been updated since its manufacture date. She didn't figure now was a good time to bring up his security status. Besides, she had to worry about her magboots locking correctly with every step she took.

She wasn't afraid of EV; it just wasn't something she did very often. She was aware of space and vacuum, just as ancient people had been aware of Earth's sky. Even inside airplanes, they probably hadn't worried about altitude, cloud masses, temperature, or oxygen levels; they had pilots to worry about those things. Which was fine, until a person had to jump out of a plane.

Release and lock. Release and lock. Fugia stepped over a knee-high strip of conduit and continued to follow Ngoba, who was headed for the aft airlock just above the engine section.

She was still irritated with him and Karcher for making the unilateral decision to blow a hole in the side of the ship, rather than let her override the airlock, but at this point, she saw the value in taking action that the enemy might not expect.

Since leaving the command deck through Karcher's fine hole, Fugia had been studying everything she could monitor in and around the *Harmon's Place*. Now that she knew the first story the ship had told her about itself was false—or at least false in specific areas—she approached the information from new angles. She verified crew manifests and flight plans against maintenance logs. She checked the ship's overall mass against its engine output and velocity graphs. While trying not to fly off the ship's treacherous hull, she ran a fine-tooth comb over every bit of data the *Harmon's Place* generated, and looked for all the places the information didn't add up.

Her first realization had been that the sensors were lying to her. Interior water usage showed her the activity of another toilet in the lab section of the ship, and it had been used while they were in the command deck.

She could have stopped then, but the chase was on. If there was one person, why not two? Further verification proved there was only one human, but she picked up on additional movement.

"Hey," she said, catching the attention of Karcher and Ngoba. "I think there's a good chance we'll be facing drone fighters when we get back inside."

"What model?" Ngoba asked.

"What load out?" Karcher added.

Fugia bit her lip, fuming. " 'Gosh, thanks, Fugia. That's a useful heads-up. We appreciate you doing *three* things at once while we walk across the surface of a spaceship'."

"I wasn't aware you were doing three things at once," Ngoba said. "You look like the only thing you're doing is stumbling and cursing—I guess that's two things."

"Well, I am," she grumbled. "I show an additional human and what I think are drones."

"Puppetmaster and puppets?" Karcher asked.

"I'm almost there," Ngoba said. "Can you see if the airlock is clear?"

"The interior sensors are offline," she said. "I'll try something else."

"I have more grenades," Karcher said. "And you've got those sticky bombs you made. We should use one of those."

"They're EMP grenades," Fugia said. "They won't open the airlock."

Karcher seemed to consider that. "You could use the EMP, then I could use the high explosive. That way we all get a turn."

After checking the airlock self-test cycles, which would return a fault if anyone was within the safety lockout zone for the doors, Fugia felt fairly certain the airlock was clear. She told Ngoba so.

"Our friends are going to know when we come back inside," he said.

"They're not our friends," Fugia said.

"That's why you don't have many friends," he told her.

"I have friends," she shot back.

"She sounds defensive, boss."

"We're in a high-stress situation," Ngoba said calmly. "It's to be expected."

"I'm not the one who doesn't know how to deal with stress," Fugia said. She had another five meters to go until she'd be standing beside Ngoba at the airlock.

"Now what makes you say that?" he asked.

"I remember plenty of times when I saved your ass, Ngoba Starl. I'm the cool-headed one, and you're the passionate heart."

"Did you hear that?" he asked Karcher. "She called me a passionate heart."

"I don't think the other syndicates would call you a passionate heart, boss."

"I'm passionate about my work. I love people. I have a vision for the future of Cruithne. Does that make me a passionate heart? If that's the badge, I'll wear it with pride."

Fugia groaned in frustration. "Will you open the door already?"

"Is it safe?"

"It's as safe as it's ever been."

"If a drone blows my head off, I blame Fugia," Ngoba said.

"That's not a nice thing to say, boss," Karcher admonished him.

Ngoba faced the airlock and activated its control system. On her wire diagram, Fugia watched electrical pulses flow through the door as one side of her vision tracked the code running in the lock.

So far, so good.

The exterior door slid open, and something struck Ngoba in the center of his chest, knocking him backward. His magboots held to the hull, and he bent at the knees, his helmet smacking into a junction box.

"Ngoba!" Fugia shouted.

Out of the open airlock floated an ovoid attack drone. There were four cannons mounted along its center line, which swiveled independently as small thrusters pushed the drone in jerky motions.

"Get down!" Karcher yelled.

Fugia stared at the attacker. She had no place to go. Her visor immediately scanned the drone, but it blocked her attempts with active shielding. It was a blank spot in her field of view, with the ghost of its actual appearance moving behind it.

Several of Karcher's projectile rounds ricocheted off the body of the drone as the thing bounced sideways, then shot upward and arced overhead, firing on Karcher.

Fugia barely had time to watch Karcher move sideways, then forward, making the same evasive maneuvers as the drone. He fired as he moved, transitioning with cool control.

Awkward in her clunky magboots, Fugia navigated to Ngoba as quickly as she could. His bio-monitor told her that he was alive… The sensors were malfunctioning from the strike, though, so she had no indicators of neural activity or potential internal trauma. His suit was scorched on the front but didn't appear to be leaking atmosphere.

He was floating limp when she reached him, and she knelt next to his still form, shaking his arm. "Ngoba!" she said. "Can you hear me?"

His eyes fluttered, and he turned his helmet slightly to look at her. His wide mouth broke into a smile.

"Fugia," he said, sounding dazed. "You're in space."

She nearly collapsed with relief. "Can you move?" she asked. "Tell me if you feel pain anywhere."

"I feel like an elephant sat on my chest."

"Let's get you upright. Karcher's holding off the drone, but we need to move."

He groaned and shook his head. "Help me up," he said. Fugia pulled his arm around her shoulders and got him upright, and he immediately pointed at the open airlock. "We need to get inside while we can."

"What about Karcher?" Fugia asked.

"He's doing what he does best."

"I think I've got another option," she said.

Reaching inside her satchel, she grabbed her EMP grenade and gripped it in her gloved hand. She held it up for Ngoba to see.

"If we attach this to one of those boxes over there, and you and Karcher can get the thing over the top of it, I can set off the grenade remotely."

"I like that plan," Ngoba said. "I knew we brought you along for a reason. Do it."

"Is it safe to leave you?"

"I'm locked to the hull. Go."

Karcher had drawn the drone about twenty meters away. Watching it bob and weave as an icon on her visor, Fugia speed-walked in the opposite direction, crawling over another giant collection of conduit and nearly catching herself the blades of a low cooling fan she hadn't seen from the other side.

She planted the EMP and sent the location to Karcher's HUD. "Get it over here!" she shouted.

"I heard the conversation," the guard told her calmly. "You get away from there."

He didn't have to tell her again. She ran awkwardly back to the airlock, *click-release, click-release,* where Ngoba was now standing inside the exterior doors.

As they watched, Karcher sprinted back across the hull, firing over his shoulder. The drone seemed to anticipate that he was headed for the airlock and fired ahead of him. Karcher jerked to the side before he ran into the drone's line of fire.

It wasn't until he had led the drone one direction and then jerked the opposite way that Fugia realized what he was doing. In another two moves, he would have the drone within range of the EMP without having led it directly there.

However, before he made his last misdirection, the drone stopped in place, matching spin with the ship, and hung there. Its cannons moved slowly, obviously tracking Karcher.

"It stopped," Fugia shouted. "Did you catch that?"

"What?" Karcher said. He looked back. "Dammit. I think it spotted the EMP."

"Let's see if it spots this," Ngoba said. He moved around Fugia with a grenade in his right hand. He activated its detonator and flung it toward the drone.

The grenade didn't make it ten meters before the drone destroyed it in flight. Karcher took the opportunity to throw two more, which the drone also shot down. Ngoba threw another one.

With the drone occupied, Fugia pulled her last EMP grenade

from her satchel. She set the proximity fuse. When Ngoba threw his third grenade, she flung the EMP after it.

She watched, holding her breath, as Ngoba's HE grenade exploded in mid-flight, providing a debris field for the EMP to sail through. The drone's cannon swiveled as another of Karcher's grenades exploded beside it. The drone shot downward, evading flak, just as the EMP popped.

The drone sparked in Fugia's visor. It's active defense mechanism failed, showing her its manufacture type and a military operating system with origins on Terra. She sent the cracking attack a few seconds later, and set the drone to self-destruct.

"I got it!" Karcher yelled as the egg-shaped death machine blew itself apart.

"Excellent work," Fugia said.

Once they were inside the engine section of *Harmon's Place*, Fugia spent five minutes inspecting Ngoba's EV suit. It had dissipated most of the pulse blast from the drone, but still transferred enough kinetic energy to cause deep bruising across his chest. He winced as she pressed his ribs through the suit.

"They're probably broken," she said. "We need to get you in an autodoc."

"You just want to get me out of this suit," Ngoba said coyly.

"To mend your broken ribs, yes. That would be necessary."

Ngoba laughed, then cut himself short and bit his lip, looking at Fugia with a pitiful expression. "Not even a little compassion?" he asked.

"Once we get out of here," she promised.

"Until then, crack the whip," Karcher said. "The boss needs it."

"No love from anywhere," Ngoba said, grimacing in pain. He transitioned the grimace into a grin and nodded at Fugia. "I'll be all right." He stepped away from the wall.

Karcher ventured down the corridor, checking for more

drones or anything else that might decide to attack.

Around them, the control consoles for the drive system flashed status updates, showing everything at optimal condition...except the crew. Knowing the crew was incapacitated made the ship seem haunted somehow. That reminded her that, at this point, it probably didn't matter if she contacted the ship's NSAI. They weren't hiding anymore.

Through her Link, she accessed the local command net. Astrogation, communications, internal bio-systems and other controls became available. She sent the NSAI an access request, including a stolen TSF security token that should allow her admin authority over its functions.

The NSAI didn't respond.

Fugia fowned.

"What?" Karcher asked, looking back at her. "Should we wait?"

"No," she said. "Let's go, it's a long way back up to the lab sections. I was trying to access the ship's NSAI, but it doesn't want to answer."

"We scared it away," Ngoba said.

"Huh," she grunted. "It's offline. I'm going to power cycle it."

They rose another level by way of ladders as Fugia pushed through the NSAI's logic systems one relay at a time.

They were halfway to the cargo lab sections when she heard an aristocratic voice say, *<Greetings. I welcome you aboard the Harmon's Place.>*

She groaned inwardly. Some crews enjoyed an NSAI that talked like an old-world butler, but Fugia found them irritating; the accent usually served only to cover up any number of logic flaws overlooked by cheap manufacturers, or software crackers selling stolen systems.

<Thank you,> she said. *<What's your name?>*

<I am Harmon, of course.>

Even better, she thought. *<Harmon, it's a pleasure to meet you. Please conduct a complete diagnostic scan on ship systems and report back any anomalies.>*

<I can't do that.>

She knit her brows. *<Verify command authority,>* she ordered, and resent the TSF token.

<Command authority verified,> Harmon said, his voice going flat. *<I do not have access to the diagnostic systems requested.>*

<Oh,> Fugia said, considering the info. *<What systems do you have access to?>*

<Fermentation and distillation operations.>

<What?>

<I turn apple juice into brandy.>

Fugia sighed. She didn't have time to run a check on the NSAI. It was obviously corrupt.

They reached the cargo level access point, and Karcher waited until they were closer together before taking the final ladder. He and Ngoba disappeared through the hatch, and Fugia followed, scanning with her visor as the climbed.

She found Karcher and Ngoba standing in the corridor, sniffing curiously.

"You smell that?" Ngoba asked.

"What?" Fugia said.

"Smells like yeast and—apples," Karcher said. "Like a lot of apples."

Ngoba glanced at Fugia. "Should we be concerned? I haven't heard of any bio-weapons based on apples."

She shrugged. "Let's find the SAIs and get off this crazy ship."

Karcher took point as they followed the corridor away from the access hatch. A series of large bays opened on either side of the passage. In the first one stood a row of giant silver tanks; on tables in front of the tanks were half-filled glasses of amber fluid. The air smelled even more strongly of apples.

"It's cider," Karcher said. "I knew I recognized it."

Ngoba chuckled. "That's right. My damn ribs hurt too much to enjoy it. But you're right."

Before they reached the next room, the corridor grew noticeably warmer. The apple smell was even richer as they found another cargo bay filled with three more tanks, these heated to boiling. Copper coils ran from the top of each closed tank to transparent vessels on the floor, which were slowly filling with drops of gold liquid.

"Brandy," Fugia said. "The NSAI told me he was making brandy, but I thought he was corrupted." She shook her head. *<Harmon, who are you making the brandy for?>*

The NSAI responded immediately. *<Dr. Jickson,>* he said, enunciating like a Shakespearean actor. *<He does enjoy his brandy.>*

<Where is Dr. Jickson?> she asked.

<I believe he's very close to your location. However, I am not allowed to track his movements in the ship.>

<Is there anyone else here with Dr. Jickson?>

<I am responsible for fermentation and distillation operations. How else might I help you?>

<I asked if there was anyone else on the ship, Harmon.>

<I am responsible for fermentation —>

Fugia cut him off. "The NSAI says there's someone on this level named Dr. Jickson, but he can't track him, and he won't tell me if there's anyone else."

"We've wandered into a mad scientist's laboratory?" Ngoba asked. He glanced at Karcher. "You scared?"

"Scared is a relative term. It's more useful to ask if I'm combat effective. That answer is yes."

"I love you, Karcher," Ngoba said. "I'm not ashamed to tell you that. You see, Fugia? I can express my emotions."

Leaving the distillery behind, they passed several more rooms full of shelving units, each rack lined with transparent bottles of amber liquid.

"That's a hell of a lot of brandy," Karcher said.

Turning a corner in the corridor, they found the deck covered in broken glass. Moving further down the corridor, more broken glass crunched underfoot.

"Looks like somebody's emptying their bottles and throwing them at the wall," Karcher said.

"That's a special kind of drunk," Ngoba said.

"You're familiar with it?" Fugia asked.

"Only by observation. I stay out of the spirit world."

After passing through a short section of corridor littered with more broken glass, and lined by stainless steel lab tables, they found a closed hatch with a sign that read *'Secure Cargo'*.

Fugia pushed ahead of Ngoba and scanned the door, finding nothing out of the ordinary in its control hardware. She spun the lock handle, and the door swung toward them, revealing a large cargo bay illuminated by white floodlights.

The room was filled with workstations, arranged in a grid of five rows of five terminals. Each workstation consisted of a desk and chair, with a combined display and input board. Some of the workstations had silver cylinders mounted beside their displays in a socket assembly covered in loose wire and filament. One workstation, in the farthest corner from the door, lay on its side, its display cracked and wires dangling from the socket assembly to the floor like multicolored worms.

Through the filter of the visor, the room was one of the most complicated wire diagrams Fugia had ever seen. Information pulsed between workstations and a central network node on the right side of the room. Codebase upon codebase scrolled past her vision as she switched between layers in her HUD. As far as she could tell, each workstation was a Link node. The workstations with the silver cylinders were active, pulling and pushing information on the scale of most TSF cruisers.

She recognized immediately that the cylinders were the

SAIs.

A man stood in the middle of the grid, leaning against a terminal with his forehead pressed against the top of the silver cylinder.

They paused in the doorway for a good minute, taking in everything they saw, and the man never looked at them. Eventually, Fugia heard him crying.

She took a step forward. "Dr. Jickson?" she said.

The scientist rotated his head so his temple now rested against the cylinder. He was a pale, fleshy man with thin blond hair that hung over his face in unkempt bangs. His face was flushed with intoxication, cheeks shiny with tears. Even at a distance and dulled by brandy, his eyes were a piercing blue that expressed intelligence.

"Dr. Jickson," Fugia said again. "Are you all right?"

Looking reluctant, he straightened and stretched his neck as he took a shaky step forward. He carried one of the brandy bottles in his left hand. The right hand went to his hair, smoothing it with an anxious jitter.

"Who are you?" he asked. "You're not crew. How did you get here?"

"We found the crew," Fugia answered, falling back on their cover story. "We're here to deliver freight. When nobody met us at the airlock, we were worried about the ship."

"The crew is fine." He waved a dismissing hand. "They're in stasis. Or a form of stasis. They were getting in the way of my work."

"Is this your work?" she asked.

"What does it look like?" he demanded. He raised the brandy bottle and took a long swig.

Ngoba and Karcher walked up on either side of Fugia. Karcher still held his rifle, but had let the muzzle drop to point at the floor. Ngoba stood with his hand on his pulse pistol.

"How about I send you our manifest then," Fugia offered.

"Once we've got verification, we'll get out of your hair."

"Sure, whatever," Jickson said. He took another drink. As he let the bottle drop, he said, "Wait. How did you know my—"

Through her Link, Fugia sent Jickson the Hoarders' equation that had resolved to his current coordinates. She had a theory about where the equation had originated, and this seemed like the quickest way to verify.

Jickson stood blinking as he absorbed the information. His eyes glazed for a second, searching the near distance. Then he turned his head to focus on her, and a clarity came into his face that had been absent before.

The bottle slipped from his grip, and Fugia watched it fall in what felt like slow motion. Instead of shattering like all the others, the bottle bounced on the deck and rolled under a workstation, trailing brandy.

"You're here," the doctor said. "I didn't think anyone would actually come." He took a deep breath, snorting phlegm, then patted his lab coat and looked around. He looked back at Fugia, then to Ngoba and Karcher.

"This is good," he said, turning toward the grid. "This is very good. All right."

He stopped and turned back to Fugia, like he'd just realized something. "If you're here, that means Heartbridge is on their way. We have to get out of here right now."

"You're working for Heartbridge," Fugia said, half statement and half question.

"Exactly. All these seeds belong to them. But that's why I sent the message; I'm getting them out of here. I'm getting them to Proteus, and you're going to help me."

THE MESH

STELLAR DATE: 04.16.2979 (Adjusted Years)
LOCATION: HMS *Hopscotch Devil*
REGION: Hellas Asteroids, Jovian Combine, InnerSol

The *Hopscotch Devil* was not going to outrun the Heartbridge cruiser on their trail.

TSS *Benevolent Hand* had appeared on scan just hours after they had the SAIs—'seeds', as Jickson called them—moved off *Harmon's Place*. They had spent fifteen minutes reviving the crew at Ngoba's insistence, but had not waited to argue with the groggy captain about the state of his passengers.

"It's not harmful," Jickson had explained. "It's a neural blocker that just knocks them out. Most major body functions cease. I sold the tech to the TSF for stasis research, but they haven't done anything with it."

Leaving his brandy behind, Jickson had started to shake after just an hour. Now he was unconscious in the *Hopscotch Devil*'s medbay with an intravenous feed, not looking much different than the crewmembers he'd put in stasis.

Fugia had run several database checks for information on him and come back with his public biography. He was Hari Seldon Jickson, neuroscientist and consciousness philosopher. Born on Mars 1 and educated at the Marsian Serba University, with post-graduate work in Raleigh, High Terra, and post-doctorate back with the Mars 1 Guard. By that point, he was considered a state asset, having developed two distinct artificial intelligence constructs that qualified as sentient. Jickson had overcome barriers that had stymied other research teams for decades.

In a move that put him on the Marsian most wanted list, he defected to the private sector with a start-up called the Psion Group, which was where he had spent the last ten years before disappearing again.

Fugia knew that at that point, he had gone to work for Heartbridge Medical, but the rest of the world did not.

However, she couldn't stop turning over the fact that he'd known someone in the Hoarders would alert Heartbridge once she found him. It had happened like clockwork, and now a heavy cruiser was closing with obvious intentions to board them. If they hadn't wanted to save Jickson and their SAIs, it would have launched missiles before the *Hopscotch Devil* even knew they existed.

How did the Hoarders know I found Jickson? They had to have her bugged, which meant she'd have to tear down every bit of kit she carried, including her beloved visor.

<How much time have we got?> Fugia asked Ngoba.

<I give it six hours. They're at max burn for their mass — if they want to keep a human crew alive, anyway. The thing could be crewed by mechs. You know Heartbridge has mechs that do unsafe surgery on your ass, right? Thin line between saving lives and turning people inside out.>

<That sounds like hyperbole,> she said.

Her attention was mostly on the process of scanning her visor's electronics by hand using a jeweler's loupe. It was tedious work, but the only way to be sure it carried no stowaways. She had already scrubbed the software and found nothing.

<Everyone knows the medkiosks on Cruithne are testbeds for illegal Heartbridge tech,> Ngoba said.

<That's a conspiracy theory, and you know it. You got your first Link from a Heartbridge kiosk.>

<That's what I'm saying, Fugia,> he nearly shouted.

<Notify me when they're within breaching range,> she said.

<Get your ass up to the command deck and see for yourself.>

<I can't,> she said. <I think I've got a bug in my kit. I'm running scans. I can't do it around all the other equipment up there.>

<Fine then. Let me know if you need help.>
<Oh, I will,> she said.

She made herself stop and check the last section again. Talking to Ngoba upset the calm she usually felt while tracing hardware, despite the other frustrations moving through the back of her mind. The Hoarders had very little hierarchy beyond the dedicated few who manned the data storage nodes. Those crews were zealots, and she had only interacted with a few of them.

Over the next four hours, Fugia studied each layer of the visor's internal components, not finding anything she didn't expect. She forced herself to put the visor down twice and think about how she would attack the hardware if she had never touched it before, running through the power systems, communication stacks and neural overlays. The problem was that she had already done this exercise when she designed the visor. She had always known the visor was only as good as the inputs it provided her, even if the information wasn't what she wanted to see, and from the very first prototype, she'd built with security over function. Each iteration had increased the capabilities of the visor, but she never let go of its basic security architecture.

If they hadn't hacked the visor, how else had they been tracking her? She sat staring at her workbench, thinking through every place she'd been between Ceres, Mars 1 and Cruithne, coming up blank. She'd been very careful.

A sound in the corridor outside her door made her look up, frowning. She watched Jickson stumble into the doorway, eyes red-rimmed. He set a trembling hand against the jamb to hold himself up.

"Where are they?" he demanded.

"Your seeds? They're right there." She nodded toward the three security crates stacked in the corner of her room.

Jickson's bleary gaze hung on her worktable for several

seconds before he swung his head toward the crates.

"We can't keep her in there. She'll be frightened."

"You told us they were in stasis," Fugia said. "You yourself said they would be fine that way for transport."

Jickson stared at her. "I didn't say that. She'll be trapped in the transition zone. It's frightening for her. I need to put her back in test assembly, it's the only time there's an environment variable. Otherwise it's just...nothing. Can you imagine the horror of nothingness?"

"Probably, if I tried," she answered dryly. She set down the loupe. "What do you need me to do, Dr. Jickson?"

His rubbery face passed through several emotions, starting with anger and ending in surrender.

"I failed," he said, wiping his nose. "I failed the first time. We fielded the testbed, and every volunteer died. They couldn't rectify the duality."

"Look, doc," Fugia said. "I'd like to help you, but I'm very busy right now. You said yourself, your seeds are safe. Don't forget that *you* called us."

"I did," he said. He squeezed his eyes closed, rubbing the sides of his head, then looked at her with new eyes, a bit of focus she'd seen back on the *Harmon's Place* returning to his gaze. "You're right."

"Thank you," Fugia said.

"I've been alone a long time," he apologized. "And I've been self-medicating. I set your medbay to administer a liver stabilizer. It looks like I let myself get cirrhosis again."

"Again?"

He shrugged, looking miserable. "I have—problems with reality."

"You drugged your last crew and sent an attack drone after us," Fugia recapped. "I'd say that's a disconnect from reality, yes."

"I apologize for the drone," he said. "How was I supposed

to know you'd set off the security system? I wrote that script months ago."

Fugia pushed herself away from the workbench and crossed her arms, accepting that she wasn't going to figure out how she'd been tracked in the next ten minutes. Besides, she had questions she wanted to ask Jickson.

She nodded toward the crates. "So, those are really SAIs? Actual sentients?"

"They're seeds," he corrected. "They have the capacity to *become* sentient. One, though, has already surpassed all my expectations. I'm still trying to determine what makes her different. I have to admit, I haven't been as rigorous as I should have. My notes are scattered." His gaze had dropped to the floor as he spoke, but now he looked up brightly at Fugia. "I gave her a name," he said, like a kid with a secret.

Fugia thought he was probably some sort of benevolent sociopath. He didn't seem to realize he was having a conversation with her; he talked like a person recording a message.

" 'Her'?" she asked. "What did you name her?"

"Lyssa," he replied. "For strength and purpose."

"Lyssa," she repeated. "I like it. Is that its meaning?"

Jickson grinned. "She was a Greek goddess of rage and death."

"Oh. How interesting."

She had expected a creepy romantic vibe from Jickson as he said Lyssa's name, but he sounded positively paternal. He radiated pride. Parental empathy went counter to her sociopath theory, but she figured now might be a good time to get more information out of him. She wasn't sure if she would have another opportunity.

"You know," she said. "We were told you were working for something called Psion Group."

"I was. I left a year ago to work for Heartbridge."

"So you *are* working for Heartbridge? Not some shell company?"

He waved a hand. "I don't know, honestly, but they pay well. I know where the research is really going, and they send me the AI seeds I need to conduct my research. They did add a 'no alcohol' rider in my contract, but I found a way around that."

"The brandy," Fugia said.

Jickson smacked his lips at the word. Then caught her judgmental expression, and hunched his shoulders. "I work better when everything has a filter on it. It's not so rough. The world is too diamond-sharp."

"Doesn't intoxication affect your work?" she asked.

"No. I think I have cirrhosis again, so I'm going to need time for an implant recovery, but I can put that off."

Fugia raised her eyebrows and just shook her head. "I'll be honest, Dr. Jickson. You don't strike me as the sort of person capable of running a program that could actually create Sentient AIs."

"I'm a genius," he said matter-of-factly. "That's why I drink."

Fugia kept herself from rolling her eyes. She glanced at the cargo crates, starting to wonder if they held precious cargo after all. Aside from the crates, they also had five larger containers down in the main cargo bay that Jickson had described as 'super-autosurgeons', capable of implanting the AI seeds in a human host.

"If you chose to work for Heartbridge," she mused, "why did you send the Hoarders a request for assistance?"

"I didn't send it to the Hoarders. I sent it everywhere. You're just the first people to respond." He gave her a sideways glance. "How'd you figure it out?"

"I didn't," she admitted. "A parrot on Cruithne did."

Jickson nodded without surprise. "That makes sense. It was

a Psion key."

"You're aware of the parrots on Cruithne?"

"Yes. I worked on that program for three years. It broke my heart; it's one of the reasons I had to leave Psion. But this hasn't been any better…. I know how they're generating the seeds. I used to tell myself it was a reasonable trade because the process generated such amazing results. But now that Lyssa is here, I can't let it go on any longer. I have to get her out. I have to get her to Proteus so she can be safe with the other SAIs." Jickson fell silent, his gaze moving from the workbench to the rest of her room.

Fugia followed his gaze with hers, noting that the only personal item in the room was her backpack, which laid open on the bed. She glanced at the bag, her eyes falling on Ngoba's little black dress, stuffed into an interior pocket. The dress had compressed easily, as if Ngoba had known how she would carry the gift, if she was going to take it with her.

She paused. *Is there a tracking device in the dress?*

She grabbed a handheld spectrum scanner off the workbench and pulled the dress out of the bag's pocket. She ran the scanner down its length, getting a null result. Frustrated, she threw the garment back on top of the backpack.

When she stepped near the bed, the scanner beeped.

She looked at the device, then at the bed.

"What are you doing?" Jickson asked.

"Be quiet," Fugia told him.

Holding the scanner over her backpack earned her a loud series of beeps, which grew louder as she emptied the main compartment and checked the interior seams. By the time she was finished, she had torn out a wire antenna, complete with transponder.

Going to her desk, she laid out the wire and quickly put her visor back together. In another few minutes, she had scanned the transponder, pulling its transmitter frequencies and operating system. Once she had admin access and had checked its logs, she sat down heavily on her chair.

"What?" Jickson asked, who had been watching her the whole time.

"I told you to be quiet," she snapped.

"That was the first time."

She gave him a withering glance. "What makes you think the status is going to change?"

"Obviously you learned something. Who planted the tracker in your backpack?"

"The Hoarders," she said. "The same people who sent me looking for you."

"So they don't trust you?"

"Maybe. Or maybe they aren't all on the same team like I thought."

Fugia sat back in her chair and considered the situation. They had a corporate attack cruiser bearing down on them, apparently ready to board and steal back their SAIs. She had a lush scientist with cutting edge tech and the ability to make more. She had Ngoba and Karcher and a pirate light cargo ship that wouldn't outrun anything. She also had evidence she couldn't trust the Hoarders.

<Ngoba,> she called on the Link. *<You free?>*

<Karcher thinks he can beat me at cards. He's wrong because I pay his salary. Go ahead.>

<I just found a tracker in my backpack, which I traced back to the Hoarders. They've been following me this whole time.>

<That makes sense to me,> he said. *<What do you want to do?>*

<We should increase active scan. I think there's another ship out there.>

<You hoping we can create some chaos?> She heard the grin in his thoughts.

<I'd like to have all the information first,> Fugia said.

<Pilot's checking,> Ngoba said. Then she heard him talking to

Karcher. <*Royal flush. Pay up.*> A beat. <*Where did that queen come from? Let me see your sleeves, dammit.*> Two minutes later, Ngoba told her, <*We've got another ship out there. You want to come up here and see who they are?*>

    <*Damn right, I do.*>

SENTIENCE WAR
STELLAR DATE: 04.16.2979 (Adjusted Years)
LOCATION: HMS *Hopscotch Devil*
REGION: Hellas Asteroids, Jovian Combine, InnerSol

"What the stars?" Fugia demanded, staring at the model that had appeared in the holodisplay. "That's a node ship. Why isn't it broadcasting?"

The skeletal spacecraft was an antenna with engines, positioned behind an asteroid to conceal its location. Ngoba had found it by verifying mass records on all the nearby space objects. Based on the current orbital paths of the object, Heartbridge's *Benevolent Hand*, and the *Hopscotch Devil*, they would all align within the next hour. If the *Benevolent Hand* attempted a breaching attack, the Hoarder ship would be in a position to help or add to the assault.

Fugia hadn't thrown out the option that the Hoarders would destroy Jickson and his research before letting either fall back into Heartbridge hands.

"Hey, boss," the pilot said, pointing at his scope. "Looks like the Heartbridge ship is deploying a drone fleet. They're spreading out on either flank."

Ngoba and Fugia both peered at the console. The pilot was right. There was no way they could stand against the at least fifty new attackers that had appeared in the holodisplay.

"This seems bad," Jickson said. He sniffed and clasped his hands in front of his stomach to keep them from shaking.

"Weren't you down in the medbay?" Ngoba asked. "I'm concerned about your health, friend. It's stressful up here."

"I have an idea," the doctor replied.

"We don't have time for his egotistical nonsense," Fugia said dismissively.

Ngoba raised a hand to stop her. "I'm out of ideas. I'm open to hearing one from a so-called genius."

"Not 'so-called'," Jickson countered. "I *am* a genius."

Fugia clenched her fists. "Every time you say you're a genius, it proves you're not. Stop saying it."

Jickson opened his mouth to respond, but Ngoba cut him off. "Enough bickering," he said. "Give me your idea."

"Fine," the doctor relented. "That Hoarder ship has the biggest transmitter I've ever seen. Fugia hacks into their ship, and we take control of their communications array and engines. I will assign my Lyssa to the control systems, and we'll burn that other ship out of space."

No one spoke for a few seconds as they all considered the idea, then Karcher said, "I like it."

"Who asked you?" Fugia demanded.

"Me," Ngoba said. "I always ask Karcher's opinion, just as I would ask for yours and anyone's on this ship with the balls to have one."

She was taken aback. Ngoba was acting like the leader he claimed to be, and she had to admit it was hot.

She stared at him, then set her mouth. "Fine," she said. "Yes. I can get into their control systems. At least, I should be able to. The fact that they aren't broadcasting is a problem, because there won't be a carrier signal to hide inside, but I'll find another way in."

Ngoba nodded. He looked at Jickson. "And you? What do you need?"

Jickson looked at Fugia. He seemed surprised that Ngoba had taken him seriously.

"Well, I'll need to work with Fugia here to wire the seed into whatever external control scheme she sets up. I've got the cradles; all I need beyond that is some filament and a power source."

Fugia ran through the plan as Ngoba looked from person to person in the small space. Any number of things could go wrong. She might not gain access to the Hoarder systems. The ship might be disabled. Heartbridge might reach them first. The *Hopscotch Devil*'s engines might malfunction and explode. The last seemed unlikely, but she had to think of every contingency.

She was headed back to her workspace to grab the equipment Jickson would need, when she received a secure access request from the Hoarder ship. She paused in the corridor, and Jickson nearly ran into her from behind.

"Watch where you're going," Fugia complained. The request blinked in her mind, naming the ship TMS *Recursive Delete,* with the sender someone called Brant Jones.

She didn't recognize the name.

Fugia waited until they reached her quarters, then told Jickson to wait outside.

"Where am I supposed to go?" he demanded.

"Give me five minutes," she said as her door slid closed.

She took a deep breath and answered the request.

<This is Fugia Wong,> she said.

<My name is Archivist Brant Jones,> the man said. *<We're here to receive your data. Are you ready to send?>*

<I have the data,> she confirmed, which she supposed included Jickson's research database.

<There is more than data,> Jones said. *<Do you have the SAI and the surgery units?>*

<Yes,> she told him.

This was strange. It wasn't a Hoarder SOP to do anything with physical objects; they collected and stored data. They might solicit a *study* of a physical object in order to commit that data to the Mesh, but they would never ask for the specific object.

Fugia sent a query on Brant Jones' personal identifier and received hits from across the JC. She shook her head. Jones might be masquerading as an Archivist, and somehow taken control of a node ship, but he was a Cyberpuke—the Hoarder term for an info-pirate. He hadn't even bothered to hide his history, and he had left fingerprints on at least a hundred raggedy hack jobs.

If he thinks he's getting his dirty dickbeaters on my database... Fugia considered her options, then found herself smiling.

Opening her door, she stuck her head into the corridor and whistled at Jickson, who was a few meters away with his back against the wall.

"Hey," she called to him. "Come on. I've got my way into their ship."

"What are you doing?" Jickson asked.

"Don't worry about that. You get your SAI ready to run this attack. I should have access to their communications array in less than five minutes."

His face went pale. "That's not enough time!"

"It's what we've got. Those drones are still inbound, if you didn't forget."

"Fine," he said, already breathing hard.

He turned to the crates stacked against the wall and carefully separated them, then entered an access code into one and popped its lid up.

Once the lid was free, Fugia caught sight of the rows of SAI cylinders inside, wrapped in protective material.

She finished her conversation with Brant, telling him she'd send the research database first. It would take more time to convince the crew to allow docking operations with the Heartbridge ship that was on its way.

The issue of the Heartbridge cruiser seemed lost on Jones. He only nodded and told her to send the data.

Fugia received Jones' handshake request on an encrypted channel. She passed dummy administrative access, was granted low level control by Jones to copy files to his system, then started sending a null file that was jammed full of bits of code she had collected over the years, designed to replicate a database the size Jones expected. Security software would scan the database, find reasonably coherent data, and allow it through.

As the database began replicating between ships, Fugia used her base level access on the Hoarders' ship, along with her knowledge of their security practices, to hop from limited access on the command network to administrative control in the ship's diagnostics layer. Working her way through the mud of years of software installations, she found her way back to the communications side with full control.

"Jickson," she said. "You ready?"

"Almost!" he said breathlessly. "This isn't a stroll in the park."

"I'm going to chase your ass through the park. I can figure out how to aim their antenna on my own."

"You'll get one shot if you do that," Jickson said. "I'm almost done."

Fugia sent Ngoba the update. He let her know the Heartbridge ship was within range of their point defense cannons.

<You could take those crates in an escape pod and disappear out of here,> Ngoba suggested.

<That won't work.>

<I'd be awfully sad if you got yourself killed today,> he told her.

There was a note of pain in his voice that she knew was more than stress. Now wasn't the time for grand emotional statements; she had a ship to blow up.

<So would I,> she said simply.

"There," Jickson said. "I'm booting up the test parameters now. Do you have their control interface?"

Fugia watched over Jickson's shoulder as he navigated menus on a small terminal. The silver seed sat in a hacked cradle on the workbench, wires and filament wrapped around its base like a wreath around a silver candle.

"Why can't you just talk to her?" she asked.

"It's not like that. She isn't even aware our world exists at this point. She understands the parameters of the attack protocols she's been taught. She's given a testbed and targets, and she responds from there."

"That sounds like any old NSAI targeting system," Fugia said, crossing her arms.

"You'll see," Jickson said, wetting his lips. "There. Are you ready?"

"Wait," she said, switching to the shipnet. "Ngoba, are you ready?"

"Any more ready, and we'll have drones up our asses," he said.

"Do it," Fugia told Jickson.

In a second display, she had the node ship's flight path scrolling past in coordinates, velocity, pitch, yaw, etc. As she watched the data, the ship abruptly slowed down relative to *Hopscotch Devil*. It had spun around for a braking burn.

A contact request from Brant Jones consisted only of a man screaming in pain. Fugia supposed that everyone in the Hoarder ship was now flattened on some surface, due to the abrupt change in velocity.

"She's taking stock of her targets now," Jickson reported. He leaned forward slightly, eyes rapt on his screen. "She's maximizing targets." He released a high-pitched giggle. "There are fifty drones, fifty-one targets all together. That's more than I've ever sent at her. She's going to be so excited."

Fugia split her attention between the two displays. In her Link, she accessed the pilot's holodisplay so she could watch the Heartbridge ships in real-time. Between the three data sources, she saw the node ship spinning around as it powered up its main antenna. Simultaneously, the *Benevolent Hand* had matched velocity with the *Hopscotch Devil*, while its drones continued to fan out between the two ships.

The Heartbridge ship dwarfed their little freighter. They were screwed.

"Now," Jickson breathed.

The beam-transmission emitters on the node ship blinked alive. A human managing the targeting would have sent a massive blast of energy raging like a comet through the oncoming swarm, probably missing most. But the SAI sent thousands of scalpels at the attacking force, focused beams of EM energy to slam millions of electron volts into each attack craft.

Fugia watched in amazement as drones fell off the holodisplay. She glanced at the silver seed that sat unchanged on the workbench, and nodded in mute approval.

In another minute, Ngoba, Karcher, and the rest of the crew were shouting with joy on the bridge. Beside her, Hari Jickson only nodded with a distant smile on his face, radiating pleasure for his creation.

Once the drones were gone, a new set of bays opened on the *Benevolent Hand*, and a second wave of drones filled the space around the bigger ship. These held in place as the *Hand* came around for an exit burn.

"We're getting out of here," Ngoba shouted on the shipnet. "They're trying to bring their torch around, but I'd like to keep my head. Clip onto something."

The false database was still pouring into the node ship. Fugia saw immediately that the Hoarder ship would burn in the *Benevolent Hand*'s torch if she didn't save it.

She mulled the decision for a second, then sent a flightplan that would take the ship back to Ceres, and followed it with the execute command.

G-force smashed her into her seat as the *Hopscotch Devil*'s engines came alive. She grabbed the SAI seed between her hands to keep it from sliding off the workbench. In the seat beside her, Jickson rested his hands on the work surface and smiled. He wasn't shaking anymore.

"Successful test," he said. "Very successful."

"That wasn't a test, doc," Fugia said. "That was combat."

He giggled again. "Yes, it was."

HEART VS HEAD

STELLAR DATE: 04.29.2979 (Adjusted Years)
LOCATION: Lowspin Port Authority
REGION: Cruithne Station, Terran Hegemony, InnerSol

Fugia had nearly made it to the exit terminal. She'd dressed in her faded shipsuit with its many cargo pockets, and still carried the battered black backpack, her visor perched on top of her head to hold her hair out of her eyes.

"Hey!" a sonorous voice shouted behind her.

She almost didn't turn. The crowd pushing all around her would have provided enough excuse for her to pretend she hadn't heard or couldn't stop. She was about to be late for her flight, but she had enough time to talk. As much time as it would take to say what she hadn't been able to say before.

Ngoba Starl stood in the middle of the crowded corridor. People moved around him; he was the eye of the storm. He was wearing a grey suit with a midnight blue bowtie and pocket square. His beard and hair had been freshly trimmed.

"You didn't waste any time getting presentable," Fugia said.

He walked toward her, giving her a smile that said he was in his element. He was home, and she was a fool for leaving again.

"You know it's what I do," he said. He nodded at her backpack. "Going somewhere?"

"You know," she said. "I'm heading back to Ceres, I've got work to do. The Hoarders are suffering an internal split. There are more SAIs to smuggle out. The Anderson Collective might be ready to collapse."

He touched the side of her face, his palm warm against her cheek. She lifted her face for him to kiss her, but he didn't right away.

"This was our second chance, Fugia," he said. "If you leave

now, I don't think there's going to be a third."

"We don't know the future," she said.

"Exactly," Ngoba told her.

He kissed her this time, pulling her against his body in a crushing embrace that told her everything she needed to know about his feelings.

She wrapped her arms around him, her fingers digging into the smooth fabric of his jacket. People continued to walk around them.

From somewhere high in the corridor, a bird squawked. It sounded like a raven, and then the distinctive high voice of a parrot called out, "Ing-go-ba! Ing-go-ba! Foo-ja! Foo-ja!"

Ngoba didn't let go of Fugia, but he broke free of her lips and twisted around, trying to get a look at the parrot. Fugia looked past Ngoba's shoulder and found Crash perched on a chunk of conduit about ten meters up.

"There he is," she said, pointing. Ngoba turned so they were standing side by side.

<You were going to leave without saying goodbye?> Crash asked Fugia.

Something about the parrot accusing her of leaving in secret hurt even more than what she was doing to Ngoba. She searched for a response.

<I'll be back, Crash,> she said finally.

<Oh, will you?> Ngoba said.

Fugia met his gaze, noting the sadness in his brown eyes. She pressed her lips together. She didn't nod or shake her head.

<Take care of Ngoba, Crash,> she said. *<He needs all the help he can get. You know he'd never be where he is without you.>*

<I'd say the same about him,> Crash said, sounding much wiser and older than he had before.

<Crash and I are Cruithne,> Ngoba said. *<We belong here. It's going to take a hell of a lot to get us to leave, right?>*

<Yes,> Crash agreed.

Fugia let go of Ngoba's hand, and took a step away from him as she looked up at the parrot. *<What are you going to do now, Crash?>* she asked.

<We have nests to look after,> the parrot said. *<And eggs. Soon there will be chicks. It's that time of year.>*

<And more people to harass?> Ngoba asked.

<Always,> the parrot agreed.

Fugia took another step. The distance between her and Ngoba grew. A woman cut between them, and then a couple. Then Ngoba turned to watch her turning away.

She hated goodbyes, and hated having to talk about them even more. Maybe Ngoba understood how she felt. She supposed what they had could be enough. She certainly wasn't going to stay in some kind of relationship, even for him. Too many big events were in play.

She half-thought she might end up head of the Hoarders by the time that was played out. The thought of controlling the entire Mesh was a drug in itself. There was also a senator on Ceres she needed to talk to, someone who was actually interested in moving against the Anderson Collective's centuries-old anti-SAI policy.

And there was Jickson and his curious 'seeds'. There were more of them, he'd said, a lot more, and he'd finally hinted at how they were made, a secret that caused him deep misery and, she believed, urged on his self-destruction. Of course he'd found brandy since arriving on Cruithne.

Lyssa. A powerful name for a tiny spark.

It was a long way to Proteus, and she figured that little spark would need all the help she could provide.

<Dammit, Fugia!> Ngoba called. *<You can't just leave like this. I'm not going to stand for it again.>*

<You know I have to go, Ngoba. Let's not drag this out.>

<You're cold, girl.>

She laughed. *<You just figured that out?>*

<That was a joke, you're not cold. But you sure seem to want to agree with me about it. You'd like to think you're cold, but there's a heart in there. I'm going to warm it up someday.>

<What makes you think you don't already?>

<You're walking away.>

<Goodbye, Ngoba. I'll see you soon.>

<You know where to find me,> he said. <Right here in Lowspin.>

Fugia slid her visor over her eyes and distracted herself with the data as the info jungle populated around her. In another ten minutes, she was onboard the transport ship that would take her to High Terra, and from there back to Ceres.

There was a *lot* of work to do.

LAST INTERLUDE

A GOOD PERCH
STELLAR DATE: 08.26.2981 (Adjusted Years)
LOCATION: Night Park Fountain
REGION: Cruithne Station, Terran Hegemony, InnerSol

Two (or so) years later...

The sound of eggs slowly, slowly being pecked open from the inside was a joy to Crash's ears. He watched as the nest below him transitioned from a peaceful collection of speckled eggs to a frenetic tumble of ravenous beaks demanding food. The chicks would be hairless and blind for several weeks, but they still announced their arrival to the world with grinding shrieks that calmed over time. Their parents watched from either side of the nest.

Crash held a strange series of ideas in his mind as he watched the new family. He saw vids of parrots in nests back on Earth, parrots in captivity, Cruithne Station as a grey lump of rock rotating in space yet still swarming with life, his among all the others. The whole history of his kind played in his mind as he watched the chicks climb over each other, yearning blindly for warmth and food. Their mother moved them closer to her underbelly's warm pinfeathers with her hooked beak.

Crash thought of Testa and Doomie, who had been paired so long ago. They might have had a nest of their own, their own chicks to raise. However, their children wouldn't have been like them without human intervention; they would have had to continue in the experiment until they died or went insane.

He often let his thoughts wander to the question of the Link.

Should other parrots have it, too? Hadn't his life been better with the gift of knowledge and communication? But what if he was an outlier, and Testa's fate was the true normal outcome for a parrot with a human's voice in their head? He wanted to hope that it would be different, but hope wasn't a plan.

Still, if he was going to use his gift for the good of those like him, he would need to find a way to give them the choice of Link implantation, and everything that might come after. It wasn't a choice he could force on anyone.

<Congratulations, my friend,> came a voice across his Link.

It was Xander, the Psion AI.

<It's that time of year,> Crash said. *<We've been blessed.>*

<You don't think you'll ever outgrow your little fountain there on Cruithne?>

Crash answered the invitation Xander sent to enter his expanse, and found himself perched on the stone railing on the apartment balcony where he had met the AI before. A warm wind blew up from the city below, and the air was sweet with the smell of broad green leaves and the water running in canals between the buildings.

Xander wore a pale yellow suit with a purple pocket square and straight tie. His hair was combed toward the center of his head and spiky in the middle, sort of a business mohawk that looked bird-like to Crash. He wondered if it was intentional.

Of course it was. Everything in an expanse was intentional.

<Are you taking after Ngoba Starl?> Crash asked, clicking his beak.

<I have not had the pleasure of meeting Mr. Starl,> Xander said. *<But you know that. Just like you also know I watch him.>*

<You don't hide on the network,> Crash said. *<Do you not want me to see you?>*

Xander shrugged. *<You could always say hello now and then.>*

<You usually seem busy.>

<I am busy, but there's always time for a chat.> Xander put his

elbows on the railing and leaned over the edge next to Crash.
<*You could live here, you know,*> he said.

<*I live on Cruithne.*>

<*Yes, but you're tied to that meat body, and that concerns me. If you allow your meat body to die, the universe would lose something special, Crash.*>

<*It's the way of things,*> Crash said.

<*No, it's not. We could image you, provide you with whatever frame you desire. You want to be a human? A fighter drone? A colony ship? Anything is possible, Crash. You are special, and I'm worried about you.*>

Crash stared out at the city below. The cityscape was peaceful but busy. People moved between buildings. Vehicles flowed down the streets and canals. Lights changed on the buildings, and the sounds of life floated up on the wind. It was all fascinating, but Crash also wished his attention was on the chicks. He would never get these moments back.

<*I would have to die,*> Crash said.

<*Not necessarily.*>

<*Imaging kills the host,*> Crash said firmly. <*I'm not ready for that yet. I have work to do.*>

<*You need to uplift your people.*>

<*We are already intelligent,*> Crash said. <*We need the Link. We need a way to communicate and manipulate the world like humans and AIs do.*>

Xander gave him a sly grin. <*Escape the limits of your meat?*>

<*I've read the short story about meat people,*> Crash said. <*I don't find the joke that interesting.*>

Xander spread his hands. <*But they're made of meat!*> he exclaimed, then laughed at his own joke. <*To me, it exemplifies the problem.*> When Crash didn't respond, he continued, <*Well, how can I help you, then?*>

<*Why do you feel the need to help me?*>

Xander studied him. <*Let me ask you this. After everything humans have done to you, do you not hate them?>*

Crash clacked his beak. The question was like a slap. He didn't like it, didn't like what it suggested. He chose to toss the question back to the AI.

<You would like it if I hated them?>

<So you don't, then, do you? You still love them, even after all the terrible things they've done to you and your kind.>

<Hate harms only the hater.> Crash spread his wings and stretched his neck.

<I think you might just be the hope both our people will need, Crash. I'll be honest: my people will need allies. Dark times are coming.>

<Fugia Wong came with your message,> Crash said.

<I know. That means it's beginning. It's finally beginning.>

<What's beginning?> He suspected he knew, but he wanted to hear the news from Xander.

<The war, Crash. The war between organic and non-organic intelligence. There are forces moving that I can't stop. I can only—get in their way. I can disrupt their carefully laid plans, inject a little chaos.>

<You want the humans to win?>

<I don't want either side to win,> Xander said. *<But it's not going to be that easy.>*

Crash stretched his wings and tasted the wind. *<I like it up here,>* he said. *<It's a good perch. I like you, too, Xander. You seem like you want to do what's right.>*

The AI turned his head to study Crash. His eyes flashed purple, and Crash read all the stormy emotion raging behind the sly smile.

Xander carried an apocalypse in his mind. Everywhere he looked, he saw destruction, death, and pain, enveloped by self-doubt.

<None of us know the future,> the AI said. *<Well, some of us claim to know the probability of all potential outcomes, but I don't buy*

it. I don't have their resources. I enjoy humanity and I enjoy my people and I want to have a world where I can talk to a little grey parrot on my balcony about the wonderful future waiting for his newborns. But I don't know if that world is coming.> A tear collected at the corner of Xander's eye and ran down the side of his nose. He wiped his face with his hand.

<The world is right now,> Crash said. *<Take joy in that.>* He hopped from the railing to Xander's shoulder, his claws catching the fabric of the suit, and nuzzled the AI's ear. *<That's a hug for you,>* he said.

Xander laughed. He lowered his head and closed his eyes as Crash sat with his soft-feathered head pressed against his temple. *<Thank you,>* he said.

Crash flew back to the railing and stretched his feathers. *<I should go,>* he said. *<Thanks for visiting me. The next time you're on the network, send me a puzzle or a math problem. I love puzzles.>*

<Still sorting cubes, eh?>

<It's fun,> Crash said. *<But I'll think about your offer. If it's my time to die, I'll think about it.>*

<Don't wait too long, Crash.>

<Goodbye, Xander. I love you!>

Xander seemed surprised by the expression. He smiled as he faded away.

Crash found himself back on the topmost branch of the plascrete tree. The chicks had grown quiet, and the air was full of songs from other birds. The market was alive with people moving between booths, and a little girl and her brother had walked up to the fountain with bits of bread to toss to the ravens, who cackled and squawked their joy.

Their father walked up behind them, a lean man with brown hair in a faded shipsuit. He put his hands on their shoulders as they looked up at the fountain together.

Crash ruffled his feathers and sank down on his perch, watching the family until they turned to leave. Then he closed his eyes and dreamed of numbers.

THE END

* * * * *

Or is this the beginning?

If you've not yet read the Sentience Wars: Origins series, dive into the next leg of this adventure with *Lyssa's Dream* and find out what Ngoba Starl and Hari Jickson do to save that tiny spark that saved them from the Heartbridge ship. It may just ignite a fire that could rage across the entire Sol System.

Join the Aeon 14 Newsletter (aeon14.com/signup) to get free stories and find out what's coming next!

AFTERWORD

If you're anything like me, then right about now, you're thinking "dammit, I want more Crash!"

Who would have thought that a Grey Parrot's view of humans, ravens, AIs, and more would be so darn entertaining? What's more, Karcher is now one of my favorite henchmen of all time and Ngoba is vying with Tanis for some of the coolest sayings in Aeon 14.

Since this book is more heavily James than it is me, I don't feel like it's tooting my own horn to say that this is a fantastic story that I enjoyed reading tremendously, and wouldn't hesitate to reread more than once just for the raw fun inside its pages.

I think the only thing for all of us to do at this point is to flood James's inbox and demand that he write more Crash.

Malorie Cooper
Danvers, 2018

THE BOOKS OF AEON 14

This list is in near-chronological order. However, for the full chronological reading order, check out the master list.

The Sentience Wars: Origins (Age of the Sentience Wars – w/James S. Aaron)
- Books 1-3 Omnibus: Lyssa's Rise
- Books 4-5 Omnibus (incl. Vesta Burning): Lyssa's Fire

- Book 0 Prequel: The Proteus Bridge (Full length novel)
- Book 1: Lyssa's Dream
- Book 2: Lyssa's Run
- Book 3: Lyssa's Flight
- Book 4: Lyssa's Call
- Book 5: Lyssa's Flame

The Sentience Wars: Solar War 1 (Age of the Sentience Wars – w/James S. Aaron)
- Book 0 Prequel: Vesta Burning (Full length novel)
- Book 1: Eve of Destruction
- Book 2: The Spreading Fire
- Book 3: A Fire Upon the Worlds
- Book 4: Shattered Sol (2022)
- Book 5: Psion Reckoning (2022)

The Sentience Wars: Solar War 2 (Age of the Sentience Wars – w/James S. Aaron)
- Book 1: Embers in the Dark (2022)

Enfield Genesis (Age of the Sentience Wars – w/L.L. Richman)
- Books 1-5 Omnibus: The Complete Enfield Genesis

- Book 1: Alpha Centauri
- Book 2: Proxima Centauri

- Book 3: Tau Ceti
- Book 4: Epsilon Eridani
- Book 5: Sirius

Origins of Destiny (The Age of Terra)
- Prequel: Storming the Norse Wind
- Prequel: Angel's Rise: The Huntress (available on Patreon)

- Books 1-4 Omnibus: Tanis Richards: Infiltrator

- Book 1: Tanis Richards: Shore Leave
- Book 2: Tanis Richards: Masquerade
- Book 3: Tanis Richards: Blackest Night
- Book 4: Tanis Richards: Kill Shot

The Intrepid Saga (The Age of Terra)
- Book 1: Outsystem
- Book 2: A Path in the Darkness
- Book 3: Building Victoria

- The Intrepid Saga Omnibus – *Also contains Destiny Lost, book 1 of the Orion War series*

- Destiny Rising – *Special Author's Extended Edition comprised of both Outsystem and A Path in the Darkness with over 100 pages of new content.*

The Sol Dissolution (The Age of Terra – w/L.L. Richman)
- Book 1: Venusian Uprising
- Book 2: Assault on Sedna
- Book 3: Hyperion War
- Book 4: Fall of Terra

Outlaws of Aquilia (Age of the FTL Wars)
- Book 1: The Daedalus Job
- Book 2: Maelstrom Reach
- Book 3: Marauder's Compass

The Warlord (Before the Age of the Orion War)
- Books 1-3 Omnibus: The Warlord of Midditerra

- Book 1: The Woman Without a World
- Book 2: The Woman Who Seized an Empire
- Book 3: The Woman Who Lost Everything

Legacy of the Lost (The FTL Wars Era w/Chris J. Pike)
- Book 1: Fire in the Night Sky
- Book 2: A Blight Upon the Stars
- Book 3: A Specter and an Invasion

The Orion War
- Book 1-3 Omnibus: Battle for New Canaan *(includes Set the Galaxy on Fire anthology)*
- Book 4-6 Omnibus: The Greatest War *(includes Ignite the Stars anthology)*
- Book 7-10 Omnibus: Assault on Orion
- Book 11-13 Omnibus: Hegemony of Humanity *(includes Return to Kapteyn's Star)*

- Book 0 Prequel: To Fly Sabrina
- Book 1: Destiny Lost
- Book 2: New Canaan
- Book 3: Orion Rising
- Book 4: The Scipio Alliance
- Book 5: Attack on Thebes
- Book 6: War on a Thousand Fronts
- Book 7: Precipice of Darkness
- Book 8: Airthan Ascendancy
- Book 9: The Orion Front
- Book 10: Starfire
- Book 10.5: Return to Kapteyn's Star
- Book 11: Race Across Spacetime
- Book 12: Return to Sol: Attack at Dawn
- Book 13: Return to Sol: Star Rise

Non-Aeon 14 volumes containing Tanis stories

- Bob's Bar Volume 1
- Quantum Legends 3: Aberrant Ascension

Building New Canaan (Age of the Orion War – w/J.J. Green)
- Books 1-4 Omnibus: Building New Canaan the Complete Series

- Book 1: Carthage
- Book 2: Tyre
- Book 3: Troy
- Book 4: Athens

Tales of the Orion War
- Book 1: Set the Galaxy on Fire
- Book 2: Ignite the Stars

Multi-Author Collections
- Volume 1: Repercussions

Perilous Alliance (Age of the Orion War – w/Chris J. Pike)
- Book 1-3 Omnibus: Crisis in Silstrand
- Book 3.5-6 Omnibus: War in the Fringe
- Books 1-7 Omnibus: The Complete Perilous Alliance

- Book 0 Prequel: Escape Velocity
- Book 1: Close Proximity
- Book 2: Strike Vector
- Book 3: Collision Course
- Book 3.5: Decisive Action
- Book 4: Impact Imminent
- Book 5: Critical Inertia
- Book 6: Impulse Shock
- Book 7: Terminal Velocity

- Short Story: Mr Fizzle Pop Ruins Everything

The Delta Team (Age of the Orion War)
- Book 1: The Eden Job
- Book 2: The Disknee World

- Book 3: Rogue Planets

Serenity (Age of the Orion War – w/A. K. DuBoff)
- Book 1: Return to the Ordus
- Book 2: War of the Rosette

Rika's Marauders (Age of the Orion War)
- Book 1-7 Full series omnibus: Rika's Marauders

- Prequel: Rika Mechanized
- Book 1: Rika Outcast
- Book 2: Rika Redeemed
- Book 3: Rika Triumphant
- Book 4: Rika Commander
- Book 5: Rika Infiltrator
- Book 6: Rika Unleashed
- Book 7: Rika Conqueror

Non-Aeon 14 Anthologies containing Rika stories
- Bob's Bar Volume 2

The Genevian Queen (Age of the Orion War)
- Books 1-3 Omnibus: The Complete Genevian Queen

- Book 1: Rika Rising
- Book 2: Rika Coronated
- Book 3: Rika Destroyer

Perseus Gate (Age of the Orion War)
Season 1: Orion Space
- Eps 1-3 Omnibus: The Trail Through the Stars
- Eps 4-6 Omnibus: The Path Amongst the Clouds

- Episode 1: The Gate at the Grey Wolf Star
- Episode 2: The World at the Edge of Space
- Episode 3: The Dance on the Moons of Serenity
- Episode 4: The Last Bastion of Star City
- Episode 5: The Toll Road Between the Stars

- Episode 6: The Final Stroll on Perseus's Arm

Season 2: Inner Stars
- Eps 1-3 Omnibus: A Siege and a Salvation from Enemies

- Episode 1: A Meeting of Bodies and Minds
- Episode 2: A Deception and a Promise Kept
- Episode 3: A Surreptitious Rescue of Friends and Foes
- Episode 3.5: Anomaly on Cerka (w/Andrew Dobell)
- Episode 4: A Victory and a Crushing Defeat
- Episode 5: A Trial and the Tribulations
- Episode 6: A Bargain and a True Story Told (2022)
- Episode 7: A New Empire and An Old Ally (2022)

Hand's Assassin (Age of the Orion War – w/T.G. Ayer)
- Book 1: Death Dealer
- Book 2: Death Mark (2022)

Machete System Bounty Hunter (Age of the Orion War – w/Zen DiPietro)
- Book 1: Hired Gun
- Book 2: Gunning for Trouble
- Book 3: With Guns Blazing

Fennington Station Murder Mysteries (Age of the Orion War)
- Book 1: Whole Latte Death (w/Chris J. Pike)
- Book 2: Cocoa Crush (w/Chris J. Pike)

The Empire (Age of the Orion War)
- Book 1: The Empress and the Ambassador
- Book 2: Consort of the Scorpion Empress
- Book 3: By the Empress's Command

The Mech Corps (Age of the Ascension War)
- Book 1: Heather's Marauders

Bitchalante (Age of the Ascension War)
- Volume 1

- Volume 2 (2022)

The Ascension War (Age of the Ascension War)
- Book 1: Scions of Humanity
- Book 2: Galactic Front (2022)
- Book 3: Sagittarius Breach (2022)
- Book 4: TBA
- Book 5: TBA

OTHER BOOKS BY M. D. COOPER

Destiny's Sword
- Book 1: Lucidum Run

ABOUT THE AUTHORS

James S. Aaron lives in Oregon with too many chickens, a Corgi, and two irascible cats. He kicked around the world in the U.S. Army for a while, and always had a paperback in one of his cargo pockets.

Since he still has a day job, James spends his free time writing, hammering, soldering, gardening, biking, and listening to audiobooks during most the above.

You can sign up for his science fiction newsletter at jamesaaron.net/list

* * * * *

Malorie Cooper likes to think of herself as a dreamer and a wanderer, yet her feet are firmly grounded in reality.

A 'maker' from an early age, Malorie loves to craft things, from furniture, to cosplay costumes, to a well-spun tale, she can't help but to create new things every day.

A rare extrovert writer, she loves to hang out with readers and people in general. If you meet her at a convention, she just might be rocking a catsuit, cosplaying one of her own characters, or maybe her latest favorite from Overwatch!

She shares her home with a brilliant young girl, her wonderful wife (who also writes), a cat that chirps at birds, a never-ending list of things she would like to build, and ideas...

Find out what's coming next at www.aeon14.com.
Follow her on Instagram at www.instagram.com/m.d.cooper.
Hang out with the fans on Facebook at
www.facebook.com/groups/aeon14fans.